ON Kilroy's Trail

A World of Travel

To Tait & Wilma

You will recognize many of the planes, people and far-away places. Hope you enjoy

Jon E. Robertson

On Kilroy's Trail

A World of Travel

by
Joe E. Robertson

Sunflower University Press®
1531 Yuma • P. O. Box 1009 • Manhattan, Kansas 66505-1009 USA

© 1998 by Joe E. Robertson
Printed in the United States of America on acid-free paper.

ISBN 0-89745-226-7

Edited by Sonie Liebler

Layout by Lori L. Daniel

Sunflower University Press is a wholly-owned subsidiary
of the non-profit 501(c)3 Journal of the West, Inc.

*Dedicated to our grandchildren:
Katie and C. J. Robertson*

Contents

Acknowledgments		ix
Preface		xiii
Chapter 1	The Travel Seeds	1
Chapter 2	Travel During World War II	16
Chapter 3	Family Travel in the U.S. After the War	32
Chapter 4	The Global "Kilroy" Connection: The Tropics, 1966 and 1970, and the Orient, 1973 and 1981	52
Chapter 5	Odysseys — Great Britain, Scandinavia, and Europe, 1974 Russia and Siberia, 1979 The Mediterranean, 1980	97
Chapter 6	African Safaris, 1975 and 1985	154
Chapter 7	The First Around-the-World Trip, 1977	188

Chapter 8	Latin America and the Galapagos, 1987	229
Chapter 9	The Travelers' Century Club and the Circumnavigators Club: Around the World in 18 Days, 1987	237
Chapter 10	The Canadian Northwest and Alaska, 1989	254
Chapter 11	The Walls of the World: Our Travels in the 1990s	260
Epilogue		302
Appendix	The Robertson Corporation	304
Index		312

Acknowledgments

THERE ARE MANY who have helped so much in providing material and encouragement for this book and many who have helped put it together. Those who have been involved know it, and I hope a "Thank You" stated here will provide a degree of recognition and appreciation to them as they read the result.

Although The Robertson Corporation has always been directed and managed by family members, from the beginning its officers keenly recognized the extremely important contributions of the many loyal, dedicated, and productive employees responsible for the survival, health, and growth of the company.

Throughout our travels, my tolerant wife, Virginia, kept abundant and accurate notes, and Clark and Sylvia McDonald were an integral part of the planning. Our son, "Rob" (Dr. Joe, Jr.) endured thousands of miles, with and without peer-companions, on the hot leather of the back seat as we crisscrossed the United States many times in every direction from the time he was four (and before) until he was fourteen, when the demands of many activities, including serious athletics and academics, took over.

My brothers and business associates have been very supportive of our very extensive travel — always believing, over many years, that our industry visits, data collections, and national and international networking were far more rewarding to our business than the properly allocated "expensed" part of the trips.

Fortunately, the names of most of our travel partners are documented at the beginning of each trip segment. The contribution of "neighbors" in our wonderful small town could not be overemphasized. The same is true for our friends in high school, college, the military, and teammates.

In later years, we connected with "younger" circles of friends through our son and his friends at Yale, Indiana University, Oregon Health Science University, etc. And, we became acquainted with the friends of our daughter-in-law, Dr. Margaret "Maggie" Hewitt Robertson. Maggie's parents, Dr. Charlie and Harriet Hewitt, were also enthusiastic travelers — so for that and many reasons, we really "hit it off" with the Hewitts.

Our parents, of course, contributed immensely by their travel interests. My mother's travel experiences are mentioned later, and certainly Virginia's mother, Kansas State University Professor Laura Falkenrich Baxter, was involved in travel long before most women were straying far from their own green valleys.

The book, and the many travel articles included in it, would not have been possible without the skilled and talented efforts of others in writing, discussing, reviewing, proofing, and rewriting the materials.

Early on, my business associates — executive secretaries and others — assisted me in getting the business-related material ready for publication. Clydia Love worked with me for about 35 years — anything she doesn't know about me, and where I've been and what I've done and with whom isn't worth knowing. Sherrell Perry has worked with me for over 20 years and can read my writing better than anyone. Mary Jane Wheatley has also worked with me for 20-plus years and became almost as travel-infected as I! Mary Acton was very skilled in writing down excellent expressions of ideas and had a feel for the "gypsy" in travel. Helen Potter was probably the best proofreader I have ever known. Anne Nagle was a B.A., English major, and has a flare for the romantic. There were others, and lately Darlene Atchison and Karen Harrison have been making up for my lack of skill in word processing.

Of course, we owe a special debt to Ray Snapp and Claude Parsons, both former editors of the Bedford (Indiana) *Times-Mail* who along with Mary Margaret Stipp and other *Times-Mail* staff members were always encouraging and helpful in both the preparation and publication of the travel articles. Usually the trip stories were accorded front-page space, headlines, and bold- face leads — with pictures!

Joe Persinger, editor and publisher of *The Jackson County* (Brownstown, Indiana) *Banner*, treated our stories equally well. Permission has been granted by both newspapers to reproduce and publish my stories.

The "character identifications" noted in many trip accounts are very important. Bill Altman, who now leads the International Hardwood Plywood and Veneer Association, has opined that his members constitute the most interesting and varied group of international business participants in the world.

One interesting family background associated with this book is that linked with the Darlington Veneer Plywood company of South Carolina. The late Jack Ramsey, long time Darlington owner, and his wife, Esther, traveled extensively. Their sons John and Jim now own the business. In the '60s, Jack Ramsey hired Joe Shuman, a sharp football-playing engineer from Purdue, to manage the plywood manufacturing operation. Joe, in turn, hired young Reggie Hubbard, a Carolinian, to follow in the management shoes. Reggie's wife, Carolyn, is the daughter of a World War II pilot who flew "The Hump" with General Claire Chennault's "Flying Tigers." These and many business/travel friends — Dr. Terry Sellers and Tom Maloney, and John Tritch and Larry Evans of Columbia Forest Products — were often guests at semi-annual plywood dinners we hosted at exotic convention sites over a 30-year span. Clearly, we gathered a great deal from the guests at this "'round the world round table," and they deserve credit for their contributions, as well as do the many "characters" associated with the former American Plywood Association, now APA — the Engineered Wood Association and the International Forest Products Society.

But all of this had to be "put together," and the credit for preliminary editing, "flow," and "focus" belongs to a very talented Peggy Lucas Robison who demonstrated a unique savvy for what I wanted to say and how it might be understandable.

This credit listing is certainly proof that "No man is an island."

Joe E. Robertson points to Yugoslavia, the 100th country he has visited in his international travels, on a map in his office at the Robertson Corporation, Bedford, Indiana.

Preface

KILROY WAS A TRAVELER. My fascination with Kilroy began in about 1943, during World War II, as "50-mission" fliers (those who had miraculously survived 50 bombing, recon, or escort missions) began to filter back to the States on leave, or temporary duty assignments, or as experienced instructors. These veterans brought back stories of their attacks, their landings, or their occupations, by whatever means, of very far away, dangerous, and exotic places. However, the most common observation, in whatever account of initial travel, was the incredible description of a sign on a wall — any wall — latrine, fort, garden, stone, wood, or brick, along with a primitive drawing of a "Schmoe" with a bald head and a very long nose protruding over a fence, and the inscription "*Kilroy was here*" below.

Reading like a myth, but repeated 10,000 times in reports from Burma, Morocco, Indonesia, Turkey, China, Italy, or wherever, this "maybe myth" became "gospel" to the 20 million GI's of World

War II. And at a time when the prevailing image of the American GI was that of Colossus, in helmet and uniform, standing astride of the globe.

In the mind of the GI's, Kilroy always "got there first." And he must have been an engineer — whether Army Engineer, Navy Seabee, or "dogface" driving a D-4 bulldozer — for I can personally attest to landing on a hundred airstrips as we moved from place to place in a large part of the world — and Kilroy had *always been there*! These wartime airstrips later became the small domestic and great international airports that linked the postwar world, one of the prime factors in the making of a global community. For lack of a better one to credit, I'll say "Kilroy did it."

The accounts in this collection of my worldwide travels, for the most part, were published in the Bedford (Indiana) *Times-Mail* between 1973 and 1993, and in *The Jackson County Banner* in 1995 and 1996, or reported in The Robertson Corporation's published letters and literature. Many of the trips were business-related and associated with the activities not only of The Robertson Corporation but also of the International Hardwood Plywood Manufacturers Association. Some of the more exotic visits were extensions of the business itineraries of the Association.

Clark McDonald was president-executive of the Association during that period. His wife, Sylvia, planned and arranged most of the trips, with the help of excellent travel agents. Sylvia was undoubtedly one of the most knowledgeable world travelers of that era. She knew, or could access, information regarding the business, technical, political, and historical background and potential of any place. She could establish contacts with the great and the small. She could arrange for us to "talk with crowds . . . and walk with kings." And she did. On nearly every trip, we would ask Sylvia to arrange either business or adventure visits to lesser traveled places of stories and dreams. No challenge was unacceptable, no request was dismissed — a Sultan's palace, the highest mountain, the deepest jungle, or to witness the most exciting events.

These travel accounts indicate that it is possible to order our lives, despite the many proper obligations and constraints, so that with reasonable dedication and discipline, there is time to realize "the stuff that dreams are made of." The "Tomorrow Isles" can become the exciting explorations of today.

These tales will be especially interesting to those who have a high level of travel energy, a burning desire to go and see and learn, a romantic idealism, and an adventurer's heart.

Chapter 1

The Travel Seeds

"GREAT OAKS FROM LITTLE ACORNS . . . ," and so it was. At six years of age, Virginia Baxter (Robertson) began traveling, both accompanied and then by herself, by train, between Manhattan, Kansas (across plains, prairies, the Flint Hills) and Evansville, Indiana, on the Ohio River. Her mother, a young widow, was teaching in the Evansville schools, and her grandparents, on both sides, as well as many other family members, were firmly rooted in Manhattan, Kansas.

At the same time, I was starting to travel by "Interurban" (electric train) between nearby Seymour, Indiana, and South Bend, Indiana, where I was picked up by my Aunt Jewell and Uncle Lee for a week on and around the northern Indiana lakes. From the Interurban station, I was driven in a Hudson auto past the Golden Dome of Notre Dame en route to Elkhart, Indiana. I felt I had established an early rapport with the football program, which was soon to thrill the world with stories of Knute Rockne, "The Four Horsemen," "The Gipper," and others associated with the home of "Touchdown Jesus," the prominent statue near the entrance to the university.

On those childhood trips, I learned to love lake boating and developed an early desire to someday own a mahogany in-board motor boat and to maneuver through the water in the same manner that we cruised Lake Wawasee. On one of those Elkhart trips we took an overnight Lake Michigan cruise between Chicago and Milwaukee. At that time, an ocean voyage could not have pleased me more!

My mother must have contributed most of my travel genes, for she and a number of the other young matrons had taken the Baltimore & Ohio (B&O) Railroad 250 miles west from Brownstown, Indiana, to the St. Louis World's Fair in 1903. Maybe that doesn't match Meryl Streep's (Isak Dinesen) trip in *Out of Africa*, but it was relatively daring at the time.

My father was not really travel-oriented, although his great grandfather, at 16 years old, had packed the wagons in the Virginias, made his way through the wilderness with his widowed mother, and settled in Indian Country (Indiana) in the late 1700s. My father was, however, fascinated by the reciprocal gasoline engine. As a young man, he was one of the small crowd at the first Indianapolis 500 Speedway Race in 1911. And, with a partner, he purchased a chain-drive Grabowski Motor Bus in 1912 to carry passengers the 11 miles between Brownstown and Seymour, Indiana — over Crane Hill. One day in 1913, the bus made five round trips between Brownstown and Seymour transporting passengers to the Centennial Celebration of the Battle of Tipton's Island — which reportedly had secured southern Indiana from the Indians in 1813.

There were seven U.S. Railway Postal "mail clerks" who lived within seven blocks of the Roscoe Robertson house in Brownstown. (The house is now in "best ever" condition as the home of Jon and Peggy Robison at 515 West Spring Street). These mail clerks were mostly employed on the "Mainline" B&O trains such as "The National Limited" and "The Diplomat," which connected the Western Terminal at St. Louis with the Eastern metropolitan centers of commerce and government — Washington, Philadelphia, and New York. The trains also ran through the booming river town of Cincinnati.

The Pennsylvania Railroad lines that we knew ran from Louisville, Kentucky, to Chicago, Illinois. There were many travel tales told by both men and boys (sexist?) of the wonderful world of America from the Atlantic to the Mighty Mississippi.

My parents would occasionally take us on a "Railroad Sponsored Excursion" to the Cincinnati Zoo to see the wonderful animals from around the world — seeds of future Safaris. My father did business in Louisville, Kentucky, so I was sometimes permitted to accompany him via a Marmon "8" automobile, on his calls to that river and rail center.

In the eighth grade, I had an opportunity for a really big trip — a weeklong auto excursion with my history-government teacher and four other students across the Allegheny Mountains to Washington, D.C. About two years later, I went with six or seven other young high school juniors and seniors to the Chicago World's Fair to view the Century of Progress Exhibition.

I also was given permission to ride on a motorcycle trip north past Elkhart, Indiana, to Michigan. My folks were generally pretty strict, and why they gave me permission to go with the "big boys" at age 15 to the Chicago World's Fair, or at 17 on a "Harley" trip to Michigan, I don't know.

Anyway, by now, as the song says . . . "I've been in some big towns, I've heard me some big talk." The travel seed had sprouted, and the sapling was straining to grow like Jack's beanstalk.

I had visited several college campuses in trying to make an intelligent university selection, and was fortunate that finances were available and adequate. As a class valedictorian, I felt I was academically qualified to matriculate at any university, and I thought I might be good enough to play college varsity basketball. Distance was not a deterrent, as my brothers had both gone away to school at Wabash College. It was still in Indiana, but far enough away that they usually came home no more than two or three times during the school year. In the same manner, my parents visited them on campus about twice each year.

I was attracted to my family's milling business, so I ended up looking primarily at Pennsylvania State University and Kansas State College of Agriculture and Applied Science (now Kansas State University). They were the only universities with a fully-accredited four-year curriculum in milling industry at that time.

In early July 1936, a friend, Theo Mobley, and I decided to drive out to Manhattan, Kansas, and look over the college — a distance of about 640 miles. We planned to take his family's 1936 Chevrolet.

Our plan was to have dates in Bedford, Indiana, on Saturday night, take the girls home at midnight, and start off on the journey across the plains of Illinois, Missouri, and Kansas. We took U.S. 50 to St. Louis and U.S. 40 on through Kansas City to Manhattan, arriving about 14 hours later. We checked in at the Wareham Hotel.

After a short rest, we drove around town and campus and ended up at Scheu's Cafe for a hamburger, where many college kids happily ate. I was by then familiar with the Greek fraternity system because my brothers had both been "Phi Delts." (Phi Delta Theta, Sigma Chi, and Beta Theta Pi had been founded at Miami University (Ohio) and were called the Miami Triad.) I recognized the fraternity ring on the hand of one of two young men sitting on the counter stools by us.

"Isn't that a Beta ring?" I asked.

"You bet," Leroy MacInitch answered. "This is my friend, Bill Miller. Are you boys coming to school here?"

From there the conversation developed. Pretty soon, they mentioned that there was to be a Sunrise Dance under the stars on one of the beautiful Flint Hills nearby. Jimmy Jones and his Seven Clouds of Joy band were playing. We tried to act nonchalant, but were about to jump for joy. Soon, they returned with their own dates and two of the prettiest "older" college girls we had ever seen, Maxine and Mary, one a Tri Delt and the other an Alpha Delt. Their dancing was as beautiful as their appearance (both girls were later elected college beauty queens), and when the Seven Clouds of Joy played "It's a Sin to Tell a Lie," I was sure I was dreaming or had died and gone to heaven.

Academics, basketball, career preparation, and all other factors became secondary. If this was college life, it was for me — here at K-State! My decision was made — and it turned out to be a good one, for I found all of the above factors, and one year later in Anderson Hall (The Old Main of Kansas State), I met my future wife, Virginia Baxter, a Pi Beta Phi, "Miss Manhattan," and the Honorary Colonel of the Reserve Officer's Training Corps (ROTC). She, in my opinion, was even lovelier than the beautiful girls who did have some influence on my choosing a school located "out West."

My travels were just beginning. My father had said, "There will probably only be sixteen 'away' football games during your four years in college. I would advise you to attend as many of them as you can." And I did. Big Six, Big Eight, and now Big Twelve (as the conference expanded) college football games were and are big events. I went by the Short Line rail with the crowds up to Lincoln to see our Wildcats battle the Nebraska University Cornhuskers. I went by car east down the Kaw River Valley for intense games with the University of Kansas Jayhawks. I rode the Rock Island Rocket through the Indian Nations and the great Oklahoma oil derricks to watch K-State play the University of Oklahoma Sooners at Norman, and would usually do a Kansas City overnight, in that Tom Pendergast-Harry Truman era, when en route to the University of Missouri at Columbia. MU was and still is noted for its world-class journalism school. There were Stevens and Christian Colleges for Women as well. Columbia was what everyone pictures a beautiful college town should be — including "The Old Ox Road" of romantic lore.

I made two or three trips a year between Brownstown and Manhattan. I would usually take the B&O National Limited to the St. Louis Union Station and there change to the Burlington Zephyr west to Kansas City, where I would quickly transfer to the Santa Fe Chief. All of these were new 80-mph diesel streamliners. Passengers reclined in the lap of luxury while the landscape changed from southern Indiana hills, past Illinois oil wells, over the Mighty Mississippi, along the broad Missouri River, to Kansas City and through the Flint Hills and the plains to Manhattan. These very special "Limited" trains made few stops, and Brownstown would "flag" or stop the Limited for me because my father's mill shipped grain and flour and meal on their railroad.

On my first trip to Manhattan, I took a steamer trunk and a Gladstone bag and was met at the Manhattan train station by a couple of Phi Delts in a brand new blue 1936 Deluxe Ford sport sedan. After a brief stop at the Phi Delt House, I was checked in at the hotel again, in accordance with Rush Week rules. After I had visited several good fraternities, at the end of Rush Week I pledged Phi Delt, as was expected.

My making the Kansas State Varsity basketball team was, of course, a very real contributor to my college travel experiences. At that time, freshmen were not allowed to play varsity basketball, and the travel schedules for freshmen teams were limited. Freshmen were made eligible for Varsity during World War II, and most of the large schools never went back to a separate freshman team — too bad, because that freshman year allowed time to determine if the student was college oriented: would he study, would he make grades, would he submit to the necessary discipline? A return to the freshman "trial year" would solve a lot of problems in big-time college basketball today.

Anyway, after a rather uneventful travel year as a freshman, I went home for a working summer in the mill with trips largely consisting of driving to Seymour for dates and to Heflin's Camp every Thursday and Saturday night for dances. (Heflin's was a summer camp with a beautiful covered dance pavilion and an outstanding 'big band' type orchestra, all of which contributed to unforgettable, romantic memories of youth.)

All things were different — bigger and better during my sophomore year. I remember the BIG DOUBLEHEADER at the beginning of my sophomore basketball season. We were playing a double program with KU against DePaul University and Loyola University — the "Catholics" — in the cavernous Chicago Coliseum. We played DePaul on Friday night and were scheduled to play Loyola on Saturday. Playing with and against some of the biggest names in college basketball, I was going to start against DePaul — as a sophomore! I had last played a real basketball game at the regional high school tourney in Mitchell, Indiana. It's a long way from Mitchell High School to the Chicago Coliseum — and I was scared. The game started. We got the ball. We went into our offense, the first play was executed perfectly. I found myself driving under the basket, wide open.

"Robertson shoots and misses." I knew it was on national radio, and I guess I knew there would be a loudspeaker, but not *that* loud! I knew they would hear it in New York, Manhattan, Kansas, and Brownstown, Indiana. My recollection gets a little fuzzy regarding rebounds, etc., after that, but we did recover the ball soon. Same play, same successful execution, *same result*: "Robertson shoots AND MISSES!" Next thing I knew, I was benched. I didn't start the next night against Loyola.

There were many pluses to that road trip, however. I met some of the basketball "greats." Dr. Forest "Phog" Allen introduced himself to me, and after that always called me by name whenever we played his Kansas Jayhawks during the next three years. KU's Allen Fieldhouse is named for Coach "Phog."

During Phog's long tenure at the University, he established the record for most games won. At that time, his protegé, Adolph Rupp of the University of Kentucky, was second. In later years, Jack Gardner, my coach at KSU during my last year, was the third winningest coach. During that last year I also had the pleasure of playing against one of Rupp's Kentucky

Wildcat teams in the famous old "Death Valley" gym in Lexington. The more-than-capacity crowd of 5,000 delirious fans watched the two Wildcat teams meet — but we lost there, as did everyone else. Coach Rupp knew me then by my first name, but I soon learned that all good coaches know the opposing players — and what they can do.

We had a good team that year. Unfortunately, I remember the losses. The KU Jayhawks barely beat us, and then they lost to Branch McCracken's Indiana University Hurryin' Hoosiers, in the NCAA Finals. The Oklahoma Sooners beat us, and I broke my ankle in the melée at Norman.

The names and faces of some of the great ones are still etched in my memory from exciting away games and from the Wildcat Club antics at home. Everywhere we played, home and away, there was truly mass hysteria. And this was a time when most players were really serious students. There were two engineering honor students, besides myself, on the team.

One of our substitutes, D. S. Guerrant, went on to become president of the multi-national Nestle Corporation. D. S., of course, had an excellent background — as a child he had lived awhile in my hometown of Brownstown, Indiana, where his father was the Presbyterian preacher who coached the town ladies basketball team. That was really an avant-garde action, and the lady players, including my mother, played in white middy blouses and black bloomers with long black socks — the fashion of that era.

From repeated meetings over a three-year period, covering thousands of miles from the Colorado Rockies to the Alleghenies, I came to know some outstanding players, who were also outstanding men. Billy Martin, a brother Phi Delt from Oklahoma, was an All-American who, after a stint with the Bartlettsville Oilers/Phillips 66ers, became president of the Phillips Oil Corporation. The company hired a number of players from our conference during that period, played them for awhile on their AAU basketball teams, and then made oil executives out of them — good ones, too. The winning resume: "Have basketball credits, have brains AND motivation, will travel."

But back to Phog Allen's Kansas Jayhawks, Phog had an All-American player named Ralph Miller. I "guarded" him. I use the word loosely for that's the best I could defend against him. Ralph, as a coach, went on to take his Oregon State University team to the NCAA Finals several times. About 1990, on national television at the NCAA Tournament, Ralph was given an award for the all-time "winningest" coach. He had won 700 games! I don't want to take anything away from his coaching ability, but I knew he was about my age, so one reason he won more games was that he had coached big-time basketball longer than anyone else!

Another famous player-executive was Gerald Tucker. Gerald was one of the early "big guys." He was a gentle giant — exceptional athlete, brilliant student, and talented musician. My coach and my fraternity sent me down to some little town in Oklahoma to recruit Gerald. He came to Kansas State the next year and pledged our Phi Delta Theta fraternity. He also played freshman basketball, which was as good as you could do at that time. Anyway, something happened, and the next year Gerald took all of his talents and went elsewhere. Of course, he did just as well there, as was expected.

Many of my college acquaintances later became widely traveled "military men." In the same manner as with Gerald Tucker, I assisted in pledging Bernie Rogers — later known as U.S. Army General Bernard Rogers, successor to General Dwight D. Eisenhower, a North Atlantic Treaty Organization (NATO) Commander, and a mentor of General Colin Powell. And, Congressman John Rhodes, longtime House Republican leader, was a good friend of both Virginia and myself. "Johnny" was one Virginia's escorts when she was elected Honorary Cadet Colonel of ROTC.

During my college years, I experienced a number of worthwhile travels other than those associated with basketball. I was privileged to represent our fraternity at the National Convention at Old Point Comfort, Hampton Roads, Virginia, in 1939. This was another long drive via a Studebaker Champion over the Alleghenies to the Chesapeake Bay area. One of the many attractions there, in addition to visiting with students from over 100 chapters across the land, was visiting the College of William & Mary, as well as the Colonial Williamsburg, Jamestown, and Yorktown Park areas. As I have said about so many of our trips, "I was fascinated."

One of the special away football trips was a weekend trip with Bill Beasen, in his new '39 Chrysler sport coupe, to the K-State *vs* Indiana University game in Bloomington in the fall of 1939. We took off after Friday classes for me, and festivities for Bill at Slim's "near-beer" joint in Aggieville, near the KSU campus. We drove all night in rotation. We stopped at my house in Brownstown to wash up and then drove on to

Bloomington for a visit to the Phi Delta Theta fraternity house and pre-game festivities — and then the game, and a big band dance, and back to Brownstown after midnight. We were up the next morning about 8:00, had breakfast, and were on the road for the long drive back to Manhattan. We arrived about midnight. I had tried not to have early Monday classes as a senior, so I probably only had to make a ten o'clock.

As business manager of the yearbook, *Royal Purple*, I went, totally sanctioned, faculty approved, and expenses paid, to the national convention on the Iowa State University campus at Ames. It hadn't been all fun, for we had produced an All-American yearbook that year — a lot of work by a lot of good people. We had learned our lessons well from our professors and advisors.

One of our excellent staffers was a very smart young journalist, Marianna Kistler. She later married a Beta Theta Pi, Ross Beach. Many years later they remembered their alma mater very well by giving four million dollars for the Marianna Kistler Beach Museum of Art at Kansas State University.

By my senior year, basketball travel and intercollegiate travel for other activities were adding rapidly to my list of visited states, cities, and special sights. I was becoming familiar with a good bit of U.S. geography from the Colorado Rockies to the Eastern Shore. This was before the interstate highway system, but very good federal highways provided roads to opportunities and markets for those inclined to be "the seekers." Route 66 was coming into preeminence — that 2,400-mile journey from Los Angeles to Chicago, was a special accomplishment for the young, restless, affluent, or resourceful. The rails were still efficient and economical, too, and a bus system extended to nearly every village in the land. So travel was not especially difficult for those, like myself, with the "bug."

My wife-to-be, Virginia, worked most of my senior year as a clinical technician in the famous Mayo Clinic in Rochester, Minnesota. She had graduated in Dietetics from Kansas State, completing her degree in three years while I took the usual four. Thus, during my senior year, it was not uncommon for me to borrow her mother's car and take off after class Friday afternoon for a 12- to 14-hour jaunt over the 600 miles to Minnesota.

I would spend Saturday and most of Sunday there, returning to arrive in the early morning on Monday. Sleep was never held in high regard during my college days — there were always other things more important (books, athletics, travel) and/or more fun (dances and parties).

Anyway, by the time I was graduated in June 1940, travel had become of significance in my life. Virginia was now a teaching assistant at Kansas State engaged in metabolic research and a Master's degree program. But she was in Manhattan, Kansas, and I was working at the Ewing Mill (Robertson Corporation) in Brownstown. There were over 600 miles between us, but a Studebaker Champion could make the trip with one stop in about 12 hours, and that's what happened — rather frequently — until our marriage in November 1941.

As part of the World War II generation — the one that in a large measure determined the course of world events for over a half-century — we were inordinately and positively influenced by people associated with ROTC, land grant colleges, and communities particularly exemplified by Kansas State University and Manhattan. Virginia's three generations of active ancestry in the town and her experience on the K-State faculty, put us in a position to appreciate these.

Fort Riley's proximity to Manhattan no doubt was a contributing factor to the town's influence on us as World War II-raised folks. Established in 1852, Fort Riley's history is also important. Virginia remembers when the officers competed in polo games attended by "town, gowns, and big guns" on Sundays — people who worked in town, academics from Kansas State University, and Army "Brass" from Fort Riley. My acquaintance with Fort Riley began "through the back door" on Friday or Saturday nights at "The Ogden Supper Club," where new recruits and civilian students sipped beer together and danced and sang, "You get a line and I'll get a pole, we'll go down by the crawdad hole, Honey, Sweet Baby mine."

Anyone under 60 years of age who today reads about or reviews the events just prior to World War II just naturally assumes that in 1939 and 1940 most Americans, and particularly young men of college and draft age, knew that war with Germany, Italy, and Japan was coming. But, that just wasn't so.

Many of us thought that compromise or realignment could be accomplished in Europe. We regarded Russia as possibly more of a threat than Germany, and we didn't regard Japan as a threat — obviously neither did our Naval Intelligence, or Pearl Harbor would not have happened. The world was in turmoil — but it usually is, and, Americans were largely "Isolationists": the phrase "Stay out of foreign entanglements" had been the cry since our involvement in World War I.

Italy had been playing war games with combat planes against Ethiopia's bows and arrows and many nations had been rehearsing for World War II by testing their military materiél in the Spanish Civil War.

I, for one, had not continued with ROTC at Kansas State during my junior and senior years. I hadn't needed the money and thought I could spend my time better elsewhere than running around in a uniform and polished boots. As a result, I needed a lot of practice saluting my classmates and friends after the war started. They were commissioned officers, Second Lieutenants in the Artillery and the Infantry (although it became possible to transfer to the Army Air Corps). As a Private, I volunteered to be an Air Cadet, which is somewhat lower than Private, but the rank had better chances for promotion.

My memories are not always totally accurate, but I think I remember being parked in a Pontiac with some friends near the beacon of the Seymour Airport (later Freeman Army Air Force Base — a "Kilroy" field) in September 1939, just before going back for my senior year in college. It was a beautiful night and we were probably listening to the music of Glenn Miller from the Glen Island Casino, when the program was interrupted to announce Germany's invasion of Poland. I wondered then if things would ever be the same, but I still did not regard America's entry into the war as imminent.

The next day I remember buying an "Extra" paper in Bedford, Indiana — probably my last day of work at our mill in Bedford before departing on the National Limited for Kansas State to be a "dignified senior." Large, black, bold headlines shouted, "**Britain and France Declare War on Germany**." At that point, we had not generally identified the "bads and the goods." I gave no further thought to ROTC and still believed the U.S. would "get along" with whatever European power structure that survived. My judgment regarding who was right and wrong didn't improve much for a few months, but my geography and "travel sense" started improving rapidly. World War I veterans were about the only ones, except "old rich people," who had traveled in Europe and were familiar with Germany,

France, and Belgium. Some knew about England, and a few had experienced Spain and Rome, but not much else.

Russia invaded Finland (where's that located, we asked?). Russia and Germany were actually in cahoots at this time. And in 1940, Germany occupied Normandy and Denmark (who's been there?). France surrendered or collaborated — we weren't sure which. And the Draft began to make things serious, especially for young men. "Involuntary" travel began to appear in the thoughts of the future for many.

I had graduated in June 1940, continuing the long-distance courtship with Virginia. We coped with the Draft and the now more uncertain future. Attitudes and Allies changed frequently. And work went on — actually the production capacity of the U.S. started growing at an inconceivable rate.

Pearl Harbor, the "Day of Infamy," 7 December 1941, changed just about everything for everyone. But because this record is concerned with travel, I will attempt only a brief discussion of the impact of World War II on the exploding, individual and collective, importance of geography as well as politics, economics, and sociology — and, the recognition that mobility was to become an essential element in nearly everyone's life.

Virginia and I were married on November 23, 1941. I had applied and been accepted for enlistment in the U.S. Army Air Corps and was placed on "deferred" status, awaiting official enlistment and active call-up. It was still peacetime and there were no restrictions on my activities or travel. Because we were already seasoned domestic travelers, we planned a rather extensive honeymoon trip following our marriage in Virginia's hometown of Manhattan. We spent our first night in Kansas City, Missouri, and the next night in Memphis, Tennessee, at the famous Peabody Hotel where every morning the mallard ducks ride down in the elevator and waddle out onto the red carpet to the pool in the hotel lobby.

The next night we entered the real "Old South" at the Albany Hotel in Albany, Georgia. It was a scene out of *Gone With The Wind*. We saw our first palm trees and were greeted at the entrance by red-coated liverymen wearing black stockings and top hats. In the candlelight of the quiet, carpeted, plush dining room, we were elegantly served again by red-jacketed, courteous waiters with white gloves.

Remember, this was 1941. There were good paved two-lane national highways with light traffic and no speed limits between towns. We were driving a new Studebaker Champion Tudor sedan, which would run 85 to 90 mph and in which we cruised in "overdrive" at about 70 mph, getting about 34 miles per gallon. It was no problem to drive more than 500 miles per day — even on a honeymoon — between a leisurely breakfast and an elaborate evening dinner.

The next day we drove to Tampa, Florida, and registered at the Tampa Terrace — an elegant hotel with wonderful accommodations. Our balcony opened to 80-degree sunshine — quite a change from the snow we had left behind in Kansas! There were flowers in the room — a honeymoon suite — and an orange tree with oranges beside a cold, fresh, orange juice bar in the spacious and open lobby. From Tampa we drove down the famous Tamiami Trail, through Sarasota, Venice, Fort Meyers, Naples, and across the Everglades where Seminole Indian villages and alligators alternate beside the highway.

That evening, we arrived at the miracle city of Miami Beach, with its lavish profusion of new pink and white hotels of Spanish architecture and lots of neon signs. The hotels, located beside the beautiful white sand beaches, were all advertising "specials" at less than $3 per night — not cheap at that time, but a very attractive value to honeymooners who had never before visited the Deep South or sunny Florida.

Then . . . on December 1st, I received a telegram from my folks advising I had received my "Greetings" from the President of the United States. It was my draft notice to report in ten days to a military processing center. By noon, Virginia and I had packed and started driving up U.S. Highway 1 toward Jacksonville. We breezed past Palm Beach, Daytona Beach, and St. Augustine and stopped at a motel in North Jacksonville for the night. The next day we drove about 900 miles to get home.

On December 3rd, I went to see George Schneider, First Lieutenant U.S. Army (Retired), and president of the local Draft Board. He knew my situation, but said he couldn't change the notice. Schneider did, however, give me a letter releasing me to a Louisville recruiting station. He also suggested I get to Louisville "right now," which I did.

The Air Corps recruiting sergeant looked at my letter and said, "Who the hell is this Lieutenant Schneider?"

"He is the president of my Draft Board and the authorized officer certifying that I am awaiting Air Cadet enlistment orders and am released from the Draft." (This entire story is surely a Kilroy script.)

I don't know whether what I said was correct in detail, but it was right in substance — and it sounded good, too. Anyway, the Sarge accepted it and told me to get my clothes off and get in line for a physical. This was the beginning of a few hundred times I was told to get my clothes off for one reason or another — all good GI reasons. Of course, the main reason is because with no clothes, one has no dignity or backbone or anything else and is pretty responsive to orders in one's powerless position. Also, right then I found out that although I was in pretty good shape (I was 24 years old — old for air cadet — I had lost a couple of teeth, I had an obvious broken-ankle syndrome), and although I was good enough for air cadet training, I was not qualified for pilot training — which is what most Air Corps enlistees wanted. The old story applies: "Many are called, but few are chosen" — and most of the boys were 18, 19, and 20 years old. Anyway, the real blow descended. I stepped under the measuring level and on to the scales.

"You're six feet two and you weigh only 158 pounds."

My basketball weight had been about 170, but I had worked and driven and stayed up late a lot since then.

"You've got to be 160 pounds for the Air Corps."

It was 11:00 a.m. "Can I come back after lunch, Sarge?"

"I guess so, we're out from twelve until one."

I turned quickly, went to the nearest store, bought bananas and pop and started eating and drinking. At 12:55 p.m., I got in the strip line again, tipped the scale at a bare 160, and got some printed orders from the Sarge saying I had enlisted and was awaiting orders to report for duty, etc. I went back and reported to Lieutenant Schneider, my name was removed from the Draft call, and I was very relieved and happy — relieved that I wasn't going to be drafted, and happy and very patriotically proud that I would have the opportunity to "wear a pair of silver wings."

The next two days — December 4th and 5th — were as normal as Fridays and Saturdays could be at that time. On Sunday, December 7, 1941 (by now we were in "our house"), Virginia and I went to Sunday School and church, and then, to my parents' house for Sunday dinner (they were helping out the newlyweds). We ate at noon, had finished quickly, and were back at our little house by 1:00. I hurried to get ready to go bowling with friends. I don't know what Virginia thought, but she didn't protest my going "out" and leaving my bride on Sunday afternoon, 12 days after our marriage. Anyway, we went to Seymour to bowl.

Shortly after arriving at the bowling alley, about 1:45 p.m., the word came over the radio that the Japanese had bombed Pearl Harbor a few minutes earlier — about 6:00 a.m., Hawaii time. And so, we spent the rest of the afternoon close to the radio as the horrible news of the battleship *Arizona*'s sinking and the destruction of the Pacific battleship fleet slowly unfolded. From that day forward, our country was on a wartime footing.

Chapter 2

Travel During World War II

A FEW MONTHS PASSED between the time I signed on as a volunteer with the Army Air Forces and my actual reporting for duty. However, I finally bid civilization farewell at Columbus, Ohio, and boarded an overnight train for Boca Raton, Florida. Upon arrival at the Boca station, an authoritative Sergeant took over, put us at "attention," and marched us down toward the Atlantic Ocean to the Boca Raton Club — perhaps the finest, most exclusive hotel club in the United States! However, the veneer of luxury had been largely removed and the elevator of the eight-floor building barricaded. On arrival at the Club, we were halted in an out-building, told to "strip," and given a bag to put our "feather-merchant civies" in for mailing home. We were then given GI (Government Issue) clothes in a choice of one color — khaki — and two sizes — too big and too little!

We had traveled over 1,000 miles on our first day of active duty. And travel, from then on, became a way of life. I can tell you now, with great respect for those who go through four years of the U.S. Military Academy, at West Point, that as an Air Cadet this was the first day of nine months of something resembling Purgatory, if not Hell.

The 13 weeks of Basic Officer Training at Boca Raton did not pass quickly. Reveille was at 4:45 a.m. We had 15 minutes to shower (sometimes), shave, do whatever toilet required, dress, and get down the six flights of stairs and fall into rank on parade or assembly areas (converted lawns or fairways). The roster was checked and updated, and the "chow-line" was quickly formed. The food was good — eggs, bacon, cereal, milk, fruit — whatever one could stuff down in 15 minutes. Then, quickly back to the room and return in 15 minutes ready for our first class or duty at 5:45 a.m. Classes included Officers Manual, Military Discipline, and Jungle Survival. Duties and exercises included Principles of Hand-to-Hand Combat, Swimming with Gear, and Obstacle Course. Physical Buildup included forced beach hikes, all or any increments of the distance from Del Ray to Fort Lauderdale — that was pretty much the extent of our travel while at Boca. It was a rigorous and stressful time. We needed to stay healthy and physically fit. Any failure could result in a "wash-out" and back to "enlisted" status instead of that of officer candidate. If one could not run fast enough, swim far enough, master close-order drill commands — or whatever — it was "wash out."

After completing the first phase of the nine-month Air Cadet program, we were notified to "pack up"; we were moving somewhere else. One night, under cover of darkness, we carried our duffle bags to the depot and boarded the train bound for an unknown destination. No one ever mentioned "troop movements." All such was "classified" information.

Our train was a typical stripped-down troop train. We slept sitting up that night and the next. We were provided adequate meals with "boxed food" and a chance to try out some "C" or "K Rations," which we had previously sampled at Boca. It was also our first encounter with SPAM, a canned ground ham-pork shoulder concoction, which really would have been okay on occasion, but was offered so frequently overseas that it earned an undeserved reputation of "bad taste."

Our journey ended after a long 36 or 40 hours of maybe 40-mph train movement during which the blinds were kept down as we passed through towns. As we filed out of the train on the rather early morning of the second day, in the very busy and pretty large station we saw the name — "NEW HAVEN, CONN." We knew we had arrived at Yale.

Air Cadet Training at Yale University sounded like that of the Basic Training at the Boca Raton Club. However, it was T-O-U-G-H! We were herded down through the old campus, halted in front of the venerable statue of Nathan Hale and were put through a hazing orientation. No physical abuse — just more of a humbling, not really humiliating, verbal experience. It was stressed again that we acted always "on order." We always obeyed, and that we had only three responses: "Yes Sir," "No Sir," and "No Excuse, Sir." Our Tactical Officers, mostly Second and First Lieutenants, commanded all the respect of Generals, but were as tough on us as our top Sergeants.

After a short orientation, we were assigned rooms about mid-afternoon. Somehow, I ended up in a room of my own, not knowing what to do next and with no one to ask. (During those days, we all had an unspoken expectation — the very real anticipation of possibly getting killed. Those of us who volunteered as Air Cadets just figured we'd rather be shot down in clean air than the drafted ones who might get shot up in the mud.) I was scared — and for one of the few times in my life — very homesick.

The Yale schedule was also very tight. We were in the sack at 8:00 p.m. and up at 4:00 a.m. We were not allowed to go the latrine during the night hours: "If you can't control yourself for eight hours, you can't be a Cadet!" But, there were at least two alternatives. One was to go to "Sick Bay." The other was to relieve oneself through the by-now rusted window screens.

At Yale, we began to travel. On occasion, we would be transported to nearby military airfields and flew instructional aerial mapping and reconnaissance missions. By then, my little group had become designated as Aerial Photo Reconnaissance and Intelligence Officers, vacillating between the Military Occupational Specialties (MOS) of 8502 and 8503.

My Yale suite mates consisted of Jim McIlvane from Ohio State; Weinstein, a very smart Jewish boy out of City College of New York; Sammy Romano, an Italian Yale buddy from Hempstead, Long Island; and Jim MacNeil out of Harvard, who was married to the delightful Deborah Bradford, a direct descendant of the Boston-Plymouth Colony Mayflower Bradfords. "Harvard" was not as cautious as the rest of us, and he ended up getting "washed back" two weeks, which meant we all had two weeks' rank on him when we got our commissions.

A World of Travel

Joseph Edmond Robertson as an Aviation Cadet in the United States Army Air Forces Officer Training Program at Yale University, New Haven, Connecticut, 1943.

One of my fondest memories of my six months at Yale was the wonderful Big Band music of Glenn Miller's Army Air Corps Technical Training Command Band. We were privileged to march to such tunes as "St. Louis Blues March" and "Knuckle Down Winsocki" in the great parades on the New Haven Green. In order to boost morale for those stationed there, Miller and his band played frequently on the Yale campus, which served as their wartime headquarters. The band also performed for many radio broadcasts from the university, and played for troops throughout the world during 1943 and 1944 to assist the war effort.

Unbelievable discipline was required of an Air Cadet during training. My socks "for show" were rolled and displayed in staggered drawers, as were my folded shirts and trousers. Shirts hanging in the closet were always fully buttoned. Shoes were shined to a high gloss. All these were ready "for inspection." The clothes I had worn during the day were in a laundry bag, and the ones I was going to wear were underneath the mattress on which I was sleeping — "being pressed"! We were in rigorous academic training all morning and rigorous military training all afternoon. We did have some fun playing basketball during Physical Training classes. The parades were also exciting.

One cherished memory from my Cadet training days is that of an evening when Virginia and I went to Saks Fifth Avenue and Brooks Brothers to spend my allowance to buy new officer's uniforms. This in itself was a great thrill because of the transition from being an "enlisted" man to an "officer." In addition, it was especially exciting because Glenn Miller was buying uniforms in the same store at the same time!

When wives and girlfriends came to visit on Saturday afternoon and Sunday, we could only greet them with a handshake — "no public display of affection." Like the other "cadet followers," Virginia would come up some Saturday mornings on the New York and New Haven Railroad and check in at the Taft Hotel just across the Green from Yale's famous fence. On one or two occasions we managed to go to the Taft Theatre for one of the Broadway show trials. Usually, however, it was a short visit to the Taft Bar and back to the Yale colleges. We could attend church together, and Virginia could watch the "Review" Sunday afternoon. Then, it was back to the barracks and books for me and by train to New York for her.

Yale played a great football schedule then, and probably had four games in the famous Yale Bowl while I was there. Virginia was coming from Indiana to visit me the weekend of the Yale-Army game, where the greatest athletes of the era were scheduled to play — Army's "Mr. Inside" and "Mr. Outside," Glen Davis and Doc Blanchard. There was a great air of anticipation all week before that Saturday. I was to meet Virginia Saturday at noon, after our morning schedule.

Because of my height, I had been made a flight leader with Cadet Corporal rank. It was dark when we "fell out" that Saturday morning about 5 a.m. My flight assembled smartly in rank as usual. I, out in front, wheeled and reported to the Tactical Officer, "Flight B, all present and accounted for, SIR!"

"MISTER," came the booming retort from the Tac Officer, "how do you know your flight is all present and accounted for? Can you see them in this blackness? Do you know which ones are where?"

The horns of a dilemma. I only had three possible answers. The consequences of a false report might be less than a report compounded by a false reply to a Tac Officer, so I said, "No Sir."

"Cadet Robertson, at 1200 hours, after morning duties, you will report to the Officer of the Day for four hours of policing duty which will consist of cleaning pigeon poop from the high arches of Sterling Hall."

There went my afternoon with Virginia and an opportunity of a lifetime to see Mr. Inside and Mr. Outside! That's the way it was in training at Yale.

Anyway, on November 18, 1943, I stood scared and proud during the graduation ceremony waiting anxiously — very anxiously — for my commission and my Second Lieutenant's gold bars. Finally, I got 'em! Virginia was waiting. I went by my room to get my duffle and B-4 bags, stuffed in the last clothes, and we walked or ran to the New Haven Station. I was not at ease and not sure I was really no longer a Cadet until the train was rolling down the track to New York.

I had my orders. I was to report to the Army Air Forces Base at McCook, Nebraska, with a one-week leave en route. The orders read "No deps." That meant no provision or pay for dependents. Virginia and I stopped by overnight in the New York apartment of our friends, Mr. and Mrs. Winston Brooke. Winston was an FBI agent, and I later found that, like many others, he was engaged in fringe work on the "Manhattan Project," which developed the atom bomb. The Brookes had been frequent hosts to Virginia while I was at Yale. They took us to the airport the next morning to put us on our first commercial air flight.

The New York to Indianapolis flight, in a two-engine DC-3 type aircraft, took about eight hours — so many landings and takeoffs, including Pittsburgh and Dayton — but we made it. We had two stewardesses, and we were treated with great hospitality. It really was a milestone for us.

We were met in Indianapolis by my folks, spent about four days in Brownstown, and then went quickly out to Manhattan, to see Virginia's mother for the weekend. Then, I took the train up the Short Line to Lincoln, Nebraska, and on to a hotel in McCook.

I never even got to the base. There was a Sergeant waiting in the lobby with new orders for me. Such were the fortunes of war. I had fully expected to be attached to a group as a Photo Reconnaissance & Intelligence Officer and figured that we would be shipping out for the European Theater in about 10 to 12 weeks — that's about how long it took to train the combat crews for shipment and action. Now, these orders read: "Report to Davis-Monthan Army Air Base, Tucson, Arizona, for assignment as Base Aerial Photo Training Officer." That was actually a considerable promotion, perhaps based on my trying pretty hard in academics, etc., at Yale. Anyway, those were the orders and not to be questioned by a green Second Lieutenant. I was to proceed to Omaha where I would be picked up by Air Transport Command or whatever air available. I could spend the next night before departure at the Cornhusker Hotel in Lincoln, so I called Virginia and told her to get on that little Short Line up to meet me for another goodbye in there. Our wartime experiences were filled with goodbyes.

The day after Lincoln, I had checked into an Omaha hotel. About 4:45 a.m. the next morning, my phone rang and a Sergeant said he would be by my room to pick me up at 5:00 a.m. and escort me to the airplane (I guess they wanted to be sure I didn't go AWOL). Anyway, off we went, and the plane took off for a desert I had never seen and a town I had only associated with Western movies. Despite the fact that my orders again read "No deps," I had told Virginia to come on down however she could and we would find someway for her to stay wherever she could until my "shipping out" time, whenever that might be.

The best reporting of our experiences in Tucson and training at Davis Monthan Field is found in a letter which we wrote, in March 1993:

March 17, 1993

Auna Elmore
2518 Seneca Court
Tucson, AZ 85716

Dear Ms. Elmore,

Thanks so much for the hospitality you extended our group of five strangers who appeared on the walks of your Seneca Court, Monday, March 8. We were indeed most fortunate to meet one so attractive, charming, intelligent, and interesting — and one who was willing to indulge our intense inquiry regarding the place which was our home for a while during the turbulent time of World War II.

You mentioned that you sensed a history associated with Seneca Court. Perhaps some references regarding us will be helpful to you in sorting out some of that history:

At the time we lived in Seneca Court, Major Ralph (& Betty)

Cable (Ohio) was Ass't. Director of Training at Davis Monthan Air Base; Captain John (& Betty) White (Illinois), was Special Services Officer; 1st Lt. Joe (& Virginia) Robertson (Indiana), was Aerial Photo Intelligence & Bomb & Gunnery Camera Training Officer. The women were about the age you are now — Betty White the youngest at 20.

Our Mission was to train bomber combat crews for the European Theater and then the Asian Theater. There were generally about 10 crew members — Pilot, Co-Pilot, Navigator, Bombardier (all officers), and 6 enlisted men, radio and radar operators, waist, belly, turret, and tail gunners. The first of the 4-engine warplanes were Flying Fortresses, B-17's, then Flying Boxcars, B-24's, and last the monstrous B-29's. These planes often filled the skies as they took off from Davis Monthan over Seneca Court — often 50 in a flight at 50-second intervals. There is much more to tell about the magnificent machines and the men who flew and supported them, but this gives you a background for us — the temporary residents of your Seneca Court.

All of us had academic backgrounds or relationships and these were continued somewhat at Seneca Court through keeping in touch at U. of Arizona near there. The women developed rapport doing support and Red Cross work there. Betty Cable taught school for many years. White played football and hockey at U. of Illinois. Virginia's (Robertson) mother was a Professor in Education at Kansas State and Virginia was a Clinical Technician at Mayo Clinic for a while after her BS from Kansas State. She later returned for some graduate work (as you plan). I played on the Davis Monthan basketball team — which Captain White coached, and we played a number of games there at the old Arizona U. gym. We also traveled some and played other Air Force teams, including early versions of the Harlem Globetrotters and New York Renaissance.

Tucson was "way out west" to all of us when we came — Cable out of an ROTC program, and White and I from Air Cadet Programs — mine were at Boca Raton, Florida and Yale U. (where our son later did his undergraduate work.) We came to appreciate the many attractions of Tucson and Arizona. The

350 clear-weather flying days, the cool clear nights, the nearby range from desert to snow-capped mountains — the real cowboys, real Indians, and Mexicans.

At that time none of us had children. Dogs included "Penny" Cable (Great Dane) and "Ranger" Garrison — a part or mixed small white dog that relentlessly pursued his love for Penny in total frustration.

After 18 months in Seneca Court, Virginia and I moved to Biggs AF Base in El Paso where I was on General Longfellow's 16th Wing Bombardment Operational Training Wing Staff — a part of 2nd Air Force which trained all crews for the Asian operation including the 7 crews from which was selected the one to carry the atom bomb on the Enola Gay. While we were in the area, the White Sands Missile Range was involved in atom bomb development program — with only parts of the very secret program known to any of us. In July of '45 the bomb was detonated at Trinity about 70 miles north of El Paso in the New Mexico desert. You know the following events, the war was quickly over and the world was dramatically changed forever.

After the war Cable remained in the service, raised three attractive, charming, and bright daughters in England and New England. During that time he received his Harvard MBA. He was retired as a full Colonel. The Cables now have two homes, both in golf resorts, Horseshoe, NC and Green Valley, AZ. Granddaughter Lindsey comes to visit frequently.

John White returned to manage Champaign (Ill.) Seed Co. near the U. of Illinois. He had played football and hockey at U. of I. and was very active in youth coaching programs. The Whites had three boys and lost one in an auto-bicycle accident. The older son is a hospital administrator. The younger, after following his Dad on the U. of I. football field, went into the seed business and also has a couple of Dairy Queen franchises. John died prematurely of a heart attack, and Betty was employed in the U. of I. academic community for several years until her retirement — spent mostly in travel. She has a bunch of grandchildren — five I think.

Virginia and I returned to Brownstown, Indiana to the family milling business and the Robertson home area since 1790. We have traveled extensively since on both business and pleasure to about 120 countries. Our son and daughter-in-law are both physicians in Portland, Oregon, and we visit them frequently and play with our two grandchildren; and at their mountain "cabin" on the snow slopes of Mt. Hood.

When we came to Tucson's Seneca Court my pay was about $125.00 a month, White's about $135, and Cable's $150. We paid $47.50/mo. for our Court units. The owner of the Court was Mr. Tucker — we called him B.G. (for Big Gear), a Seventh Day Adventist whom we really didn't know and who provided us adequate and affordable housing — nevertheless, since he was our landlord-capitalist, we made up rules he supposedly enforced. We named the rules "Special Orders 00-2 Late," following the military manner. Then we were totally chauvinistic and in tune with the military macho of the time. For example: wives were to make sure the larder was well-filled at all times for the proper pleasure and sustenance of the husband-officers. Husbands were forbidden to be involved in such menial tasks as taking out garbage or assisting in dish or clothes washing, etc., etc., etc. Of course, after the war, it was difficult for us to maintain the excellent military discipline of the Court. As the years passed, I lost household control totally and John's grip was eroding rapidly before his death. Only Cable has been able to maintain some of the proper male dominance in his family and household — perhaps because of his higher rank and the fact that he "accumulated" money instead of spending it freely like the rest of us.

I'm sure this is more than enough information for you to complete your historical background of the Court, and of course the nearby museum will give you plenty of information regarding the planes and activities at the base.

Joe E. Robertson

Perhaps, in Tucson, we first started seeing the beginning of the "Kilroy legend." The "50-Mission fliers" returned from overseas with "Kilroy."

Our air base was just one of the many major bases with satellite airfields scattered throughout the Southwest. And soon on every field the long-nosed sign and signature, "Kilroy was here," could be found.

Visiting Mexico was fairly common, at least for our wives, while we were at Tucson. Nogales, Sonora, Mexico, was about 70 miles south, and our wives would take our 1936 Packard (or one of the other cars) and roll right on down in little more than an hour. The shopping was good, friendly and cheap.

After more than a year at Tucson, I was transferred to Biggs Field at El Paso, Texas, and placed on General Longfellow's staff as Wing Aerial Photo Combat Training Officer of the 16th Bombardment Operational Training Wing. Our mission was (1) to develop and supervise the training of the individual crew members who were to do bomb-accuracy assessment and reconnaissance and intelligence functions; and (2) to help train the combat crews in developing combat skills in both bombing and gunnery through photographic assistance. Thus, instead of just firing at straight-flight towed targets, we mounted movie cameras on the .50-caliber machine guns so that we could hold complete fighter-interceptance training missions and record the accuracy of the waist, nose, and tail gunners. We also had a long focal-length camera rigged to the bombing system and tied into the Norden Bomb Sights and the bomb-release button. We had developed a Nadir-point Target Locater, which calculated where the bomb "would have impacted" had it been real and live.

I received a citation from "the Big Guy," General Henry H. "Hap" Arnold, for submitting this Camera Bombing System suggestion. We could do camera bombing and live-target bombing on the same mission, which included a full bomb bay of 100-pound practice bombs and all gun cameras including the "Big Bertha" bomb camera (40-inch focal length) full of film.

I occasionally accompanied the crews as we would fly over Dallas, Los Angelos, and San Francisco on training bomb missions arranged in 1944 and early 1945 to simulate runs on German targets of ammunition plants, oil refineries, weapons factories, etc., in, for example, Hamburg, Berlin, Frankfurt, or Ploesti. On this part of the exercise, the operational switch was on "Camera Bombing," but remember, the bomb bay was full of 100-pound bombs. We would then make our real bomb runs by dropping the 100-pounders on the ground targets established at Gila Bend, Yuma, Globe, Arizona, or wherever.

One day in Tucson we had about 50 B-24s ready to roll at approximately 6:00 a.m. Crews had fallen out around 4:00 a.m. and several photo instructors were scheduled to go along. I was in my flight-line office waiting for the departure of this significant training flight when Sergeant Russell came running in.

"Lt. Robertson, didn't you say just put the operational switch on Camera Bombing and the Bomb Release Mechanism will not function to release?"

"That's exactly right, Sergeant."

"Well, Sir, I just did that on a check-out drill and when I punched the Bomb Release Button, real bombs fell all over the runway."

Fortunately, that "snafu" (situation normal, all fouled up) went unreported to General Arnold, and we got it straightened out. Otherwise, we would have, in the Sergeant's words, "blown the hell out of the rail yards in San Francisco or some other city."

While assigned to the 16th Wing Headquarters in El Paso, we lived very close to the river and Mexico. "Quarters" were not available to officers, so we put our wives in black-market houses and showed up at home whenever we could. The General's wife (he was about 62 and she about 29) required officers' wives to report for frequent duty at "aid the war effort" functions. Also, she required us to have "maids" so that the wives could be available on call. That wasn't as snooty and unreasonable as it sounds, because maids were available for $5 a week and could walk over from Mexico every morning. Our maid, Lupee, spoke a little more English than I did Spanish-Mexican. She had to adjust, but my wife communicated with her very well. I never did.

We had 16 officers and 4 airplanes assigned to the Wing Staff. Of course, the mission and territory changed all the time, but the headquarters of the 2nd Air Force Training Command, was located at Peterson Field, Colorado Springs, Colorado. Our Wing included bases at El Paso; Tucson, Arizona; and Albuquerque, Roswell, Alamogordo, New Mexico, (near the

Trinity Atom Bomb Site); and sometimes Mountain Home, Utah, and Proscuto, California.

We soon established training priorities. Flights to the Colorado Springs Headquarters were most important. And, funny thing, we almost always got "weathered in" there because the famous Broadmoor Hotel would put up Army Air Forces officers for $2 per night. (The last time I stayed there, we paid $200!)

After Colorado Springs, we found that March Air Force Base, Riverside, California, needed quite a lot of supervision. At that time, L.A. was less than an hour away and the great hotels were also rate-friendly to us. Motor pool cars were available "on official Air Forces business" or "to quarters" in L.A. Coconut Grove gave us military admission, too. Somehow, the base needing the least attention was Wendover Field at Mountain Home, Utah. Those guys had to be fast learners, because there was little to attract instructors at that base.

Although the twin-engine planes or bombers in which we flew throughout the Southwest cruised at only 200 to 275 mph, we covered a lot of territory in six or seven big states. Many times, we would leave El Paso before dawn and return after dusk following a full day's work at some distant base. Other times we would stay over a night or two. Actually, about the only place we would really be "weathered in" was Colorado Springs.

In early '45, we heard some talk indicating an early Allied victory, but having heard of the disastrous "Battle of the Bulge," in December 1944, we weren't buying into it too well. Even after we started switching over training from the big "heavy" bombers (B-24s) to the very heavy super bombers (B-29s), we didn't have enough "big picture" knowledge to know that the plan would be for sure "all Asia." However, we did know that the training in the 200 mph "winds aloft" was not for typical European missions, and we did know that the 90-mile classified stretch of White Sands we were flying around every day (over, if the General was along) was restricted for a good reason.

When Germany surrendered on V-E Day, May 8, 1945, the European war was suddenly behind us and preparations for escalating the Asian effort were going forward at a rapid pace. The Training Command, including our Wing, was involved in preparing seven combat crews for a possible "big mission" over Japan. Of course, everything was a "big mission" and all of us knew there was much more war ahead. Our victories in the Pacific included Coral Sea, Midway, the Solomon Islands, and later Guam, the Marianas, and Iwo Jima. A series of island-hopping carrier attacks and victorious battles by August 1944 had secured the Marianas, which lay within bomber distance of Japan. From these bases, our B-29s were able to reach Japan and return, generally unescorted, in one very long day. We had to train air crews very well not only to fly the great warbirds, but to deliver the bomb load to the target and man the guns effectively against the attacking Zeros. The "rate of return" when the B-29s flew over Japan was much improved over that of the B-17s and B-24s during the early stages of the European War, when sometimes 50 planes were sent out and perhaps 12 returned unscathed. "The 50 Mission and Home" requirement had to be lowered to 25. The great heroics of personnel and aircraft like that of B-17 Flying Fortress, "The Memphis Belle" let all of us know how courageous the American crews were in their "wonderful flying machines."

Like so many other officers in the 2nd Air Force, I managed to sign up on good combat outfits headed for both Europe and Asia. However, our shipping orders passed under the scrutiny of General Longfellow. Along with others, I would be called in and chewed out. "You're staying here, Robertson, until *I* ship you out. These young boys must be taught how to fly, to hit bomb targets, and machine gun Zeros, and they must be better, much better, than the enemy."

Combat Crew Training was not without risk. That's one reason everyone had parachutes. The 19, 20, and 21-year old pilots had only taken off and, more crucially, landed these planes a few times. Any landing was a good one, and bouncing in was commonplace. Most of the poor flight instructors undoubtedly died prematurely from heart damage sustained as they sat there daily behind or beside the green pilots or engineers. Of course, I have also heard the response of the student navigator when he was questioned high over the Rockies at about midnight, "What's our position?"

"Sir, I haven't the foggiest idea."

Although I didn't fly daily, I experienced taking off without flaps, losing engines in flight, etc. There were those who said they would be afraid to jump out in a parachute. Not me. If I heard a change in the engine symphony or saw a feathered prop, I rapidly strapped on the 'chute and awaited command.

Most of us were expecting at least two or three more years of costly war and a million casualties when things started happening quickly.

We were sleeping in El Paso, Texas, about 5 a.m. the morning after July 4th, 1945. There was a great boom that shook the windows and walls — then quiet. Later in the day, radio and newspapers reported that an ammunition dump had exploded near the Alamogordo Air Base. Of course, I had visited that base many times and it sounded reasonable to me. After all, *all of* Kilroy's Bases had plenty of ammo.

Well, you know the rest of the story. President Harry S. Truman decided we had sacrificed enough American blood toward obtaining an honorable peace with Japan's Emperor Hirohito. We were in the war to win. On August 6, the B-29 *Enola Gay* dropped the Atomic bomb on Hiroshima, and another struck Nagasaki three days later. Within a week, the shooting had stopped. The superiority of not only Kilroy's boys but of all the Americans involved in the war effort from "Rosie the Riveter" to General Eisenhower had been demonstrated when the fighting was for a just cause and no suitable alternatives could be found.

The war effort wound down quickly, though orderly discharge and return to civilian life actually took more adjustment than most people had anticipated. Most military folks were anxious to get out; but some, fortunately, had contracted "the Kilroy syndrome" and were hoping they would get to "stay in." I was among those anxious to get out and go back home. My discharge orders read December 16, 1945, and I was back in the milling business before the year's end.

On the way home from El Paso, Texas, Virginia and I had to stop every 75 miles and put a quart of oil in the 1936 Packard. Tires were no better and replacements were unavailable. My last tire blew 75 miles from home. Civilians couldn't buy shotgun shells, and I had some, so I traded a service station guy two boxes of 12-gauge shells for one worn tire. I called my folks and told them if we weren't home in an hour and a half to start out Highway 50 West in search. The tire held out, and I later sold the Packard for $444 (OPA Ceiling Price) which was $44 more than I had paid for it.

My own wartime experience in North America and the experiences related to me by my flying friends just added to my amazement at the American accomplishments in establishing the Kilroy fields all over the world during the years from 1941 to 1945. Furthermore, I don't understand where enough D4 Caterpillar (or any kind) bulldozers came from to build those fields. I knew that the U.S. built almost one million airplanes — fighter, bomber, cargo, recon, training — little and big, new or modified during the war years. Permits, licenses, and most of the usual roadblocks were waived or disregarded. There was a lot of paper work — in fact, it was said if we ran out of ammunition, we could win the war by smothering our enemies with paper.

Fliers came home who had been with Claire L. Chennault's Flying Tigers in China, from flying the "Hump" with heavily laden cargo planes over the Himalayas between Burma and China, from the sand fields of Casablanca, the jungles of New Guinea, the "temporary" bases at Truk and other Pacific atolls, as well as from the snow fields of Alaska. Aviators came home with stories more exciting than those of "One Thousand and One Nights," stories as varied as the locales. But there was always one common denominator — "Kilroy was here."

Chapter 3

Family Travel in the U.S. After the War

IN FEBRUARY 1947, Virginia and I started on the first of what became annual trips to Florida. We had no children yet and hadn't built a house, so we were financially able to take off for the better part of a month and go wherever we pleased.

At that time, we decided to go via New Orleans and take in the Mardi Gras. We took my mother and dad with us and had a great time. My dad bought feed molasses from an import broker in New Orleans.

We didn't know how treasured admission was to the exclusive Rex Ball, so Dad just flat out asked the broker if she would get us four tickets so that we could celebrate Fat (Shrove) Tuesday and pay homage to the King and Queen of the Mardi Gras. "Ask and you will receive." Somehow, the lady came up with the four ducats, and we went to the ball in our rented tuxedos. Dad's pants were a pretty snug fit and, early in the evening, he seriously split the main bottom seam. When it came time to pass in review before the royalty and make a deep bow, Dad's was more of a dip so as to minimize the white exposure of his B.V.D.s.

Leaving New Orleans, we drove across the Mississippi Gulf Coast on picturesque U.S. 90, past the Biloxi Gulf shores and the beaches of Panama City to the magnolias of Tallahassee, Florida — all in one day. We passed three military bases. Biloxi had enjoyed considerable growth as a result of the World War II Kilroy field, Kessler Air Force Base, still in operation today.

Pensacola, then as now, was a Naval Air Station. Eglin Field between the Fort Walton and Panama City beaches was also a large and active air base. Both bases are active today. Panama Beach, with its beautiful white sand beaches, was mostly a "summer place" at that time, and the relatively few seaside cottages were, for the most part, "boarded up" from November until March.

From Tallahassee, we drove south the next day to our first destination — Fort Myers, Florida, where we visited the wonderful Shanklin family, Captain Jack, Betty, 5-year old Susan, and little Mary. They put up all four of us in grand style. We went out to Fort Myers Beach, crossed by ferry (no bridges) to go shelling on Sanibel and Captiva Islands and went deep-sea fishing — quite a program for "snow birds" or "tourists," but Betty always insisted on calling us "winter visitors." There were only about 12,000 people in Fort Myers at that time. Now, there are about one-half million in the metropolitan area.

We liked it so well we kept coming back every year for decades until, in 1980, Betty and the society editor of the *Fort Myers Bugle* printed a headline on the Society Page heralding: "Robertsons make 33rd Annual Visit to The Shanklin Residence." We did reduce the frequency and length of our sojourns thereafter.

On one of the 1950s Florida trips, we noticed a billboard advertising "International Travel: "Leave The Country — Freeport, Grand Bahamas, Less Than One Hour From Fort Lauderdale." That did it. After leaving Fort Myers, we drove east via the Tamiami Trail, rearranged our clothes and luggage, parked our car at the airport, and took off for Freeport. The airfield, a former Kilroy World War II base, was a long way from our resort-casino-hotel. In those days, the $35 taxi fare was really expensive — still is. Anyway, the weather was warm, the sand white, and the water blue — those elements do a lot for winter living. That short, early venture into "international" commercial air travel demonstrated to us that we could go about anywhere at anytime, if we had the funds and the time.

On our return trip from Florida, we began to explore business potential. We determined that the furniture industry was constructing and using a lot of hardwood plywood and that the Southeast's center of the industry was in northwest North Carolina, with some spill-over into southern Virginia and also into South Carolina. The industry was exploding, and our product — GLU-X adhesive extender — was a natural to meet their needs. The manufacturers had been using low-grade "wheat flour" of sometimes unknown and highly variable characteristics and specifications. We introduced them to a "Special" Extender, milled to meet their needs with a quality and uniformity far superior to what they had been using. Of course, our price was much higher, and we were a long distance away, but we did accomplish the rather "hard sell." Soon, our trucks were lumbering over the Smoky Mountains with loads of GLU-X bound for household-name furniture plants such as Broyhill, Drexel, Lane, Stanley, and many others.

In making a week of business calls to the Carolina Heartland, we soon learned we could visit Gatlinburg, Tennessee, the Great Smoky Mountains National Park, South Carolina, and/or Asheville on the weekend before business calls and head for Myrtle Beach, South Carolina, after the working week was over. This business-pleasure arrangement began to develop into a visiting relationship, too. As we called on customers throughout the nation, we began to develop a travel-visit relationship with many of them in a manner similar to the business-golf syndrome so prevalent in the business community.

Our son, "Rob" (Joe, Jr.), was born in 1952, and he soon was a regular passenger-companion on our many trips, which, by now, were extending to most of the nation. Of course, as we passed by former WWII air base locations, my military curiosity would prevail, and we would drop in for a quick look at the commercial aviation installations that have since developed — noticing the enlargement of the original airstrip used by piston engine planes to the longer runways now required by jet aircraft.

On the longer, harder trips, we could fortunately leave young Rob in the excellent care of my mother or our sisters-in-law. However, he became accustomed to making the 640-mile trip to Manhattan, Kansas, in a day.

To facilitate that journey, and others of extended length, we rigged a piece of plywood in the back seat, overlaid with a child's mattress surrounded by plenty of pillows to avoid injury and toys to provide enjoyment.

We had always made stops at the Kilroy air bases, but we began to visit historical battlefields. On our New England trips, we visited Bunker Hill, while in Boston, and drove out to see Lexington and the Concord Bridge, where the first shots were fired to begin the American Revolutionary War, in April 1775.

As we moved down the Eastern states, we covered many Civil War battle sites, including Gettysburg (more than once) in Pennsylvania, and on to Bull Run, then to Richmond, the Confederate capital, and Petersburg, in Virginia — then, Lookout Mountain near Chattanooga, Tennessee, and Atlanta, Georgia. As we covered the more western territory of Civil War battles, we stopped at Pittsburg Landing, in Tennessee, and Vicksburg, Mississippi. We finished our Civil War tour at Appomattox Courthouse in Virginia, where General Robert E. Lee surrendered to General Ulysses S. Grant on April 9, 1865, ending the War Between the States.

During that ten or twelve-year period, we had visited many Revolutionary War battlefields also and the sites of several conflicts during the Plains Indian Wars, in the late 1800s, if it isn't too politically incorrect to still call them that. Regardless of circumstances, justice, or politics, those conflicts in the Old West were important in determining "The Birth of A Nation" and "How The West Was Won."

The historical names and places mentioned were, of course, only some of many visited and discussed with son Rob during his childhood. However, the experiences undoubtedly gave him an excellent background for a valid understanding of the people and places involved in our American history.

An illustration of his early grasp of what we were doing happened when we were checking in at the Holiday Inn in Orangeburg, South Carolina. We had been driving up and down the Carolina coast, both calling on customers and reading roadside markers that documented the movements of Revolutionary and Civil War armies in those parts. We had been discussing some of the guerrilla tactics of Francis Marion, the "Swamp Fox," who had gained his nickname leading Colonist raiders against the British Army in South Carolina, in 1780, during the American Revolutionary War. At any rate, I was registering and Rob was standing beside me on tiptoe, his head barely over the desk.

"How are you, Sonny, and what are you doing down here in the South?"

"Well," Rob replied, "My Dad's a 'histryan' and he's down here to sell GLU-X — it's the best." I think he might have been five years old at the time, but he had the whole program in a nutshell!

Rob's history background was undoubtedly further strengthened by the fact that he was brought up in an authentic pioneer log house which we had purchased in 1949. In its reconstruction the huge poplar logs were numbered, dismantled, moved, and rebuilt, pegs and all, with quite a few additions and alterations to its present location. Joseph Weaver had originally built the log home, in 1836, on a land grant signed by President Martin Van Buren.

For us, our home became a place of interesting collections — at first, for old and/or antique pieces linked to Indiana history in general and our family history in particular — the decor ranged from "Early American" to "Around the World." Later, our home became a repository for bits and pieces of souvenirs, minor art, presents, and memorabilia from our travels in many parts of the world, which included the 50 states, many U.S. territories, all Canadian provinces, most of Mexico and about 140 countries. Some of our building concepts and collection policies were undoubtedly influenced by the following excerpts from Don Blanding's poem, "Vagabond House" (Dodd, Mead and Company/Penguin Putnam, Inc.):

> When I have a house . . . as I sometime may . . .
> I'll suit my fancy in every way.
> I'll fill it with things that have caught my eye
> In drifting from Iceland to Molokai
> It won't be correct or in period style,
> But . . . oh, I've thought for a long, long while
> Of all the corners and all the nooks,
> Of all the bookshelves and all the books,
> The great big table, the deep, soft chairs,
> And the Chinese rug at the foot of the stairs;
> It's an old, old rug from far Chow Wan
> That a Chinese princess once walked on.
>
> My house will stand on the side of a hill
> By a slow, broad river, deep and still,
> With a tall lone pine on guard near by

Where the birds can sing and the stormwinds cry.
A flagstone walk with lazy curves
Will lead to the door where a Pan's head serves
As a knocker there like a vibrant drum
To let me know that a friend has come;
And the door will squeak as I swing it wide
To welcome you to the cheer inside.

For I'll have good friends who can sit and chat
Or simply sit, when it comes to that,
By the fireplace where the fir logs blaze
And the smoke rolls up in a weaving haze.

• • •

A paperweight of meteorite
That seared and scored the sky one night,
A Moro kris — my paper knife —
Once slit the throat of a Rajah's wife.

The beams of my house will be fragrant wood
That once in a teeming jungle stood
As a proud, tall tree where the leopards couched,
And the parrot screamed, and the black men crouched.
The roof must have a rakish dip
To shadowy eaves where the rain can drip
In a damp, persistent, tuneful way;
It's a cheerful sound on a gloomy day.
And I want a shingle loose somewhere
To wail like a banshee in despair
When the wind is high and the storm gods race,
And I am snug by my fireplace.

• • •

I'll have a window seat broad and deep
Where I can sprawl to read or sleep,
With windows placed so I can turn
And watch the sunsets blaze and burn
Beyond high peaks that scar the sky
Like bare white wolf fangs that defy
The very gods. I'll have a nook

For a savage idol that I took
From a ruined temple in Peru,
A demon chaser named Mang-Chu,
To guard my house by night and day
And keep all evil things away.

Pewter and bronze and hammered brass,
Old carved wood and gleaming glass,
Candles in polychrome candlesticks,
And peasant lamps in floating wicks,
Dragons in silk on a Mandarin suit,
In a chest that is filled with vagabond loot;
All of the beautiful, useless things
That a vagabond's aimless drifting brings.

• • •

And the hot gold light will fall on my face
And make me think of some heathen place
That I've failed to see — that I've missed someway —
A place that I'd planned to find someday;
And I'll feel the lure of it drawing me,
Oh damn, I know what the end will be.

• • •

While I follow the sun, while I drift and roam
To the ends of the earth like a chip on a stream,
Like a straw on the wind, like a vagrant dream;
And the thought will strike with a swift, sharp pain
That I probably never will build again
This house that I'll have in some far day.
Well — it's just a dream house, anyway.

In 1955, our hometown — Brownstown, Indiana — had entered the All-American Cities Contest. The town was selected as a finalist and invited to the competition in Seattle. I was to make our presentation, so Virginia and I planned the transcontinental trip by train, in a dome car this time, instead of our now-usual travel by air.

The train ride out was fabulous — through Chicago and westward on

A World of Travel 39

the Burlington and the Great Northern Railroads, continuing on into the Big Sky Country, and through Glacier National and Yellowstone Parks. Crossing the Cascade Mountains on our second and last night aboard, we stayed up all through the beautiful moonlit night to see the spectacular views from our glassed-in dome car.

Our town was named a runner-up in the contest which pleased us immensely as, of course, we were the smallest city in the contest. Following the presentation, Virginia and I took a short cruise from Seattle to Victoria Island at Vancouver. It was here that we started staying in the great Canadian National hotels beginning with the famous "Empress" at Victoria. On a later trip, we stayed at the Chateau Frontenac in Quebec.

As we rode the Canadian National Railroad eastward through Southern Canada, we made stops in Alberta at Lake Louise and the Banff Springs Hotel on the Bow River.

Perhaps I should pause and tell a story that relates to many of the great "happenstance" incidents that turned out to be most unusual and exciting. Before the Seattle-Canadian trip, Virginia and I had been repeatedly told by many ticket and booking agencies that "everything" was sold out at the Banff Springs Hotel all summer. Well, we booked a stop-over there anyway. Virginia noted that she had stayed up on trains all night on several occasions during the war, and if the great and famous hotel couldn't accommodate us, we would sleep in the depot. Soooo . . . we got off the train with our bags and caught a taxi up to the imposing hotel. There were long lines of tour people lined up in front of the desk clerks. The "tourists" were prebooked and prepaid. No real money was in evidence. When I got to the desk, I just discreetly placed three dollars — that's right, three one-dollar bills — on the desk and said, "We would like a room."

The money was picked up discreetly and pocketed rapidly. "Yes Sir," he replied, "Would you like one overlooking the Bow River?"

We agreed, and the view from that room was the same beautiful calendar scene that we have seen forever advertising the grandeur of the Canadian Rockies.

"Cash on the palm," "cash on the tabletop," or "cash on the barrelhead" has been known for centuries as an "enabler." It shouldn't be but sometimes it is, and for those of us who sometimes pass a place or an opportunity only once, it can make the difference between mission accomplished or missed. However, it works best in places known for corruption and vice — Las Vegas and New Orleans, for example — and other such places which many Americans try to accept as "respectable" when we're "away from home." I guess I want to know about such places, but I hope I'm never deceived into thinking they present wholesome entertainment.

After visiting Calgary, the site of the glorious "Calgary Stampede" with its world class rodeo and world famous "Chuckwagon Race," we rolled on across the border south into Minneapolis, Minnesota, and boarded the Chicago, Milwaukee, St. Paul and Pacific Railroad "400" — the crack train which ran that 400-mile route in 400 minutes, for a great ride to Chicago.

After 1955, we traveled mostly with Rob as previously mentioned, at least during the summer, and most of the travel was business, battlefield, and airfield related.

In 1964, we decided to do a "very big trip," two weeks encompassing three weekends, combining business and visits to some of the great Kilroy airfields of the Southwest and on to Los Angeles and San Francisco. From home, we drove down the Natchez Trace to make business calls in Louisiana and East Texas.

We then continued west out of Houston to Sheridan, Texas (near Columbus), where Virginia and her aunt had title to a small acreage with supposed oil potential. It was still pretty barren between Houston and San Antonio at that time. About 70 miles west out of Houston, we pulled up at a filling station.

"I'm looking for Sheridan, Texas," I told the gas station operator.

"You're standing right in the middle of it," he replied.

"Well," I said, "my wife owns supposed oil property here."

"So does everyone else in the country," the local added. "I have a map with names and numbers here just for the pass-through oil property hopefuls."

So, we located the property, and found out a Mr. Briscoe was looking after it and was grazing cattle on the pastures. We found Briscoe at his small store. He readily agreed to show us the land — 10 acres in Virginia's name and 10 acres belonging to "Aunt Mabel Baxter" — later willed to Rob.

I invited Briscoe to get in our car but he shook his head. "We need to go in my pickup," he said.

It was 114 degrees and the truck had no air conditioning. The pickup bed had a metal floor. Briscoe motioned for 12-year-old Rob to hop in. Rob did so and from then on continued a foot-and-hand dance to keep from frying on either the truck bed or cab top.

We proceeded a mile or so to a swinging iron gate where Briscoe motioned me out to open and close it. There was one problem. A Brahma Bull, weight by my estimate at one ton, was standing just inside the gate. I not only hesitated, I stopped. (Remember, this was about 25 years before I "ran with (from) the Bulls in Pamplona.")

"He won't hurt you," Briscoe said.

"Maybe not," I ventured, "but I only play toreador on Saturdays."

So, Briscoe had to tend gate as well as the truck. Keep in mind that Rob is continuing his dance all this while. We then proceeded into some pretty rough country — mesquite, scrub palmetto, dry creek beds, etc. I thought right then that the land would never raise taxes or anything else. Virginia, however, was sure there was a lake of golden crude somewhere under the surface and that the Shell Oil Refinery three miles away had been built there especially to process the golden flow from her field. She would, however, consider selling the town lots — two of Aunt Mabel's, two of her own.

So I started negotiating with Briscoe. (This is true!)

"Is there a market for the town lots?"

"Sometimes. I buy one or two now and then."

"What's the going price?"

"I've bought some recently for 'two and a half'."

"Well, two of these lots are corner lots. Do you think you could go five?"

"Oh I guess five dollars wouldn't be too much."

I didn't either faint or fudge, just casually said we weren't ready to sell yet! Virginia did sell all four of the town lots later at a somewhat respectable price. Rob and Virginia still have the acreage and are waiting for another "Spindletop," like that of the huge field of gushers near Beaumont, Texas, someday. In the meantime, the Briscoe family has rented the land for 20 dollars per annum. They have improved the pasture considerably to where it would support not only that old Brahma bull, but a harem of cows, too.

From Sheridan, we went west and stopped for gas in Gonzales, Texas. Across the highway was a building with beer signs on its sides. It looked like a saloon, but appeared to be the only place where one could get a drink of any kind. Virginia took Rob by the hand and in they went through the swinging doors. The Cokes and water were cold and consumed quickly. The saloon keeper was very nice, but he wasn't catering to the family trade.

It was a good piece to San Antonio, then a full day to El Paso, where we stayed overnight.

The next morning we went out to Biggs Field where I had spent six months as Wing Photo Recon and Intelligence Officer. At that time, it was a very secure base. I flashed my Reserve Air Force Officer ID card and called for the Base Commander. I reached the Officer of The Day, who sent a jeep out to the gate to pick us up and take us to headquarters. When I came out of the office where I had been talking with some "Brass," Virginia and Rob were nowhere to be seen. At that time, General Curtis "Iron Ass" LeMay was running the Strategic Air Command, noted for its "instant readiness." Our Long Range Bombers could be airborne in 20 minutes at any of the SAC bases, ready to counter a Soviet threat during the politically tense 1960s. When alarms went off, vehicles and men moved quickly. For sure, there were not to be civilians in the streets. But Virginia knew the base well and was showing Rob around. Quickly, a Military Police (MP) Captain rounded them up and then courteously escorted the three of us around the field and along the familiar flight line. It was a great day.

From Biggs, we traveled west along lonely U.S. 90 to another Kilroy field, which had been a tow target base, at Deming, New Mexico. From Deming Air Base to Tucson, the road of long straight stretches ran through American desert country, north of the Chiricahua Mountains where the famous Apache chiefs, Cochise and Geronimo, had played out their roles of the "good" and "bad" Indians. We drove through purple sage, towering saguaro cacti, and Joshua trees which had formed the authentic backdrop for a hundred semi-authentic Western movies with cowboys and indians. It was, and still is, easy to vicariously live with the Pony Soldiers of the Seventh Cavalry or the cowboy bands of Tom Mix, Buck Jones, and Roy Rogers as they rode the barren ranges of Arizona.

Also, it was the land of rich lodes of copper and silver which nurtured the violent frontier towns such as Tombstone in the Southwest. In the popular televison series "Gunsmoke," Marshall Matt Dillon left Miss Kitty and rode down from Dodge City to "shoot it out" with the lawless Clantons in the O.K. Corral. Yes, we could see the Old West as it was while we drove between the Santa Rita and the Rin Con Mountains toward the Tucson Range which harbored the reconstructed "Old Tucson," featuring the saloons, dance halls, boarding houses, and bawdy houses of an era long past but kept alive by the wonderful imagery of Hollywood.

When we reached Tucson, we, of course, stayed in a modern Holiday Inn in the shadow of Tucson's "A" Mountain. The next day, we visited the Davis-Monthan Air Force Base and were accorded the same military courtesy and camaraderie of our Biggs Field visit. Davis-Monthan, named for two local World War I fliers, was now a SAC base. The base is still a functioning establishment today, but with a far different mission as a "graveyard" for perhaps a thousand warbirds in a mothball fleet — bombers, super bombers, and some fighters from the Kilroy days of the "Fly Boys" in their crushed caps, bombardier coats, and Eisenhower jackets. Even though 20 years had passed, the camaraderie and spirit of that place and time had stayed with me until this return visit — and, indeed, until now, and will remain forever.

From Tucson, the next day, we drove north towards Phoenix. As I noted the familiar landscape and towns, memories came flooding back. From our high-altitude bombers, it had been easy to see the many Kilroy airstrips, with bombing ranges nearby — Globe, Williams, Gila Bend, and so many others — seemingly in close proximity. However, the expanse of the Southwest and our side trips made it a long trek by car.

In the distance, the Superstition Mountains reached skyward. The location of the Lost Dutchman Mine, a treasure trove beyond measure is still enshrouded somewhere in the mysterious range. In the shadow of the mountains, Tortilla Flat, the epitome of poverty as portrayed in John Steinbeck's novel of the same name, had been home to disappointed and unsuccessful prospectors.

Perhaps Virginia and Rob sensed the intensity of my interest in reliving the history and geography of my Air Corps-Air Force days. Boredom, there was not on this trip. The excitement of the military jeep ride close up to the monstrous bombers and sleek fighters had been just one of many experiences through which young Rob sensed the life of his parents' during wartime in the Southwest.

But back to current reality. We headed west over the desert to March

Field at Riverside, California, then, on the freeways of Los Angeles, the "City of Angels," to glittering Disneyland.

The day at Disneyland was certainly a highlight of our trip. I had to make a business call, so I purchased three all-day tickets covering many of the features of the Magic Kingdom. Virginia and Rob also had 40 or 50 dollars spending money (a good amount then). The plan was for them to eyeball the set-up, go to whatever attractions and rides seemed like the most fun and where the lines were short. In the evening, we planned to go together to those they had bypassed that day.

When I returned that night, they were not back yet. However, in a few minutes they showed up in the motel van. It seems that because of a very hot day, the lines were short and they were able to go quickly from one ride or show to another. They had used up all their combination ticket books and had spent all of their money, with none left for tram or taxi. So they had called the motel for emergency (and free) transportation. What a day!

We needed to move north quickly. So after a quick dip in the Pacific Ocean (we have always made a practice of at least wading if not swimming in all the waters we have visited throughout the world) we drove up Route 101 through Big Sur, Carmel, and Monterey and headed over the Sierra Madre Range toward Bakersfield on Old Road 99.

We had a RON (Kilroy abbreviation for Remain Overnight) to visit relatives in Modesto. The next day, we gloried in the Old West of the Gold Rush country on our drive among the giant sequoias to the Roaring Angel's Camp, made famous by Mark Twain's wonderful story, "The Celebrated Jumping Frog of Calaveras County." Placer sites, saloons, dance halls, and re-enactments were more than adequate to stir our imaginations of times past.

The next day, we visited more shirt-tail relatives — faculty members on the then famous or infamous campus of the University of California at Berkeley. Infamous, perhaps, because the long-haired and unkempt Hippies, together with news-hungry television crews had decided to use an area just off the campus to launch the counter-cultural revolution "against the Establishment." The fact of the matter was, then as now, there were more serious students than serious Hippies, neither of whom really knew what "the Establishment" was. However, the power of the media was clearly demonstrated in the twisted melodramas and staged riots broadcast from Berkeley which rolled across the country as a tide and converted many to "the cause" — for a while.

San Francisco, as always, was one marvelous experience after another. Knob Hill, the little Cable Cars, Fishermans' Wharf, Telegraph Hill, and across the Golden Gate through Sausalito, and on to the giant redwoods of Muir Woods National Monument, can all be experienced in one day (just as one can hit the high spots of Boston in one day). We visited all these and more. Rob was only 12 the time, but I'm sure his younger mind registered more exciting memories than we adults could match.

The next day we were up early and on U.S. 50 to Sacramento. We drove through the dangerous pass where the Donner Party had been stranded, in many feet of beautiful but deadly snow in that tragic winter of 1846.

From there we traveled down the mountain to a RON just outside rip-roarin' Reno, Nevada — "The Biggest Little City In The World" — Dodge City of an earlier age moved west. The city thrived on tourists looking for gambling, girls, liquor, and divorce (a six-week decree wait in Nevada at that time). In the late 1800s, Dodge City had made its fame and fortune from cowboys driving the Texas longhorns up the trail to the railhead where they found the gambling, the girls, and the liquor, and the deadly gunplay that sometimes ended in the Boot Hill Cemetery.

Children (minors) were not welcome in the Reno of that time. Then, as now, they were forbidden to play the slots. However, the one-armed bandits were everywhere, and young Rob kept pleading to put in a few nickels and pull the lever. Finally, I relented with a stern admonition that this would teach him a lesson, "These things always take your money." I gave him one nickel to break the law and gain dependable knowledge. He happily put the nickel in the slot, pulled the handle, and, wouldn't you know it, the bars lined up and nickels started pouring out everywhere. One more well-intended parental effort thwarted!

From Reno, it was east again on "our own" highway 50. We called it "our own" because it runs through Main Street in our hometown. Highway 50 was not as famous as Route 66 or the "National Highway" U.S. 40 but was a longer, if lesser well-known, coast-to-coast highway from the nation's capital to the California Gold Coast. However, it is one of those familiar roads that one returns to now and then in extensive U.S. travel where and when one knows he is close to home. It's a feeling similar to that experienced by international air travelers in the 70's and 80's when they transferred from Chinese Air Cathay, Russian Air Lines, or Japanese Air Lines (small seats) back onto Pan Am No. 1 or No. 2, both of which proudly carried the "Stars and Stripes" on globe-circling trips every day. Whether in Tokyo, New Delhi, or Frankfurt, when one came aboard he felt he was heading home.

After veering north toward Salt Lake City, Utah, and after 300 or more miles of intermittent mountainous driving, we rolled down into desert country by Wendover Air Force Base, another Kilroy field born of military necessity in the 1940s. I had landed there in various size bombers during my service time. It was now a restricted area, and since we had just visited my war-training fields at both El Paso and Tucson, we passed by into the Great Salt Desert.

We had stopped at a filling station for gas when a pick-up towing the longest, sleekest, bullet-looking car (racer) I had ever seen pulled in. It appeared as something out of Buck Rogers' 21st Century.

"We must be near that place I've heard of called the Bonneville Salt Flats," I thought. Rob immediately and excitedly asked the station attendant the directions to the test site.

The Bonneville experience was incredible. The speed of the futuristic cars was beyond our imagination — setting records near 400 mph, but we were also spellbound by the wide variety of motor vehicles participating in the program and the easy access of the few spectators to *all* the vehicles. At that time, there seemed to be no regard for security. It was assumed that those present were very interested and would only "look." And, the confidence was justified.

We saw parachute braking for the first time. We witnessed a 1919 Indian motorcycle record a speed of 119 mph. We saw the telescope steering by which the drivers of the nearly flying machines sighted on targets two miles or more down the salt flats and then took off in a deafening roar. We saw what appeared to be a twin to Frank Lockhart's "Bluebird," the car which had been clocked at 325 mph before the man and machine had careened into the surf by the white sands of Daytona Beach. We were probably there a little more than an hour experiencing sights that would remain in our memories forever. It occurred to me that if Kilroy had been there he wouldn't have believed we had cars traveling faster than WWII bombers.

Spectators looked and asked all kinds of questions. Drivers, mechanics, and owners answered. Automotive engineers, theorists, death-defying drivers, grease monkeys and mechanical ignoramuses — like us — seemed to be all one happy family.

Continuing on our way, it wasn't far across the desert flats until we saw the "heavy" waters of the Great Salt Lake. We jumped out of the car at the first public beach, donned our suits, and were soon floating effortlessly, like sea otters, in the salty sea. It's true, you don't sink! The salt-saturated water makes floating easy even for non-swimmers. Similar to the Dead Sea between Israel and Jordan, water flows into the Great Salt Lake from the Jordan River and other streams as snow melts off the surrounding mountains. The lake is salty because it is not drained by out-flowing streams. Salt deposits are left behind as some of the water evaporates.

Soon after showering and *trying* to wash off the salt, we arrived in the midst of scrupulously clean Salt Lake City with its prominent spires of the Mormon Temple. The Temple is the private sanctuary of the Mormon hierarchy from whence comes the policies that drive the vigorous congregations of the followers of Joseph Smith and Brigham Young — Supreme Elders of The Church of Jesus Christ of Latter-day Saints. The Mormons are active in religious and medical missionary work. Young men, as they come of age, go out two by two to spread their particular gospel throughout the world. They are effective missionaries and generally are achievers. Much of our Western society might call them "chauvinistic." Our American feminist society can scarcely understand how such a male-dominated religion can still believe in "a woman's place" and "a man's place," but they do. (We should remember, too, that over one billion followers of Islam firmly share such a view and are committed to its preservation.)

Regardless of creed and beliefs, the Mormons have built a wonderful "New Jerusalem" in Salt Lake City. In the mid-1800s when Brigham Young brought his people in wagon trains after persecution in Nauvoo, Illinois, to the Wasatch Mountains and looked down upon both the salt and the rich soil of the beautiful valley, a voice from the Lord whispered, "This is the place." Whether fact or fantasy, the reality is that they have, in a manner, confirmed the prophesy. I don't know all the implications and interpretations of the beehive symbol of the Mormons, but it stands for hard work and industry. I can't say whether their women have been "protected" or "exploited," but without doubt they have built a kingdom of sorts that is wondrous to behold.

We were fortunate in being able to enter the acoustical excellence of the tabernacle and hear the beautiful music of the Mormon Tabernacle Choir. We also took tours and listened to learned teachers expound on the virtues of the faith. These experiences are not easily forgotten.

From Salt Lake City, we proceeded eastward to the Colorado Rockies and on to the Mile-High City of Denver for a RON. It was another time warp visit for me. As an Air Corps officer, I had been on temporary duty here at another famous Kilroy air base, Lowry Field, where the Air Corps Technical School put students through pressure-cooker technical training in two weeks of total immersion. The air in Denver during the early 60's was still clean before the industrial fog developed from the dense fossil fuel emissions over the past 20 years. We saw the famous Brown Palace Hotel, named for the *Titanic* survivor, Molly Brown (portrayed by Debbie Reynolds in the movie *The Unsinkable Molly Brown*).

From Denver, we slowly descended from the high country into the "breadbasket" of the nation (except for the Dust Bowl years depicted in John Steinbeck's *The Grapes of Wrath*) and through the seemingly endless and beautiful wheatfields of western Kansas. On through Junction City, home of Fort Riley, the training and staging ground for the Pony Soldiers, the U.S. Cavalry, who "won the West." We stopped in Manhattan to visit our Alma Mater, Kansas State University.

Manhattan is located at the junction of the Blue and the Kansas (Kaw) Rivers. In 1858, the city founders came up the Kaw on the steamboat *Hartford* until the stern-wheeler ran aground on a sandbar near the settlement of Boston. Originally headed for a platted townsite named Manhattan at the junction of the Smoky Hill and Kansas Rivers, the low-water stage precluded further progress by the steamer. Knowing they would never reach their original destination, the officers agreed to join the Boston settlers if they would change the name to Manhattan. Among the boat passengers was writer Damon Runyon's father.

Manhattan, called "the Little Apple," lies in the divided valley with the Flint Hills (barren but beautiful) rising to the north, west, and south, and the fertile Kaw Valley stretching eastward. To the north, in the Wildcat Creek plain, and bordering the Kansas State campus, there were many clusters of hemp plants, either disregarded entirely or, at the time, lightly regarded as either rope plants or weeds until after World War II when they were essentially eradicated.

Manhattan was "not exactly" on either the Santa Fe or the Oregon Trail but was between them and close enough to welcome some of those who recovered from "trail fever" in the early stages. The town's proximity to military roads leading to nearby Fort Riley also gave it communication with the outside world that was not equalled by many frontier towns of the Civil War era.

Perhaps because of location and intellectual advantage, those in authority established Kansas State Agricultural College in 1863. Its status as a "land grant" college provided substantial income from the rather large land entitlements around it.The school flourished and was nourished by good farmers, and later cattlemen, many direct Irish, Russian, and German immigrants who brought skills, spirituality, and work ethic to this area. Undoubtedly, the vision and effort of the early equivalent of the K-State Extension Service was in a large measure responsible for the seeding of the Kansas Prairie with the miraculous Turkey-Red winter wheat from the steppes of Russia.

The long day's drive home to Brownstown from Manhattan took us eastward through the beautiful bluestem grass of the Flint Hills. The flourishing wheat fields are green in May. By the 4th of July, the harvest of the golden grain is in full swing. The prairie grasses are still green unless it has been a very dry season. We drove past Forbes Air Force Base, another example of a great Kilroy airfield, on the south edge of Topeka.

At Topeka, Interstate 70 and the Kansas Turnpike become one and pass not far from the massive red brick halls of the University of Kansas perched on the hill named Mount Oread at Lawrence — the home of the Jayhawks and the Haskell Indian Nations University where Jim Thorpe learned to play football before going on to Carlisle, Pennsylvania.

At the junction of the Kansas and Missouri Rivers, the two Kansas Cities, — of each state, face each other across the bridges. It was here that many of "The Trail People" brought their covered wagons and assembled at the early towns of Independence and Westport for departure on both of the routes that carried Americans westward — the Oregon Trail to the northwest and the Santa Fe Trail to the southwest — to carve from the wilderness the greatest nation in history.

From Kansas City, we traveled on I-70 eastward through the broad Missouri Valley, and north of the Ozarks, bridging the Missouri River at St. Charles and breezing past the pre-Kilroy airport, Lambert Field, from which "Lucky Lindy," Charles A. Lindbergh, and his aircraft, "Spirit of St. Louis" departed for Roosevelt Field, Long Island, New York, to begin the first crossing of the Atlantic Ocean in 1927.

From St. Louis, U.S. 50 rolls through southern Illinois and the southern Indiana hills right into Brownstown's Main Street. We were home again from a summer's business/pleasure cross-country trip which had taken us almost to Mexico, across the American desert, to the Pacific, and back over the Rockies and through the Great Plains— 15 states in 15 days! This takes lots of desire, lots of energy, and lots of tolerance — but it was lots of fun.

I usually drove long distances every day but we had planned activities for Virginia and Rob while I made business calls. I left Virginia and Rob at a pool, a seashore, a miniature golf course, a theme park, or something equally interesting and/or entertaining. We did stop for lunch and usually planned a nice dinner at a good hotel or motel with a pool and/or play areas.

Summer days are long. We tended to use most of the daylight, stopping for scenic views, historical markers, and other points of interest. We talked a lot — about many things, but particularly about the country we were passing through, the pioneers, the Indians, the river people, the cowboys, the soldiers, and the trail blazers. We had a few in-car games, not many, but no "Walkman." The car radio was used very infrequently — at times only for weather and news briefs.

We stopped to see people, too. Friends and relatives, but very briefly unless overnight. We had a "four minute plan" for shopping, for sight-seeing, for visiting. The time wasn't set in stone but the plan kept us moving.

This cross-country trip to California was possibly the most intense of our family trips but there were others, many and varied, with and without friends and companions. However, as Rob's high school age approached, his increasingly demanding schedule soon crowded out the opportunities for other trips with us. His year-round athletic training began — basketball, football, golf, swimming, and other sports. Working toward an Eagle Scout Badge was also time consuming for Rob.

During these formative years for Rob, both parents and child gained an education in American geography as well as our nation's history. We had criss-crossed some areas of the contiguous 48 states many times. Often our destinations were at scenic points along the seashore. The East, West, and Gulf Coasts of the United States provide spectacular and varied scenery as well as historical points of interest.

After many wonderful road trips and great times shared by the three of us, the "family trip" era ended without plan or announcement. From then on, Virginia and I started our twosome trips. They became longer and more frequent, with or without business associates.

We found it pleasurable to drive down U.S. 1 from the rocky coasts of Maine, along the lonely windswept shores of Nags Head and Cape Hatteras and the outer banks of North Carolina, past the white strands of South Carolina, to Georgia's golden isles, and south along the beautiful beaches of Florida and on through the Keys to land's end at Key West. We also traveled U.S. 90 around the Gulf of Mexico to Texas.

On the West Coast, we drove the high road, U.S. 101, north from Los Angeles through San Francisco, California, to Oregon's beautiful coasts to the Washington-Canadian border.

Virginia, Rob, and I have been blessed in being able to travel throughout our great land, which left an indelible impression on us that can only be summed up by the words of the song, "America the Beautiful . . . from sea to shining sea."

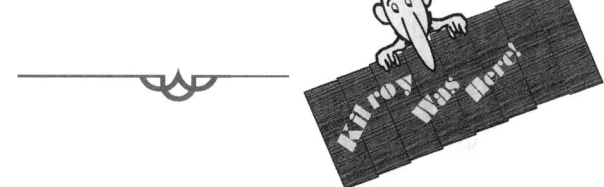

Chapter 4

The Global "Kilroy" Connection: The Tropics, 1966 and 1970, and the Orient, 1973 and 1981

WHEN VIRGINIA AND I began participating in what was to become a continuing series of international business study tours, I contemplated the international structures, relationships, and infrastructures which afforded us the practical opportunity, as ordinary U.S. citizens and business people, to freely travel throughout the entire world. We would be able to move between and among very foreign countries and cultures in relative safety with access to nearly all segments of world societies (not only those we regarded as civilized, but also those we had come to think of as "third world" and even uncivilized).

As we boarded various types of airplanes and landed at large airports and on small airstrips, it became increasingly apparent that the mighty American military machine of the World War II era had been responsible for building and establishing these installations. The airfields had become the facilitators for accomplishing "the Great

Commission" of Christendom: "Go ye into all the world . . ." and the building of the modern trade channels and communications which superceded and far excelled the ancient trade routes such as the Silk Road and the seaways of the Spanish Main. The motivation of the rainbow's end in gold, frankincense, and myrrh as well as jewels, ivory, and silver paled in comparison to the trade in stock, oil, grain, and intellectual property that is the global trade of the present and the future.

In all of this, beside the all-encompassing spiritual guidance of God, was the practical earthy symbolism of Kilroy. Wherever we would land, whether at the great airports of Tokyo and Singapore, at Jamaica, Mexico, Yucatan, the sand strip at Timbuktu, or the one runway at the little Truk International Airport in the South Pacific, in my mind, I visualized — a schmoe with a long nose over a fence and the scrawled script, "Kilroy was here."

Marco Polo, Christopher Columbus, and other explorers, had no such resources as we now have at our disposal. Kilroy, as the symbol of American mission, had cleared the runways for countless generations to follow.

To avoid redundancy, Kilroy will not be mentioned in most of the following accounts, but the reader should bear in mind that in nearly all instances "Kilroy had been there."

Tropical Trips
Jamaica

In 1966, I was invited to present a technical paper at the spring meeting of the International Hardwood Plywood Manufacturers Association (HPMA) — The Robertson Corporation was a manufacturer of protein-starch extenders for plywood adhesives. The plant manager of Georgia Pacific's Savannah Plywood Mill was chairing the panel on "Plywood Adhesive Systems." This was an opening into policy level of the major international plywood manufacturing network, and I quickly accepted the invitation.

The meeting was to be held in the Playboy Club Hotel of Ocho Rios, Jamaica. Dressed in Caribbean colors, the "bunnies," beautiful, charming, and generally very well-educated, were very helpful. The surroundings were about as deluxe and pleasant as possible at that time. The tropical climate and atmosphere were "as ordered."

Many of my customers (and their spouses) were there, as well as many prospects from the leading plywood and furniture manufacturing companies. Furthermore, my paper was to be published in the *International Plywood and Panel Magazine*. How could anyone plan a better scenario for mixing business and pleasure? We still belong to the organization and have probably used the Association's international business trips as a springboard into a hundred countries.

Jamaica is an idyllic and exotic tropical island — palm trees, banana trees, and white sand beaches lapped by the usually tranquil waves of the Caribbean Sea. We had no screens on the windows of our beach side rooms attached to the hotel, and we had neither flies nor bugs. This was before general air conditioning, but the breezes from the sea, through open doors and windows, kept us most comfortable in our room. Our open-door policy netted one small and friendly wild pig who wandered into our "parlor." He was, however, no trouble to shoo out so that he could wander on down the beach.

Virginia toured green mountains covered with coffee trees, while I spoke, studied, and conferred with other conference participants. We went "down Kingston Way" and to Montego Bay with friends and business associates. The dinners and fruit buffets were spectacular and delicious. We danced the moonlit nights away on the beach and under the palms to the marimba bands and the rhythm of steel drums. This was tropical paradise "as advertised."

The Yucatan Ruins

In 1970, Virginia and I made a trip targeted for Merida, Mexico, and the ruins of the Yucatan. However, we decided to make a stopover at the Panama Canal Zone before proceeding into Mexico. The Panama airstrips were Kilroy fields and were very effective in protecting the Canal, which had remained open throughout World War II.

We had been invited to Panama City by Roy Hammack, a long-time friend and plywood manufacturer. Roy had been born in Alabama, where he learned the wood business and had later migrated to Panama. He was soon engaged in the international wood product trade. His daughter was very gracious to us during our stay; she was married to a U.S. Navy officer, which opened the way for us to visit the Naval Officers Club beside the Canal and have a spectacular view of the ships passing through.

Roy had been very insistent on our visiting him and he had told us what we thought were pretty expansive tales of the accommodations he could provide. It became apparent to us upon our arrival at the Panama City Airport that he was truly a man of some importance. As Virginia and I disembarked, most of the people were going through routine Customs procedures. Roy came out onto the field to meet us with his entourage of assistants who seized our luggage as it came off the plane, loaded it and us onto trucks, and drove us around everybody else! Roy's repeated instruction to his assistants was *"Rapido! Rapido!"* — which we understood as "Hurry up!"

Virginia and I were taken to a waiting limousine and were transported up the mountainside to a beautiful view of the Canal and the Pacific Ocean. Roy's main house had once been the residence of the president of the Republic of Panama. He also had a guest house, about a quarter of a mile away, in another beautiful setting. We had every reason to believe Roy when he told us the guest house could accommodate 50 people. We were privileged to stay in the main house, with many servants catering to whatever one's needs might be — beautiful serving girls and men servants. We were presented a rather formal Spanish meal that evening — delicious, beautifully served, and very enjoyable.

Roy had been married to an American but didn't seem to be married at that time. His daughter served as hostess, and two other female companions were present. After dinner, we retired into a spacious bedroom. We were awakened at 6:30 the next morning with a knock on the door. In came Roy, accompanied by a servant. Roy personally carried a tray with our coffee. He served us in bed, chatted with us a few minutes, and told us we would be expected downstairs for breakfast at 7:30. The stay there was one delightful experience after another as Roy and his daughter showed us about the city, the Canal, where we watched the locking process, and the surrounding area, which extended into the jungles. We did visit his plywood mills (which he later sold). After staying there two nights, we were put back onto the plane and traveled on to Merida in the Yucatan Peninsula of Mexico.

Upon arriving at Merida, Virginia and I were met once more by gracious hosts, Dr. and Mrs. Ernest Matthews, with whom we had had previous correspondence. The Matthews were Presbyterian missionaries in the

Yucatan, and their headquarters was in the suburbs of Merida, which is a beautiful city about 30 miles inland from the port city of Progreso. There were jungles nearby, and there were also two plywood mills in that area. (They have since ceased to operate.) The Matthews were delightful hosts and well-informed guides. They had been in the area for more than 20 years and knew both the geography of the land and certainly the characteristics of the people.

We stayed at a Spanish-type hotel in the old quarter downtown, which had been built around a center court with pool. There was a small wall air-conditioner unit which didn't function well, but it was not essential because of the good ventilation generally afforded by the Spanish architecture of the tropical regions.

After shopping and being shown around the city, we went out to the Presbyterian mission, which consisted partly of the Hope Clinic, a very small medical facility, and the Priscilla Bible School. The Clinic had mainly obstetric facilities and some other capabilities. The families of the expectant mothers would come to the Clinic with them and would sleep on the porch and ground until the babies were delivered. Following a brief stay, they would all return to their homes in the jungle. The Mayan people were extremely friendly and pleasant. The Matthews had done a great job in bringing the Christian message to them.

Dr. Matthews was an outstanding linguistic scholar. Between his wife and himself, they spoke nine languages fluently. He had translated large parts of the Bible from English, through the use of Spanish and Mexican dialects, into the Mayan language so the natives could read the Bible in their own language.

In the Priscilla Bible School, Mrs. Matthews was instrumental in seeing that young Mayan girls aged 8 to 16 were instructed in the principles of home economics and Christian principles of the Bible. After completing their equivalent of high school, these young people would return to their villages in the jungle and teach their people how to do the best job of managing their households. The small "houses" were made of adobe. Hammocks were used for sleeping. Most of the clothing worn by the people, who were very clean, was white cotton, and in many places we saw them washing their clothes. The people carried ground corn, their main food staple, from the little mills back to their houses where it was cooked and made into tortillas. Beans, prepared similarly to our hominy, was another staple food.

The Matthews then took us out to the Mexican ruins at Uxmal, which had lain undiscovered from the demise of the Mayan civilization until about 1930. One of the discoverers of these ruins was the aviator Charles Lindbergh who had noticed many unexplained mounds as he flew over the Yucatan jungles. When these mounds were explored, they were found to be overgrowths covering large pyramids.

Other famous sites in the Yucatan were pyramids, some with tunnels — Chichén Itzá, Tulum, Oaxaca, and Teotihuacan near Mexico City. Chichén Itzá contains a jeweled panther with a large jewel in its belly, among other artifacts.

After visiting Uxmal with the Matthews, we returned to Merida and were privileged to meet three young men who were excellent role models as missionaries. These young men had been brought out of the Mayan jungle by the Matthews and educated in Merida. Later, one was sent to medical school, one to law school, and the other, named Pedro, became the mayor of Progreso. I developed a friendship with Pedro and since we had visited Mexico many times near the U.S. border, we had quite a lot to discuss with him in regard to Mexico.

A Business Trip to the Orient, 1973

With the Jamaica, Panama, Yucatan, and Mexico trips under our belts, Virginia and I now had a liking for international travel. All of our journeys up to this point had sharpened our skills and had prepared us to take some significant trips abroad.

Many of these accounts that follow, reprinted from the Bedford *Times-Mail* (1973-1993) and the *Jackson County Banner* (1995 and 1996), document these international trips as we began what would eventually become a portfolio containing visits to more than 150 countries, including all continents except Antarctica (which we plan to visit in 1998). Most of our travels have included both pleasure and business. The affiliation between The Robertson Corporation and the Hardwood Plywood Manufacturers Association (HPMA) has enabled us to visit many corners of the world we might not have visited otherwise.

The following articles were published in the *Daily Times-Mail* during late 1973.

Local Businessman Back from Orient Study Tour:
Never So Many Doing So Much in Such Little Space

By Joe Robertson

"They're tearing Raffles down, you know. . . ." The Singapore taxi driver was obviously pleased with the scheduled demolition of the typical Oriental hotel made famous in Somerset Maugham's books — good riddance of another symbol of the former English Colonialism and the past.

To the Singaporean the delightful hostelry was just one more reminder of previous subjection and something to be erased from memory as soon as possible. It was time to think only of progress, of reform, of high rises, housing, industry and production. This was the mood over Asia in the fall of 1973.

From the liftoff time of Japan Air Lines' Flight 1-747, we were immediately immersed in the Oriental world and before the Golden Gate was out of sight, the petite Japanese stewardess had given us an "Oshinori" (hot damp cloth) to symbolically cleanse our entry to the Far East.

I looked out at the red rising sun marking on the swept wing and recalled that 30 years ago we were intensively trained to destroy such aircraft rather than ride in them.

When the Big Bird settled in Tokyo, I was amazed at the number of 747's and other large airplanes at the Tokyo airport — many more than I had ever seen in any American airport. The jolt of the landing gear was nothing, however, compared to the succession of shocks coming in rapid order. Never so many automobiles. Never so many doing so much in such a little space. More cars (small ones) than I had ever seen — really jammed, but moving. Advertising signs everywhere and essentially no open spaces, parking lots or vacant lots. Many skyscrapers and superthruways.

Generally, we were not prepared for the amazing progress of the Japanese industrial complex or the contrasting near-primitive state of most agriculture — as compared to conditions in the U.S.

The Tokyo Hilton at least gave us an English name reference for home base. This was the last hotel with a home town name. Our view of Fuji — the famous sacred mountain — was better than that obtained from many points.

Other deep impressions of Japan included the near universality of western clothes, the absence of police or any military presence (soldiers), and the almost complete absence of motorcycles — it seems they sell them all to the United States.

We had a morning conference with people from the Japanese Plywood Manufacturers Association and as a prelude to the industrial plant visits which were scheduled.

We learned that Japanese wages, particularly in the Tokyo area, were fast approaching American standards. About $7,000 U.S. per year was being paid for skilled workers in the plywood plants.

The day of cheap Japanese labor is past. They are pleased. They work about 28 days per month with two, three or four days off per month depending on holidays and production schedules. Their days are long, often more than eight hours.

Although there are many Buddhist temples and Shinto shrines in Japan, religion appears of little concern or import. And, the temple and shrines have nothing comparable to Sunday service.

Many factories work on Sundays just as any other day. Schools are not in session, however, so the streets and parks are even more crowded than on work days. The workers in the Tokyo factories and plants were alert, fast, skilled and happy. The machinery was very modern, and production per plant was more than in many U.S. plants.

Although we had been briefed, we were not ready to accept Japanese industrial production per unit as equal to ours. Their progress is undoubtedly aided by their discipline and dedication.

Among other things, some of our group visited in a Japanese home, a tea house, and a Buddhist temple where the "ting tang" music and dim candles reminded us of the days of Fu Manchu. The Geisha girls are still a very real part of today's life, as are Las Vegas-type night clubs with hundreds of "hostesses."

The contrasting cultures in Japanese life today would seem to create sociological problems beyond our comprehension. It doesn't seem real that a girl's career choices could vary between being a respected Geisha girl or a factory production worker; or that a woman may choose between being employed as an aggressive stock broker or as a resident housewife who walks behind her husband, remains quiet, and does not go out at night with him.

Impressions of Orient Study Tour:
Dairy Industry Has Made Reasonable Progress in Japan

After Tokyo we hopped 600 miles to Sapporo, Hokkaido, the beautiful site of the 1972 Olympics. From the air we could see that Japan was over 70 per cent mountainous and that only about 15 per cent of the land area was suitable for productive agriculture in the United States manner.

The Hokkaido plywood plants paid a little lower hourly wage than those in Tokyo but annual wages were about equal because longer hours were worked. This part of Japan allows one a little room for living but even Sapporo has over one million people.

Hokkaido is the best agriculture area in Japan. The dairy industry has made reasonable progress there, and "Snow Brand" dairy products are good and well marketed in Japan — with good reason. Dr. Sato, chairman of Snow Brand's board, attended Ohio State. We were fortunate to meet Mr. M. Tjime, a division manager for Snow Brand. We also talked with our people at the U.S. Consulate and as usual found them most helpful.

We could easily see that our Sepro-X (Soy Protein-Energy Feed) could be most helpful to the poultry, beef and swine industries. These phases of agriculture are hardly recognizable to U.S. visitors.

It was the time of the rice harvest, and harvesting methods were 19th century at best. It is difficult to believe that rice was being harvested by hand in fields only a few hundred yards from factories with production-line methods second to none in the world.

From Hokkaido an hour's jet flight places one at Osaki Airport near the Shrine-studded city of Kyoto, site of Japan's former Imperial Palace and ancient capital.

Kyoto now has over five million people. It is on the outskirts of a population and industrial complex (Kyoto-Osaka-Nara) unlike any in our country. We drove toward a plywood mill for four hours from our Mykata Hotel without ever seeing open country or leaving heavy traffic.

One must remember that while the seven main islands of Japan stretch out over 1,000 miles, the population of over 100 million is contained in an area no larger than California. More than 95 per cent of those people are crowded into less than 5 per cent of the land area — following the same useless overcrowding policy that we do in the United States, and more so.

We needed visas for our Korean visit for it is here that American troops,

A World of Travel

The last outpost — Panmunjom, Korea, Demilitarized Zone, November 1973.

under the Joint Security Administration, are in daily contact with the North Koreans at Panmunjom.

"In front of them all" is the motto of the U.S. troops there and they are really a crack outfit. The village of Panmunjom is not a village at all but merely some nice buildings where thirty soldiers from each side have outposts and hold conferences.

We stepped across the line at the conference table and were in North Korea for a few minutes. The Communists said nothing but watched us closely — even with binoculars from only a few yards away.

The tense security of the area is impressive. A few hundred yards back from the line in the DMZ [*Demilitarized Zone*], the heavy fortifications start — tanks, barriers, mine fields, soldiers with bazookas ready, succeeding military checkpoints, barbed wire — all in a state of readiness for combat — pretty much the same as our GIs left it in 1953. Little else, however, would be recognizable.

Seoul, a city of six million, is only an hour's drive from the uneasy post at the front. There are probably 40,000 U.S. troops in Korea and most within gun range of the front — an explosive situation.

Seoul was an American household word in 1950 — as were other

In front of the Presidential Palace in Seoul, Korea, November 1973. From the left, Sylvia McDonald, Virginia and Joe Robertson, and Mary Koss.

famous Korean War battlegrounds such as Heartbreak Ridge and Pork Chop Hill. The tens of thousands of GIs who fought in the streets of Seoul and saw it reduced to ruins would be amazed at this now-modern city with skyscrapers, theaters, shopping centers and hotels.

Our hotel, "Chosun" — which takes its name from the description of Korea, "the land of the morning calm," had some of the best shopping in the world. The Korean smoky topaz is one of the most beautiful and sought-after gems in the world and Korea is the place to buy it. The Korean Brass was also the most beautiful we saw anywhere.

The Korean money has a low value compared to the dollar. Four-hundred won was equal to $1 U.S. when we were there. In comparison, 264 Japanese yen were traded for $1 U.S., when we entered Japan. (Incidentally, our dollar value had increased to 280 yen by the time we left — but things were still much higher in Japan than in any other Asian country).

We were most fortunate to have with us a world wood industry expert who had been a U.S. Navy officer on duty repatriating Japanese from

Korea to Japan after the war in 1946. He noted the vast changes and improvements which had taken place, particularly regarding the health and nutrition of the nation.

In 1946 it was a sorrowful morning task to clean the streets of those who had died in the night of starvation. Today the people, while many are still very poor, appear healthy and well-fed.

The farmers still cling to the past. Outside Seoul we saw many working knee-deep in mud, behind their struggling oxen, in the same manner as their ancestors. All, however, appear in the same state of readiness, truly one hand on the plow and one on the sword in preparation for conflict which many view as inevitable.

Perhaps our troops provide needed stability here, but the wisdom of trying to maintain a political system in a land so foreign and distant seems questionable at best.

In Pusan we visited what is undoubtedly the largest plywood plant in the world — 120,000 4-by-8 panels are produced daily. Seventy per cent of these are sold to the U.S. Young women comprise a large part of the 3,000 workers. They are housed in dormitories, work eleven to twelve hours daily (with breaks), are given about three days off each month and are paid the equivalent of $40 American money per month, $10 of which is paid back for room and board.

However, these girls appear healthy and satisfied. Maybe not quite as petite and pretty as the Japanese, but very alert and attractive.

Conditions were similar in the Inchon Mills. Military-type uniforms were worn by all the rank assigned to employees and bosses and saluting practiced in the usual military manner throughout the factories.

Inflation rates varied quite a little from country to country but were generally reported to be in the 16 per cent range. Interest rates were reported to be all the way from 7 to 18 per cent.

In Republic of China:
Military Presence Obvious, But Business Brisk

Moving on to the Republic of (Nationalist) China (Taiwan), the military presence was again obvious but brisk. Prices were cheap for chicken heads and feet, snake oil and other things for which Americans have no use.

However, for items which Americans like, prices were also American-style.

For example, first class hotel rooms in Taipei were about $1,000 NT dollars (New Taiwan dollars at 38 to $1 U.S.) . . . and $25 U.S. for a hotel room isn't exactly cheap.

One of our finest true Chinese dinners was given for us by the Taiwan Plywood Manufacturers at the Mandarin Palace in Taipei. There were 9 to 15 courses, depending on the counter and the eater, and the hosts and hostesses were charming.

Mrs. Pei Yu Lin, wife of the manager of a wood industry complex with 20,000 employees, assisted and advised us at dinner. She was a delightful and attractive person who made the unfamiliar Mandarin dishes (not Cantonese) exciting to the taste.

Conditions in the plywood plants in the Republic of China were similar to those in Korea. Wages were a little higher and education was perhaps a little broader. Motor bikes were very prevalent here as they were generally in the low income countries.

Women employed as secretaries were among the highest paid people here — more than teachers or factory workers. They were apparently considered most essential in generating export business.

If a Chinese family can earn the equivalent of $1,200 U.S., needs can be adequately met. We were told that per capita income was about $370 U.S. annually.

It was repeatedly mentioned that soldiers and visitors of previous decades would no longer recognize the industrial progress of the nations bordering the China Seas. They would, however, as our wives did, recognize the Oriental culture which is preserved not only in shrine, but also in spirit throughout the East.

Stability in Taiwan is also perhaps aided by our fleet in the Formosa Straits and some remaining military personnel. The proud people were quick to show us hillside caves which had been used for bomb and shell protection and which, they feared, might be needed again.

We had previously exported a little of our GLU-X to the Philippines and my nephew, Phil Robertson, had become very familiar with the Islands in the 60's while serving as an Air Force officer there. Nevertheless, we were again amazed at the contrast and progress of the last few years. How an island country could generate the money for such an outstanding building program was beyond comprehension.

Corregidor and the South China Sea are in view from Manila. South the road winds up to Tagaytay City, where the famous volcanic crater lake contains an island with another lake and island.

"The Filipinas," women of the Philippines, are considered by some to be the most beautiful in the Orient — a blend of Malay, Spanish, Chinese, Japanese and American. In Cebu these women are also musical and the Cebuana girls may be heard singing and strumming on native guitars. The guitars, a product of the island's cottage industry, are shipped all over the world.

We flew 700 miles south, toward Mindanoa nearly to the equator, to view forests full of gigantic Philippine mahogany (Luan) and the plywood mills on the Davoa Gulf. After a fast day at mills, we were entertained under the palms on the tropical beach while we exchanged information gathered in the mills.

Here we were only about 80 miles from the "Tasi Dei" — the recently found cave people who had no contact with the outside world and were still living in the Stone Age.

The forest industries are very important in the Philippines as log and plywood exports are tremendous. The future trend will be to export more processed wood and fewer logs — to use Philippine labor.

The Philippine peso is worth about 15 cents American. The plywood workers make about $1.50 to $2.25 per day or $10 to $14 per week. There are about fifty plywood plants in the Philippines and their operations had already been curtailed by fuel and urea (nitrogen) shortages.

Back toward the sunset was Hong Kong. The Philippine Airways jet (every country has an airline with a policy of providing less space per passenger than that in Pan Am) gave us an excellent view of Kowloon and the harbor.

We were seated next to the charming wife of a British Government Foreign Service official. She was most pleased that we were staying at "The Peninsula — one of the last places in the world where one can still enjoy gracious living."

And so it was. We were met, to our surprise and delight, by a Rolls Royce from the hotel and sinfully spoiled for the weekend by Chinese service in the manner of the Ming Dynasty. However, the Peninsula, like "Raffles," is scheduled for destruction to give way to a more modern and economical structure. Those who want to see "The Old East" had best hurry.

After going out to the Red China border, where the Kowloon and Canton Railroad chugs unconcerned into the land of The Sleeping Giant, we came back and hired a "san pan" to carry us out into the harbor, where thousands of san pans and junks are home to the Red Chinese refugees who manage to live on fish and rations and care provided by the benevolent British.

We of course carried some fear of being near Red China, but our driver said it was no trick for him to get back and forth, and my business contact, John Berry of the Australian Division of the Bunge Corporation, said he had regularly made business trips inside since 1958.

Incidentally, money changing was easy in Hong Kong. Hong Kong dollars were good metal coins worth 25 cents U.S. The silks and suits still appeared to be excellent values, and the jade, as in Taiwan, was beautiful. The Dragon Lady must have found her gowns and jewels here.

Singapore, Another Stop on Business Man's Tour

From Hong Kong, our flight plan took us over South Vietnam, where we could plainly look down on the Mekong Delta and the jungles where so many Americans had given so much.

In Singapore, we were met by a most gracious British lady standing in for her English son, who had been educated in America and was running a Norwegian-owned mill in Singapore.

By now we were traveling only with Jack and Mary Koss. We were staying in the Shangri La Hotel and it was all anyone could wish in Eastern accommodation.

Jack, another Hoosier and a brilliant Purdue engineer, is president of Capitol Machine Co. and he was especially pleased with Singapore after he sold a veneer slicing layout to one of the large mills there. His company makes veneer machines which are apparently better than German or Japanese or other foreign makes because his slicers are accepted the world over as the superior standard.

This is a good example of where American design know-how and effective and intelligent labor input competes effectively with any combination of circumstances elsewhere in the world — without special subsidy.

Singapore was beautiful and clean. Although the snake charmers and

A World of Travel

Sylvia McDonald and Bruce Markel are pictured in front of a Sultan's Palace in Jahore Baharu. The gentleman in the jumpsuit (on the left) was the crown prince at the time and also high commissioner of the forests and forestry industry. He personally conducted the group through the palace. He later became the Sultan of Jahore Baharu and then King of all Maylasia.

other mysteries of the Orient were still in evidence, they were, as the cabbie said, "tearing Raffles down," and the city was teeming with the business of today's world. [*But plans changed; they did not tear Raffles down.*]

Singaporeans are noted for their industry. Everyone in the Republic of Singapore works or leaves, we were told, and they are interested in their work. The mill managers there were so concerned with the glue situation (gas and oil bases plus urea shortage) that one made a special trip to our hotel to have a hurry-up conference with me before our take-off.

Urea is 46 per cent nitrogen and serves both as a chemical base for many glues and as a fertilizer. In Singapore it was selling for $400 per ton — about three times what it is now bringing here. This underlines the kind of fertilizer and chemical shortages and prices which we can expect here soon.

The port is a hub of activity — a contact point where ships from the Western World take on both exotic prizes and basic commodities from the East.

The Plywood mills have done well here in using the great logs from Malaysia and Indonesia. Here one may see people of many races in a few minutes — Malaysians, Japanese, Indians, Indonesians, Chinese, Eurasians, and others.

They claim no prejudice, but each is jealously proud of his heritage. And, when I handed a Malaysian couple my card with Japanese printing (card exchanging is ritual with Japanese), she exclaimed, "We're not Japanese, we're Malaysian." She was pretty enough that I continued the conversation and managed to learn a lot from her husband about plywood business in Malaysia — so we decided to go there.

A total of 2.35 Singapore dollars were equal to $1 U.S. Values were good but when we were taken out to dinner by some industry people, we could see that food prices, for what we considered good food, were also high here. The money trick in Singapore was to think in terms of Singapore dollars, not American dollars.

In Malaysia we saw our first Sultan's Palace and walked and talked with crowds of individuals of Moslem faith. During the trip we had visited in Shinto homes, dined with Buddhists, and talked rationally with Sons of Islam as we inspected their mosques.

These encounters with different religious influences included the apparent near-absence of religion in Japan.

Orient Tour Group Eager to Learn from Customers and Suppliers

At this point it should be mentioned that we were frequently asked if we were on "business or pleasure." In our instance it was business for the men and pleasure for the women but there was a great deal of pleasure derived from our very pressing business schedule.

Never have I witnessed a group so eager to learn from our customers, our suppliers, our prospects or our counterparts (depending on our position and viewpoint) in the Orient. We were always received with ceremony and courtesy at the plants. American flags were displayed and all personnel alerted. Welcoming addresses were given and refreshments served. Question and answer sessions were arranged.

I'm afraid, in our American haste, we were sometimes not as courteous as our guests. Clark McDonald, our executive managing director, did his best to keep us in line. Clark is extremely sharp — a Phi Beta Kappa with an M.S. [*actually M.B.A*] from Harvard School of Business — and he would try to keep us within protocol and within the schedules and areas of both the plant and discussion on the agenda.

However, we sometimes descended on those plants like a plague of locusts. Before Clark could get tour hosts properly thanked, cards exchanged, and interpretations made, I would be headed for the glue section and the laboratories; Koss would be on top of a veneer slicer; Jean Perron (the French-Canadian president of Canadian Wood Products Association) would be timing production, and others spread out for equally fervent inspections of various departments. Dick Weber, our Stanford-educated Wisconsin representative, got the real feel of the labor movement in the Orient — he played tennis or other games with the employees on the factory fields. He said one learns a lot that way and I agree for I tried a game or two myself.

Paul Koenig, our man from the U.S. Department of Commerce, would get the data on wages, hours, conditions, interest, government participation, etc. And so it went.

To illustrate the depth of our personnel resources, the list of others pictured in the Grand Hotel group [*following page*] includes:

Row 1 — McDonald; Bill Lowrey — curved plywood; Koss; Koenig; Mrs. Lowry — our child labor critic; Weber; Bob Gross — veneers; R. Goodman — millwork.

Row 2 — Interpreter; George Erath — veneers; Bob O'Donoghue, president, HPMA; Dan Tyler — S.C. plywood manufacturer (Dan knew how Japanese plywood had made great inroads in the U.S. market in the '50's); Dick Bowers — wood industry accountant; Mike Van Beuren — manufacturer of plywood in Mexico; Perron; "Tomjon"; Jim Stenerson (beard) — veneers; George Walters (kneeling) — plastic laminations and general entertainer; Robertson (hat); J. Burrell; Kinley — exotic veneer specialist.

There were others not in the picture and not mentioned who were just as helpful in the exchange and in-gathering of information. A Carolinian attorney, Don McCoy, accompanied us, too, and he was most helpful in objectivity. His friend, Thomas Johns, was not only a knowledgeable plywood person, but had the distinction of having the biggest feet on the expedition and the name always seized upon by the Orientals.

The shoe shine boys held a viewing convention at the base of McArthur's statue in Taiwan when one shiner discovered he had contracted to

American plywood study group (Joe Robertson is at right rear with hat) in front of Chiang Kai-shek Grand Hotel. The hotel expresses the hopes, unity, frustrations and "face" of the Republic of China. "It is beautiful, expressive and impressive, but reportedly construction has been stalled for some time with only three floors completed and ready for occupancy," Robertson said at the time. It was fully completed later.

shine Tom's No. 14's for 3 cents. He had heard us call Tom by name and he started shouting, "Tomjon, Velly Beeg Feet."

The Chinese children came running from every direction to see these shoes, which were at least three times bigger than those they were accustomed to seeing.

Jim Burrell, editor of "Plywood & Panel," was seldom in our pictures, for he took many of them. He was, however, the official chronicler of our trip. Wood industrialists Prince, Lenderink, Campbell, Huey and Thompson rounded out the group. From the above references, one can determine that we had American expertise in every department.

At night we would return to our hotels to have delightful dinners with our wives and to gather the "cultural data" on the country we were visiting. The wives were a charming and compatible group that contributed a great deal to the success of our venture. We also had forums in which the total information gathered was collected and confirmed.

We of course did not know in how many areas we impressed the Orientals, but they were always impressed with our height. Wherever we went, factory workers and students alike would look up in wonder at how we towered over them, and they would then smile and nudge one another. We had the feeling, however, despite the ever-present and deplorable language barriers, that we were liked — and we liked them.

The trip back was most enjoyable. Like the rest of the plywood group we stopped for a short rest in Hawaii. Despite commercialism, Waikiki Beach is still delightful and Diamond Head beautiful. Surfing is fun, as are the outriggers.

From Honolulu, we moved to our 50th state, Alaska. Here we spent a week-end layover, visited glaciers and felt the pulse of these modern pioneer people waiting for the oil pipeline start which will boom Alaska more than the Klondike. From the ski slopes at Alyeska we returned over the Arctic Circle back to O'Hare and home.

It was indeed a stimulating and exciting trip. We loved the lands and the peoples. However, we will keep loving America, and leaving it to find out what others are doing and how we can all get along better. We were really glad to be home.

The Orient, 1981

In 1981, Virginia and I again toured the Orient with the Study Group, after attending the annual meeting of the HPMA in Vancouver, British Columbia.

On this trip, however, we visited Hong Kong, Shanghai, the Peoples Republic of China, India, Nepal, and returned home through Germany with sightseeing excursions into Switzerland, Luxembourg, and Belgium. The following article appeared in the *Times-Mail*, November 25, 1981.

Hong Kong Has Amazing Prosperity

As a child I was aware of a legend which promised that by digging a hole deep enough one could eventually "dig to China" — the other side of the world. As an adult of some travel experience, I now know it does take some digging to get into the People's Republic of China and it really is "the other side of the world" — economically, politically, technically, geographically, culturally, philosophically and religiously.

The first group to go to Shanghai included five from Indiana: The Robertsons, Mr. and Mrs. Bruce Markel, and Werner Lorenz. Others included Mr. and Mrs. Marcel Lafleur of Canada; Don Bell of Louisville, Kentucky; Mr. and Mrs. Pete Armstrong of North Carolina; and Sue Hazard of Corporate Travel. In our previous trip to Communist Russia the group always had two aids or interpreters, watchers or whatever. In China there were always three or four.

The flight from Hong Kong to Shanghai was rather uneventful. We were on China Airlines Flight No. 502 — a crowded jet which covered the 1250 kilometers (830 miles) in about two hours. The pre-flight inspections were a bit more numerous and thorough than usual. Baggage control was pretty tight — and baggage limited. Flight attendants were efficient and more than courteous. Storage of baggage was about equally divided between "underseat" and "overhead." Hard hats might have been in order and additional seating space would have been welcome. In-flight food was

Chinese but okay. Drinks included tea, coffee or Chinese beer. Food was chicken and well-cooked beef and a small dish of litchis and tangerine segments.

During the flight we had time to reflect on our observations in Tokyo and Hong Kong. Several changes had occurred since our last visit in 1973. The Tokyo area now has 27 million people living productive and highly-motivated lives. Through their hard work and intelligent improvements on many American inventions, they have obtained much of what was formerly U.S. business. Japanese inroads into American markets for cars, television sets, office machines, cameras, etc., are well known. Many Japanese now follow Shinto religion as a way of life since it permits modernization and earthly enjoyments while retaining cultural ties with the family and the past. Buddhism is favored in later years as it promises eternal salvation under certain conditions.

Hong Kong has prospered even more than Tokyo. This city demonstrates what free enterprise and Capitalism can accomplish, even under a flood of illegal immigration, as compared to the restraining Socialism of neighboring Red China. Hong Kong has problems and poverty but it also has an amazing prosperity and vitality. Hong Kong is neither the China of yesterday nor the China of today's People's Republic. It more closely resembles a booming American Chinatown of skyscraper luxury hotels and bustling commercial activity.

Many of the people look oriental and sharp — beautiful women and well-groomed men in western dress. Many of the people still look like coolies — even an occasional rick-shaw-puller. Then there are also the thousands of boat people and the disadvantaged residents of Cat Alley — but back to the Hong Kong-Shanghai flight. At the termination of the flight, the health and passport checks were okay, but baggage handling was all by hand and total chaos. Customs people were courteous but there were no orderly lines. It was everyone crowd their baggage through one small door for clearance.

Once the baggage cleared, everything was very pleasant again. We were met outside the Shanghai airport by a delegation representing the China National Forestry Import and Export Corporation. Three of these people came all the way from Peking (Beijing) to meet us: Zhang (Chong) Lihua, project manager, China National Forestry Import and Export Operations; Liu Minggang, an assistant; and Chao (Chow) Yung Ching (translated this comes out Miss Evergreen Chow). Last or family names are always listed first. Madam Cho, deputy of Shanghai Light Industry Commission, was also present.

Our quarters for the first night were most impressive. The Xing Guo Guest House was more than a mansion and was probably built by a wealthy English nobleman about 1930. It was part of a walled " club" district which contained perhaps a dozen mansions and expansive lawns and gardens. The luxurious setting was straight out of the movies and told a story of a privileged class of unbelievable wealth, a walled-in contrast to the impoverished conditions of those outside the compound. After the Revolution, the house was used as a residence for China's vice premier.

All meals were multi-course affairs and food was different and tasty. We were allowed freedom to walk about the streets and to visit with the very friendly natives — many of whom knew a little English.

On the second day we were joined by another interpreter, Zhang (Chong) Tung Jiang with the Foreign Affairs Office of The Shanghai Bureau of Light Industry. We toured much of the great city of 11,400,000. Private autos were seldom seen and are used only by high government officials. Huai Hai (Quay Hay) Street and Nanking Street are the main throughfares and Sun Yat-sen Drive, along the Huang Pu (Poo) River, is faced by many beautiful buildings. We celebrated Pete Armstrong's birthday October 15 at the 17th Floor Roof Garden Restaurant of the Shanghai Mansion Hotel overlooking the river in downtown Shanghai. After the sumptuous 12-course dinner, we retired to an adjacent "Resting Room" in the Eastern fashion. By now, it was apparent that "The Chinese Way" prescribes pleasantries before business.

A visit to the zoo was one of the highlights, particularly because of the rare Pandas. We were also privileged to see one of the rare Snow Leopards from the Himalayas and many other exciting animals from the forests, deserts and mountains of China.

We were told the average wage was about 65 Yuan ($40.00) per month, but many services, including medical, were provided free and a month's rent was only two or three Yuan for an apartment. Single family dwellings are no longer constructed. A shirt costs about 6 Yuan (58 cents per Yuan) and a black and white TV costs about 3200 Yuan. Most families have only one child now although two may be permitted without serious penalty. Venereal disease has been essentially wiped out through required examinations and treatment. There certainly was no-sex emphasis apparent in China society — in contrast to that in most other cultures. We were told that there was a very low incidence of promiscuity and that the divorce rate was very low in most areas. The crime rate was also reported to be low and the experience of our group bore this out as no problems of any kind were encountered.

That the urban population of Shanghai was poor is perhaps an understatement, but it appeared that the millions in the street were healthy and happy. They were walking — pedestrians overflowing the sidewalks and crowding a million bicycles in the streets. An occasional car and overcrowded buses honked a perpetual chorus of confusion.

The Chinese Never Wear Red

Our insights to Red China industrial patterns started with visits to Shanghai's number one wood processing company and the Yang Zhi Timber Factory. These plywood and furniture manufacturing plants had good personnel organization and labor management, but equipment and methods were older and labor intensive.

After two days of plywood plant study and an interesting tour of Shanghai's Industrial Exhibition, we took a day off for a river cruise down the Huang Pu into the mouth of the Yangtze and the Great East China Sea. During the cruise we introduced some of our friends to American dance — they were apt pupils. Much of the Chinese Navy seemed to be moored in Shanghai Harbor. Submarines, destroyers, sampans and junks were all present in profusion.

The next day we boarded the train from Shanghai to Suzhou. The train ride on the "Shanghai Express" was fascinating. A varied landscape of rural China rolled by the window. Rice fields, canals, vegetable plots and orchards all testified to the maximum utilizations of The Good Earth. Terraces, ridges and ditches were used by the commune residents to stop erosion and make flat, tillable ground on all hillsides and in valleys.

Suzhou (Soochow) City is one of the most beautiful, most historical and most popular cities in Southeast China. The tower atop Tiger Hill is the city's most famous attraction. It predates and it rivals the Leaning Tower of Pisa in its "angle of repose" — leaning leeward more than seven feet. The Buddhist Temple Monastery there is the site of perhaps the earliest "College of Buddhist Scholars." Five hundred monks met in Suzhou about

700 A.D. to establish some order of doctrine. Statues of the monks resemble those of the Saints at St. Peter's. The propaganda director of the city and his assistant accompanied us in Soochow, as did our three Chinese associates. That made five Chinese escorts for our party of 11.

The so-called Gardens of Soochow were once the residences of the powerful leaders of government and politics. The Oriental splendor of one's imagination comes to reality here. An old Chinese proverb says, "In Heaven there is paradise, on earth Suzhou." It is bordered by the Grand Canal which runs through Yangtze Basin and with connecting waterways provides a navigable waterway all the way to Peking. Much of China's transportation is by the many canals, which also provide irrigation.

The noon banquet at the Soochow Hotel was unbelievable. We were able to keep a copy of the menu. We ate some of every item and the dishes were generally very tasty. The special Suzhou Fish Dish is called "Dazhaxie" — served whole, of course, as is the duck, but both are good. Crabs, pigeon eggs and vegetable soup also were served before the rice, bean curd, Tangbao dumplings and desserts. That Suzhou was a favored retreat for emperors of many dynasties is no surprise. It is a 3,000-year old city which has retained some of the glories of ages past.

The rural populations in most farm areas were probably even poorer than in the cities. From our train and bus windows we saw lots of China, covering maybe 600 or 700 miles with representative stops along the highways and byways. We saw only a half dozen small farm tractors in two days of touring farm areas. Small pitchfork-fed threshing machines were in wide use. Wheat, rice and corn were placed in shocks, and "threshing floors," mentioned often in the Bible, were not uncommon.

There are so many unusual things about China and the Chinese. Tipping really is not customary — a "thank you" is appreciated. "Face" is still important — not understood by most of us. And, "yes" means only "yes, I heard you" — not "I agree," or "that is correct." Bargaining is not the custom. Dress was mainly pants and jackets in dark blue although some dark greys and greens were seen with a small smattering of western dress.

Chinese men are just never seen in anything red and I caused some considerable comment when I appeared one day in a red jacket — "only for children and young girls," our young woman interpreter said in reproof. Polaroid pictures create much excitement. As a matter of fact, any American can easily feel like a movie star just by standing on the street, in a

Our study group made a surprising discovery of women plant managers in China. From left to right, plant manager, J. D. Prince, Chinese guide, Marcel Lafleur, Pierre Legeard, Joe Robertson, and Chinese plant superintendent.

store, or anywhere for just a few minutes. Friendly Chinese will gather around and smile and stare.

As we moved along on our study tour and as we attempted to talk "business" occasionally, it became apparent that American and Chinese behavior and attitudes were very different in many respects. From my own experience, I remembered that it was about seven years from the time the Red Chinese started talking about U.S. grain purchases until they actually took substantial deliveries. This time, as we would try to talk about things related to the plywood business, we usually got the impression that "in due time" or "after additional discussions," something might happen. Also, [*the Chinese*] do not like to be asked the same question twice — we often do this in order to clarify a point. We were also told that "Americans are impatient." When we totally couldn't understand something, our associates would often close the discussion with, "is the Chinese way."

Walls are another "Chinese way." It seemed that every Chinese peasant tried to see that there was an (adobe type) wall around his home and especially around the village. Formerly walls were around all the states or provinces and finally there was The Great Wall across China.

By the time we visited the plywood mill in Xian, we were becoming more aware of "Chinese ways." The Chinese forest industry people assigned to us did carefully provide us with quite a lot of pertinent information. Of course they were quite diligent in obtaining quite a bit of information from our group. We found, for example, that they did have an extensive construction program underway throughout China and we knew that they did not have plywood capacity to meet the needs of that program, that American plywood could help, and that trade credits could be arranged by way of Chinese Exotic Veneer shipments to the U.S. — camphor, sandalwood and rosewood for example. Also we know Chinese handcrafted furniture could find a market in the U.S. and not hurt American mass markets.

These things did not particularly interest the Chinese at this point. They were interested in telling us about the strides they had made in improving their forest coverage and in developing forest education research programs in their universities and colleges. Management and fire protection programs have been promoted. They are making progress in wood industry development as well as in growing more trees — they particularly like to line streets with trees. This is done almost without exception. We were admonished, "In the U.S. you have many streets without trees alongside."

Flying to Xian, we boarded a converted 4-engine C-54 type airplane. It was exciting, however, to once again hear the sound of those reciprocal engines. as the pilot revved them up individually; then, the easy take-off and the synchronization of the hum of the motors with the vibration of the fuselage. It's been a long time since WWII, but there were a number of old USAAF airplanes still around China.

Around Xian we had a chance to view "The Good Earth" first hand. Horse and water buffalo provided most of the power for plowing although some was being done by hand. There were many people in the fields. There was, however, lots of smoke-belching industry in the area. We tried to pick up English maps and literature of the area but a representative from the U.S. Embassy in Peking told us that such materials were very difficult to find.

A World of Travel

Part of the life-sized terra cotta army in burial sites of early Chinese emperors who built magnificent tombs near Xian in Central China, found by peasants in 1974.

Buried Armies of Chin Dynasty Shrouded in Mystery

Two hundred years before Christ, the first Emperor of the Qin (Chin) Dynasty was leading a powerful China to amazing accomplishments almost unknown to Western Civilizations. He had unified China and was the first builder of The Great Wall.

Like the Pharoahs of Egypt, he was obsessed with assuring immortality through construction of a great tomb. The project required the labor of 700,000 people for more than 40 years. In the manner of the Mayan Pyramids in Yucatan, it went on for centuries almost unrecognized and unnoticed — seen only as a "mound" about 150 feet high and four miles in circumference.

It is located only a short distance from Xian — the ancient walled city in the Shanxi Province of Central China. After the Qins, dynasties of Han, Sui and Tang continued to maintain fabulous Oriental palaces in Xian (Sian), and to build tombs near there.

Until recently, most of us did not even know of the existence of Xian, yet over 2.5 million Chinese live in urban Xian and hundreds of thousands of productive acres surround the city and the many outlying "tombs" which are seen as mysterious "mounds" in the plateau between the city and the nearby mountains — mountains which constitute one of the few remaining wild and remote bamboo forest homes of the giant panda.

Although we had done some "home work" our group was generally unprepared for the rapid exposure to the many unknowns and mysteries we encountered in our three days at Xian. I predict that as yet unpublicized and uncovered archeological discoveries of this area will surpass the Central American discoveries of the 20th century and rival the revelations of Egypt's pyramids.

Although the tomb sites of Xian are the focus of attention, the industrial progress in this area should not be overlooked. One of the plywood factories we visited was of relatively new construction and although the machines and layout were generally set up to utilize a lot of labor, the operations were well organized for mass production.

Forty kilometers northeast of the city is the spectacular site of the 2,200-year old ceramic army of 8,000 life-size warriors, fully equipped with weapons, horses, and chariots. Previous emperors had followed the practice of burying "live" armies to protect the king after his earthly demise. Emperor Qin Shi Huang won the hearts of his people by subsituting the ersatz soldiers. This vast burial complex was not discovered until local peasants unearthed it in 1974. Qin (Chin) records do not record the existence of the Terra Cotta Army. Well diggers supposedly made the find. This may be true, and admittedly there is much confusion of fact and fiction, and we do lose much in question-answer translations, but we suspected that the discovery may have resulted from excavation of the tombsites by peasants making home sites. We saw literally hundreds of "cave" houses in the area which certainly appeared to be parts of huge underground complexes — they were large rooms 20 to 30 feet below present day ground levels.

The Qin Ling or Chienling Tomb, is the resting place of the third emperor of the Tang Dynasty and his consort, Empress Wu — about 675 A.D. There are twin peaks facing each other across an avenue lined with huge and exquisite stone statues of winged horses, lions, birds and generals. To the north is a magnificent peak housing the main body of the tomb. Tang Dynasty records report that the complex had 378 rooms — I believe that and also that about 278 of them are being lived in today as cavehouses. Seventeen satellite tombs for related royalty are nearby.

We went down into the tomb of a royal princess — the arrangement, the carvings, the art, the outer coffins, etc., were almost duplicates of what we found in The Valley of The Kings and at Giza. The parallels between these tombs and those of Egypt and Yucatan were almost "spooky" — visible evidence supporting the world-circling legend of "The Mongol Spot."

Back at our hotel, Shan Xi Bin Guan (Shanxi Guest House) we were quickly brought back to current reality by unheated rooms and bath water. Further, although the ancient walls, shops, museums and streets of downtown Xian were most interesting, the authentic Chinese food at The May First Restaurant (including Shark fins, bamboo shoots, fungus, sea cucumber and steamed carp) left something to be desired by some of us who were "meat and potatoes" people.

Our groups were again united for a brief meeting in the Xian Airport. In the dusk they came south from modern Peking to Ancient Xian while we had flown westward from Shanghai to the Treasure City. Some business discoveries in Peking confirmed the old saw about political policies hampering trade but seldom stopping it. Our visitors found evidence of recent platform and plywood shipments from plywood-surplus Taiwan to the plywood-deficient Peoples Republic of China.

The group also came with stories of expensive "Peking Duck" to enter in our proposed book entitled "Eating Your Way Through China."

Whether Peking or Beijing, It's Different

As we left our southbound friends in Xian, we were given some last minute instruction by Clyde Howell of "Deep South" Alabama on adjusting to the culture and cuisine we were about to encounter in modern Peking. Clyde's father, "Hong Kong Harry," was still impressed by everyone's ability to handle the chopsticks. "Quantitative intake is no problem," he said, "but from here on I'm sure we'll be concerned with quality."

By now most of us had Chinese nicknames and we had dubbed our very competent leader "Ding Dong" (Don) Bell of Louisville. Don had been busy getting useful information from Jack Davidson, George Bonitz and especially from Jack and Mary Koss who really qualify as "China Watchers," having made three in-depth visits since 1979. These people may know and understand as much about the wood business in China as anyone in the U.S.

We left Xian with mixed emotions — relief perhaps in leaving behind the harsh poverty, and sadness perhaps in leaving the many unsolved riddles of the magnificent tombs laden with treasures beyond comprehension. The Eastern terminus of The Silk Road had stirred our imaginations and refreshed the history of an ancient trade route which crossed great deserts, deep rivers and the highest mountain ranges to bring luxurious silk to the courts of Europe and to return with gold and trade goods for national enrichment — all without disclosing the secret of the silkworm and the mulberry bush. Can anyone think the Chinese do not know how to trade?

We arrived at Peking airport without really knowing how to spell it. In my lifetime the name has appeared in text books as Peiping, Peking and Pekin and now as Beijing — the current Chinese-English spelling and pronounced "Bay Jing" — at least by us.

The Beijing Airport has been described as large and sterile. By now we were having no security, baggage or paper problems — we must have been preceded by the word that we were "clean." We were met at the airport by Mr. Li Guihe, Director of Import Department, China National Forestry Import and Export Corporation. Mr. Li was a charming Chinese gentleman. He had visited the U.S. and even Indiana. He put us at ease before telling us that it would be necessary for some of us to go to a sub-standard hotel for the first night. Markels and ourselves were luckily sent to the Xin Qiao (Hsin Chiao) Hotel which has the reputation for the best food of any hotel in town.

The rooms were okay, service good and there were excellent shops in the lobby. The hotel was within walking distance of Tian Anmen Square (larger than, if not as interesting as, Moscow's Red Square). Another "Chinese Way" is the ritual of turning in the room key to the "floor boy" or "floor girl" when one leaves his room. On returning, one asks for the room key and is assured that the key is now neatly hanging on the doorknob (announcing to all the room is unoccupied and here's the key). However, one finds everything in the room all there and apparently undisturbed.

The next day we had an interesting visit to the vast Beijing Woodworking and Furniture Factory. Here 3,500 workers produce a complete range of wood products including the plywood and furniture which were of paramount interest to us. Again, word had apparently been forwarded that our

The Temple of the Forbidden City in Beijing.

Canadian, Marcel Lafleur, and our German, Werner Lorenz, were experts and perhaps had something extra to offer over and above the technical expertise of the rest of us from the U.S. The Chinese had apparently solved their formaldehyde emission problems, but methods were not adaptable for use in efficient industry, and product quality characteristics were not always those desired by Western consumers. Production from this 195-acre site was sizable even by our standards. Machinery was mostly Chinese and labor intensive. Their Ming Dynasty furniture reproductions were very attractive, but we were unable to generate any real interest in trade at this point.

After other plant inspections had been completed, our hosts again took us to see the unforgettable sights of Beijing. The Tian Anmen Gate (Gate of Heavenly Peace on The Square) is the second most famous structure in all China. Here Chairman Mao Tse-Tung proclaimed The People's Republic of China in 1949. It looks down on the square which holds rallies of more than a million people and where thousands come every morning to do "Wu Shu" (martial arts), wan exercises and other forms of physical activity.

The Imperial Palace of the Ming emperors, "The Forbidden City," is almost beyond adequate description. Large elaborate, beautiful with so much symbolism — dragons, lions, butterflies in sculpture and mosaic — and the Lhama Buddhist Temple. The Summer Palace and The Temple of Heaven where sacrifices were made to The Gods of Heaven, Wind, Rain, etc.

All these sights are without comparison in other parts of the world. Beijing is modern with wide, well-lighted streets. It is clean in the central city, has modern buildings, and is very orderly.

Peking Duck, Ming Tombs

Beyond all the wonders of Beijing, three events stand out as salient — visits to the Peking Duck Restaurant, the Ming Tombs and the Great Wall.

At the Peking Duck Restaurant, we were honored to be in the company of Mr. Qin (Chin) Fengzhu, Vice-President of China's National Forestry Import and Export Corporation, as well as our other distinguished Chinese associates. Don Bell had studied and had briefed us well. We were courteous and hopefully on our best behavior but not strained. Our Chinese friends followed protocol, pleasantly. We followed suit.

It is a ceremonial dinner of many courses introduced by the presentation of "THE DUCK," which has been force-fed and baked in honey. The duck was toasted, our great friendship was toasted, etc. A couple of toasts were made "bottoms up" with Mao Tais or Mao cocktails consisting of a rice liquor which must have been 199 proof alcohol. Other less fire-feeding beverages included beer, wine and blah orange drinks for some of us. The Peking Duck Dinner represents the culmination of all that's best in Chinese culinary achievement.

The Ming Tombs are located only a few miles outside the city and are approached through a marble arch and a beautiful avenue of animals — reminding one of similar avenues on the Upper Nile in Egypt. Only two tombs have been opened. The tales and evidences of tomb-robbers, as well as the elaborate efforts of ancient architects to avoid such plunder, may also be noted at these fabulous resting places of the Ming Dynasty. Ming vases, held in such universal high regard, are beheld in size and abundance beyond those in possession of museums, shops or collectors elsewhere in the world.

The Great Wall

And finally, the Great Wall. The best-known approach is about 55 miles from Beijing at Badaling. "The Wall" never disappoints anyone. It is the only man-made structure on Earth visible from space. It is officially about 3,900 miles long, in segments and in differing states of repair. It was joined together from many shorter walls by the first Chin Emperor about 220 B.C. It was later repaired and extended by the Mings to keep out the Mongols, whom they had replaced, as well as other enemies. We walked or climbed up the 20-foot wide wall to the towers. The towers were located about every 450 feet and the ascent between them is steep. We ran up both sides on a beautiful cold day in a wind so strong that it added to the breathtaking experience.

We have visited a number of important walls of the world, including the politically important one at Berlin, but the implication of the building and maintenance of this wall is certainly a Wonder of the World.

HPMA study group ascending from the Ming Tombs.

A World of Travel

This picture of China's Great Wall was taken by Joe Robertson near Beijing. Robertson's HPMA associates include, from left, Liu Minggang, Chinese forestry expert and interpreter; Bruce Markel; Mrs. Pete Armstrong; Don Bell (kneeling); Mrs. Robertson (in back); Werner Lorenz; Pete Armstrong; Mrs. Markel; and Mrs. Pierette Lafleur.

These "China Chronicles" cannot do justice to the mysteries, mystique and "face" associated with the Chinese. From the dawn of civilization Westerners have had only fleeting glances into the lives and legends of the yellow-skinned masses with the slanting eyes. These people appear as friendly. The men range from mostly small to large, the women from ordinary to beautiful, and the children are captivating. But, we must remember that these people are atheists and they are communistic. They are non-religious but highly political so they are quite different. We do not comprehend their perceptions, traditions or motives.

Our impressions have been colored by adventurers and missionaries from Marco Polo to Pearl Buck. We conjure up visions of the Mongol Hordes, Dr. Fu Manchu, the Courts of Khan, and the Ming Dynasty, and we do not soon expect an adequacy of oil for the lamps of China. We see no chance for a meeting of minds between East and West for some time.

However, the Bamboo Curtain has parted and we're fortunate to have entered in to see a billion people being sustained by labor, land and an inherent cunning which developed rocketry while others were still fashioning arrowheads.

Americans have a keen interest in China now. Several Lawrence County (Indiana) travelers have journeyed to Red China recently. We were in and around China for nearly a month. We visited factories and palaces, talked with peasants and with high government officials. We observed the communes and millions of people at work and play along the highway, byways, airways and rivers. We ate rice with the masses and enjoyed state dinners. Never once did we encounter chop suey or chow mein.

From China West Through Shangri-La

The standard route out of Red China is back through Hong Kong. Beijing is more modern than the rest of China, but Hong Kong more modern than Beijing. There was no hassle in leaving Beijing and certainly none in entering Hong Kong.

We had a wonderful reunion banquet of both groups in the luxurious setting of the Kowloon Regent. Toasts and poems were rendered with abandon. Art McNair, one of Canada's most seasoned and reserved world ambassadors, freely conceded this experience with the "Chinese Chaps" was unusually interesting, and Mooresville's Mathers admitted that Indiana was never like this. Unfortunately, the "Hong Kong Flu," or some mutation thereof, had caught up with the McEvers from Oregon. The rest of us had sustained ourselves very well with our chop sticks, purified water and various and sundry victuals and beverages.

The day following we took a trip to view the Portuguese colony of

A World of Travel

The infamous Casino in Macau — 45 minutes by hydrofoil from Hong Kong.

Macau, which also lies on Red China's border and which supports a high-rolling gambling community rivaled only by Monte Carlo and Las Vegas. Returning to the Hong Kong Airport, we were pleased to once again set foot on full-sized American aircraft — Pan Am Flight One, undoubtedly the best and deservedly the most famous world-circling flight. The Pan Am Fleet continues under the name of the schedule-breaking tall ships of a previous century — the China Clippers. Pan Am World Flights are excellent ambassadors to foreign people everywhere.

It was a long but comfortable flight — more than eight hours over "The Hump" from Hong Kong to Delhi, India. We had only a four-hour rest in Delhi before taking off, back northeast by north into the almost unknown region of Nepal, where most entering surface travel is still by foot or beast and in the air only by planes capable of rising above the high passes of the Himalayas — that greatest of ranges.

Our introduction to the Land of Shangri-La's Gateway was as auspicious as the mysterious country itself. At last we were headed for Kathmandu. We were in Row Four of the Royal Nepal Airline Jet. Our take-off from Delhi, India, was delayed a few minutes and we were pleasantly surprised by the arrival of the Nepal Prime Minister, Surya Bahadur Thapa, and his party who were seated in the rows just ahead of us. They were not heavily guarded and on our arrival were politely greeted by a moderately large crowd.

During the flight we approached the hidden valley through a pass in the high Himalaya Range and at 30,000 feet looked out our plane window straight and level to the majestic peak of peaks, Mt. Everest, highest in the world — about twice as high as the highest of our tallest Rockies. We later took a flight in a plane especially fitted for viewing Everest and the surrounding ranges.

Kathmandu — Mt. Everest

Kathmandu and Patan live up to their mythical reputations as towns where time has stood still. Many buildings dating back to the second century are still in use as temples, government buildings and even residences. The narrow streets were bedecked with the trappings of a Double Holiday — the time of the Lighting of Candles for the Hindus and the New Year

A World of Travel

Mount Everest, the snow peak in the background, looms 15,000 feet above the upward path on the Himalayas. The Robertson-Markel party ascended to this path level.

Migrant Tibetians coming down from the Lhasa regions.

for the Buddhists. Monkeys overran the Stupas and Temples. Places of worship for Hindu and Buddhist stood side by side and at times were tended by priests of both religions. The Lamas are here from Tibet, too. Streets were crowded with merrymakers in the colorful dress of their regions.

On our second day in Nepal, we traveled some forty kilometers northeast and upward to a beautiful spot on the terraced Himalaya slopes where we could leisurely view Mount Everest and also observe the Mountain Mongol people. It was apparent that the Himalayas are adequate protection for the remote land of the Far Pavilions, where reality certainly is as strange as the myth and legends.

Some progress and improvements are being made in Nepal. The government is managing some forests, which cover 31% of the land, and even fencing acres to keep out the Sacred Cows. The Snow Leopard is said to still roam these mighty mountains with little fear of being hunted. Although wheat is cultivated on the terraced mountains up to 14,500 feet, none but the hardiest can scale the precipitous cliffs up to the 16,000-foot timber lines. Red Pandas and Black Deer also live in the hidden valleys. The vista unveiled mile after mile of mountains and valleys as we looked over into Tibet from our vantage point only about forty kilometers from the border.

Our guide, Aryal Shara Ram (last name first) was very bright. He was a young banker on vacation and he also moonlighted as a college lecturer of economics in the local municipal college. He was Hindu, very religious, and was also very familiar with the Buddhist and Lama practices in the local area. His economic information certainly confirmed our impression of underdevelopment.

The average income in Nepal is in the range of $120 per capita. The Nepal Rupee is worth about eight cents and an average worker might receive 20 Rupees daily. For this they produce some of the finest wood carvings. The refugee Tibetians, among the world's most skillful and patient weavers, have settled in Patan, where they produce some of the most coveted Oriental rugs. Nepalese and English are both taught in the schools, but the country is about 90% illiterate.

These people believe in a Living Goddess who dwells among them — a young maiden selected at five years of age to dwell in a temple as a diety until puberty. The king and queen recognize and pay homage to her. Our guide called and she came to the window. Culture shocks in Nepal come rapidly. This land is generally filthy in the urban valleys and immaculate in the lofty mountains. Somewhere near here James Hilton vaguely placed his Shangri-La of Lost Horizon.

In 1961 the border between Tibet (China) and Nepal was placed on the crest of Mt. Everest. If Everest was not the talisman of Shangri-La, perhaps it was nearby Mt. Lhotse? The Hindus know their god, Shiva, dwells in this remotest of regions, and Lama's God of Longevity must also live here where only the hairy yak can provide sustenance and where secrets are still protected by fear of the Yeti — the Abominable Snowman.

We used the coffee shop of the Everest Sheraton as a retreat from total Nepalese exposure. Here an efficient and accommodating maitre d' presided in his "Pancha Ratna," (interpreted as "Five jewels of Nepal — the Diamond, Emerald, Ruby, Sapphire and Topaz.") He was the first and only captain in all Nepal to use women as waitresses. His name was Raju, C. His food was delicious even to the Shahjahani — chicken, curry, rice and mango pickles. His pretty and diminutive girls were learning rapidly

The Living Goddess, girl-child diety of Nepal (Kathmandu).

to serve properly, and with captivating smiles. They could have been models for Hilton's Lo-Tsen.

Our guide had shown us many unusual things. For example, a Poinsettia Tree — not a potted plant; Eucalyptus Trees so tall and straight as to be excellent building timber. He had described how the scent of Sandalwood Incense and the pineapple could be deadly in attracting cobras as could also the piping of the flutes which are common in the country. He

A World of Travel

The "Dying Houses" and cremation floors outside Kathmandu.

had shown us the erotica which was in evidence everywhere, on hand in the temples and public buildings as well as hotels and shops. It was at least "startling" and while they perhaps did not regard it as pornographic (certainly not as objectionable), we would have so labeled it if it appeared on U.S. TV or news stands. China had shown us no sex — this country was immersed in it.

Now, as a departing visit, Ram wanted to take us through what was really Nepal's Valley of Death. In this area we stood near a dozen memorial stupas and watched as the sick and aged were brought to "The Dying Houses." Here death comes usually within 48 hours. Voodoo is weird. Black Magic is unfathomable, and so is the death wish of these peoples. The dying houses are located beside the Holy River, a tributary to the Ganges. There are stone cots beside the river where the dying are placed in the hope that they may die touching the Holy Water and thus break the cycle of reincarnation and attain the reward of eternal life.

Within three hours after death, the family places the body on a cremation block in the river and watches until the burning is completed. The ashes are then scraped into the river. We observed all phases of the process without resentment on the part of any present. It was one of the most eerie and depressing scenes we had ever witnessed — but for the Nepalese it was the favored way to encounter death and dying.

We had anticipated attending a Forest Industries Technical Conference in our Ashoka Hotel back in Delhi. However, an 11-hour take-off delay in Nepal and a four-hour "crush" at the inexcusably inefficient Delhi Airport consumed all the time we had allotted. It was now back on comfortable Pan Am No. 1 to Germany.

The mysterious, the exotic and the business part of the trip was over. Now it was Markels and Robertsons on a flying fun visit of Central Europe. We rented a station wagon in Frankfurt and took off down the Autobahn for Heidelberg. Then we spent some time taking Markel to revisit some quaint little villages in Alsace-Lorraine, where he had commanded artillery along the Maginot and Siegfried Lines in WWII.

We proceeded through the Black Forest with a quick look at the Swiss Alps near Zurich, then on back up to Luxembourg and Belgium and over to Cologne and down to see again the Castles on the Rhine and the Lorelei. Another Pan Am Flight carried us to West Berlin, certainly an ever-improving and exciting city, and then through Check-Point Charlie, through The Berlin Wall and into East Germany to see the special show-places of Communist Germany, but again to feel the somberness of an oppressive society. From Berlin it was on to the cheerful and boisterous Biergartens of Munich and another look at the Austrian Alps. From Munich another beautiful Pan Am Flight carried us back to The Clipper Club in New York and then on to Indiana.

There are a lot of interesting places in the world. Of the ones we have seen, there is no land like our land and no society or government as great and as good — regardless of our many flaws and imperfections. It's always good to be back.

Chapter 5

Odysseys — Great Britain, Scandinavia, and Europe, 1974 Russia and Siberia, 1979 The Mediterranean, 1980

IN LATE 1974, Virginia and I joined members of the Hardwood Plywood Manufacturer's Association and the Canadian Hardwood Plywood Association on a study tour of the United Kingdom, Scandinavia, and the European Continent. The *Daily Times-Mail* ran the following articles:

Europeans Prefer to Deal in Their Own Currency

By Joe Robertson

"And how do you find things, Yank?"

This was the query in the delightful lounge of the Queens Hotel of Dubartonshire where we had "retired for coffee" and a view of the Firth of Clyde. Our Scottish friend, Victor Lake, was engaged in shipbuilding design and engineering for an international firm. He had just returned from the States and was leaving for a fortnight in Japan the next day. He was interested in world conditions, economic and social, as were we.

At dinner we had been guests of Mr. and Mrs. Tom Blackadder, residents of Helensburgh at the edge of Scotland's Southern Highlands. Tom is a real Scot and president of Diamond Power Specialities in the United Kingdom (England-Scotland-Northern Ireland) and he, too, had international interests and was leaving the next day for London, then Copenhagen.

Tom's wife, Pat, is from Brownstown, and both of them were most charming and gracious in giving us a view of Scotland which included their own beautiful 19th century stone home, the bonny banks of Loch Lomond and Inveraray Castle — the stronghold of the Campbells who mauled the McDonalds at Glencoe in 1692.

Clark McDonald is our managing director. He and Sylvia do a superb job of scheduling our business and pleasure trips respectively, but the McDonalds want it clearly understood they had nothing to do with our visit to the Campbell Castle.

We were traveling on a study tour of European plywood mills which had originated in Montreal Canada at the International Convention of the Hardwood Plywood Manufacturers Association.

Frankly, in the U.K. and Scandinavian countries, things were much better than most of us expected. Of course, U.S. travel to the U.K. is extensive and most people have some reasonable conception of life and times in England and Scotland. However, most of us are not prepared for the rapid changes occurring in all places. The England, or Scotland, or Scandinavia or Europe, or Asia of the 40's and 50's and 60's and even the early 70's is gone. The WW II reconstruction period is over. All of the countries we visited are now, and possibly for sometime have been, "on their own."

Certainly American policies and practices influence them, but perhaps not so much more than European Community actions affect us. This national control of international relationship is a prevailing condition we Americans find a bit difficult to realize.

After WW II the U.S. Greenback was the yardstick of value for Europe and the world. This may be still true to some extent in the Orient, but Europeans now prefer to deal in their own currency, and the ordinary citizen and tradesman is not even sure official exchange rates are suitable — so he tends to discount the dollar rather than consider it a premium currency as was the case in years past.

There were forty-eight of us in London where we visited plywood and woodworking plants. Since we had briefing sessions with the management before and after each plant visit, we were able to get an impression of current economic and political conditions. The British were anticipating recession but the heavy street traffic, filled hotels and restaurants and crowded stores indicated that they were still getting on pretty well. One plant manager indicated that he planned to lay off 25 per cent of his people the following week but he hadn't done so as yet.

Our Canadian associates, Jack McCracken, Art McNair and Burt Armstrong, had especially valuable viewpoints of U.K. conditions while the French Canadians, Marcel Lafleur and Roland LeHay, added French flavor to our contingent. However, Hoosiers in the group almost outnumbered the Canadians. Jim Burrell, our Plywood and Panel Magazine publisher; Jack Koss, president of Capital Veneer Machine Company in Indianapolis; and Jim Curry of Curry Veneer, New Albany, had opinions similar to ours so that we could often establish an "Indiana position" in many discussions.

We were most fortunate in London to be present for the Queen's ceremonial opening of Parliament and could easily determine that the British people love and appreciate their Queen and all the royal pomp and tradition that she represents. The procession of the Royal Mounted Household Guards and the forty-one gun charge and salute in Hyde Park were all quite impressive.

One of the highlights of the British visit was a tour of the venerable and highly respected Oxford University where we were fortunate to meet with a Rhodes Scholar who had been a friend of our son when both were undergraduates at Yale. The "college" plan at Oxford has been copied at many great universities throughout the world. The students at Oxford are truly students with great promise.

While our plywood men were visiting industrial plants in England for a couple of days, the ladies slipped off to "Camelot Country" — the castled area around Marlborough with its legends of King Arthur's Court. The mysterious columns were viewed at Stonehenge and a typical British luncheon of beef and Yorkshire pudding was enjoyed in the typical cathedral town of Salisbury at The Red Lion Inn.

The next day was spent in becoming acquainted with the environs of Shakespeare around Stratford-upon-Avon. We were pleased to share the family interest of "Cherb" [*C. Herb*] and Dian Warwick in seeing

Warwick Castle — the great Norman Castle still serving as home for one of the Warwick cousins. After checking out the castle, "Cherb" decided he would still rather make pre-finished plywood in his plant in Vancouver, Washington, than make plans for "riding to the hounds" at Castle Warwick.

Going back and forth into London from plants and points of interest became almost routine as we became familiar with the landmarks — Big Ben, Trafalgar Square, Buckingham Palace, Tower of London, Waterloo Bridge — and the difference between the "Subways" which were merely understreet passages and the "Underground" which, in typical English reverse, is the Subway.

Freddy Hart at Thames Plywood Co. told us that "fringe benefits" in U.K. constituted about 20 per cent of the labor costs. Socialized medicine is also well established in the U.K., but complaints regarding physicians' availability and service were commonplace.

Some members of our plywood team returned to North America when we departed for Copenhagen. The men had inspected London pretty thoroughly from the industrial sections to the Soho Vice District.

The women had utilized the double-decked buses and taxis for shopping tours which ran from Harrods' through Bond Street to the other extreme at Carnaby Street. London Theatre had been sampled and roasted chestnuts eaten on the streets. Although the London fog is a thing of the past (a pollution ban on coal has cleared the smoke pot chimneys of the city), England still had much of the tradition to offer the casual visitor and the business visitor must not discount the influence of "The City" — London's Wall Street.

The group which terminated the tour in London included most of our Memphis delegation. Memphis and West Memphis are part of an important U.S. plywood area and these representatives were sorely missed.

"Lucky" Robin Jackson of Evans Products Company had won his trip fair and square in a membership contest lottery, but Robin's astute perception in noting particular English manufacturing techniques proved a valuable asset to the group. Andy and Tom Welsh are primarily importers of forest products but allegedly made some investments in English thoroughbreds while talking with friends of Lord Derby.

Walter Lee of Bradford Plywood in Vermont also decided not to continue to Scandinavia. Walter is a real expert on cut-to-size plywood and can quickly size up what plant procedures are substandard and what practices are worthy of emulation.

Contrary to the "plant secret" philosophy held by some, this type of idea interchange between competent professionals is regarded as mutually beneficial by most of our international plywood team.

Frank Sheridan, a foreign veneer specialist from New York and our Wisconsin plywood manufacturers Prexy Dick Weber and Jim Lester, also found it necessary to cut off the Scandinavian extension.

Agriculture Is Still Doing Well in Denmark

The sleek Scandinavian jet which carried us across the North Sea to Copenhagen, Denmark was a suitable child of the Viking ships which centuries before had plied the cold waters below. The cloud cover of the Gulf Stream was clearly visible warming the Jutland but separating the sun and the Danish peninsula in the all too usual manner.

As usual, Jim Kroell, the efficient and personable V.P. of our travel agency, TTI, had made proper arrangements for us to be met at the Copenhagen Airport and our baggage transferred without trouble or incident to the Sheraton-Copenhagen.

The Danes believe in a "Schnapps and Beer" reception so several of our group obliged by joining the ritual. The "Schnapps" supposedly is a high alcohol content vodka-type brew from potatoes. We all appreciated the gesture of hospitality but some reported the taste of Danish Schnapps seems to faintly resemble kerosene.

"The Little Mermaid" in the harbor at Copenhagen is certainly a sculpture of rare beauty and worthy of the fame it holds. Compared to our Statue of Liberty it is minuscule in size but equally dear to the travelers who regard it as a symbol.

Eric Nielson of the Northern Sawmill and Veneer Works (Nordisk Sav & Finervaerk) provided not only an excellent industry reference in Denmark but a real help to our better understanding of Danish history, economics and sociology.

We thought prices were very high in London but the tags appeared even loftier in Denmark. The English system of a pound being worth about $2.40 and the decimal system thereafter had come rather easily for most.

Happily in London there were still some shillings floating around worth about a quarter and a few "tupence" worth about a nickel. Now, however, in a strange land and very unfamiliar language, we started to deal with the Danish Krona — worth about 20 cents.

Jim Huey of Wilco Machines always seemed to have a good grip on exchange rates because of the frequent visits he makes to his foreign customers. Jim's "know-how" in exchange at the bank is matched by his wife's "know-how" at the shops. Unfortunately for me and for most of the men, the other touring wives picked up Scandinavian shopping expertise quickly from Mildred of Memphis.

If the reader gains an impression that this study tour was slightly loaded with southerners, he has made a correct assumption. As a matter of fact, most of the people we met now think Americans have eliminated the R from the alphabet, and that "y'all" and "damyankee" are both single words — that's because they listened a lot more to the southern drawl of the charming ladies than they did to the sharp questions of the men.

Before we left Montreal, we had dined with a one hundred per cent southern plywood group including Dibba John of southern North Carolina, Rose and Pat Speltz of southern Memphis and Beverly Howell of southern South Alabama. Only Dibba accompanied us on the trip, but I had been so thoroughly influenced that I was still ordering grits and black-eyed peas in Denmark — without success incidentally; but plenty of ham was available because the Danish pigs outnumber the Danish people, eight million to five million.

We checked in with an owner-executive of one of the few large independent feed manufacturers in Denmark. He confirmed our opinion that agriculture was still doing well in Denmark. The climate permits cultivation of a wide variety of crops, including both spring and winter wheat, and the farmsteads appear neat, comfortable and well-kept.

There were many contrasts between the very new and the very old. For example, the famous Danish pigs are generally raised in confinement — metal housing, Butler and A.O. Smith bins and silos and the whole modern works. A traveler seldom sees a pig as they are inside the modern buildings. On the other hand, the neat farm house may be very old and still have a thatched roof — they like the thatched roofs.

Since our return we have noted the resignation of the Danish prime minister. We were not aware of any unusual political dissatisfaction during our visit. Queen Margretha is apparently highly regarded and the parliament appears to function at least as well as most legislative bodies in these times.

King Christian 4th is a highly revered Danish king and the chapel of the Royal Fredricksburg Castle was breathtakingly beautiful and certainly indicated that the monarchy generally held Christianity in high regard and didn't use the noun as the meaningless word. I think Denmark can properly be called, among other things, a Christian nation, essentially all people are Lutheran — ninety-six per cent was the figure we were given. We were told, however, that church attendance has dropped sharply in recent years.

In Copenhagen are many beautiful churches and perhaps, for the lover of modern architecture, the Grundsvic Kirchen is the most beautiful in the world. A bright young neighbor of mine, Ted Spicer, had reported the outstanding beauty of the church when he visited Copenhagen several years ago — it was all that he reported.

Hans Christian Andersen, the Danish writer of fairy tales, undoubtedly received inspiration from the sea, the lakes and streams, the drifting snow forms and rising mists with enough warmth and sunshine to lift the spirit. Danish scenes brought back memories of the illustrations in the wonderful children's story books.

While Fredericksburg Castle was very interesting, it was Kronborg Castle near Elsinor which really kindled the historical imagination. In this strategic location ancient Danish kings collected tribute from the ships which had to pass through the two-mile channel separating Denmark and Sweden at this point en route between the North and Baltic Seas. The castle also served as the locale for Shakespeare's Hamlet and it is still eerie to imagine the intrigue, mystery and action which filled the royal halls in former years.

J.D. Prince, owner and executive of Plywood Panels Inc. in New Orleans, served as a seafood critic on this trip. J.D. had established his position as a seafood gourmet last spring when he treated the plywood manufacturers to a riverboat shrimp and "crawdad" feast. J.D. approved of Scandinavian lobster and Copenhagen crayfish but was sure they were no better than the Cajun varieties.

At this point, J.D. had shipped young John Prince and John's charming wife, Donna, back to look after the business while he continued to absorb a little "couth" regarding cathedrals and castles as well as more familiarity with Scandinavian manufacturing practices. He indicated that the new U.S., and particularly New Orleans, practices suited his fancy better than the industry and history of Scandinavia, but he faithfully joined the tour, and "on time."

In leaving Denmark, we had been impressed by many things but now had begun to firmly recognize the vast difference between U.K. and Scandinavian factory conditions and those we had observed in Asia last year. The Asian worker is younger and not as well educated but eager to learn. The workers of the Asian countries tend to center their lives around their work. The European worker generally is more mature, skilled, deliberate and regards the job as only one part of a life with more interests.

Bill Lowry, a Michigan Manufacturer of curved plywood is an expert in evaluating the character, mood and productiveness of a labor force — because his wife chides him about labor relations — but Bill had left us in London so we had to make our individual evaluations thereafter.

Swedes Complain More About Sugar Prices Than Petroleum

By the time we arrived in Stockholm we were becoming convinced that our American recession had not reached Scandinavia yet. As was the case in London and Copenhagen, Stockholm was "bustling."

American automobiles were seldom seen but the Volvos were everywhere and the Saabs running second. It was also obvious that German, French and Italian automakers had done an outstanding job of exporting their cars to Scandinavia, and just as obvious that Detroit's Big Ones wouldn't sell there at our prices in these times.

The high gasoline prices did not seem to deter driving. Traffic was heavy and many cars carried only one person. On this tour we found gas prices ranging generally from $1.20 to $1.50 per gallon, but not pricing the cars off the roads. People were much more inclined to complain about sugar and edible oil prices than petroleum. There appeared to be a resignation that it would be necessary for some time to bear high petroleum costs. They were also optimistic about prospects for off-shore oil supplies in the North Sea.

Most of us had the preconceived notion that the Swedes were liberal thinkers in regard to sex. The theatres, TV, magazines, and advertising tended to confirm our beliefs. However, the other outstanding features of the country and the characteristics of these fine people soon placed this subject in proper perspective.

The marquee of our Stockholm hotel was a large replica of a Viking ship — truly representative of the importance of the sea to the Swedes. In the harbor, just a distance of a few blocks, the government has sponsored the creation of a multi-million dollar museum around the raised hulk of a 17th century Swedish battleship — the Wasa.

Three hundred and fifty years ago the ancient warship sank within a few hundred yards of launching and there remained until recently. It has been recovered in near-perfect condition — giving the world an authentic picture of the state of naval development in 1638 just lifted out of the past for the world to see today.

From Stockholm, our plywood team flew to Karlstad and continued by bus to Otterbacken to visit Vanerply — the most modern plywood mill in Europe specializing in sheathing grade plywood. This great manufacturing co-op has twenty-four thousand forest-farmer owners (one man, one vote, regardless of shares owned) and largely follows the process pattern of the new breed of southern pine plywood mills which have been constructed in our U.S. Southland during the past twenty years.

We were especially interested in the Vanerply Mills because the feasibility study on the large Swedish spruce and pine logs had been conducted in a large U.S. mill where our GLU-X was included in the glue mix. Mr. Svante Funcke, a civil engineer, had visited many U.S. mills where our glue extender was in use so we were able to develop an especially meaningful communication regarding not only the gluing technology being employed but process procedures generally.

I have never seen a more modern or efficient gluing operation. Ecology considerations had been given proper emphasis and glue wash water and other residue liquids were being totally recycled to accomplish "zero discharge" with no water pollution. U.S. quality standards were being met.

In this country we are often concerned about the small log size in the South. In Sweden, the many extra large diameter logs had been considered a trouble source until recently. The logging is done in late winter or early spring and yearly supply contracts are executed with the forest-farmer owners. Computer data is collected on each log and maximum utilization planned.

A plywood marketing session with Swedish executives proved mutually beneficial. The Swedes were concerned about the lagging tendency of their architects and builders to incorporate plywood in Scandinavian construction. We assured them that we projected increased utilization not only because of the many benefits and cost-saving advantages of the construction grades, but also because of the beauty and permanence associated with decorative plywood panels.

The keen understanding of Swedish plywood management for the proper relationship of quality to costs became apparent to me through their selection of their glue ingredients. They were using a proper application of a good American basic phenolic, and while they were not using our GLU-X, the quality and specifications of their glue extender was far better than the extender quality we have found in most samples we have collected in our plant visits over much of Asia and Europe — as a result, they had excellent gluing quality control, little waste, fewer failures and fewer clean-up and pollution problems.

Scandinavia is regarded as the "Cradle of Co-Operatives." I can well remember my college agricultural economics profs and particularly my university president pointing to the Swedish Co-Op in 1940 as being the near-perfect pattern for our ag-industry to follow. This ownership resting in a one-man, one-vote idea struck me as extremely liberal, to say the least, at that time.

American agriculture, however, and even publicly held stock companies, has picked up many ideas from Scandinavia and made them work in America. On the other hand, it was easy to see that American corporate ideas were prominent in administration and management of the Swedish Co-Op.

Any discussion of Sweden must include Swedish smorgasbord and other traditional Scandinavian foods. Some of our people visited Operakallaren (ranked by Fortune as one of the world's ten best restaurants). It was reported as very good — but one must keep in mind the time, the dishes ordered, etc. As one of our waiters noted, "There are probably at least one hundred and ten "ten best restaurants." We agree. However, here are a few of these Swedish delicacies from the menue Gastronomique: Oxtail soup, smoked eel, black roe, herring, smoked reindeer, lightly smoked salmon braised in white wine, souffle of snow grouse with morel sauce, Russian pancakes, and cloudberry parfait.

Other restaurants were visited and judged equally good. The Sotare (chimney sweepers) at Diana's was a winner — an oldtime Baltic herring specialty. The "Paillard du boeuf" ground beefsteak with egg yolk, etc. (all uncooked) struck me as "unusual." However, regardless of one's opinion of the so-called "specialties," the food generally must be fairly judged as very delicious.

The dessert question had been solved by the time we reached Sweden. "Catbird" Tomjon of North Carolina always passed judgment on dessert and never passed it up. Catbird rendered the decision that Grand Marnier Souffle was best in any country. This fluffy egg and liqueur concoction did gain a wide following, even including group leader Clark McDonald, who liked to embellish the flames with a couple of scoops of ice cream.

Our guide in Sweden was a handsome Swedish girl — Vera. She had visited the U.S. and had been interviewed with her husband on a talk show. She said she had been particularly confused with American words of identical sounds yet vastly different meanings. On the Johnny Carson Show, in the presence of her husband, she was asked (she thought), "What do you think of the American mail?" "Best in the World!" was her enthusiastic reply — which brought all of the house down, except her husband. Johnny's query in American pertained to the American male.

She was an excellent guide, as was the usual for our English-speaking guides. Her posture was enviable and her accent Swedish-enough to be charming, yet understandable. She took the ladies on a tour through the ancient university town of Uppsala and out to a quaint wooden church, near the Beowolf Mounds. Runic Stones — very old slabs with Nordic markings — were frequently seen in the countryside.

In the medical school at Uppsala, so it is claimed, teaching doctors first performed surgery in an observation amphitheater where students on steep steps viewed the operations. The simple grave of Dag Hammarskjold lies in a family plot at Uppsala. The Swedes feel, as do many of us, that the mystery surrounding the death of this great international statesman may never be solved.

The City Hall in Stockholm is magnificent — small wonder it has been chosen as an appropriate place for awarding the Nobel prize every year — and particularly for holding the Nobel Prize Ball. Of course, in visiting the six-hundred-room palace, one is exposed to the fascinating tales of Sweden's prominence as a world power in earlier centuries. Vera held the close attention of her American friends as she related the romantic story of Desiree, the beautiful Swedish queen from Marseille who had earlier been the fiancé of Napoleon before her father turned her attention to General

Bernadotte and Napoleon turned his attention to Josephine. Desiree always missed her sunny France and made the perceptive statement that Sweden had two winters — a white and a green one.

As we progressed on our trip, different men would receive business calls making necessary their departure from the group. The time spent on these study tours is as valuable as any, but plywood business, like most others, operates under almost hourly change schedules and pressures.

By now, Bob and Jeanne Brown, also of Memphis, had found it necessary to leave the tour in order to take care of some business in another country. Every person on the trip appeared highly interested in our proceedings and Bob and Jeanne were sorely missed as were the others — each made a unique contribution to the success of the trip.

Now, however, the cold weather, the short days, long nights and fast pace had caught up with some others in our crowd, and Jim Burrell, the Indianapolis magazine editor, gave in to pneumonia and boarded a plane back to the States. The rest of us buttoned up our overcoats and took on some additional food and-or fuel for the still farther north — Helsinki and beyond.

Finland Is Prominent in World Industry and Trade

"Outokumpo Metor." You may not recognize the words, but if you travel by air, you have probably passed through one during your airport security check. The metor is the metal detector used in most of the world's airports and gives a hint that Finland is more prominent in world industry and trade than most of us realize.

I had never given any real thought to going to Finland, but it was most exciting and informative. Most of us think of the Finns favorably for their repayment of War Debt and their heroic stand against the Russians at the start of WW II. They also want to be considered for other reasons.

Helsinki has been properly called the "Pearl of the Baltic" and the "Daughter of the Baltic." It is a modern capital of a modern republic — the country has been controlled by neighboring Sweden and Russia in times past but it gained independence in 1917. These independent people still feel that they must be vigilant to maintain their freedom from what they consider the envious appetite of military neighbors.

The days were growing increasingly short in the land of summer midnight sun and winter darkness. Nonetheless, we were amazed at the bright attitude and splendid appearance of the people. As in the other Scandinavian countries, many of the women were extremely well dressed. The beautiful fur coats are seldom equaled elsewhere in the world and fashionable longer skirts and smart boots were appropriately worn for street wear in the chilly weather.

The Finns are noted for their school of architecture. Hvittrask the former studio-residence of Saarinen and Lindgren and Gesellius is an outstanding architectural creation and is now also an exhibition center for Finnish art and handicraft. This architectural competence has probably served as a stimulant for the highly developed Finnish plywood industry, which does a brisk export business to many parts of the world — including the U.S.

We visited Tapiola Garden City, which is regarded as a triumph in modern architecture and ideal urban planning — it seems to be all of that. It's a stunning accomplishment in building a modern city as a pleasant place to live.

Jack Koss, whose Indianapolis Capital Clippers, lathes and other veneer machines have established an enviable world-wide reputation, rented a car for a special drive north on an inspection trip of a furniture factory, a plywood mill and a machinery plant.

This may seem like a routine travel note but if you have never started out driving in a strange large city, not knowing anything about the city, the countryside, the language (not the usual French, Spanish, etc.), the laws or road signs, and with all written names sounding different than the spelling, then you have no idea of the adventure on which he embarked. Add snow flurries and darkness to compound the confusion.

Ted Lenderink, a Michigan veneer and plywood man; Tom Odom, also associated with Linwood, and Clark McDonald "rode along" as "guides" having somewhat less road knowledge than Jack. The destination was Lahti about eighty miles north.

Stout fellows Jack and Clark returned from the victorious crusade about midnight. Ted and Tom decided discretion was the better part of valor and remained in the Northland to seek most any alternate transportation in the light of the following day.

The rest of our plywood team took a rather less hazardous air journey to Lappeenranta — about ninety miles northeast of Helsinki to the Russian border. By now we were accustomed to being surprised by the size, productivity and efficiency of foreign plants. One mill was laying veneer on blockboard with extended urea-resin and the "Kerrotex" mill at Joutseno was producing a board containing a refined sawdust core which was covered with an adhesive film and then surfaced with a birch veneer to which an extended poly-vinyl had been applied. The very large production was mostly on Finnish equipment and ninety per cent of the product was scheduled for export sale. The management people were very hospitable as were the Raute Machinery personnel.

At every meal, unusual food and drink was provided. I could write a whole chapter on how all people but Yankees louse up coffee, but most readers already know this and will readily agree that most foreign restaurants, for all their graciousness, charm and superb dishes, do not know WHEN coffee should be served, that it doesn't NEED to be that strong and a full size cup should be served — full.

We were close enough to Russia, however, that most were much more concerned with "toast" than coffee. I guess the Finnish Schnapps tasted every bit as good as the Danish — possibly a little more like lighter fuel than kerosene. We should have brought a sample back to Quay MacMaster of South Carolina, who reputedly studied distillery — flavor trade secrets involved in southern "white lightnin'" production at the same time he learned the plywood business.

At this point, Jack Koss and I had to cut out on a Finnair night flight to make an appointment in Switzerland. The Raute people provided a car and chauffeur to drive me across the delightful Finnish countryside to meet Mary K. and Virginia at the Helsinki Airport. Surprise again! In this reindeer land, I guess I expected to see mostly backward people living under sub-standard conditions. Instead I saw people who appeared healthy and prosperous, in nice homes, good looking villages, lots of good little cars on excellent highways — pretty much like typical U.S. scenes in winter.

The Scandinavian experience was completed. The Canadians with their cold weather experience would have been helpful to us in these northern climes, but the others previously mentioned, along with Ted and Margot Samuel, had left us back in the U.K. when we started north. It also started to dawn on me why we had dwindled to a group of mostly Southerners (good group that we were). Those Wolverines, Badgers and other Northern U.S. snowbirds already knew what winter climate was — in any Northern country. But, we loved it and learned.

The Finnish Plywood Association gave our people a gala reception as a send-off. The official study group headed homeward. Huey to the Deutsche-land with his engineering design, and we to the rest of the European Common Market.

Switzerland

Switzerland was something! Mount Blanc was beautiful from our Geneva Hotel. Carlo Iseli, chairman of Zurich Veneer Mill, Ltd., arranged an unbelievable Swiss business and pleasure tour for us. From Zurich, over two hundred miles away, he sent Deiter Baumann to pick us up and drive us through the most beautiful Swiss alpine scenes one could imagine — even *Heidi* [*the novel*] was never like this. A one meter (39-inch) snow had fallen in the Alps.

After all of the small cars I had crowded my long legs into for so long, the Chrysler New Yorker looked and felt like the *Queen Elizabeth* — four snow tires for the high passes. Deiter was undoubtedly the most qualified chauffeur, guide and companion in Switzerland. A race driver, world traveler and skier, the young Swiss knew the country, the roads, the people and the places. He was fluent in English and he handled the car like the pro that he was.

He took us around Lake Geneva and up and over the heart of the ski country. He showed us where the Swiss ski — and they were skiing — not St. Moritz where one must wait long for the lifts, but to Gstadd — the beautiful "in" spot of the stars and jet-setters, and many other places just as exciting — through Zeng around the Zurich Sea and into the Splugenschloss — one of the most charming hotels I have ever visited. . . small, individual, European and most attractively furnished with European period pieces. Beds beyond belief. Mr. Iseli's attractive daughter, Madelon Sutter, was our hotel owner and hostess.

We spent an evening with one of Carlo's sons, Rico, who writes for a Swiss finance publication. After discussing many interesting items of business and finance with a representative of the famous Swiss banking community, we formed the opinion that the Swiss still have a high regard for the American economy and U.S. production capacity as compared to that of most other countries.

We were entertained by Mr. Iseli and his charming wife, Thais, in their most impressive home, and then we were taken to the Old Castle for dinner with the Iselis and their son, Daniel, who had just returned from his first duty tour in the Swiss Army. The next day Carlo took us to the airport for our take-off to Germany.

Germany

As we were preparing to board our plane for Frankfurt, we ran into Marcel Elefant, whose General Woods Company had been our hosts for a visit through their plant back in Montreal.

Canadians know how to do international business and they also have good wood process plants. We had visited Okaply before we left Montreal, and Bill Caine, president of Canada's Commonwealth Plywood Co., had invited us all out to the opening of their brand-spanking new plant — another model of design efficiency.

Frankfurt is a business-oriented city and, of course, well known by many U.S. servicemen. Plenty of English-speaking businessmen here are ready to discuss the impact of the Petrodollar or the price and prospects for building materials in marks or dollars. They have their economic problems, too, but their inflation rate is less than ours and their unemployment percentage considerably lower.

We were met in Frankfurt by Albert Kalkhof of the Kling Furnier-Werk. Albert gets around the world considerably and we had previously met him, quite by accident, on a flight from Chicago to Indianapolis.

In noting accomplishments of the foreign forest products industry, we do not want to leave any impression that others have out-stripped our U.S. industry in international business. Our HPMA board members — Deane Brink of Champion-International, Lynn Black of Georgia-Pacific, Bill Turnstill of Evans and some others were not on this particular trip, but they all have many associates selling and buying many items in many parts of the world.

We were certainly leaders in world forest utilization and are vitally interested in the most efficient wood production and marketing in all areas from the tropical rain forests to the timber stands of the snow countries. We all, however, have much to gain through world exchange in commerce and technology.

The Mercedes seemed to us to be the most highly regarded car in Europe, but we were very happy with the little Rekord we were able to rent for a drive down the Rhine. The Castles on the Rhine are still wonders to behold, and looking up and down the busy river from the top of the Lorelei

(Loreley) one can still imagine the siren songs luring sailors to destruction on the rocks below.

After pledging to forget business for a few days we drove down the Autobahn to old and interesting Heidelburg. We visited the castle, university, and other points of interest and climaxed the visit with an evening in the Red Ox Inn amid familiar scenes from "The Student Prince." The tables had student carvings dating back hundreds of years.

A crack European train, the Rheinblitz, carried us quickly and smoothly to Munich (Munchen). The 1972 Olympic site is still beautiful. The Glockenspiel, the Hofbrauhaus and Nymphenburg Castle are places to be remembered. Munich is an outstanding example of total reconstruction from near-total destruction. It is German. If a Sauna House is the symbol of Finland, then the Beer Garden or Rathauskeller must be the symbol of Munich.

We touched base again with the business world in Munich. The Herald-Tribune — an English newspaper published jointly by the New York Times and Washington Post — is distributed internationally and we could usually keep within about twenty-four hours of U.S. market whenever we could find an issue.

Austria

In Vienna, the world of the Old Music Masters comes to life. It is truly a romantic city. One may waltz in the park beneath the statue of Johann Strauss, ride on or beside the Blue Danube and be entertained with beautiful music by the strolling musicians in a wine cellar.

We toured the Vienna (Wein) Woods where Crown Prince Rudolph met his death with Mary Vetsera at Mayerling. The prince was convinced that the romanticism of the monarchy would be eroded by democratic yearnings of the Austrian masses. The Castle of the Hapsburgs contains an imperial treasury, including the Crown of The Holy Roman Empire, which reminds one of the vast wealth and power once controlled by the princes of Austria, Germany and Hungary. The Schonbrunn Palace is another fabulous reminder of the heyday of the double-eagle monarchy.

In Vienna, one must also see the Royal Lipizzaner stallions at the Spanish Riding Academy and spend some time in Grinzing Village where new wine, song and laughter rule the mood of the visitors. Before leaving Vienna, we ate one wickedly expensive Sacher Torte at "Demel's."

Through the Common Market, European nations are again rebuilding the barriers of nationalism. Everywhere the threats of recession and economic pressures on business and particularly jobs, were kindling flames of resentment against "aliens" — job holders and job seekers from neighboring nations were being asked to "go home."

Italy

When we landed in Rome, we found summer again. And it was welcome. Italy is bankrupt, so it is said. If this is true, it was not readily apparent to the casual visitor in November, 1974. Streets were filled with Fiats. We were getting about 650 Lira for our dollars, but wishing for more to cover the high hotel and food prices.

We were inconvenienced a little by a half-hearted strike of bus drivers — then baggage handlers. We thought, "These emotional Italianos — always striking." Then we picked up the Herald-Tribune — "Coal Strike in U.S." . . . "Bus drivers strike in U.S." Guess things are much the same all over.

The Eternal City is indeed that — and impressive. The Vatican, the Appian Way, the Catacombs, the Colosseum, Forum and other inspiring ruins are effective in reminding one of "the glory that was Rome." We climbed the Spanish Steps and threw coins in the Fountain and did the things tourists are supposed to do. Incidentally, the spaghetti was good in Italy, as was the Wiener Schnitzel in Austria.

Perhaps the current unrest in Italy will eventually bring a Mussolini-type leader again to the Romans. However, today the Communists, not the Fascists, pose a challenge and the Communists may be a 30 per cent factor in Italian politics. Nevertheless, as far as political unrest, we just didn't see any — not as much, for example, as the rather large student demonstration in Frankfurt, Germany.

We were lucky to be able to attend a High Mass in St. Peter's with a benediction by the Pope. None of us were Catholic, but we were highly impressed by this experience in these surroundings.

Monaco

Monaco is truly a story-book kingdom. The drive from the airport in Nice along the French Riviera is spell-binding as one looks down from the cliff-hugging roads to the blue Mediterranean below. Our good fortune with celebrities continued in Monaco. Just as we had seen the Queen in

London and the Pope in Rome, it was National Fete Day in Monaco and we went to church with Princess Grace.

The night before we had witnessed the fireworks from a roof-top restaurant overlooking the harbor — the lights on the palace made the whole thing look as if it were the Magic Kingdom at Disney World, only life-size. Of course, we lost at roulette in the renowned Monte Carlo Casino.

Majorca

About one hundred miles south of Spain's Sun Coast, the island of Majorca (Mallorca) lies nestled in the warm Mediterranean waters. The isle is favored with one of the finest climates in the world, and is populated with inhabitants who are friendly and hospitable. The sea and the mountains are both beautiful and a thousand ancient windmills harness the power of tradewinds to water fertile lands of wheat and grapes and olives from trees more than one thousand years old.

Only about three per cent of the visitors here are American — this is enlightening to those of us who have always had the idea that world tourist business is essentially supported by the Yankees.

Spain's Iberia Airlines carried us from Majorca to Madrid — the last stop on our journey. While we still prefer U.S. airlines, it is worthy of note that Iberia was the only line which didn't take most of the stewardesses' and passengers' time in booze trading.

The passage through customs was as routine as passing through a turnstile at a football game. It was no more difficult for us to pass from one European country to another than for us to go from one state to another inside the U.S. — nothing like the hassle one encounters on returning from overseas into New York, or Honolulu, for example.

The Castles in Spain are there to be seen, but El Toro is yielding to El Soccer as the national sport. Traffic in Spain moves in millions of Seats — Spanish version of the Fiat. The Royal Palace takes on added significance as Franco's old age makes the reinstatement of the House of Hapsburg imminent.

The Spanish seemed to us to anticipate the probable return to a monarchy as a natural and unexciting turn of events. They were, however, highly concerned about the turn of political events in Portugal. Catholicism remains the predominant faith in Spain and divorce is still almost nonexistent — it is, of course, illegal.

Temple Fielding, in his most helpful travel guide, has said that Spain is California, and Arizona with bits of Virginia, Colorado and Florida thrown in. With this in mind, our Hoosier foursome became ready for a return to the "good 'ol" U.S. of A. The TWA 747 moved us swiftly into Kennedy, through customs, then via helicopter to LaGuardia and on to Indianapolis where a delightful surprise homecoming awaited us.

General conclusions are never too meaningful without explanations and details, but again we found the European business community friendly, receptive and more advanced in most respects than we had anticipated. We will need to be productive and exercise good financial stewardship to keep our position as a leader in world commerce.

We believe good communications with our neighbors around the world can help all of us toward maximum development of our individual potentials. It is always great to go — but better to get back.

Russia and Siberia

In the spring of 1979, our HPMA-sponsored study group visited Holland and the Soviet Union, with emphasis on Siberian forests. The following articles appeared in the *Times-Mail*.

Holland First Stop on Wood Industry Study Tour

In prior years, small groups of plywood industry representatives have traveled to many parts of the world to study tropical and temperate hardwood forests and forest product processing facilities. Above the rainforest and temperate hardwood belts, there are vast wooded areas often regarded as substantially softwood, or conifer.

However, birch and other species are intermixed with the pines of this sub-arctic belt and provide perhaps unrealized resources of hard and soft woods for both decorative and construction purposes.

As the petrochemical and energy crunch worsens, it is imperative that the world becomes aware of wood as a basic renewable resource. Hopefully, Americans can be educated to develop an attitude favorable to maximum utilization of trees wherever they may be — for recreation and wildlife cover as the trees grow, and for desperately needed shelter and fiber as they mature and are harvested under a multi-use, human-benefit concept of management.

The plywood group started this sub-arctic study tour with 21 adventuresome souls, having a wide range of backgrounds and qualifications. This diversity contributed a great deal to challenged viewpoints and qualified consensus opinions rather than superficial conclusions drawn from first and biased impressions. In addition to managers directly associated with plywood business, the group included a lawyer, a doctor, a journalist and a number of women with wide interests and varying fields of competence. And in this group, women insisted on at least "equal rights."

The trip took place during the NCAA and NIT tournaments, which were the source of much anxiety. Communication was poor, very poor, and since representatives of most major 1979 athletic conferences were in the group, any time a call went through the first word was necessarily concerned with game results. The representatives of the Atlanta Coast Conference and Southeastern Conference fell early. The Ivy League representative followed with Big Eight down the tube and Robertson had great fun when the word arrived that the Big Ten's Indiana had won the NIT. Flowers and condolences, however, were proffered when the word of Indiana State's demise came through at a homeward-bound touchdown in Newfoundland.

In addition to Joe and Virginia Robertson, Indiana's other representatives were Jack and Mary Koss of Indianapolis. This was his third trip to Russia, and with Mary he has traveled over a great deal of six continents.

George and Shirley Earth own Earth Veneer in North Carolina. George had early college training at Indiana University before taking up with the Tar Heels. Charles and Jerry Guyer are Georgia (Univ.) Bulldogs primarily and also run Alexander Wood products. Mabel Thornton, another Georgian and board chairman of Alexander Wood, also accompanied the group.

Ed and Carolyn Hanley, Yankee Veneer people, tried to balance some of the group's distinctly Dixie flavor. Clay Howell's dad runs a plywood mill in Alabama. Clay left his dad at home and took his mother, Beverly, because she was originally from Florida and Clay and Harry had decided that one conservative was adequate representation. Others included Jim and Mildred Huey and Tom and Dibba John.

Dr. Thomas John, Jr. also accompanied the group and passed out quite

A row of Holland's famous windmills are lined up in welcome for our adventuresome HPMA study group.

a bit of free medical advice when conditions were stressful — as often was the case. He and Judge Don McCoy gave a professional flavor to the group and perhaps untarnished the "Capitalistic Business" image of the rest of the party. Kathryn McCoy was an excellent observer of flora and fauna and Sylvia McDonald managed the study tour in a very effective manner.

From the above names and references, it can easily be determined that opinion and conceptions have seen the light of challenge and debate from many competent quarters and the words "I think" were often met with "Why, and what is the basis of that conclusion?"

The trip will be judged a successful one if impressions from this study should provide some enlightenment regarding future wood resources and the attitudes and practices of "wood people" in distant parts of the world.

Holland

Amsterdam was not only interesting but also pleasant and comfortable in contrast with some latter parts of the tour. The Krasnapolski Hotel, in the center of the city, provided a convenient base for excursion in every direction.

Shopping along the picturesque streets was enjoyable and the hot pea soup served from the small and unique streetside cafes was delicious and exhilarating.

The delightful boat trip through a few of the 100 canals permitted unhurried views of unusual architecture and historical sights. Outside the city, the neat and antique windmills made everyone an instant Don Quixote riding forth from LaMancha to change the world.

Canals criss-crossed the countryside, and the enterprise of the Dutch people was plainly evidenced by the intense utilization of the land which had been so painstakingly reclaimed from the sea — even the fields between the airport runways were cultivated.

The fabled flowers of Spring in the Netherlands were emerging everywhere. The dikes on the Zuyder [*Zuider*] Zee were, just as we had imagined, standing fortresses for people, villages and farms against the everpresent pressure of the North Sea. Childhood memories came rushing back of the story of the brave little Dutch boy who plugged the dike to save his village. Wooden shoes and native costumes were still being worn by many of the villagers as they came from the churches along the seaside route of our Sunday tour.

Any visit to Amsterdam would be incomplete without a visit to a diamond-cutting factory and the Rijks Museum, where so many paintings of the famous Dutch Masters hang, and where one may stand in awe before Rembrandt's "Night Watch." The Van Gogh museum is probably the most modern public building in Amsterdam and it too proved a refuge for our "art lovers." The home which provided sanctuary to the little girl writer of "The Diary of Anne Frank" was also among the "must" sights nestled among the gabled houses dating back to 1600.

The Dutch East Indies Company long ago brought back the recipes for the Indonesian food and "The Rystaffel" or "rice table" at the Sama Sebo Restaurant was up to its reputation. Many of our party attested that the food was as flavorful (and as hot) as that which they had last enjoyed in Bali [*a trip we took in 1977*].

The group motored southward through historical battle areas of World War II for a full day's visit to the VanHout Veneer, Plywood and Furniture Complex in Mill, Holland. The mill visit was rewarding in many ways. Personable Tony VanHout and his associates were genial hosts in the interesting business which evolved from a maker of wooden shoes, yes wooden shoes, into a modern and sophisticated wood processing complex.

Egy Henrichse, a company director, had accompanied us all the way from the U.S.A. Peter Jansen proved to us that Dutch ingenuity and engineering is comparable to that in America. Young Adrian VanHout had recently completed an extensive work and study experience in the U.S. to make sure that this continues to be true.

The next morning, a mill visit and conference at the large Bruynzell Multi-Panel Co. (Plywood, Doors, Funiture) furnished some new insights on business in the Netherlands. Obviously the priority concern of the company was "pleasing the workers."

Employment is full in Holland and government programs assure a reasonably comfortable life for all those willing to meet the qualifications. The current social-political climate favors early retirements, forty-hour work weeks, plenty of vacation time and good working conditions — whenever the Dutchmen choose to work. They are, however, intelligent and very productive workers, when they work. And, they surely realize that workers are also customers so there must be a grave concern for serving the customer's interest or else the workers ultimately are hurt.

In any event, the Bruynzell plant has brightly painted work areas, gardens and shared leadership responsibility, among other things, to keep their workers "at it." We had particularly interesting and rewarding discussions with J. H. Verhoeven, managing director; B. Loerts, marketing manager, and A. A. Folge, head of quality control. Adhesive technology developments were discussed with W. Boonstra of their Central Laboratories. All of these people were fluent in English and there were open discussions of industry problems. After the discussions, we rushed to the airport to board KLM (Royal Dutch Airlines) for the not-so-secure flight over the Iron Curtain and into the enigma that is Russia

Many Surprises, Schedule Changes on Russian Trip

An old saying, "There is no 'cow' in Moscow," is intended as an aid in pronunciation. But, as an aid in understanding, one might add, "There is a lot of 'bull'."

Our KLM jet touched down in Warsaw enroute from Amsterdam to Moscow. This was the first of many surprises and schedule changes during our Russian trip. We were pleased to see a little bit of Poland and the people.

A few purchases were made as some of our adventurers immediately "tested" the effectiveness of "the restraining system" by wandering from the prescribed waiting area through a closed and rather narrow gate into "the shops." This maneuver separated our conformists from our professional world shoppers — the conformists then passing the word to gather in the stragglers at boarding time. Once on the plane, all enjoyed checking the "good buys."

The airliner settled down in early darkness at Moscow. Nearly all landings at major aiports were in darkness — whether by plan or coincidence we never quite decided.

Through the entry procedures and customs, as always in Russia, we were courteously treated — no hostility but then no real exhibition of friendliness. Some of us were asked pointedly if we carried any Bibles. Clay Howell admitted he had some magazines so his baggage was searched and his literature reviewed. Fortunately he had previously discarded Playboy.

The agents asked me to remove my hat so they could confirm that I really did resemble the Kojak character pictured on my passport and visa photo. Then we looked for "Alex," the man we were to meet. No man.

Outside the turnstiles we were met by an attractive young woman. In excellent English she announced, "I am Elena. I will be your Intourist Guide while you are in our country. Alex is in the hospital." Elena was with us thereafter until we left USSR.

Americans, rightly or wrongly, are suspicious of "official Russians." We were indeed sorry that Alex was ill and unable to meet us. However, Elena was to prove herself a most capable and considerate Russian resource person. Most of us soon grew to love and respect her as an intelligent and beautiful person, one we could look to with confidence for guidance and enlightenment within the limits of her proper duties and prescribed behavior under political affiliation and system.

There were additional guides who met and accompanied us in all the cities or republics which we visited — specialists, political, cultural, industrial. These "specialists" were very well informed but for the most part their responses to our questions were rather formal, conditioned and certainly flavored with Communism, as we should have expected.

Our itinerary, as constantly revised, finally included three stops in Moscow or Moska or Mockba — every sign I saw seemed to spell it differently. This isn't surprising when one realizes over 100 languages (the principal ones are Slavic) and five alphabets are used.

The first Moscow hotel, Intourist, was adequate, not The Hilton. It was indeed exciting, however, when drawing back the curtains in the room to see a truly striking view of Red Square with the ruby red star glowing over the moonlit, snow-covered Kremlin grounds and St. Basil's Cathedral.

It was late but Elena had arranged for a surprisingly good and efficiently-served dinner. We gulped it down, American style, traded in our room keys (for which we had traded our passports) for our hotel identification cards, rushed past the hotel guard en masse, under Karl Marx Avenue and up the "metro" (subway) stairs, on across Red Square in time to hear the booming strokes of midnight from the Kremlin Tower and to watch the impressive changing of the guard at Lenin's Tomb.

The feeling is that of finding one's self at a far away and famous place — "at last I am really here, at the place I have read about for so long or have seen long ago in the newsreels or watched by satellite TV."

At first appearance, coming in through the suburbs from the airport, Judge McCoy properly characterized Russia for all of us, "Drab and cold." The coldness was to get much colder as we traveled north and west but the drab veneer was to be peeled back and overlooked as we began to

A World of Travel

The study group on a tour of Moscow in front of St. Basil's Cathedral just outside Red Square.

discover the history and pulse of a land and people, mysterious and alien but extremely interesting.

In Washington, D.C., our orientation visit to the Russian Embassy should have prepared us somewhat for some of the first-visit shocks we were to encounter. There we had to return a second time for an appointment. The Red Embassy stated flatly "we" had failed to show at the appointed time. "We" were just as sure "they" had changed the appointment time without advising us. However, "they" put on a good show.

They asked that we compare Soviet progress and conditions not to the United States, but to pre-revolutionary Russia. This proved to be a thought-provoking admonition. In a general statement, one may say that Russians do not have private cars as we have them, nor private one-family houses, nor living space, nor dishwashers, nor clothes dryers, nor many decorative panel walls, nor many pieces of beautiful wood furniture, but what they have is adequate and, in material possessions, far more than Russian peasants ever dreamed of and far more than the ordinary citizens of most non-western countries have.

Furthermore, and more important, we in what we term "democratic" countries must remember the Russian Communistic System permits the government to place priority wherever "they," the government, see fit without much regard to accommodating the consumer. This permits them to match anyone in a technical or industrial endeavor — without too much worry about level of available consumer goods, little nuclear fallout, OSHA, EPA, FDA, etc.

This must be remembered for our survival but we must also remember how much better we like our kind of freedom, rights, privileges, and life style and not fall into the trap of turning our ways into Communistic patterns in order to achieve priority results.

The Russian experience convinced most of us that God-fearing, hard-working Capitalism, for all of its faults, has out-performed and will out-perform any other system, for the good of the people and the stability and survival of the government. But soft and creeping Socialism is no match for the priority-oriented productivity of the disciplined Communism which we witnessed.

Many Americans have visited Russia in recent years and to recall the many Moscow sights would be repetitive for many. The accommodations are adequate, but Spartan. Life, including tourist and business visitor handling, is regimented.

We met with the U.S.-U.S.S.R. Trade and Economic Council personnel in Moscow. Excellent interpretation was available although we felt that the Russian participants understood our comments and questions in English.

N.M. Zhizhenkov, director, Furniture and Wood Products Department, was present and chief spokesman for "their" group. Other wood specialists were also there. Most of us understood Mr. Zhizhenkov to indicate that Russian plywoods, fiberboard and veneers were not moving directly into Canada or the U.S. Some of our people did not think this was in fact the current situation but did not discuss the difference in opinion. This was how we listened to much of the "bull" mentioned earlier. We did, however, have enlightening discussions of forest resources, factory conditions, costs, etc. The Russian director and his cohorts could not be described as open-minded or ready to compromise. They had what we would call "propaganda positions" and held to them even if irrelevant and erroneous.

By now we had an official description of the Russian wood business. We had sensed the political climate. We knew a Ruble cost $1.50 U.S. and a Kopek was 1/100th of a Ruble. We had tried the food and accommodations. Moscow is the Russian showcase. This is the picture most travelers get and the one most Olympic visitors will get. We saw the large Olympic stadium, the lesser stadiums and some of the athletic housing. These will surely be ready to take care of the athletes in typical regimented manner. [*The Summer Olympics were held in Moscow, in 1980.*]

About the spectators — officially Russia maintains that visitors will be accommodated. After getting details, I cancelled my game reservations and got my money back. One must remember he doesn't step out and hail a taxi or rent a car at will, or anything else without prearrangement. The subway and buses will probably do the job. Undoubtedly, the Olympic visitor will be okay if he is willing to sleep and eat wherever the crowds are put and if he is willing to go to whatever the events are scheduled for him, etc.

Our schedule was to move out of the Great Capital City toward lesser and more distant places. And so, it was on north to Tallinn.

A Visit to Tallinn is Like Walking Through Time Barrier

Tallinn is the capital of the Soviet State or Republic of Estonia and it is also an important, well-equipped and relatively ice-free seaport. In its 700 years of history, it previously has been under the flags of Denmark, Sweden, and Germany.

Tallinn was acquired for Russia by Peter The Great as a "Window on Europe." More than all else, however, Tallinn is a delightful, friendly, and unique old city. It is truly the "Jewel of The Baltic."

Tallinn was comfortable and filled with tradition. It was removed insofar as possible from all but the basic restraints of Moscow's political system. Here we freely entered a beautiful old Russian Orthodox Church during a service attended mostly by the elderly. Here we took pictures of a functioning (barely and rarely) Methodist Church and here we wandered freely and carelessly into Old Tallinn, which was like walking through a time barrier and into the Baltic World of 1500 A.D.

The old streets were filled with pedestrians — automotive vehicles came by only infrequently, but then cars are not commonplace in Russia except for Moscow and a few other places. The castles of the Old Aristocracy sat upon a hill where the fortress towers named "Tall Herman" and "Fat Margaret" stood.

The dinner in the Viru Hotel was very good. Caviar, cold peas (always everywhere), beef stroganoff, brown bread, sweet cakes. Perhaps the most inaccurate pre-trip notion we had was that we would have food problems. Not so. Elena or someone saw to it that we had good food — Russian, of course, but certainly things an American can eat and, if any kind of sport, relish?

Water was the problem. Some people drink risky water — this I avoid. I classify Moscow as having risky water (for Americans) together with most but not all Russia.

There are all kinds of public health bulletins about the water at Leningrad. And the international Aeroflot planes carry tap water warnings. We are accustomed to buying mineral water, but it was neither good nor easy to get in Russia.

I would say my first two concerns in Russia and Siberia were: No.1, "Where do I get my next water supply? No. 2, "Where's a good bathroom?"

But back to food, it was even interesting. The wine might have been all right but for thirst-quenching it would have been disastrous with its 13 percent alcohol level. The vodka must have been great judging from the quantities being sold — incidentally, one is supposed to account for his spending in Russia except no receipts are required for booze. At this point it should probably be said that there is an evident alcohol problem generally in Russia but this was not apparent in Tallinn.

After one delightful dinner at the Viru Hotel, we decided to go into the "roof-top night club." Well, that's just what it was and a nice one with a good live band which struck up "San Francisco" the first time we hit the floor — they had the words memorized, too.

There was some orderly confusion in seating us because our reservation request numbers were round, casual and "pull up a chair," while their requirements were exact. Anyway, they got us seated by the numbers, properly, courteously and happily.

Then in came eight Russian young ladies and occupied the table next to ours. They were dressed and made up in "western" fashion, at least we would say "un-Russian." Our veteran travelers said the trend was definitely to more make-up, hairstyle and color variations and more color and fashion in dress. The girls danced disco to American-type, well-amplified music as the band played to repertoire ranging from Benny Goodman to the Beatles.

A couple in our party was determined to have detente and the action was either easy or reflected the finesse of the social diplomats. Soon Catbird Tom John representing North Carolina and Clay Auburn Howell, the southern gentleman from South Alabama, were dancing away the Cold War, spellbinding those girls with terpsichorean talent, and eyeball-to-eyeball tall stories as well as teaching them "Dixie" and of all things, "Yankee Doodle Dandy."

It was a complete victory for visitors and was properly toasted with chug-a-lug vodka and salty mineral water. [*President Jimmy*] Carter and [*Henry A.*] Kissinger should take lessons.

After the vodka cleared, the group was up early Monday morning and out to study a Russian furniture factory. We went to the furniture factory but were not permitted to see the plywood operation of the factory — more of the Russian "bull" (probably should be the symbol of Russia instead of the bear).

The missed plywood operation stimulated the shopping in The Beryoska (where American money is used) and The Magazines (Russian store). In both places it takes standing in line three times to get what one wants. First, one lines up to get the clerk to set back what one selects and write up a ticket. Second, queue up in the line to pay a cashier for the goods; third, line up again to get the clerk's attention, give her the cash and ticket and get the goods. This is no spoof or exaggeration.

From Tallinn, we moved to the Europa Hotel in Leningrad — a great city with innumerable points of interest, all of which are overshadowed by the magnificent and overwhelming Winter Palace which now is The Hermitage — one of the truly great art museums in the world.

Leningrad is a great wood-working center and, as Russian wood-product exports grow, it will undoubtedly become a major ship-loading facility for the forest products of the land.

Through our plant visits and management conferences we were finding that Russian workers in wood processing factories received an average monthly wage of around 217 Rubles ($325 U.S.) with a range from 110 Rubles ($165) for the least skilled worker to 690 Rubles ($1035) for the top manager. Benefits were estimated to be worth maybe 65 percent of the salaries. Income taxes are less than 10 percent. The State, of course, gets perhaps 50 percent of all plant profits (social benefits?) to start. Housing is mostly in very small apartments, which cost less than 5 percent of the worker's income.

In perspective however, one should keep in mind that both husband and wife work in most Russian families and yet only one Russian family in eight has a private car as contrasted to the two vehicles owned by most American families — other comparisons would be similar. These Russians, however, are not "wanting" for necessities or basics necessary to a fruitful life. They might be termed "efficient livers" — small apartments, public transportation, parks and other public facilities for recreation, etc.

Perceptive McCoy once more summed up a characterization and contrast: "In Holland the objective was to please and reward the worker. In Russia, supposedly the land of The Worker, the objective was or seemed to be, to please and reward The State."

The ballet in Leningrad compares favorably to Moscow's Bolshoi, older and steeped in the tradition of Russian dance supremacy. It was impressive and very entertaining. Several of our real musicians reported the orchestra was probably unexcelled anywhere. Jack Koss and George Earth were particularly overwhelmed with the beauty and grace of the ballerinas and the unbelievable athletic ability of the male dancers.

In all of Russia, but especially in Leningrad (undoubtedly in Stalingrad), one cannot escape being impressed by the reverence directed toward those millions who died in heroic defense of their country. In Leningrad's great military cemetery the outstretched arms of the gigantic statue of a weeping "Mother Russia" beckon to the innumerable rows and names of the sons and daughters who gave all.

The eternal flame there is guarded by an ever-present elite Red guard. There are signs of a patriotism and family affinity, and of a stoic dedication, determination, discipline and forbearance that will be remembered and must be regarded with respect.

The metro (subway) in Leningrad was also comparable to that in Moscow and riding subways in either city is a challenge and an adventure, a place where one may leave the guide and strike into the unknown of strange voices, fast turns, quick stops at many stations and very, very foreign-reading signs.

Shirley Earth and Beverly Howell were trying to keep some semblance or order and accountability in our largely otherwise irresponsible group when we, sans guide, stepped on the seemingly half-mile long, mile-a-minute, roller-coaster steep escalator that delivered us to the subterranean depths where trains departed in both directions. I agreed with Shirley and Beverly that the station was "Bbiboxoa" or something like that because the signs said so. The plan was to get on a train going one way, ride through several stops, get off, and look for a train going back to "Bbiboxoa" or something.

With much hilarity and some trepidation, we sped under the great city. After some ages later we finally got off at a large station, and started looking for a train bound for, or a sign giving directions for return to, "Bbiboxoa." We saw the sign all right, pointing in every direction — the word means "exit." We finally started back, got off, got lost, found familiar street signs and, luckily, took off in the right direction toward our hotel.

I think most of our group would agree that when an American is lost in Russia he is apprehensive, justified or no. We have learned enough to be convinced that one is not supposed to wander about freely in the cities under their tight political and security system. We do not have confidence in their plan to return us if we have strayed far from their guidelines, or in our own embassy's ability to find and recover us.

Anyway, it was "get nervous" time again. Elena was gathering us together for the jet thrust into the great and fearsome unknown. Off to the land of the Salt Mines of the Czars and the Gulags of the Soviets — Siberia.

Trip on the Trans-Siberian Express Fascinating

There is a vastness in Siberia perhaps unequalled elsewhere in the world. The pole stations are remote and climatically dangerous, but so is the great wilderness which lies bounded by the European Urals on the West, the Pacific on the East, the Arctic Ocean on the north and Outer Mongolia on the South. The remote region spans a continent and dwarfs any country in a comparison of size.

As a part of the history of Russia, Siberia is linked with the millions dead and tortured in the slave camps of The Czars and the Soviet Gulags. The capability of the foreboding land to swallow millions is as incomprehensible to most of us as its bitter cold and barren expanses. We are perhaps just as ignorant of its resources.

In searching deep within Siberia for forest product potentials, our group found forests described by Russians as "inexhaustible" and forest product factories much larger than any in the U.S. In making these findings we essentially stumbled across a monstrous hydro-electric power system which, though not concealed from the world, is not recognized by the world — having lots of energy to export to Europe from rivers.

Our original objective was to zero in our study tour on Russia, but our diversion to Siberia provided a revealing shock that fabulous frozen frontiers remain on the earth, inaccessible by ordinary conception, but not as inaccessible as space and not inaccessible to the hardy breed which has survived the persecution and adversities. This is an awakening land which harbors super resistant beings in testing the concept of "survival of the fittest."

"Omsk, Siberia" always sounded as if it were the coldest town in the world — now having been there and having waited out on a runway for 20 minutes at minus 20 degrees with 40-mile winds, I am convinced it is. This incident was in late March — Spring! As a college senior anticipating military service, I frequently discussed with a fraternity brother the worst that might happen to us in the service. We never mentioned prison or death — it was always the possibility of being shipped to Omsk. I sent him a postcard from there but at last report the postcard had not arrived in the U.S. — possibly because it was sent by way of dog sled after the KGB (Russian Secret Police) read my remarks.

At Omsk we were four hours out of Moscow by jet. After we had flown another two hours to Bratsk, we began to "feel" the immensity of Siberia. We now had a 13-hour time difference with Eastern Standard and were undoubtedly as far from home as one can get.

Unexpected incidents and poor communication up to this point were too much for two of our men who were trying to keep in touch with their businesses and home bases. Ed Hanley had to get back to Vermont, and anyway by this time his wife, Carolyn, Aeroflot baggage restrictions not withstanding, had acquired four bags full of souvenirs and shopping items.

Ed was sure that neither his business attitude nor his baggage-carrying capacity could survive Siberia so he did manage, after many arrangement sessions with guide Elena and others of the Intourist System, to separate from us back to Moscow and catch a flight out to Copenhagen. Jim Huey, equally frustrated after numerous telex and telephone delays and schedule changes, was not as lucky.

Finally, after three days and three ulcers, Jim and Mildred separated from our group at Irkutsk, Siberia and started the long journey back from exile country — their experiences in getting out "alone" (accompanied by four 'officials' at times) make another story.

Bratsk, Siberia, is a tremendous industrial city — new since 1950, born out of the "Taiga" (like "Tiger" but meaning wilderness forest) and powered by taming a raging river and confining its water in the largest manmade lake in the world. A gigantic aluminum complex as well as the huge wood and paper complex are just two of the Bratsk industries. A superficial inspection of the new grain storage and milling facility there gave the impression that it may also rank high in the world.

Some of the people in our group have probably visited most of the major plywood mills in the world. However, after a friendly and informative briefing, we were led into a plant which flabbergasted us by its size. The machinery looked good; it was mostly Finnish.

The management people appeared extremely competent as did the technical personnel. The plywood products were mostly exterior construction type and the "plan" was to make maximum utilization of the "inexhausbile" forest which surrounds the plant in every direction — far beyond the visible horizon even from jet altitudes. The plant, however, was not operating at any rate near capacity.

For perspective, it is true we were awed by the size of the Bratsk plywood plant but our tour convinced us that total plywood capacity in Russia, either decorative hardwood plywood or construction type, was not remotely comparable to that in the U.S. and the production was largely intended for foreign trade advantage rather than consumer living advancement.

From Bratsk we flew another hour to Irkutsk, an interesting and very old city near the border of Outer Mongolia. Here we saw many Oriental Russians, and we were reminded of the ethnic conflicts inherent in the great country — as satirized with much truth by the comic poem referring to Abdul and Ivan — "The bravest by far in the ranks of the Shah was Abdul Abulbul Amier," and "My man, did you know you have trod on the toe of Ivan Petruski Skavar."

The only prominent picture of Christ we saw in all Russia was at Irkutsk — a large exterior portrait on the side of an Orthodox church. It was being preserved as "evidence of historical interest in the culture of the past."

Lake Baikal has to be one of the most beautiful places in the world, not a scene Americans associate with Siberia. On the road from Irkutsk, we stopped high on a majestic mountain in the geographical center of Asia to take pictures of the Taiga Forest sloping down in every direction but particularly toward the shining inland sea which contains one sixth of the world's fresh water and is crystal clear, transparent to a depth of 90 feet.

There was no drinking water problem here — natives were cutting through the six feet of ice and drawing the water directly from the lake. They were also driving their few unique and antique vehicles across the frozen surface.

The hotel there was beautifully located, and the dining room and lobby were inviting and comfortable. Our room, however, was ice cold. In the TV room, I was given a special showing of the "Truth of The China-Vietnamese Conflict."

There would be little point in reporting the program — everyone knows whose side the Russians are on. They have been mad at the Chinese and Mongols ever since Genghis Khan conquered much of Russia and Siberia about 1200 A.D.

We attended the theater while in Siberia and have a Russian program to prove it. Dr. Tom John, Jr. interpreted the billing as "Karl and the Marx Brothers in Lenin Least." It is really a satire on New Yorkers titled, "My Wife the Liar!" We could recognize the comic portrayal of many triangles and American affluence. The audience really enjoyed it and we laughed with them.

Back at Irkutsk, we boarded the famous "Trans-Siberian Express." We had read a lot about it and Betty Beldon of Mitchell had given us the very helpful benefit of her previous experience on this fabled train which runs almost 7,000 miles across the entire length of Asia. For more than two days and two nights we were crowded in the soft (first) class compartment, four people and baggage in a double bunked 6 ft x 6 ft space. The toilet (no bath for three days) was down the aisle at the end of a long line of our people and Red Army officers.

In spite of the travel hardships, the train trip was fascinating and educational beyond belief. On this, the longest and perhaps most efficient rail system in the world, freights passed our westbound passenger on the double or the triple tracks every five minutes. They were heading east toward China and the Pacific. Unending forests rolled past our window. Deep within these forests were many strange and exotic furbearing animals including those of the Siberian emblem — the Babr-a-Beast with the near-priceless sable in its teeth. Every few miles a village would appear with great factories for processing wood and other natural resources.

The diner was truly more comfortable and a Russian gourmet delight — in sharp contrast to our crowded and unkept compartments. The fare included borscht, of course, varieties of cheese, pelmeni, kepir (buttermilk?), elk and bear, blini (pancake with meat or jam), one cup of either tea or coffee (no choice) and the usual bread and sweet cakes.

Elena arranged our dining times at our convenience and as elsewhere at airports, theaters, and restaurants, the Russian lines moved back for the American "guests" with no apparent hostility.

The stops along the way were short and absolutely punctual. One disembarked with one eye on the attendants and one on the clock for the three-to-ten minutes before the restart which came without signal or warning. Everyone knew that failure to get aboard could mean days of delay and red tape in finding another spot on the overcrowded trains.

We ended our journey at Novosibirsk (New Siberia), another very large and impressive Siberian city. A science institute here draws international scientists from the world over. We visited the institute but to us the big attraction was the circus. The Russian dancing bears and the Cossack riders and dancers were all one had ever imagined. Our shopping was finished up here, too, with purchases of Matryuska (nesting) dolls and Icon replicas.

Mabel Thornton and Charlie and Jerry Guyer discovered some charming wooden doll chess sets here — we bought them out. Then it was catch another night plane to Moscow and finally a bath in Hotel Russia (a good one) and, after a three-hour sleep, off early on the famous or infamous Aeroflot No. 315 for New York.

No. 315 was the flight which brought the five exchange dissidents to the U.S. a few days ago — a grim reminder that the Gulag still exists despite the many signs of national progress and thawing of international relations. It was the exhausting finale to a truly great adventure. Our hope is that the Russian system will move more rapidly toward capitalism than our system moves toward communism. We again returned very thankful for the freedom we do have and determined to help stop our regulatory trend if possible.

THE BAWDY BALLAD OF THE BALTIC
or TALLINN'S CLAY & CATBIRD EPIC

by Josef Ivan Robinski*
En route from Tallinn to Leningrad
Friday, March 23, 1979

T'was a Beautiful Nite Neath The Northern Lights
At a place on the Baltic Sea
Where Russian maids did their promenade
As they danced in exotic glee.

There were visitors two from around the blue,
Adrift on a Foreign Sphere
Who found joys divine in the dance of wine
As they mounted the ballroom floor.

One was older and so was bolder
Than his less experienced buddy
But Birds of a Feather Flock Together
Without getting the water muddy.

Tom would boast with a Vodka Toast
While the other's lids would flicker.
There were wide Russian Eyes as Clay told lies
And Tom showed nary a snicker.

Tom topped the thing with a Highland Fling
While Clay wooed Comrade Sandy;
Then the girls all swooned when Howell crooned
A tune for Doodle Dandy.

McCoy keen smoked his pipe serene
As he watched the Climax build
He knew Dibba was certain to close the curtain
Whenever, however she willed.

And so she did and she clamped the lid
On Tallinn's Greatest Show,

> But Tom and Clay had one great day
> And the Catbird now can crow.
>
> All the girls departed broken hearted
> And so did Tom and Clay;
> For a Russian maid who's been betrayed
> Remembers a year and a day.
>
> Now when Tallinn's cold, these tales are told
> How Americans bright and able
> Bestowed delight on a Russian Nite
> Till they both slid under the Table.
>
> * Joe Robertson

The Mediterranean

In May 1980, Virginia and I returned from a HPMA-sponsored study tour of the wood industry, its markets and production facilities in the Mediterranean countries of Italy, Israel, Egypt, and Morocco. Our observations on the religious, political, and cultural as well as the economic aspects of the countries are reflected in my articles published in the *Times-Mail*.

Visit to Pompeii Ruins Was a Timely Lesson

A group of 18 enthusiastic travelers took off for Rome from New York's Kennedy Airport late Friday, April 18. Some had exceptional language capabilities and extensive travel experience but the common denominator for all of us was a continuing desire to learn of conditions, contrasts and cultures in foreign places. Such travel can often entail less-than-comfortable accommodations and less-than-secure atmospheres.

Our people were oriented to the wood products industry and dedicated to maximum utilization of renewable resources everywhere in the world, but we were also interested in the building traditions which have established the importance of building material combinations such as wood and stone for maximum utility and beauty. We looked into the early history of

"The Stonecutters" not only in Italy but also in Egypt, where gifted carvers produced great masterpieces of stone work and woodcrafters created veneered furniture of striking beauty during some of the earliest dynasties.

Some individuals in the group have visited many major plywood plants in remote and far away places. For example, the range of visitations would include a gigantic Russian plant deep in the frozen Taiga of Siberia; busy veneer mills in the teeming jungles of the Philippines, Africa and the Amazon; plants with vast swarms of "little people" working intently in Japan, Korea and The Republic of China; efficient Scandinavian plants where the "Big Swedes" work; and plants in the emerging forest industry of Indonesia. The group could speak and listen in a dozen languages and understand from experiences in many countries.

In the Mediterranean, the crucible and cradle of civilization, most sources and symbols of progress and problems, past and present, are in evidence. From medieval cathedrals of Italy through the synagogues of Israel, across the Sinai to the Pyramids and Mosques of Egypt, and the Casbah of Casablanca, there is a thread of conflict, conquest and commerce which has fostered ever-increasing trade despite many periods of uneasy peace or actual war.

Our group was most interested in plywood and veneers, but we were also interested in spreading a philosophy of the truth regarding wood as a renewable resource. People everywhere must learn not to waste wood and not to regard trees as useless idol objects. As long as there are people requiring homes of utility and beauty in this world, there is no right to waste wood or worship trees. The old forest must make way for the new as shelter and aesthetic needs must be met.

Italy still gives the impression of a happy land abounding with happy people despite the problems and adversities encountered through the centuries, especially through the 20th century and perhaps through the last few years. For example, on our previous visit we encountered a near-bankruptcy of the government, a drastic currency devaluation and a bus drivers' strike. This time the inflation and interest rates were high, and airline and taxi personnel were striking and settling between breakfast and dinner — it is said most Italian strikes are settled by noon because they will not walk a picket line if it means missing a meal. However, the communists and other minority parties do keep the nation in turmoil as the Christian Democrat premier tries to bring order out of political chaos.

After the landing at Leonardo da Vinci Airport, we immediately started toward Pompeii. Monte Cassino soon appeared in the East — a prominent reminder of its strategic importance when religious consideration for the Benedictine Monastery painfully halted the Allied advance for months in 1944. Beyond, Vesuvius loomed large to the south with the great crater evidencing the incalculable power of the eruption which blew off the top third of the volcano and buried Pompeii and its people in an obscurity of lava, ash and soil during August of 79 A.D.

After being lost for centuries, the preserved ruins were discovered, and archeological excavations starting about 1600 A.D. have revealed the horror of the tragedy and its lightning rapidity. The ruins show an amazing panorama of family life, business, government, and a disproportionate dedication to questionable sexual practices just as if the revelations were locked in a time machine to be revealed to those of us coming by a millennium later.

It was a timely lesson, just before the St. Helens blowout; it can happen here. And, these awesome displays of power, not-so-deep within the earth, are perhaps omens to a world seeking frantically for energy and maybe overlooking the obvious.

From Pompeii it was on through beautiful Sorrento and a hydrofoil trip across the Bay of Naples to the legendary Isle of Capri for a delightful weekend. Sunday afternoon a long drive and flight north to Milan placed us in Italy's second largest city. Our hotel was named The Leonardo da Vinci in honor of the great artist-inventor who did the famous fresco, The Last Supper, on the wall of Milan's Church of Santa Maria delle Grazie. Of course, many of his works are hung in the museum bearing his name. The Great Cathedral of Milan is awe-inspiring with its 135 pinnacles reaching skyward for 354 feet. The La Scala Opera House and busy piazzo are only two of many impressive sights.

The stone work in the historic edifices is outstanding. Of course, the descendants of the Italian artisans were some of the immigrants who brought their skill and talent to help establish Bedford, Indiana, as the "Limestone Capital of the World."

Monday morning we hurried outside Milan to the little village of Lentate sul Seveso. Here, Fratelli Tragni (The Tragni Brothers — Ettore and Giuseppe) manufacture some of the world's best veneer and plywood from exotic African trees and from walnut and other fine hardwoods out of southern Indiana. Many of the veneers are sliced on Capital Equipment out of Indianapolis.

Gondolier Robertson pours forth song for his group on the Grand Canal in Venice.

After a thorough tour of the interesting mill, the hospitable Tragni Brothers hosted us to a delightful meal in nearby Cantu Village at the Trattoria Fossano (Fossano Family Restaurant). The delicious antipasto, pasta, meats, sauces, cheese and vino were served with a cheerfulness and flourish seldom equaled. The many toasts by the generous Fratelli in vintage wines, and the friendly efficiency of personable Italian waitresses such as Anna di Stasio and others of the Fossano Family soon established a glowing spirit of fellowship — and a spontaneous trip to nearby Lugano, Switzerland. At a late supper that night in the hotel, Ettore Tragni introduced his charming family to the group — two adult daughters Laura and Josephine, one a lawyer and one a student, and a bright young high school lad of 14.

After more sight-seeing in Milan, we headed southeast Tuesday afternoon across the Po Valley to the Eurocomp Plywood Mills at Padova. This mill was much larger than most American hardwood mills and utilized a combination of hardwood plywood and construction plywood production machinery.

That night we boarded a motor launch for the trip to our Europa-Regina Hotel on the Grand Canal of Venice. In typical tourist fashion we boarded the gondolas and sang with the gondoliers as we moved through many of the canals in the floating city of churches, palaces, art treasures and beautiful Venetian glass. Here early Venetian merchants built and launched ships on trade routes through the then-known world, and travel ambassadors such as Marco Polo brought news of exciting worlds beyond.

We fed the friendly pigeons in St. Mark's Square and crossed the Bridge of Sighs where prisoners took their last walk to the Doge's dungeons from which no one ever escaped — except Casanova and a few of us.

After Venice, it was back to Central Italy and Michelangelo's Florence (Firenze), Jewel of the Italian Renaissance. The Excelsior Hotel was magnificent. The art treasures from the work of Michelangelo, Raphael, da Vinci and others are almost innumerable. The cathedrals are massive and beautiful. The leather work and mosaic art proved attractive to several. The city's history highlights included the Scourge of The Black Death, which killed about 60% of the population in 1348. The Medici family ruled Florence for many years and fostered an incredible growth in commercial, intellectual and artistic development.

On the road to Rome from Florence (The Cassian Way) we visited a

The "Bridge of Sighs" to the Doge's Dungeon, from which none returned except the rascal, Casanova.

bustling plywood mill at the foot of a Castle Hill near Siena. The plywood company, ICAS, s.p.a., was processing large African logs as well as native Lombardy Poplars. Piero Giacobbi was one of the managers who led us through the well-equipped hardwood mill and then graciously extended Italian hospitality in what might be called a wine-tasting conference — where Italian vintage wines and international plywood were discussed with equal interest. We were then led up the hill to the very old castle, still functioning as a village, where we discovered an ancient grain elevator and flour mill within the castle walls.

Since a previous Rome visit [*in November 1974*] was reported in a former *Times-Mail* article, our comments will be directed toward events rather than the always interesting sights of the Eternal City. We were fortunate again. The Pope was appearing in St. Peter's. Some of our group were in the first few rows of the thousands of followers gathered that day. That night, the news of the aborted Iranian hostage rescue attempt had all Rome buzzing — crowds everywhere watching TV sets in all public places. We held a caucus to determine if we should proceed on our route which would take us through Israel to some Arab lands.

A World of Travel 141

Bruce Markel, center; Clyde Howell, right rear; and Joe Robertson, with hat, show Beverly Howell and Susie Markel the festival of the flowers on Rome's famous Spanish Steps.

    Some of us were concerned. Bruce Markel and some others figured, "whatever will be, will be." So, Sylvia McDonald and I went to the U.S. Embassy the next morning while some continued sight-seeing, and Markel rented a car to drive himself through the crazy traffic and out to Anzio and other Kilroy places in which he had been vitally interested during WW II. After getting the go-ahead from the embassy, we returned for a conference with Dr. Domenico Bosi and his associates of BOSI, s.p.a., another Italian plywood company.

    These people were extremely interested in buying American oak to supplement their production based on Lombardy Poplar and African logs. Rome was never prettier — the Spanish Steps were obscured by a huge blanket of flowers, the spray from the fountains was turned into mist by the gentle spring breezes and the emotional Italianos were passing out friendly greetings everywhere. We reluctantly departed for the large airport which had been rebuilt over the remains of U.S. military airstrips first visited by Kilroy.

The Places Where Christ Walked Are Awe-Inspiring

The 747 from Rome delivered us from the heartland of Catholicism to Jewish Zion in about 3 1/2 hours. It was Sunday and we had departed after mass at St. Peter's and lunch at a delightful sidewalk cafe. If one works it right in this corner of the world, three-day weekends are easy.

The Moslems' Holy Day is Friday, the Jewish Sabbath is Saturday and the Christians worship on Sunday. All worship the same God and all look back to Father Abraham, but there are differences — and the differences are important. Many have died for them. International conferences are progressing today which hopefully will arrange for these different groups to accommodate one another.

From Ben Gurion Airport near Tel Aviv we went directly to Old Joppa, where Jonah the Jew sailed off on a whaling trip because he didn't like his Ninevah assignment.

At the Diplomat Hotel in Tel Aviv (much like a very modern hotel in New York or Miami Beach) we encountered the "Kosher Division" when we ignorantly ordered a hamburger and milk only to be politely advised there were two restaurants — one in which we could order meat and one in which we could order dairy products.

The next day, our drive took us south along the Mediterranean Sea through the Philistine Country — Ashdod where the Ark of The Covenant was held in the house of the Pagan God, Dagon, and Gaza where Samson pulled down the Temple. We visited Askalon Plywood Ltd., a large and thoroughly modern mill employing 500 people and manufacturing many plywood and furniture products. David Kremerman, the managing director, had been educated at Georgetown University, so we had the opportunity to get "near-American" explanations to many of our questions.

Our advisers told us both inflation and interest rates exceeded 100%. Also, as is the perhaps unnoticed trend in this country, government financing for up to 85% of costs at favorable interest was available to those who would establish enterprises of the kind and in places desired by the government.

A new "currency reform" was just being put in place in Israel. Americans should observe and hope we will not follow suit (again). For example, following disastrous inflation, a new Israeli note (10 Shekel paper money) was issued. It looked exactly like the 100-pound note but was supposed to be worth ten times as much, $2.30, instead of 23 cents.

The result will be to retire the old note at lesser value and in effect it will take fewer pieces of paper (new money) to buy a banana than it did when pounds were used, so inflation will have been accommodated and money will not need to be hauled in wheelbarrows, but savers and debt holders will receive payment (values) in shekels instead of pounds.

Already the new money is being discounted. Of course, Americans have placidly accepted similar maneuvers in the past. Most of us remember when a silver dollar was worth $1 — they looked like all other dollars. Then, Silver Certificates were recalled. Good hard silver dollars went out of circulation because they are worth 10 to 20 paper dollars. Previously gold dollars were also made as illegal as moonshine whiskey back in the thirties. Currency reforms are usually bad news in Israel or the United States or anywhere else.

Our college professor guide — a political expert — taught us a great deal. Like many visitors to the Holy Land we were probably looking for, and mainly impressed by, the Christian heritage so delightfully visible to us as Christians. Tourists need also to see the age-old problems of this land of such deep-rooted loves and conflicts . . . a land which has been home, the inheritance, promise, plunder and fulfillment to the estranged children of Abraham through Ishmael and Isaac, Jacob and Esau and later the Gentile Christians.

The Gaza Strip is still contested as in the days of Samson. The Jews have a tenuous hold on the land of Israel (Jacob), which was Jordan and Palestine only a generation back and which before that witnessed centuries of Crusader conflict between such immortal figures as Saladin and Richard-the-Lionhearted. Before that, Moses brought the Hebrews back from Egypt to wrest the land from the Canaanites and ad infinitum into the dim beginning of history when Adam the man was driven from Eden.

Returning north to Caesarea we sang in the same Roman amphitheatre where Paul preached Christianity. Our tour then proceeded through Samaria and many interesting places up to Jerusalem. From our headquarters in the Jerusalem Hilton — also a very modern and Kosher establishment — we visited the many inspiring sights of The Holy City — holy not only to the Christian, but also to the Jews and the Moslems. Bethlehem, Bethany and the many other places where Christ walked are awe-inspiring.

The peace talks between [*Prime Minister Menachem*] Begin and [*Pre-

mier Gamal] Nasser, Israel and Egypt, continue to be held together only by slender threads and are refereed by misunderstanding Christians — all under the watchful eye of godless Communists. Other powerful Arabs, such as King Hussein, will not participate in the discussions because Jordan feels the West Bank should be returned to them and the Palestinians think they should have autonomy in the villages.

It is not a scenario of promise. The West Bank problem is real. The Palestinians are refugees, poor refugees, and there are many of them — although they do not make the most of their opportunities. (Is the West Bank Jewish or Jordanian?) The fact that Moses pointed his people toward the only oil-free land in the Middle East is probably the main reason the situation has not exploded again.

It was exciting to travel down the Jericho Road to the place where Moses looked over Jordan and where Joshua won his victory after having been saved by Rahab. We stumbled on the remains of an ancient flour mill in Qumran where the Dead Sea Scrolls were discovered. The scrolls gave new authenticity to the Bible. We crawled under the barbed wire defenses to wade in The Dead Sea in the manner of really interested tourists.

We were one of the first groups who were permitted to drive across the disputed Sinai Desert from Israel to Egypt. The border was only "opened" this spring and we were carefully inspected before and after walking (and carrying our own luggage) through the 100 yards of No Man's Land between the armies near El Arish.

The desert road was "sorta" paved but constant clearing was necessary to keep the sands from covering it up. The destroyed track and roadbed of the Beirut-Cairo Railway were visible on occasion. Destroyed tanks and weapon carriers were everywhere — remnants of the previous Israeli-Egypt Wars.

It was a long day from dawn in Jerusalem until dark in Cairo — our advice to carry food and water was appropriate.

The barren Sinai will soon be regarded as Egyptian again. Beyond El Arish it was typical desert all the way to the Suez — there it was, the thin lifeline of the world's shipping commerce. The appearance was actually that of a caravan of ships moving through the desert. The Arabs, tents, goats and camels had been present all along the way but here all were crowded on the canal bank waiting for an *African Queen*-type boat to ferry them across. Fortunately for us, foreigners were given preference and we were first on the crowded vessel. Across the canal, the Egyptian fortifications became even more dense than on the East. But the desert was soon to merge into the green Nile Delta.

Comparing the Great Cheops to the Local Pyramid

Bedford's [*Indiana*] plan to build a reduced-size replica of the great Cheops Pyramid is an exciting challenge for today's "Limestone Capital of The World" [*in 1980*]. The quarry workers, architects, transportation experts, stonecutters and builders of ancient Egypt were certainly competent in building one of the "Seven Wonders of The World" but today's craftsmen and engineers are surely more knowledgeable and capable.

Continued interest in the pyramid project can be anticipated for many have traveled thousands of miles to the Nile to see the great stonework of the ancients and surely many will travel to Lawrence County, Indiana, to see how the moderns do it. [*Unfortunately, this project was never completed.*]

The Egyptians resent the implication that the massive structures were built by slave labor — and they particularly resent the inference that Hebrew slaves were used to do this proud work.

There are many conflicting accounts of where the stone came from and how it was constructed into the pyramids. It is likely that much of the limestone was quarried in the great quarry just east of Cairo and transported over most of the eight or ten miles by boat (the location of the pyramids on the plateau of Giza lies just above the flood mark of the Nile). The granite was undoubtedly brought hundreds of miles down the Nile from Aswan.

The Great Pyramid (Cheops) is the largest ever built. It was built 4,660 years ago, 2680 B.C., on 13 acres. There are about two million blocks (mostly limestone) piled to a peak 482-foot high on a square base with 756-foot sides. The blocks were individually hewn and were generally around 40 inches high (1 meter) and were laid without mortar. Some blocks varied, however, from two to 30 tons each.

The four-foot Bedford blocks will be similar in size to those of the Great Cheops and the modern administration building apparently will be in place of an original funerary chapel. The 100-foot long corridor connecting this building to the new pyramid will also be historically and architecturally correct.

The scene was almost unbelievable when we pulled the drapes in our hotel (Mena House) room the night of our arrival. There were the gigantic pyramids looming up just across the way — maybe a half-mile. It was a bright night and the three great rock piles stood out boldly on the desert against the moonlit sky — Cheops first, then Chephren (the one with the polished limestone cap remaining) and the smallest one built by the Monarch, Mycernius.

Two more Canadian friends joined our group in Cairo. Bill Caine and Karin Vogler, representing Commonwealth Plywood of St. Therese, Quebec, were just as excited as the rest of us to "see the pyramids along the Nile" and reflect on the works of the Pharaohs.

The next morning we scrambled up and around the pyramids and into the passageways of Cheops — crawling through one passageway to an outside hole high up on one face. The Great Sphinx was also subject to our scrutiny, and camel-riding in the area was the order of the day. Alabama Clyde Howell, who earlier had been knighted "Southern Sheik" by a friendly Arab, was a "natural" on camelback and led the charge of the Humpers with the clarion call, "Camels Ho, Y'All!"

Cairo is a great and bustling city. It has been visited by many Americans, and presents many faces to the interested visitor. The great Mosques, the Citadel, the City of The Dead (Moslem Cemetery), and the Egyptian Bazaar were viewed with appreciation.

The uncompleted apartments and the many vacant building lots in Cairo (antiquated buildings had been removed from the lots) served as signals to our group that Egypt held tremendous market potential for American plywood. A [*President Anwar*] Sadat Speech Day (in which he promised workers a 50% bonus — from what funds?), a Moslem Holiday and poor phone service all combined to scratch our plywood plant appointment, but we could certainly see the market — the logs undoubtedly would be imported.

We were now anxious to move south and up the Nile which defied exploration for so long and kept its source hidden until the mid-nineteenth century.

Our next stop was far south or up-river at the site of the ancient Egyptian capital, Thebes. Today Karnak occupies the eastern part of the Thebes Site and Luxor the western part. The Karnak Temple or The Great Temple of Amon is considered one of the finest examples of Egyptian architecture. There is a vast court and a hippostyle hall with 134 columns arranged in sixteen rows. Here is the Avenue of Sphinx. Just a buggy ride away is the Temple of Luxor, generally regarded as the greatest monument of antiquity. It was built as a Temple of Amon, but was much altered later, especially by Ramses II who had many colossal statues of himself erected on the grounds.

The Valley of The Kings is located on the West bank of the Nile. It was the Necropolis of Ancient Thebes with most of the cave-cut tombs opening toward the rising sun and the Nile. The Valleys of The Queens and The Nobles are also nearby. Here in 1922 in the Valley of Kings, Howard Carter discovered the greatest hidden treasure in history — the Tomb of King Tut.

We had viewed many of the treasure pieces of Tutankhamen in The Egyptian Museum in Cairo — the museum contains many more objects than even those in the successful display of the recent U.S. Tour. However, the tomb itself was a revelation. One of the gold masks was there in the sarcophagus in the great frescoed burial chamber at the end of the entrance corridor — which corridor had a number of false halls and rooms carved out to lead searchers away from the true chamber where the Great Pharaoh had awaited his reunion with Amon from 1350 B.C. until 1922 A.D. When Carter opened the box he was overwhelmed by the immensity of the find — one of the gold masks weighed two hundred and forty pounds.

From Luxor, our Nile River Boat moved up river to Esna where Khnum Temple was preserved through centuries by the sands which covered it. It was getting really hot now — well over 100 degrees.

Our Egyptian guide, Iman Hashish, was a bright young Moslem woman. She was undoubtedly the best resource we had. A 23-year-old graduate of the University of Cairo and obviously well-educated, she did not regard herself as "liberated" and she seemed to see women of good Moslem families as "protected" rather than exploited. She had a strong belief in Mohammed as the last prophet of God and in the Koran as God's Word.

Each day after returning from the hot and exhausting visits to the ever-amazing sights along the Nile, we would gather in the comfortable and air conditioned boat lounge and listen intently as Iman discussed Moslem sects, beliefs, traditions and hopes. Although she was independent, hundreds of miles from home, unprotected from "Western" exposure, she could expound on the merits of women wearing clothes covering all but hands and feet — and even veils. Understanding another culture is very difficult and perhaps not even desirable — but having some contact knowledge of such culture is most interesting.

From Esna, we continued on up the mysterious Nile to ruins at Edfu ad Kom Ombo. At Edfu we visited perhaps the most primitive sawmill and wood-working plant we had ever seen. Power in the miniature log yard was by donkey and the "mechanized" saw was powered by an ancient gasoline engine. The dramatic changes brought about by the High Aswan Dam were made apparent to us.

The Nile no longer floods the great basin all the way to the Delta. However, while the ravages of the annual floods are avoided, the resulting situation is not all good. There may be developing salinity and soil exhaustion because the yearly deposits of rich new soil from the upper regions no longer come down with the floods.

The high dam at Aswan was imposing. The resulting Nasser Lake has all but eliminated Hubia, and the lake backs up well into Sudan. The Russians financed the project and supposedly bested us politically in doing so — but as is often the case, the benefactor didn't come off too well and we are probably better off for having missed that one. Of course, friendly nations have done a great job of moving some of the priceless tombs from the Nile basin to the lake shore — almost unbelievable.

The market at Aswan was a good one but everywhere the call for "Basheesh" (tip) was evident. Iman urged us not to give "Basheesh," for the people, and especially the children, often find it is much easier to ask for Basheesh than to work.

The old Cataract Hotel Veranda at Aswan overlooks the Nile Cataracts and across the river the fabulous marble tomb of the Agha Khan dominates a desert hilltop. The Cataract Hotel figured prominently in Agatha Christie's "Death on The Nile."

From Aswan, we flew by jet from one of the world's most basic airports, also of Kilroy origin, to Abu Simbel near the Southern border of Egypt where we visited the tombs of Ramses II and his wife. We felt dwarfed by the colossal statues of The Pharaoh-God — and were amused by the usual miniature statues of his wife, coming only to Ramses' kneecap. Sudan was visible from this point. It was 130 degrees F. that day!

Returning by plane to Cairo, we found the Nile Hilton to be beautiful

A World of Travel   149

The HPMA Study Group at Abu Simbel. Notice the miniature statues of the Princess, child, and our group in contrast to the colossal size of Pharaoh.

and refreshing. Lunch in the famous Shepherds Hotel Bar was exciting and brought back memories of earlier days when Americans gathered and rested here before or after action in other places where Kilroy had been first.

The next day we flew fifteen hundred miles across North Africa to Morocco — the land of The Rift and The Berbers. The former American Airbase at Casablanca is a huge sprawling complex symbolic of the American power structure which protected much of the world through the postwar development period. We traveled around some of Morocco, through Rabat, and through the famous Casbah of Casablanca.

It was with some difficulty that we persuaded our new guide to "come away to the Casbah." The modern Moroccans would much rather point out the modern achievements, and they have many of them — it is a relatively progressive country but still with a a strong and conservative Islamic tradition.

Nevertheless, we wanted to mingle in the mysterious and narrow passages of the Ancient Arab Quarter where it is said that all things are bought and sold — even strong men and beautiful women, and one may be lost forever in the twinkling of an eye. After the trek through the old market, we searched diligently for Rick's American Cafe and other locale associated with the movie, "Casablanca." There are young people on the streets who have never heard of the film and we didn't find Bogie or Ingrid but piano players are still there who can "play it again, Sam. As Time Goes By."

It was a fantastic, educational and exhausting trip. Air Moroc brought us back to the States in one long hop — we left Casablanca at 9:00 a.m., turned back the clock six hours and arrived in New York about 1:00 p.m. From there it was back to Charleston and the Mills House Hotel from where we had started. Would you believe, we walked in the hotel room, flipped on the TV, and the words came right out, "We are now pleased to present a replay of that famous film classic, 'Casablanca'" and we watched it with even more interest than ever before.

The following poem did not appear in the newspaper account but was

A World of Travel

mailed to those on the trip upon our return. It illustrates some of the many amusing events that happened and also reveals how some of the travelers were characterized by their fellow trippers.

HPMA Tales of the Med Round Robin

Joe Robertson

Sylvia Mac took her HPMA Pack
On a trek for trees in The Med,
And the Plywood Group was a model troop
As along the route we sped.

An initial spree on the Isle Capri
Just whetted the appetites
For Italian scenes, spaghetti and beans
As we started a series of flights.

By Milano's Past a spell was cast
And the Tragnis played fortissimo
That charmed the bunch through a special lunch
To honor Maria and Jack Kossissimo.

Then J.B. led as we forged ahead
And Joan was prone to stay
Where Gondaliers sing of eternal spring
And others stretched the day.

Between business jaunts and hucksters' taunts
The arts of Florence were tasted
And Helen told of Masters Old;
On none her knowledge wasted.

And sure enough when times were tough
And Gabriella prodded
As when "Playwood Hard" was on the card
Ahead our students plodded.

It seemed like home when back in Rome

Some looked for church, some bar,
And the Noble Pope almost lost hope
When Markel rented a car.

Here Lise and Mike the wine did spike
In a cafe near St. Pete,
Margaret and Hube watched the Pope on the tube,
Susie watched from across the street.

Marcel and Pierrette did a minuette
When they reached the land of no-rainin'
And Judy recalled how Moses bawled
When Canada came out "K-K-Canaan."

Now the Honor Supreme — 'twas a thrilling scene
When a merchant wise and meek
Sold Clydius Howell a Magic Towel
And knighted him "Arab Sheik."

As Beverly tried to bribe the guide
(Virginia shushed up Joe)
For some extra rolls — the Dead Sea Scrolls
And a swim, plus Jericho.

Then Adventurers gay threw caution away,
And for better or for worse
From Israel high they crossed Sinai —
Moses did it in reverse!

At Egypt's Nile they paused awhile
For Karin and Bill to see
The pyramids too, and a savvy crew
Who mixed business well with glee.

And now Sunday dawn will a parting spawn,
But a parting for only awhile,
Till we join again in the sun or rain
And remember the scenes at The Nile.

And we will be Winkum and Blinkum and Nod
And we'll sail on the moon's gold stream,
Through a thousand nights of incredible sights
We'll remember a wonderful dream.

Names referred to are:

> J. B. & Joan Alexander
> Beverly & Clyde Howell
> Mary & Jack Koss
> Pierrette & Marcel Lafleur
> Susie & Bruce Markel
> Virginia & Joe Robertson
> Lise & Mike Van Beuren
> Helen Whitehead
> Sylvia McDonald
> Bill Caine & Karin Vogler
> Margaret & Hubert Morgan
> Ettore & Peppino Tragni, plywood hosts
> Gabriella, our Italian guide
> Judy, our guide in Israel

Chapter 6

African Safaris, 1975 and 1985

*I*N THE FALL OF 1975, Virginia and I joined the HPMA study tour of seven African countries. We visited the plywood, veneer, and forest industries and mills located in the jungle as well as on the coast.

On our return trip through Brazil, more plants were visited near Rio de Janeiro and Vitoria.

From the *Daily Times-Mail*:

Culture Contrasts Startling in Land of Jungles

Introduction

Africa speaks — in a few languages and a thousand dialects, and in money. The ability to communicate reduces the money requirement substantially. Africa speaks of and as developing nations, united in desire if not in action, to shape a dream of important destiny into a reality. A strong, zealous sense of nationalism (Africanism) in economic matters is combined with a probably unjustified tendency to blame colonial exploitation for the slowness of the Dark Continent to bring material rewards and social advances to the native population.

The culture contrasts are startling in this land of jungles, savannahs, mountains and deserts. The question remains as to whether these peoples, who fiercely protected their small tribal clannishness for years and were willing to enslave and sell neighboring tribes for centuries, are now ready to unite, pay the prices for unity and self-government, and work — work hard to move forward and upward toward what developed nations regard as social-economic improvement. "Americans must remember," an African said, "the worst kind of colonialism and imperialism is the U.S. telling others what they want, what they need, and how to get it."

The African nations are taking over industries established by foreign investment; they are replacing foreign technicians and supervisory personnel with natives; they are requiring that exports carry "value added" in African processing or labor — timber as logs, for example, will no longer move overseas — timber exports will be in the form of processed plywood, veneer or other timber products. While it seems that the French influence of the Colonial Era is not appreciated by the Africans, the French leaders undoubtedly rendered great service in providing a common language of communication throughout the West African region which otherwise was and would have remained a monstrous Babel.

Africa is in the headlines of today's news. It is imprudent, if not impossible, to continue in the caravan of civilization without some knowledge of this baffling land. It is a land immersed in a boiling cauldron of troubles and tensions between factions of left and right; Moslems, Christians, Animists; the Colonial, Tribal, Continental and National Allegiance. As independence sweeps the not-ready continent, names and boundaries change, governments rise and fall quickly, often violently, and without ceremony. Government leaders, mostly with dictatorial powers, are vocal in demanding a redistribution of western wealth within Africa and from without. They seem more concerned with income distribution than income growth. The focus of the future from the prevailing African viewpoint does not include a great deal of guidance from, participation or friendly association with the Western World. Regardless of merit and all else, one soon recognizes that the mood of the emerging nations is: "We have been exploited — we are entitled to more!"

Senegal

Appropriately, it was dark as our "Air Afrique" jetliner nosed down over the Atlantic onto the runway at Dakar, Senegal — at the western tip of West Africa. This was our introduction into the "dark world" — homeland of the black African people.

Dakar — familiar to many U.S. flyboys who ferried their bombers across the sea to the action in North Africa and southern Europe in 1943; land gateway — to the northeast, World War II names of Casablanca, Tobruk, and El Alamein; to the east, the Sahara; to the southeast, the Ivory Coast and the treasures of the jungles.

Our hotel was the "Teranga," a word meaning "welcome" — which we were, but in a reserved manner. We encountered the language, culture and currency barriers at once. French was the official language but other dialects were prevalent. The CFA — loosely termed the African franc — exchanged at about 215 for one dollar. Real prices, however, were high.

The hotel was well managed and staffed by competent Senegalese (Black Africans). Rooms and food were satisfactory, but "bottle water" was necessary.

It was early Sunday morning and we looked around for a Christian Church — none were observed en route from the airport or in the vicinity of the hotel (the people are eighty per cent Muslim), so we persuaded a tour guide to find a Christian Church for us. He drove us to a small French Protestant Church where about sixty Senegalese assembled for a service in French. The man in the pulpit was white and after the service I discovered he was a graduate of the Fuller Presbyterian Seminary in California and was stopping to make a report while en route to the World Council of Churches meeting in Nairobi, Kenya.

Walking back to the hotel alone in the first few hours of my first introduction to a new continent was an exciting experience and perhaps done with some apprehension. The people on the strange streets were racially different, culturally different, were dressed or undressed differently and didn't speak my language. I kept my hand near my billfold and passport but encountered no problems in getting back to the hotel.

At noon we were treated to a native "agogo" buffet. It was authentic — cast with terrific dancers authentically costumed (barely) and scored (drums), and with gymnastics which would have qualified them for Olympic competition.

By now we had discovered how fortunate we were to have Agnes Monnin, Lad Maleniecki and the Van Beurens with us. Agnes is a vivacious New York businesswoman who owns and operates an export-import veneer business with substantial African interests. She speaks French fluently and travels Africa frequently. Mike and Lisa Van Beuren operate plywood and timber product manufacturing properties in Mexico City, and were also entirely at home with spoken or written French and many other languages.

Lad, who represents Capital Veneer Machines of Indianapolis in Europe and Africa, could also read, write or speak, and really understand about anything. We also rediscovered the study-tour "know-how" of our HPMA managing director, Clark McDonald, who schedules these trips for maximum business exposure, and his charming and talented wife, Sylvia, who arranges the educational, recreational and shopping sidetrips for the wives.

We traveled out about fifty kilometers through the tropical savannah to a fishing village — Cayar. The mud and thatch huts were to be seen frequently at roadside — no electricity, no plumbing. An uncrowded and unhurried population appeared reasonably healthy. We also saw several African "stockyards" or "feed lots" where herdsmen drove in cattle in lots generally of three to fifteen from great distances — even a thousand miles from Mali — to sell to the meat buyers in Dakar, much in the same manner as early ranchers in the American Southwest brought longhorns up the Chisholm Trail to the railhead at Dodge City. These cattle were also horned, on the thin side and with the characteristic Brahma-type hump.

The Atlantic Beach at Cayar was busy with bathers and fishermen but unspoiled. The fishermen were doing what they have done for centuries — bringing in their catches — loaded down with marine prizes in their colorful and highly decorated dug-out canoes. Swordfish, dolphins and many other fish were unloaded and displayed proudly to the buyers for the market and processors in Dakar. We saw many of the same fish in the busy, crowded and open market in Dakar the next day. In the tropical heat and existing market conditions, the fish no longer looked (or smelled) so fresh.

At Gorea — the island off Dakar which guards Cape Verde — we had an interesting tour of the Fortress-Castle-Prison. Here for centuries the Colonial Powers received and held the African slaves (more than twenty million of them) for reshipment to slave markets the world over. The African chiefs would capture and enslave whole tribes and bring them to the port for sale to the highest bidder. We visited the still-standing slave holding quarters — a stark reminder of man's inhumanity to man, not only that inhumanity of white slave traders but also that of the black chiefs who enslaved their neighbors. Perhaps some progress has been made.

Gorea, Dakar, and Senegal have been battle prizes for many nations over the years. Portuguese, British and French conquered and reconquered the area. In 1960, the Senegal portion of Old French West Africa was granted independence. It is a struggling nation with only five million inhabitants, but it is a contact point for western civilization and it will probably make it. The country served us well for an introduction into Africa and a jumping-off place for our study-tour.

Logging Operation, Plywood Mill Viewed

Harry Robinson and Dick St. John of Van Ply, Inc. had left the HPMA Convention site in Bermuda ahead of us. They had gone directly to Greenville, Liberia, to alert Van Ply of Liberia (Van Ply is a related industry to Skelly Oil) that the Americans were coming.

We had stayed at the Bermuda convention until the closing minutes to enjoy the sessions at this island paradise. HPMA President Dick Weber of Wisconsin and Charlie Guyer of Georgia, convention chairmen (together with their wives), had made sure that we had an excellent learning convention.

Some liked Bermuda so well that they came early and stayed late. As usual, the "Southern Rebels" were in the majority and some seceded from the post-convention trip — Alabama's Harry Howells, Tennessee's O'Donoghues, Hueys and Hardaways, and South Carolina's McMasters led the secession movement and established a new temporary confederate capital in Hamilton, Bermuda where sun, sand and serenity prevailed.

Our Royal Van Ply-Liberian reception started at the Monrovia, Liberia Airport (Robertsfield) where the men were picked up by two chartered planes. (The women were picked up by bus to tour the fabulous one-million-acre Firestone rubber plantation). The sleek twin-engine aircraft flew us low over the coastal jungles for the two hundred miles to Greenville. We swooped down and circled interesting villages and points of interest to and from Greenville.

It was an overall aerial view of the land which only a seasoned bush pilot can give, and it gave us an immediate and somewhat penetrating

A World of Travel   159

insight into the topography and general rural activity of this land. Iron mines, coconut plantations, and small banana farms would show up occasionally in the otherwise deep and primitive jungle. U.S. interests in Liberia are aided by a competent embassy staff. Maurice Bean of Gary, Indiana is our deputy ambassador and he visited Van Ply with us.

When the expansive Van Ply complex came into view we were indeed impressed. Here in the Sinoe River Country of Liberia was a vast exhibition of foreign venture capital in Africa. More than twenty million dollars had been invested in the logging operation, sawmill and plywood mill by the three investors, including Van Ply.

The plywood mill expects to start producing more than eighty-five million square feet of plywood annually on January 1, 1976. The logging and sawmill operations were underway and ships were standing by in the nearby port where giant cranes were loading the lumber for distant markets.

The Liberian timber concession to Van Ply contains 1,600,000 acres. Ten per cent of this vast tropical rain forest consists of great trees averaging eight feet in diameter and over one hundred and seventy feet tall. The rainfall is so heavy in the rainy season (about 200 inches annually) and the growth so lush that vines and orchids grow all the way to the top of the skyscraper trees. (Shades of Tarzan vine-swinging through the jungle — it seemed I could hear the "ahh-oo-ah" but I couldn't find Jane). Seventeen varieties of hardwoods were said to be available and suitable for commercial use.

Pete Nickel, an American, headed up the plywood operation which resembles a U.S. southern pine plant. Kees Hanschoten, general manager and a Van Ply vice-president, along with Personnel Manager Deryl Shyrock had made sure that our visit was fruitful and enjoyable — the resources and information placed at our immediate disposal would have required, under ordinary circumstances, untold time and expense. We were exposed to all of it in a matter of hours — speed learning at its best. It's too bad Dee Curry of New Albany's Curry Veneer was not on hand to take voluminous notes as she had done on our Scandinavian tour.

The Van Ply "Village," like the other African lumber operations we were to see later, was a complete self-sustaining unit. Native labor from out of the bush was utilized but modern housing and facilities were provided for the supervisory and technical personnel. The native unskilled laborers were being paid about 30 cents per hour and provided with many fringe benefits including some education and training, food and medical care. This placed their income far above the average Liberian income.

Back in Monrovia, the capital, our ladies had by now become connoisseurs of authentic African art and had started collections of Africana — arts of motion and use, rich in symbolism. The masks and figures are used in rituals by tribal peoples. The art materials range from wood (ebony, mahogany, etc.) through ivory, brass, beads and feathers.

The Liberian Ducor Hotel had been built just a few years ago as a very extraordinary hotel, but the native staff could have improved the maintenance and operation. It was on a beautiful site, overlooking the city, and we were told that a renovation program was underway. In Monrovia there were some isolated and outstanding examples of architectural beauty such as the Presidential Palace which had been built under the regime of longtime President William Tubman.

Liberia was founded in 1821 by the American Colonization Society which intended to furnish a haven for the return of American slaves to their homeland. The first American Negroes landed in 1822 and their descendants have been important in economic and political affairs ever since. There were, however, rumors of slavery in Liberia persisting as late as the 1930's when a League of Nations investigation was held. (There are still rumors of slavery in deep jungles elsewhere in Africa today).

We were treated to a buffet supper in Monrovia which rivaled any entertainment we have experienced anywhere in the world. Tony and Dilys Lewis, Dilton-Liberia Lumber, Inc., entertained our group along with some of the most cosmopolitan and stimulating people we have ever encountered. The interesting educational backgrounds included all kinds of schools from missions to our eastern universities.

Two couples named Sherman were owners of substantial Liberian timber operations. Their precise English made us ashamed of ours. The same was true for Victor Han, a Liberian attorney and his charming wife. Han and Maryke Steinz were from Holland, and Mr. and Mrs. Gary Pearson were from Scotland — Gary came dressed in kilts and opened the party with a bagpipe rendition of (imagine) "Yankee Doodle Dandy."

All through the tour, we were entertained royally by lumber people with origins in many different countries. The next night in Abidjan, for example, we were treated to an outdoor dinner by Julian Dazzi and his beautiful wife, Laura (Italians), associates of our tour-member, Agnes Monnin. Julian and Agnes put on a fabulous party at the Palm Beach Club. Another associate of Julian's, Kata Forde (not too sure of spelling on African and Moslem names) held us spellbound with his explanation of some of the Muslim marriage practices.

Forde was rather vague as to the plurality of his wives but explained that some Moslem Brotherhoods allowed four wives in that area with a possible ten concubines for each wife. He stoutly maintained that one wife would be worse than one hundred because the one would always be wanting to know where the man was going or had been and what he was going to do or had done. He frowned on this search for knowledge of a free man's activity.

Just so the reader will not gain the impression that we traveled from one party to another, let me quickly point out that many of our flights were pre-dawn and most of our days ended after dark. It was a strenuous schedule, and movement is not carefree in the many African countries under military rule. For example, twenty-two pictures, six visas, regular passport, six immunizations, a malaria pill program and two letters of introduction, intent and credit-worthiness were among many details required for African-International travel.

Ivory Coast Modernizing — But It Has a Lot of the Past

Today The Ivory Coast is more limited. It is a Republic — independent since 1960. Abidjan is a truly modern city — half a million people, international airport and The Ivoire, one of the world's finest hotels! This is the surface, the modern present and future. There are other modern spots but there is also a great deal of the past. The elephants, the buffalo, the crocodile, the snakes are all still there. The tribal villages and the jungle people are still there. The majority of the people are still animistic — masked dancers and some witch doctors. The Moslems have made some conversions but the influence of Christianity in the interior is not important.

Our group went north, more than two hundred miles, over the dustiest roads I have ever traveled, roads that were seldom sunlit because of the great overhanging trees and grass fifteen feet tall — grass which would swallow up the few roads were it not constantly cut down by natives.

The most accessible forests have been harvested but the remaining wood resource is still beyond belief.

Our first stop was at the CIB Veneer Mills near Gagnoa. Here we witnessed veneering operations turning out plywood cores and faces which had to be trucked to Abidjan or other distant ports on the Atlantic coast. The Italians there hosted an unforgettable three-hour lunch for us. The native musicians came out of the bush to demonstrate their prowess on the Tom Tom — the "talking Drum" which can be heard for thirty miles and serves as the telegraph of the jungle.

The local tribal chieftain was in attendance. He was a colorful, well-fleshed, fortyish character who could dance like a demon. He had walked into the luncheon first with his wife and he knew enough English for pleasant introductions and limited conversation. Paul and Millie Gilfillin of Transco Industries (Nakomis, Florida and Louisville, Ky.) were extremely interested in his dance and talking, but Millie became speechless when he brought in two attractive young girls — maybe half his age — and introduced them as his newest wives. The girls seemed very happy and friendly toward one another — strange culture.

After the plant inspection we continued north over more dusty and jungle-bordered roads. The bus brakes burned out and we pulled over in a small village to attempt repairs (the repairs were eventually completed by some of our own engineers rather than the native driver). It was getting late in the afternoon but the light was sufficient for Helen Livingston, a Hasty Plywood director, to get many pictures of the crowds of native children who surrounded our disabled bus. Someone had failed to tell them that the natives were supposed to be camera shy. They crowded around Helen, and also around the strange bus, even pursued after us for some distance when we pulled away.

As we drove through the jungle, dusk and then total darkness and isolation enveloped us. We were aware that real elephants and other types of wildlife were out there but we really didn't talk about it. We could still smell the burned brake linings and didn't relish another stop. At about nine o'clock we spied the huge lumber industry encampment of The Danzer Company. It was a welcome sight and we were ready to scrape off some of the encrusted jungle road dirt, but after a short clean-up period and a delicious supper, the men went on a night plant tour.

Incidentally, we learned later that a guard at our camp had been seriously bitten by a poisonous Mamba Snake — just before our arrival in the camp.

A World of Travel 163

This giant Fuma tree, more than 15 feet in base diameter and 160 feet tall, was felled in a logging operation visited by a study team from the Hardwood Plywood Manufacturers Association. Trees like this are common in Ivory Coast tropical forests. The human measuring chain includes (left to right) Clark McDonald of Arlington, VA.; Jack Koss of Indianapolis, IN; Joe Robertson of The Robertson Corporation; Bob Gross of High Point, NC.; and Harry Robinson of Charlotte, NC.

A hearty breakfast was served at six-thirty the next morning and we were off to finish up the plant tour and then into the bush to witness the logging of the biggest trees (except California Redwoods) that I have ever seen. Two of these giant Fuma trees, more than fifteen feet in diameter and one hundred sixty feet high, were felled while we watched. The operation required about fifteen minutes and the earth fairly quaked when the giants crashed down in the cleared lanes as planned.

Root sections of the trees were cut out and sharpened and handed to us. We held these pointed ends up over our mouths and drank freely from a delicious sapwater that fairly poured out of the root — the best drink in The Ivory Coast. One need not worry about the harvesting of these great trees — they need to be harvested for more economical and regenerating growth of new forest. These trees were about one hundred fifty years old and stood within one hundred yards of one another.

Mr. Bogislaw von Bonin was the German manager of the efficient Danzer Plant. The manager of the forest was a Frenchman. These men typified the excellent forest product management personnel which have aided African development. Africa will find it difficult to train native personnel for such jobs in the future. However, they intend to try.

Before leaving the Ivory Coast we attended a reception given by the Economic Section Chief of the U.S. Embassy, John Crawford. Gilbert Donahue of the section accompanied us on our bush tour, and Goodwin Cooke, the Deputy U.S. Ambassador, was also present at the reception. Our African embassies are doing a very credible job under difficult conditions.

In the interim between Ivory Coast and Ghana, we visited the African Riviera. It was an extensive beach with all kinds of beautiful scenery. The beach is separated and protected from the jungle by a long lagoon-type body of water. This we had to cross at night. We had expected a ferry. Not so. We unloaded our baggage and waited at a wood dock in the dark.

We heard the chug-chug of an engine and out of the shadows appeared what must have been the original "African Queen." We fully expected to see Bogey at the tiller. We didn't experience any Tsetse flies during the crossing but the Anopheles mosquitoes were present. Both of these insect species are very serious health threats in Africa. We also saw the very destructive Driver and Soldier Ants in many parts of Africa. Room-size ant hills were commonplace.

The Gold Coast of Ghana

Ghana was formerly a British colony called "The Gold Coast." The capital city is Accra. Accra has nearly one million of the country's eleven million people. Shirley Temple Black is the ambassador but we missed her — she was in California. The money in Ghana is the "cedi." It is supposed to be worth eighty-five cents, but dollars still worked well here.

The market merchandise in Ghana is long on excellent wood carvings and recently killed bush rats (rodents the size of ground hogs). All prices are subject to hard bargaining.

The Ghanian hand-carved stools are sought after. In West Africa a king is not "crowned" but "stooled" on a piece carved out of a single wood block.

The military government rules from a great white old slave fort called Christianborg Castle. It is somewhat of a shrine for many black Americans because the body of Dr. W. E. B. DuBois, founder of the NAACP, is entombed there. Our hotel was The Continental, which was a dandy after the management became convinced we were entitled to have our reservations. We found African hotels prone to turn away visitors.

Plane reservations were also now becoming unreliable and we were short several spaces on part of our Ghanian tour. Our group went out to Takoradi to visit Takoradi Veneer and Lumber where Mr. L. G. Eperson was Managing Director and B. Annin-Bonso was the native Deputy Managing Director. The plant was making plywood panels from African Red Hardwoods. A nearby plant, Ghana Primeboard Products, was making plywood, veneer and flush doors. Shipments were mostly to England. Both companies complained of the difficulty in obtaining replacement parts — a common complaint throughout Africa, largely due to government restrictions and red tape.

Takoradi is another of the Slave Fort cities. The Gold Coast, like Gorea island, was also infamous as a holding and shipping area for the slave trade.

In Samreboi the Ghana plant of The African Timber and Plywood Company was visited. The roads in this area were also very, very rough.

Some logs were still being shipped from Ghana ports. However, before our group departed, Mr. Botang of the African Timber Marketing Board assured our group that log exports will be eliminated by 1980 and that U.S. machines for this veneer and plywood are being actively pursued. Some of the best forest product technical and promotional material we have ever seen was being published in Ghana under the editing of Regina Thompson.

A View from Timbuktu, the Mysterious City

Timbuktu — the mysterious. A place name in everyone's vocabulary; a synonym for end-of-the-earth remoteness; inaccessible. Sometimes it is imagined to be legendary, mythical or unreal. It is almost all these things, but not quite. There is a Timbuktu. It was a lost city to the Western World for centuries. After Western Europe emerged from The Dark Ages and through the Crusades and the Renaissance, an occasional traveler or journeyman band would pass with tales of a great city, deep in an unknown country, where gold, ivory, jewels, spices, exotic wood, fabrics and yes, people, were traded by powerful men of fabulous wealth.

Much of this was true. Timbuktu (or Tombouctou as it is spelled in English letters by the natives) did exist, in a remote African country now called Mali. It lies just above the most northern ports of the Great Niger River and almost on the south edge of the Sahara Desert.

In the 14th, 15th, and 16th centuries, it was the near-secret but flourishing meeting place for exotic trading between the Arab and African worlds. Slave trading of the highest order transpired. Beautiful women were sold for delivery to the harems of Arabia and giant Africans purchased for palace guards. The unfortunates of Africa were pawns at Timbuktu in the trade game between jungle chieftains and Arabian Sheiks.

From the forests, mines and hunting grounds of west, central and south Africa, the gold, ivory and slaves were brought by boat up the rivers or by trail on bearers through the jungle. At Timbuktu, in the great central market, the barter was completed with the white and blue robed men from the North for the exotic spices, salt and beautiful silks from the far east.

The city teemed with the doings of 100,000 people — part facing Mecca for prayer five times daily, and part placing their religious faith in animistic rituals and powers of the Witch Doctors. Western whites entered only on penalty of death or slavery. Caravans consisting of legions of camels and up to 60,000 men formed in Timbuktu and traveled at night, like ships at sea guided by the stars, through the trackless Sahara, emerg-

A World of Travel   167

ing weeks or months later from "out of nowhere" on the Mediterranean shore.

Today, the glory has departed but much of the mystery of Timbuktu remains. A great university was established there by Askia Muhammed The Great to make Timbuktu the center of learning for a powerful and far-reaching Songhai Empire. The gigantic university building still stands but in partial ruins with the scrolls and books long since looted and gone. Part of it serves as a Mosque. The power, pomp and the ceremony associated with the fabled Mali Empire are well documented in Muslim history and substantiated by modern archeology, but Europe was almost totally ignorant of its existence.

The first Englishman successfully completed a journey to Timbuktu in 1836. It cost him his life. The first American made the trip in 1912, and returned, for in the late 1800's the French Foreign Legion had managed to gain a tenuous foothold in the Western Sudan. Not too many Americans have "gone to Timbuktu" even today.

While there was some confusion and delay in the airline scheduling for Ghana and Nigeria, Jack and Mary Koss, Virginia and I decided to attempt "The Timbuktu Caper." In the Ivory Coast, we engaged Nafi Kamara, a very bright and highly educated African girl, to assist and guide us. Nafi was 23, competent and confident. She plans to do graduate work in the U.S. We had not had much luck in getting firm confirmation of arrangements ourselves, but Nafi seemed to expedite things quickly and we were off.

The first flight was by Air Afrique to Bamako — the capital of Mali, about six hundred miles. The reception there was not too friendly at either the airport or the "Grand" Hotel. The Grand did have plumbing — we flushed the toilet by pouring a bucket of water down the drain. There were a number of other "inconveniences" to say the least.

Some of our colleagues back in Bermuda had warned us of the rough time we might expect in Africa. As I recall, Joe Balle of Georgia-Pacific and Jack Rutledge of Champion International opined that similar effort might be more comfortably rewarded near the U.S. Also, Don McCoy — an attorney from North Carolina — offered a low-priced curbstone opinion (prophetically) that we might need more legal protection than he or our other U.S. connections could offer.

Kathryn, his wife, added consolation by reminding us that our fellow-traveler, Dibba John, previously considered a stay in a Holiday Inn with black and white TV as "roughing it." These jewels of wisdom were at least remembered in such places as Ivory Coast, Ghana and Timbuktu.

Timbuktu was, if nothing else, a great adventure. We were essentially rolling back the clock for centuries. The now largely vacant village contained relics and things with origins and purposes veiled in an ancient and misty past.

The landing strip was of course unpaved as were all streets — just sand. Our Air Mali pilot was black and he expertly handled his Russian prop aircraft. There are supposedly three planes weekly into Timbuktu. Getting in and out on these planes seemed rather difficult, but Nafi handled it. We shared our plane with sacked live goats. En route at a desert landing strip by Goundam Village, we were accidentally met by American Baptist missionaries — Rev. and Mrs. Frank Marshall. They were expecting two more missionaries — a man and wife team, Bill and Ruth Klopp. It's a small world. Ruth is the daughter of Mrs. Delbert Roush, who lives off Highway 50 between Bedford and Brownstown.

There were six other "tourists" at "The Timbuktu Hotel" and in all the town for that matter — three, maybe wisely, didn't leave the hotel. Our guide in Timbuktu was, no foolin', Mohammed Ali — actually a common name. His English, French, etc., were entirely adequate. He was accompanied by his driver for our Land Rover — one of the two vehicles we saw in Timbuktu. Mohammed suited us. He answered questions briefly, talked some, didn't do much to ease our apprehension, but showed us all we expected to see and more.

The sleeping rooms at "The Timbuktu Hotel" were the stone and mud-brick barracks of the old French Foreign Legion officers' quarters. It was rough, but we were pleased to be there. We toured the near-vacant city (about ten thousand population) in the Land Rover and on foot, going down the twisting sand ways between the thousands of centuries-old buildings. The old central market where the slaves and great treasures had been traded, the old university, the little mill where a millet-type meal was being ground, the gold, brass and iron artisans plying their ancient trade, the conical outdoor ovens — commercial bakeries of the town, the town well with naked children drawing water — these were just a few of the sights, sounds and smells of Timbuktu.

Mohammed Ali directed the Land Rover into the vast Sahara. No trails were visible, only sand and a few scrub bush and trees in front of us. We drove for miles and saw no sign of life — actually about fifty kilometers.

A World of Travel 169

Public Water Company, Timbuktu, 1974. Virginia and Joe Robertson at right.

A desert Sheik's abode for No. 1 wife, 40 miles north of Timbuktu in the Sahara Desert, 1,000 miles from civilization.

Then, we overtook an honest-to-goodness camel caravan! Those ships of the desert still carry burdens of merchandise from Timbuktu to somewhere North. However, I doubt that there is much future in the camel caravan business.

A little farther, we came upon an oasis with a well. As for centuries, a desert man was using a burro to pull up a bucket of water which a small boy then poured into a real goatskin. For the people and the animals this water was life — for us it would have been death, or deathly sickness at least. After a few miles more, we saw what we had looked forward to seeing — the bright blue robes of "The Blue Men of the Desert." These famed nomadic tribesmen — the Tuaregs — were aristocrats and once rulers of much of the Sahara, but the severe droughts of the early seventies had forced them to slaughter their herds and move south in relative poverty.

This Blue Man had set up his camp for a day or two. His central "tent" of hide and fabric was maybe four feet in height and fifteen feet in circumference. Here was one woman and her child. Another woman and child occupied a nearby tent of maybe pup-tent size. Fifty yards distant, another woman and child were quartered under a bush — much in the same manner we remember Hagar and Ishmael when ousted by Abraham. The Blue Man was however, proud and after proper formalities were exchanged with him by Mohammed Ali and Nafi, we were invited to sit down and share his mats — and tea — no furniture, of course.

These people can take care of themselves to say the least and he wore two daggers. We didn't exactly disarm him but Virginia and Mary ended up buying both daggers. Nafi then proceeded to buy his goat butter churn and two of his "door pots" that held up part of his tent. The weapons we bought were authentic and old, but he undoubtedly figured that the money he received would get him replacements from another nomad or a passing caravan.

In the twilight we traveled south to watch a beautiful sunset on the port at the Niger. Here we were reminded of American good intentions. Several tons of well-packaged sorghum flour were stacked on the dock plainly marked, "A Gift From The People of the U.S.A." The irony is that most desert people can't read and few read English. Mohammed smiled slightly. We correctly or incorrectly assumed, "The food will be sold." Speaking of food, we won't, for among other inedibles, we were served sorghum bread — it too was sandy.

We drove back north again to take a night camel ride into the desert.

Jack noted the contrast between the plodding camel and a bright satellite speeding across the desert sky.

That night as we dropped exhausted into the sand-laden bed clothes of the old Foreign Legion quarters, above the muted bawling of distant camels, we really heard a muted taps-like bugle call from the city military post. Our dreams were naturally of Beau Geste.

Nigeria

Lagos, Nigeria, according to Bob Gross of North Carolina, has the highest density of cars and accident-prone drivers of any area in the world. There are essentially no cars in ninety-five per cent of Nigeria but everyone in Lagos apparently has one or more vehicles which they drive with one foot on the accelerator and one hand on the horn. An auto is THE status symbol. The cars often serve as homes.

The primary interest of the HPMA was of course centered in the wood industries. At Sapele, Nigeria, near the ancient city of Benin (origin of some of the world's finest bronze plaques), the group visited the African Timber and Plywood Mill. This plant is possibly the largest wood products complex in Africa.

Two thousand are employed in the plant and one thousand work in the forests. Since about ten people are supported by every one employed here, approximately thirty thousand natives are supported by this enterprise. The mill has a very large production capacity of plywood and lumber. Flush doors, rotary and sliced veneers, furniture and prefab housing are also manufactured. Much of the plant's production is for the local market. A. L. Broadley, a Scot, was plywood mill manager at Sapele.

The Nigerian workers were busy and productive. Plant policy is moving rapidly toward native direction with a reduction of foreign supervisors to less than twenty. Although many Nigerians are still backward and uneducated, they have a heritage of accomplishment and grandeur reaching back into antiquity. However, about three hundred years ago the once-powerful kingdom of Benin perished in a flood of human sacrifice as its kings and priests attempted to ward off evil by appeasing ancient gods.

Another jolly tribal chieftain was encountered at Nigeria. One of our HMPA chiefs, "Catbird Tomjon," struck up a charade conversation with the chief, and our Mr. John introduced his wife to the Nigerian chief. Later Dibba John was relating how her husband had at least introduced her as his Number One wife. "No so," interrupted daughter Helen Livingston, "I distinctly heard Daddy introduce you as "one" of his wives." Tom explained this was a matter of saving face — after all, the chief probably wouldn't even speak to a one-wife man.

Safari is Something to Remember

Safari — the hunt for big game. Bwana McDonald and Assistant Bwana Per Kalstrup (Webb Co., VP, Edinburg, Indiana — experienced hunter in vicinity of Indiana's Monroe Reservoir) led us toward the bushveld of South Africa.

Africa is a vast continent. A full day's jet flight with two stops (one scary one in Zaire — Belgian Congo) was required to get us to the gold city of Johannesburg. Some of our group found it necessary to return home from Nigeria but the rest of us donned our Safari suits, or reasonable replicas, and signed on as Great White Hunters.

We checked in at The Landrost in Jo'burg after viewing a few gold mines and mine dumps enroute from the airport. The hotel was great and we were pleased to share it with just-married Liz and Dick [*Elizabeth Taylor and Richard Burton*]. They had the 17th floor and we had one room on the eighth. At daybreak we were up for our flight — two hundred miles into the heart of eight thousand square miles of Kruger's Wild Game Preserve! It was to be a weekend long remembered.

Our excellent guide, Bok, was waiting with the safari wagon and our supplies at Skukuza. In a few miles, the excitement started — all of us straining our eyes for a sighting, each taking a sector, with instructions to properly and softly announce, not shout, a sighting with directions.

The first wild animal sighted was an impala — the fleet and beautiful African antelope for which the [*Chevrolet*] car is named. Then, at intervals, we sighted more animals — hyena, ferocious wart-hogs, buffalo, hippo, crocodile, giraffe and kudu. By 11 a.m. the game was seeking shade and rest from the heat of the day and so were we. After 3 p.m. we started again, excited but wanting desperately to see an elephant or the King of the Jungle.

Then it happened. We were off the trail with our safari wagon near a riverbed.

"Jumbo on the left at nine o'clock" — a soft whispered warning because any unusual or loud noise may provoke a charge.

There, not forty yards away, was the Great Beast. Standing trunk up and ear flaps ventilating. Everyone aimed and instead of the great booms of former years, the "clicks" of the cameras were heard. It's certainly different from the zoo.

That animal out there is wild — in the raw, and he weighs tons more than our wagon and people all put together. Furthermore, he can run twenty-five miles per hour and we can't back out that fast. But after we did back out and were safely away, we shouted. Almost the same procedure was followed when we sighted the King of Beasts — the lion and his mate at a waterhole where baboons and wildebeasts and impalas were present in abundance.

The lions out there are also real. They eat other animals and can't really distinguish people. My primary concern at this time was to remain, as with the jungle cannibals, the eater, not the eatee.

What a day. The next morning after spending a night in a safely fenced enclosure and sleeping in [*concrete*] Rondovals, and having a barbecue of hippo sausage and buffalo steak, we were off again at daybreak. Our luck was amazing. Some got good close pictures of about everything.

At one time we got in a pocket and were accidentally "surrounded" by four elephants, munching and crunching bush and trees around us with reckless abandon. Someone kicked a can and someone whispered in nervous excitement — much to the irritation and concern of Mrs. Bwana McDonald — she was ready to turn us all in to the game warden — would have served us right.

The next day we were back at work and study. We turned out early for a visit to the Raymond Plywood Company. Here Klaus Kuhn, managing director, led us on an interesting tour. We spent most of one day and part of an evening with the BruPly Board Group. Mike Lillard of California is director of this company. They are large manufacturers of plywood, and use both phenolic and urea resin glues.

I had a field day here for their research and development facilities for plywood adhesives were tremendous — far more than I have ever seen at plant level in the U.S. G. R. Saunders, R and D director, and Rory Kroon opened up their research and development work to me and I discovered that they had made amazing progress in some soon-to-be-announced adhesive developments.

There was more political stability and more economic well-being (by far) in South Africa than in any other African country. The signs of wealth and achievement are everywhere. This amazing progress has been brought about under the direction of the English and Dutch. The winds of change, however, may be sweeping toward this country for it may be difficult for its "Apartheid" to survive in a continent where native blacks have gained independence and ruling power in virtually every country — even though in some cases, the native people may be poorer and more oppressed than under colonial rule.

The Zulus and Xhosas are the majority in South Africa, and few outsiders can understand the cultural and political society existing there. A native folklore play, Ipi Tombi, perhaps did more for our understanding than all else. It explained the deep desire of the natives to keep things simple. Another thing we won't forget — the Jacaranda trees (Rosewood) were in full bloom and they were beautiful.

Brazil — Last Stop

The Brazil visit, enroute home from South Africa, was an enlightening experience. Flying into Rio is thrilling. The mountain-top statue of Christ faces across the bay and over Copacabana Beach to Sugar Loaf Mountain. The bustling city of six million has bumper-to-bumper traffic possibly wilder and more irresponsible than any in America. This is a city and a country of growth.

Rampant inflation and interest rates — both in the 30 per cent range — fail to stem Brazil's gross national product growth because people are working in industry and agriculture with amazing results. The resources, the will and the motivation here all seem to match the dream of the people for progress. Brazilia is perhaps the most modern city in the world, and Sao Paulo is expected to soon be the largest.

The scenery on Copacabana Beach, and the other beaches, is as beautiful as it is reputed to be. The girls' beachwear is the "tanga" (mostly string) and the billboards everywhere proclaim the Brazilian philosophy — "The sun is free — take advantage of it." The constellations of the night sky are different of course, and a revelation to northerners. The celestial beauty is highlighted by the famous Southern Cross.

The United States has been doing a large volume of business with

Brazil, but this is becoming more difficult as Brazil is concerned over its deficit in foreign trade balances.

We visited the Laserma Company on the Rio — Sao Paulo Highway while Per Kalstrup (Edinburgh, Indiana) flew off to visit his parent company's Danzer Veneer Mill in Sao Paulo. Leonardo Tamier, director and Otto Mermelstein, an American, conducted us through this growing Laserma wood products plant. Closer to Rio, we stopped to see Roland "Ding" Hamann of the N & N Veneer Company. "Ding", who formerly worked in southern Indiana, showed us some tremendous logs which had been trucked into the plant from the Amazon Basin — more than 2,000 miles away.

Our last stop, and one of the most memorable, was at Karl Heinz Moehring's Atlantic Veneer Mill in Vitoria. Under the able direction of Michael Bol, it is an outstanding example of the tremendous industrial growth possible in today's Brazil.

This complex is only seven years old but now employs more than 1,600 people making veneer, plywood, particle board and furniture. Innovation, motivation, efficiency and expanded energy are some of the keys here.

In addition to the good housing, food, and health services, a remarkable elementary school system is provided. Moehring and Bol told us that this school was an attempt to pass on the spirit of American food aid which had been provided to European kids after the war — so, U.S. foreign aid is not always in vain.

Jack Koss, Indianapolis Capital Veneer Kingpin, fairly "busted his buttons" at the Atlantic Veneer Plant. We had seen many Capital machines elsewhere on this trip and heard frequent compliments. However, at this showplace I counted about fourteen of these Capital Slicers and Lathes — all from Indiana, U.S.A. — a tribute to American ingenuity, quality and hard work.

Mrs. Bol and Mrs. Moehring were our charming and gracious hostesses at a delightful Brazilian luncheon. Paula Craig, an American secretary, efficiently looked after all details of our visit. It was great.

We were now ready for the home trip. It was a beautiful Pan Am flight — but nine hours long over the Amazon forests (here grows 18 per cent of the world's forest resources), the Caribbean and the Atlantic Ocean back to the outstretched torch of Lady Liberty.

It is always good to get back to the best place — home. The Hoosiers and Carolinians were again in the majority on this study tour, but Jim

Lester guarantees that our numbers will be more than matched by representatives from Wisconsin and other Yankee states next time.

Our second trip to Africa, actually ten years after our first, was chronicled in 1985 in the *Times-Mail*.

A Flight to Adventure in the Dark Continent

*By Joe Robertson,
with informational notes supplied by Virginia Robertson*

Introduction

It is pleasant to feel a close acquaintance with far away places. It brings reality to an otherwise cloudy view of what lies beyond the hills, the mountains, the plains and the oceans of our usual horizon.

Africa is still the "Dark Continent" in the minds of many who perceive it as a land of mystery, myth and shadows. A trip there reveals that a great deal of light has fallen upon this developing continent, but it is still a place of adventure and excitement and a study of the unfamiliar.

Tarzan, Bwana and the Great White Hunters of the South, along with the Egyptian Sorcerers and Sahara Camel Trains in the North, have passed into the realm of legend. Today, the real worlds of politics and economics place a spotlight on the changing cultures — in Africa we have seen civilization make more changes in one generation than in any previous century.

This time, our entry to Africa was the Cape Verde Islands off Africa's Big Western Bulge. The particular place we sought, after an eight-hour flight, was the Isla do Sal — The Isle of Salt. It is one of the Cape Verde Islands, formerly held by Portugal.

It was truly a windy, barren and desolate place, and finding it was a tribute to the navigational skill of the plane crew that found the tiny "speck" on time and schedule — it is only one of many such remote refueling stops throughout the world that was first a Kilroy U.S. airfield scraped out by the "dog faces" driving D-4 Caterpillar Bulldozers in the 1940's. After this

A World of Travel

The heaviest wild animal concentration and the greatest migration track in the world is found in the Serengeti Plain.

stop, we still had to fly another 8 1/2 hours down the African coast and across the wild and barren land of Southwest Africa beneath the Kalahari Desert to Johannesburg.

From 41,000 feet and particularly over the ocean, one can easily recognize the curvature of the earth's horizon. As we turned inward and eastward, it seemed we could still see that curvature in the desolate nothingness of Namibia (Southwest Africa).

Great dunes and desert wastes marked the roadless expanse. From our height, no signs of life were apparent for more than 100 miles until the sands of desolation gave way to fair greens and reds, and signs of roads started to appear — stark evidence that man will truly go to the ends of the earth to seek land unassigned and stake a claim.

Arrival in the spectacular Johannesburg Airport is a relative pleasure. Everything is spotless and attractive, and customs processing almost non-existent for Americans — much less trouble actually than returning to any international airport in the U.S. We merely showed our passport, picked up our baggage from the carousel, placed it on a Hertz-marked cart and were waved on by inspectors and out to the terminal area.

Here, a polite and helpful man guided us maybe 100 feet to a van waiting directly at the door with "Air Port Sun," our motel, painted plainly in English on the side. There are two principal languages here — English and Afrikaans are official languages, Zulu and Swahili are spoken by some blacks, and there are many other dialects. We heard two young girls conversing in a beautiful language in the airport — upon inquiry, we were told it was Zulu.

The facilities, food and treatment at the Airport Sun were comparable to those found in any of the major U.S. hotels — Hilton, Hyatt, Holiday Inn, etc. Well, they should compare, for that very day an announcement was made that the Sun chain was taking over the 23 Holiday Inns in South Africa.

There was an additional sadness for Americans in South Africa that day — Pan Am closed its gates and discontinued a major route of its worldwide network. We talked with two ground transportation executives that day, and they were sure the route had been discontinued for "economic" reasons — that is partly true, but politics must be considered a major factor.

Variety of Wildlife on Safari in Kenya

The friends one makes in international travel are legion. They come from a myriad of places and backgrounds. On our flight to Africa and Nairobi, we talked at length with a real big game hunter — he organizes and leads gun hunts (safari).

His seat mate was an M.D., a specialist in infectious disease, concerned with new vaccine-resistant strains. We soon became accustomed to being a definite minority — white Americans in a foreign land overwhelmingly black with a few Caucasians from lands other than ours.

"Shoot Nothing But Pictures, Leave Nothing But Footprints." That is the philosophy of Kenya Safari Country. It seems to be working well for the animals, and the quantity and variety of visible wildlife is incredible.

We thought perhaps we had waited too long to come to Nairobi, Kenya, for the bustling city of one million is a far cry from the English outpost depicted in early movies where the narrow gauge trains unloaded the white hunters, explorers, British commissioners and their beautiful companions.

However, the Norfolk Hotel still stands in Colonial splendor with memorabilia of rickshaws, wagons, and equipment which the bush-bound parties loaded on porters before starting their search for the ivory, hides and trophies to be found in the danger of the hunt.

We followed the same trails that the white hunters blazed. Today, however, within an hour by Land Rover from city-center, in almost any direction, one may see more big game and exotic birds and beasts than the walking hunters could have found in a trek of many days.

The animals are wild as always, and undoubtedly they offered a dangerous challenge to the early stalkers. But now the beasts would be fairly easy prey for one wishing to shoot to kill. It is not difficult to approach within 30 yards of elephants, lions, cheetahs, buffalo or wild hogs to obtain close-up shots of one or many.

At Nairobi, we joined an English couple for our first trek — bound for Tree Tops, the typical English shooting lodge. Most folk strike out to chase the game — the English gentry thought it more appropriate to have the game come to them, so they had a comfortable lodge built on sturdy poles near a water hole and apparently sent word to the animal kingdom to pass in review below, for that is exactly what happens.

The "hide-away" photo box permits one to come almost face to face with the animals. It is a pill box arrangement and is supposed to be "safe." However, I was thoroughly scared to be looking at a large bull elephant almost in the eye at 20 paces from my place of relative security. Occasionally a bull becomes enraged at this edifice. It forces him to deviate a few yards from his "Elephant Walk," the trail that is genetically fixed in his brain in much the same manner as the guidance systems for migratory fowl or salmon.

When the elephant is angry, structural poles are bashed and broken and it becomes necessary for "Col." J. Pickett, the hunter-supervisor, to shoot him — which is done quickly and expertly. Any time a visitor is on the grounds at Tree Tops, the colonel is escorting with his fully-loaded weapon at the ready.

It was at Tree Tops that Queen Elizabeth became a monarch. She ascended the ladder-like stair one night as a princess. Her father died during the night and she descended the stair the next morning as Queen of the British Commonwealth.

After Tree Tops, we passed the forested Mt. Kenya and joined up with different companions for a continuation of our safari — on to Amboseli, a game-rich area situated directly on the north base of Africa's greatest mountain. It was here that Clark Gable brought his beautiful bride [*Carole Lombard*] to pursue the black-maned lions, leopards, rhinos, cheetahs, the dangerous Cape Buffalo and the elephants as they moved stealthily about beneath "The Snows of Kilimanjaro." The Mystery Mountain is just south of the equator and reaches nearly four miles upward into the ever-present clouds which keep the crater top capped in snow through all seasons.

I had waited all my adult life to see the splendor of "the mountain" and feel the spirit and spell which pervades the area. We were not disappointed. Here, Africa speaks with the sounds of the hunter and the hunted, and finally with the howls of the hyenas and jackals which keep the mountain clean.

In our lodge, sleep came rapidly from exhaustion of mind and body in a land and culture which defies understanding by most of us, "the outsiders."

Conditions in Kenya Primitive Beyond Belief

After Kilimanjaro, our Kikuyu guide steered us through the Masai Country toward Masai Mara on the Tanzania Border. We were on our own now with Kamau Munene. He not only had a great talent for finding big game, but also a good knowledge of the tribal cultures and the history of Kenya.

Kenya's government is based on representation from 43 tribes. The most powerful tribe is perhaps the Kikuyu. Although the violent Mau Mau actions of the 50's (which undoubtedly contributed to independence) are still shrouded in mystery, there is widespread belief that the farmer-

A prized close-up photo of the rare black-maned lion taken by Joe and Virginia Robertson on their 1,200-mile photo safari through Kenya. This animal is found on the slopes of Kilimanjaro at the border of Kenya and Tanzania, and makes forays into the Masai Mara country adjacent to the Serengeti Plains. This lion had made an early morning kill of a zebra and was likely to remain lazy and satisfied until late evening or the following dawn.

warrior Kikuyu were involved in many incidents such as those portrayed in Robert Ruark's "Something of Value."

While all tribes generally supported the independence moves against the English, there is still inter-tribal hostility. Our information came from many sources and different people we encountered along the way. As usual, different folks have different perspectives, but all were interesting. A young anthropologist living with Masai gave us a great deal of reliable information on that tribe.

These young maidens of the Masai Tribe in Kenya are in ritualistic regalia, going through pre-nuptial ceremonies. They will be married to older men who can "afford" them, and their fathers will be given a number of cows. The "manyattas" in the background serve as homes for the nomadic families. The construction is of mud, dung, sticks, and thatch. Joe and Virginia Robertson visited in several Masai villages during their safari in Kenya.

The Masai people live in the savannah and bush and are nomadic. They have roving herds of good, fat cattle which are tended by boys and girls, and guarded by warriors wearing skins and carrying spears and skin shields in the same manner as their ancestors of One Thousand B.C. The lions and leopards prey on the cattle but are fended off and frequently killed by the warriors.

Conditions are primitive beyond belief. One may discount the few modern settlements, and realize that 30 miles from civilization he has returned to Africa as it was in Christ's time.

We witnessed ceremonial dances as young men and women prepared for ancient rites of circumcision and the entry into adult life. The role of the women is beyond comprehension. At 12 or 14, the girl is given to an older warrior who can afford the 10-cow price. The older man often shares her with younger warriors so long as they are not of the same family.

The women create great circular holes in their ears for cosmetic purposes, and likewise cover their bodies with different shades of color and dress or undress as they take options of covered, bare or half-covered breasts.

The housing is temporary, of thatch, mud and dung, with central charcoal fire and open flue.

Just west of Nairobi, one descends abruptly into the Great Rift Valley. This is one of the most prominent and unusual formations on the surface of the earth, and was caused perhaps by a great intercontinental shift in prehistoric times. It extends from Turkey through Suez and on down through Africa until it leaves the continent near Madagascar. At times it resembles the Grand Canyon with near-sheer walls of up to 5,000 feet, but the distance across the floor of the valley is more often in the 10 to 20-mile range. It varies from barren to fruitful, and sometimes serves as a barrier and other times as a highway for men and beasts. In Kenya, the valley is fertile in times of rain and serves as a farm-garden for man and for animals. We passed an occasional volcano as we journeyed through the valley toward our next "hunt."

Masai Mara is a region of incredible game population. There are wildebeasts by the thousands and great numbers of other fascinating animals. I had always dreamed of seeing "The Serengeti," that region so frequently photographed and shown in public TV specials and National Geographic presentations.

As we looked out across the Masai Mara onto the high plain of the Serengeti, our highest expectations were fulfilled. It was like looking out on great herds of cattle, except the animals were wild beasts spread across the horizon, grazing in manner and numbers reminiscent of the thundering buffalo herds on our own frontiers. The zebras, giraffe, and cape buffalo were everywhere. We saw four hippos showing their broad backs in the hippo pools. It is rare to see hippos in daylight because they do not like to expose their tender skin to the sun. There was plenty of evidence, however, that at least 1,000 of the monsters were lying under the surface of the nearby river.

The elephants pictured are just a few of the 52 mammoth beasts that surrounded Joe and Virginia Robertson at one point on their 1,200-mile photo safari through Kenya. These elephants were part of the herds that inhabit and migrate through the Masai Mara region, adjacent to the Serengeti Plain, in southern Kenya near the Tanzania border.

Families or prides of lions were frequently sighted at close range. At one time we were surrounded on three sides by 52 elephants ranging in estimated age from one week to 80 years. We always kept a retreat path open for the safari van. It was an unending series of exciting and rewarding "hunts."

It was time to leave the wilds of Africa now. Back to Nairobi, the Norfolk Hotel and back to an airport taking us out of a South Africa which we didn't understand but which we knew better than Kenya.

Kenya is a fascinating country — another far-away place, a place of fulfillment for adventurers and romantics. One leaves many of the remote areas with mixed feelings of satisfaction and sadness, for the realization is there — "I will not pass this way again."

Plenty of Potential Seen in South Africa

The flight from Nairobi, Kenya, back to Johannesburg, South Africa, offered a fascinating aerial study of the ever-changing African terrain below. Kenya had been blessed with rains but the lands below the equator appeared generally dry as we passed over Tanzania and Zimbabwe (formerly Rhodesia) with Mozambique to the East.

South Africa is dry, too — very dry — but excellent water management in this country minimizes the drought that has been so disastrous in many other parts of Africa.

Our entry again was smooth and easy — obviously we were welcome here. Representatives from the Council of Scientific and Industrial Research were on hand to welcome us, and start us on a week of an intense learning and teaching experience in a community of scientists assembled from throughout the world.

The purpose of our symposium was to review forest product research, and to discuss accomplishments and objectives in meeting the world needs for shelter and fuel from the renewable forest resources. These needs must of course be met in the most economical, efficient and ecologically-acceptable manner.

We had determined to remain aloof from politics during our visit to South Africa. However, conversation everywhere would tend to drift toward discussion of "Apartheid" (separation of races), with local explanations of the plans and progress in race relations. The basic declarations were that property rights could be protected, and progress continued only by a franchise limited to responsible voters.

It was pointed out that of the 56 African nations, only South Africa had achieved a leading role in commerce. While so many African nations were experiencing anarchy, purges, ill health, extreme poverty and widespread starvation, essentially all native South Africans were adequately fed and have access to health care and education.

South Africans have developed a mining industry in strategic materials second to none. They are the world's sixth largest grain exporters, and have furnished a stable base for protecting sea and air lanes around the Cape area. Active disapproval of Apartheid is general in the U.S. but a study of possible alternatives is prudent. We disapprove of many practices in most of Africa but doubt that we have the plan or ability to solve their problems.

U.S.-South African relations are changing rapidly. At the time of our trip it was possible to fly to South Africa in an American airline and stay in an American motel chain. That is no longer possible. We flew with black people and blacks stayed in the same hotels and ate in the same dining rooms with us, so obviously some companies are following the voluntary code of fair treatment and employment practices known as the "Sullivan Principles."

The Voortrekkers (pioneers) of South Africa had much in common with American pioneers. Only a relatively few Hottentots and Bushmen were present when Europeans started settling around the Cape of Good Hope about 1500. The Europeans pushed north later, and by then they were encountering black Africans of other tribes who were migrating southward.

Malays were brought in as slaves from the Far East. These peoples intermarried with other slaves. Slavery was outlawed about 1840 (25 years before U.S. Emancipation), but the offspring from the slave marriages are now designated as "coloured." "Asian" is another race classification.

Of the total 25 million people in South Africa, about five million are "whites," three million "coloureds," one million "Asian" and perhaps 16 million "blacks" representing a number of distinct tribal nations such as Zulu (six million) and Xhosa (three million).

Accurate numbers are difficult to establish as tribal blacks move between urban and rural cultures, and migrant tribe movements rival our own illegal alien situation. Consensus is difficult in any area because tribal differences are just as great as social differences.

The sightseeing possibilities are almost unlimited — mountains, deserts, beaches, forests, savannahs. Wild animals of all kinds roam in profusion in vast national parks which are well maintained and protected. We had enjoyed an exciting safari in Kruger Park on a previous trip, so this time we chose to explore Capetown and environs after we had completed our symposium.

Besides the great scenic beauty here, we wanted to inspect the grain shipping facilities of this major export harbor and also check on some unique wood product processes which hold promise for utilization in the U.S.

The Cape of Good Hope is an inspiring landmark for all who pass around or above it in this southern-most part of the continent. The meeting here of the placid waters of the Indian Ocean and the tumultuous South Atlantic makes a beautiful but treacherous seascape. Even the temperature of the two great waters differ — by 12 degrees in a few hundred yards.

South Africa is an amazing land blessed with plenty of sunshine, natural resources and some of the most productive people in the world. Seldom have so few accomplished so much. These highly motivated folks carved a great nation out of an aboriginal wilderness amidst many conflicts which continue to this day. The problems are real, but there is plenty of potential — peoples, resources, attitudes — to resolve differences and solve problems. There is promise of a great future in South Africa for all the citizens.

Chapter 7

The First Around-the-World Trip, 1977

VIRGINIA AND I RETURNED FROM our first around-the-world trek in the fall of 1977. Sponsored by the HPMA, our study group visited plywood and veneer plants and forest industries in the South Pacific, New Zealand, Australia, Southeast Asia, the Mediterranean countries, and Eastern Europe — all in 35 days!
From *The Times-Mail*:

Tahiti First Stop in Wood Business Journey Around the World

Introduction

There is a belt of rain forests around the world which may provide a promise for the future — a promise of renewable resource which far exceeds current practical concepts. These tropical hardwood forests are capable of furnishing housing materials, millions of productive jobs in related industry, new energy and other benefits.

The conifer forests and the temperate hardwood forests are also earth-circling and may be equally important. However, the petrochemical situation and alternate energy studies have focused attention on the tremendous potential of a natural resource which, under multi-use management and maximum utilization (not just conservation), may present solutions to many current material problems.

As a matter of fact, the tree may be re-discovered as the primary converter of solar energy. Fast-growth forest, nurtured by near-direct sunrays and one hundred or two hundred inches of rain annually, may be a keystone in building a future world economy.

In search of up-to-date knowledge regarding forest product manufacturing techniques and marketing trends, as well as future availabilities and potentials, a group of plywood manufacturers and associates embarked on a Fall Study Tour from the 1977 Hardwood Plywood Manufacturers Association Convention in Seattle. In rapid succession they visited plywood plants, veneer plants, wood product specialists, and interesting forests in New Zealand, Australia, Indonesia, Singapore, Malaysia, Thailand, India and East Europe.

Studies in previous years had covered productive areas of the China Seas, Africa, Europe and Central and South America. This year the group followed the paths of Magellan, Captain Cook, Captain Bligh, the U.S. Navy's Pacific Fleet and others into the bewitching islands of the South Pacific and the unfathomable cultures of Southeast Asia.

Temperatures ranged from torrid near the equator to freezing near Antarctic. In these varied regions one may find old and new forest-based industry. One may also find some keys to expanding business and promoting positive and profitable interaction with Australia, the South Pacific and countries east of the Aegean.

However, with the discovery of promises, one also uncovers disturbing trends. For example, it appears that the English language is passing into descendancy as many of the former English Colonies adopt and promote a national language selected from a myriad of dialects.

The same is true for French — it, too, is being phased out or de-emphasized in favor of the native tongue. This language change appears to be associated with the world-prevalent Spirit of Nationalism. The change places new barriers to communication and understanding just as many walls of prejudice, fear and distrust were being dissolved.

Governments are certainly trending toward more socialism, even in Australia and New Zealand. Governments of many other countries were called People's Democracies — which they are not, by our definition. Power is passing quickly and increasingly to dictators of various sorts, some benevolent, some not so good.

Stable and reliable government is still a dream in Southeast Asia, at least for those of us who think that individuals should be free to pursue sound economic endeavors and to trade, work and worship in an atmosphere where honesty and human rights are respected.

As always, far away places present strange cultures for those of us who are strangers in the land. The cultures are varied, in a state of flux and contrast as natives try to adjust to changing pressures from a western world. And the Western World perhaps is not properly attentive to the deep-rooted mores and cultures of the East. More often than not, we do not understand. . . .

Mark Twain's Ne'er-To-Meet East and West have met and are meeting. Those of us who have journeyed through the distant lands around the world do not have the answers. At most, we perhaps understand the questions a little better than before and hope we can help a little for having passed that way.

Tahiti

Tahiti is far from Seattle, U.S.A. It is five thousand miles, as the stratojet flies, south across the equator and westward to the fabled island paradise. It really is a delight as one imagines after reading Michener's "South Pacific."

The flight, for a group of 23 plywood manufacturers and suppliers, was the first leg on a study tour which was to carry them to many exciting places in New Zealand and Australia. Some were to return from Australia by way of Fiji. Others were scheduled to make business visits in many other places westward around the world — chasing the sun.

The over-ocean planes were always large — usually different models of DC-10's or 747's. And, the fast and high-flying jets (altitudes usually 35,000 to 40,000 feet) were usually operated and flown by the country of

A World of Travel

debarkation or embarkation. The schedule was as full as practical and rather tight and trying in some instances (flights often leaving before sunrise and often arriving after dark) but never dull — after all, how many times in one's life can he see the sunrise behind him exploding over the brim of the ocean or ride the wind through limitless sky in pursuit of a splashing sunset?

The plywood people had worked hard at the very interesting Seattle convention. They met, studied and resolved to continue the search for ever-better solutions to production, marketing and political problems. They were ready for a weekend of recreation before proceeding in the search for industry-related information. Tahiti fulfilled all expectations for the interlude.

One must adjust to a complete re-orientation as he goes "down under" the equatorial horizon. Polaris, the North Star, the best-known reference point in the Northern Hemisphere, is no more. Now, to know where one is one looks for the "Southern Cross." "Up North" is hot, "Down South" is cold. Other concepts are equally reversed. For example, where does a traveler expect to get stamps?

Southern Gentlemen

Harry Howell, a Southern gentleman who makes plywood in Alabama, stepped up to the hotel desk and asked, "Whea may Ah pauchase some staymps?" "Sir," the Polynesian replied in his best but broken English, "the stamp machine is around the corner to the right in the men's room."

Harry was sure the native had misunderstood him. Harry's wife, Beverly, speaking a similar Alabama dialect with a University of Florida accent, tried the question. The same answer. Harry then had the question repeated in "Nawthen" English by a "Damyankee" friend. The reply was the same and the stamps were there.

They were, however, to be purchased with Polynesian (French Pacific) francs. Beverly reported that she received a "ho big bunch" of francs for $20. The exchange rate at the hotel was 425 for a dollar.

Place names around the "down under" sun belt once brought to mind only visions of "The Vahine" (Polynesian Beauty), placid lagoons, blue water, the bluest skies interlaced with the whitest of clouds, mist-shrouded mountains descending to white beaches and a beautiful surf over a coral reef in the South Pacific.

"Tahiti" is such a place — as magical as its name. It is the principal island in the Society Islands of French Polynesia in the South Pacific. It is half way between California and Australia and "all the way" different. Now, of course, ships ply the trade routes laden with cargoes of copra, coconut oil, timber and other tropical produce.

There are those who complain that Tahiti is "commercialized," and perhaps it is. One might recall, however, that Captain Bligh's "Bounty" was out of Tahiti and bound for Jamaica with a cargo of breadfruit plant — and that commercial venture was in 1789! "Mister Christian" and the crew, however, decided that Tahitian women and the South Pacific islands were much to be preferred over bringing breadfruit to a western society willing to pay for the legendary tropical food.

It is much the same today. Little can be "carried back" except commercial goods, but for those who, like the natives, enjoy the gentle breeze and the gentler tide, the sun and palm shade temperature always in the 70's — this is "the place."

Modern Tahiti still retains some Polynesian charm. One must, of course, move out of the shadow of the airport and harbor to the meeting place of surf, seashore, and mountain. Civilization has paused here as if to consider whether to engulf Paradise.

"Planned progress" has left its scars of improved conditions, according to viewpoint. Nevertheless, just beyond the bustle of the harbor and airport, there still exists a spirit free and dedicated to pleasure.

"Bali Hai" is there in the distance. It's more beautiful than one can imagine. It really is there — just off Tahiti beyond the surf and the reef, a magic mountain, its crown enshrouded in misty clouds. Across the waters, the outriggers are still there, too, manned by natives. It's easy to hitch a ride. You're welcome.

The Polynesian dancers appear frequently — their China eyes, raven black hair, flashing smiles and vibrating hips soon "bemuse one into a sensitivity of the worthwhile," according to Don McCoy, a prominent and conventional North Carolina attorney.

Judgment Respected

His judgment in North Carolina is respected and regarded as astute. He was accompanied by his lively wife, Kathryn, a shelling expert, his son, Donald, Jr. a now-New Yorker associated with the TV industry.

These "solid citizens," together with Helen Livingston, a North Carolina-Florida Plywood Manufacturer, had secured snorkel gear and engaged a native and a canoe for transportation out to some diving floats located near the coral reef. The boat unceremoniously deposited them on one of the several floats loaded with brown-skinned men and maids diving into the sea. Then members of the McCoy party found themselves to be the only living souls in those waters wearing a stitch of clothes.

Judge McCoy was interrogated by Bruce Markel, a fellow attorney from Brownstown, Indiana, as to numbers, description, etc. "Under such conditions," the judge said, "one attempts to appear unimpressed and to look straight ahead." After that he took the Fifth. There is an old shipwreck near the diving site. It probably ran aground when an early sea captain saw and heard sirens diving in the surf, and scuttled his ship when, like McCoy, he realized he had discovered The Place of the Mermaids. "McCoy's Reef" is now the official name for the beautiful coral strip just off Beachcomber Beach in Tahiti.

The group spent a delightful evening on the beach at a "Tamaaran." The feast (MAA for food) featured such items as "Maiti" (a rum-based punch), "Eia Ota" (marinated fish), "Pua" (the suckling pig cooked whole), "Uru" (the fabled breadfruit — a cross between bread and potatoes), and other delicacies including "Po'e" (boiled papaya) served with coconut milk.

Tahitian Girls

After the feast, the music and fires on the beach had attracted a number of Tahitian girls ready to put on a dance — which they did. It was fantastic. George, our guide, told that "before progress" the dancers would often dance all night — just for fun. "Tahitian girls love Polynesian dancing just as American boys love baseball." He said it must be inherent.

Sunday was as exciting as Saturday night. The group sailed across the reef to Kia Ora Village and Hotel on Moorea Island at the base of "Bali Hai." It is undoubtedly one of the most delightful places in the world. Here again there was a feast defying description beneath the shade of the Magic Mountain.

But the casual regard for clothing (rather unnecessary in this climate) was still apparent. There were no "his and hers" showers, just showers. And, for those bound to segregation by tradition, fright, or moral code, it was a quick trick to get a shower completed without exposure to the opposite sex.

The sun was not yet up when the morning call went out at 5 a.m. Monday. The "Iaorana" (welcome) was still there but civilization and schedules were calling. Goodbyes were said with some regret and the group took off again just as other early birds were getting up and going to work all over the world.

"The explorers" were now bound for New Zealand with much anticipation, but not without looking down and back at the Tahitian beach and surf and finally watching Bali Hai fade out of sight and back into the realm of memory and imagination.

New Zealand Not Famous, But It Will Steal a Traveler's Heart

It was a long way to work on Monday, September 12 — more than 4,000 miles of Pacific Ocean lie between Tahiti and New Zealand. Volcanic islands and atolls appear occasionally and jet vapor trails mark up an otherwise tranquil sky.

Besides, Monday was lost forever as the UTA (French) Airliner crossed the International Dateline en route to the very metropolitan Auckland on New Zealand's North Island.

As we had almost kept up with the sun, we arrived, after eight hours, only a little later than we had started. But, it was Tuesday, September 13 instead of Monday, September 12. This means jet-lag coupled with time-space confusion. We were hurried off at once to Best Wood Company.

Here Ernie Jelinek, managing director and a transplanted European, explained how he employed mostly Maoris and Samoans (Polynesian ancestry) successfully and how he insisted that English be the language of communication in the plant.

The next stop was the large Henderson and Pollard Plywood Plant right in the center of the city. At Pollard, Tony Coyte and others told us a great deal about the plywood industry in New Zealand as well as pertinent facts regarding general business conditions. Tony was an excellent resource person as he is chairman of the New Zealand Manufacturer's Association.

New Zealand is not a famous land, but it will steal a traveler's heart. Most foreign visitors know little about it and expectations fall far short of the realities encountered. It is agriculture-oriented and most Americans do find a bit of home here whether they are looking for green, green grass (as in Montana or Wisconsin) which they find in the temperate zone of the Central Region, or the warm climates (as in South Carolina or California) in the North, or Alpine Vistas (in the south).

The two main islands are positioned North and South. A person is always near the sea as the divided land mass varies generally from 100 to 200 miles in width.

The mainstream of the New Zealand population traces roots back to the U.K. It was an important British military outpost from 1850 until the early 20th century. There are only three million people in all of New Zealand and almost one million of them now live in Auckland.

Some of the greenest hills in the world support a sheep population of 57 million, almost twenty times as many sheep as people. It was Spring and lambing season "down under," and the little hills south of Auckland toward Rotorua were dotted with the white-wooled newborns. Near Rotorua, thermal springs rivaling Yellowstone greeted the visitors with columns of steam rising from multi-colored beds of hot lava.

At Rotorua one also finds the Kiwi Fruit (Chinese mulberries) named for New Zealand's famous Kiwi birds — large, nocturnal, flightless fowls, long extinct elsewhere.

The Maori people, Polynesian Islanders overrun by the Europeans about 1860, have preserved much of their identity, culture, and tradition. There is some conflict and tension, as a social-minded government tries to make amends for injustices dating back four generations.

The government has instituted land restitution and housing aid programs which are none too popular with many of the "work-ethic" New Zealanders who have to buy land and pay high prices for their housing.

The group attended a Maori Folk Show performance, illustrating native dances, songs, and culture. The Maori stick out their tongues and make strange noises as favorite means of expressing affection, hatred and other feelings. The plywood people went about for days after the show sticking out tongues, popping eyes and yelling at one another.

J. D. Prince of New Orleans and Harry Howell of Dothan, Ala., passed up the show after deciding that clean underwear was more to be desired than mere culture: The absent twosome located a vintage laundromat with a squeeze-type wringer (dryer rolls). J. D. operated the washing machine and fed the rolls while Harry was off-bearer for the production of the machine.

The boys took a number of refreshment breaks. However, Harry soon decided he was overworked and underpaid so he took unannounced, early retirement. Harry reported that J. D. fueled up and continued solo production until wife, Doris, returned from the culture show and alleviated the undried bottleneck of shorts, socks, and shirts which had been washed in the experimental alcohol-base detergent, "Howell's WOW," for hot or cold washings.

Frits de Fluiter, general manager of H.T. Plywood, LTD., gave us additional economic and forestry background, as did the management people at New Zealand Forest Products, LTD. While the exotic hardwoods were responsible for the establishment of the veneer and plywood industry in New Zealand, it now appears that a new structural plywood industry is emerging based on Radiata Pine, a North American specie similar to U.S. Southern Pine. The climate and soil permit a short commercial harvest cycle of about 30 years.

New Zealand plywood and veneer imports are strictly controlled because of trade deficits. However, veneer and plywood imports are at an 18 percent level while current exports of these materials are at about 9 percent.

At this point, it might be well to mention that the United States is about the only country permitting relatively free export of logs while placing some restrictions on plywood imports. Most other countries have plans requiring "value added" to the natural forest resource — native jobs and further processing into veneer or plywood before export.

Christchurch is New Zealand's second largest city and principal city of the Canterbury district. The Church of England carefully selected immigrants for the colonization of Canterbury and shipped them there with the purpose of establishing a colony which represented a cross section of English Society.

The settlement plan was successful — it is a typical English town, a garden city built around the Canterbury Cathedral. It is the home of the world-famed Canterbury Lamb and, not so incidentally, a supply base for some of the U.S. Navy's "Operation Deep Freeze" in Antarctica.

Duncan Blackmore of Dominion Products, LTD., made excellent business arrangements for the group in the Christchurch area and provided introductions to other New Zealand plywood people.

The "Southern Alps" around Queenstown, near the southern tip of New Zealand's south island, provided some of the most exciting experiences of the entire trip. None of us had expected to be taken to a skier's paradise, south of majestic Mt. Cook, and only a few hundred miles north of the Antarctic Circle.

Queenstown, established in the early 1900's during a gold rush, is a miniature St. Moritz, Aspen and Stowe all rolled into one. The scenery (snow-capped peaks, clear lakes and fjords) is breathtaking. It is sharp and cold, but exhilarating.

The morning after our Queenstown arrival, we taxied out to the little airport to find three small two-engine airplanes waiting to take us on a scenic flight over the "Southern Alps." One of the flights was destined for involvement in the "Milford Sound Expedition."

Our small airplanes probably had effective operating ceilings of around 10,000 feet and no oxygen. The mountain altitudes reached a couple thousand feet above this in some areas so we were flying around glaciers and peaks just as if we had good sense.

Most of us were perfectly content to enjoy the spectacular scenes of the Norwegian-type fjords below, but there was one planeload of adventurers who decided to be the lead plane and brave the hairy descent into the landing field at Milford Sound — a deep and beautiful fjord cutting back into the shore from the nearby Tasman Sea.

An unnamed native pilot, under the command of our own itinerant Captain James Huey (Wilson Machines, Inc. of Memphis), was ordered by captain and crew to undertake the risk of letting down in the crosswind to the very, very short and narrow air strip in the very, very deep valley. The remaining crew members included a mostly-mad Mildred Huey, the Louisiana Princess, Helen Livingston, the Alabama Howells — some folks are always where the trouble starts.

Huey claimed WW II flight experience; however, the rumor is that the closest he came to flight training was a Red Baron Link Trainer correspondence course by Captain Eddie and Snoopy.

Anyway, being the very senior officer, he directed the landing — a frozen stick trick; and they made it down as the native pilot radioed the other planes, "Don't dare try it." The crew was so shaken up by the crosswinds, up drafts, down drafts, "clear air turbulence" and just plain turbulence that they were speechless when asked whether they wanted to stay down or try to get out.

Since the choice was pretty much whether to freeze to death down there or try to climb up around the glaciers in a warm plane, they made the "up" decision. Out they came on wings of an up-wind. When all returned to

Queenstown, the survivors of the expedition were the whitest of all the whites in New Zealand.

From Queenstown it was back up to Christchurch and reality again. It was a nice land to visit, but there are problems there just as at home and abroad — the problems are much the same, the seriousness of the problems differ.

Amazingly the problems in many countries are being approached in the same manner as in the U.S. For example, New Zealand has an inflation rate of 17 percent. Credit restraint is being implemented which curtails housing and so on. The twin island country does, however, have much to offer.

It was time to board the plane in Christchurch and take off again. Always westward, chasing the sun, across the Tasman Sea — next stop, Australia.

Australia Is a Land of Contrasts and Unending Surprises

"There's the 'Roo Country!" "Catbird" Tom John, president of North Carolina's Hasty Plywood, made the announcement as the lights of Brisbane appeared on the portside of our 747, making an early evening approach from the South Pacific toward Australia's Gold Coast — Surfers' Paradise of the famous continent 'down under.'

It really is "Roo Country," and the fact was evidenced as soon as we "hit the street" in front of the airport. On that busy Saturday night many of the cars, and essentially all pick-up trucks, were equipped with "Kangaroo Catchers" — somewhat similar in design and purpose to the "Cow Catcher" device attached to the front of older railroad locomotives in the U.S.

Nearly one million of Australia's 14 million people live in Brisbane. Like much of Australia, Brisbane was established as a penal colony. It is a busy, beautiful metropolitan city with many of its famous people tracing roots back to the "founding prisoners" in 1824.

Most of the plywood group had looked forward to Australia as the high point of the trip — the place they most wanted to see. They were not disappointed. It is an interesting and unique land, the smallest, flattest and overall driest continent in the world. It is a land of contrasts, unending surprises, and fulfilled expectations for the first-time visitor.

A World of Travel

Harry Howell and Virginia Robertson demonstrate bravery by petting a kangaroo in the "Roo Zoo."

However, some of the illusions of independence which the group had held regarding Australia faded fast. Tom John and his charming wife Dibba, visited in the homes of two Australian MD's and confirmed that the trend toward "socialized medicine" was probably considerably advanced over the state of government health administration in the U.S.

Jack Koss and his lovely wife, Mary, of Capital Machines, Indianapolis, spent a day in the company of some business friends and they also found that the business community was feeling the pressure of many government regulations.

As the rest of the party also made business contacts in the plants, it became apparent through casual and formal conversation that Australia was no longer the Last Frontier of Independent Capitalism. Nonetheless, the many charms and attractions of the continent draw one to it like a magnet.

The Koala Bears, and other marsupials like the kangaroo, are still there and the cuddly little bears are just as sleepy and soft as you imagine from reading the Qantas ads.

The Forestry Commission of New South Wales, Sydney, Australia. From left, Tom John, Joe Robertson, Donald McCoy, Dr. Jim Gooch, Marcel Lafleur, Jack Koss, and Pierre Legeard.

The Lone Pine Sanctuary is essentially an open area, not a zoo, and it comprises acres and acres where the Koala Bears are not caged — just climbing and chewing away on the eucalyptus trees, and kangaroos, big and little, inside and out, are everywhere.

These marsupials carry their young in a pouch for about six months and like the platypus, emus and other "living fossils," survived on this island continent where they were protected from predators.

One finds it hard to believe that he may pick up a Koala Bear or pet a kangaroo at will but, as a matter of fact, it's hard to avoid the kangaroo in the sanctuary and many other similar places in Australia.

It was back to work on Monday morning, September 19 as the men motored out to a Brisbane suburb for an interesting mill tour at Hancock Brothers Pty. Ltd. The "Pty." means Proprietary, much the same implication as "Company" or "Co." in the U.S. and the "Ltd." means "Limited" or somewhat the same as "Incorporated."

Hancock Brothers is an old line Australian wood products company and we were particularly pleased to discuss their plywood operations with John Hancock, a principal and immediate past president of the Plywood Association of Australia — PAA.

Hancock related some of the problems confronting the Australian plywood industry. He cited inflation and balance of payment deficits as deterrents to economic progress in Australia. Although the Australian dollar has been devalued, it was still worth about $1.15 U.S.

We had been told that conditions were pretty much the same in New Zealand by the PANZ (Plywood Association of New Zealand) and the New Zealand dollar was worth about the same as the U.S. dollar at that time.

Australian interest rates for building were running bout 14 percent — these rates were blamed for much of the dramatic downturn in Australian housing, and Australian industry was also concerned about the high cost of Australian production which brought about increased imports from the cheaper labor countries such as Taiwan, Japan, and Korea.

Shortly after our visit, many of the countries we visited sent representatives to the Asian Plywood Conference in Kuala Lumpur, Malaysia, where the theme, "Asian Solidarity Through Plywood," suggests that more and more countries are taking lessons from oil-producing nations in attempting to obtain increased revenue from their resource marketings.

The Asian plywood people are, however, considering two possible responsibilities — obligations on the part of exporting interests — to (1) contribute to improved product utilization in the importing countries, and (2) increase efforts to avoid or alleviate the possible global shortage of suitable wood raw material, which they say may develop before the year 2000.

Austral Plywood was the next plant visited, and after that visit the group was treated to a very Australian reception and lunch at Merio's. The lunch, featuring exotic seafood appetizers, rack of lamb, Barr Mundi (fish) and other Australian specialities, was a "smashing success."

Phil Cameron, secretary of the PAA, was emcee for the friendly Aussie event. There was table talk of the big tuna hitting off The Great Barrier Reef and, in the warm glow of luncheon comraderie, one enthusiastic fisherman booked an immediate flight to the reef to "give it a go."

He rejoined the group at Sydney and reportedly caught three mackerel and a bad cold, but it was another great adventure. The "Reef McCoys" also journeyed out to The Great Barrier Reef, perhaps thinking they might find coral mermaids again as they had in Tahiti.

It was an hour's flight Monday night to Sydney — 500 miles "down south" to colder climate. The lights of the spectacular Sydney Harbor Bridge were easily visible from the air as was the urban sprawl of the 25 percent of Australia's people who live there.

The harbor itself is also very beautiful and less than a mile from the great bridge is the Sydney Opera House — undoubtedly the most expensive and elaborate opera house in the world, built at a cost of $102 million.

Tuesday morning, Ralph Symonds, Ltd. conducted a tour of its extensive building operations and manufacturing facilities for flat and large-mold curved plywoods. This mill is a pioneer in factory-constructed buildings, and the company has unusual capabilities such as making plywood panels fifty feet long and molding room roofs of plywood.

In the afternoon the group toured the facilities of the Forestry Commission of New South Wales. (Sydney is in New South Wales and Brisbane is in Queensland). Here Dr. Jim Gooch outlined the forest resources of Australia and the ongoing research at the station for developing better trees and improved forest management methods. Like New Zealand, the Australians have turned to our North American Radiatta Pine for the backbone of their forestry program. Of course, native rain forest veneers are still available and in demand.

Wednesday, September 21 was "Outback Day." (The mobility of this plywood group was unbelievable and the available resources almost unlimited — usually provided by local associated contacts). We flew several hundred miles west for breakfast. (Just as we had flown 500 miles on Monday night from Brisbane to Sydney for dinner).

Over the coastal ranges the country flattened into the plains-type country we expected. From our breakfast stop at Dubbo, we traveled west under the guidance of "Margaret," a young and attractive Australian housewife turned part-time tour guide. She seemed to know everybody and everything in "The Outback" — it was as exciting as the Old West must have been.

The Outback adventure was just one more example of the dedication and resourcefulness of our HPMA's managing director's wife, Mrs. Clark McDonald. Sylvia had done her homework well in working with Sue Lynn, the active and attractive young manager of Washington's Bliss Travel Agency.

While Sue looked after the many details, Sylvia was the personable and charming one, serving as leader, spokesman, hostess and complaint department depending on the requirement of the occasion.

Margaret led us westward and showed us the things we wanted to see. The birdwatchers had a field day, and for those with a quick eye (or in some cases, a vivid imagination) it was easy to spot the cockatoos, kangaroos and other unusual flora and fauna.

We stopped at a very nice home which belonged to one of Margaret's rancher friends. The ranch contained about 8,000 acres, farmed mostly by the owner and his son. A private airstrip was used in ranch management (probably essential for success) and a swimming pool and other niceties provided some of the pleasures usually found in the far-removed city.

The man talked to us, very much in the manner of a Kansas or Lawrence County [*Indiana*] Republican, explaining how the country was going downhill and the government "taking over." He gave us a dandy ranch tour. We watched his two sheep dogs (a sheep collie and a kelpie) move thousands of sheep more easily than most of us could drive a cow to the barn. He showed us his vast wheat lands and we did notice that while farm equipment in Australia was good and adequate and far above that found elsewhere, it was not comparable to U.S. equipment, at least in our opinion.

Petite Pierette Lafleur, wife of Victo Veneer's Marcel Lafleur, was especially enthralled with the work of the sheep dogs. All of the ladies admired

On their way to visit the Integrated Forest Products Pty., Ltd., plant, (left to right) Jim Huey, Harry and Beverly Howell, Mary Koss, Sylvia McDonald, Tom John, and Jack Koss pause at an overlook of the government buildings, Canberra, Australia.

A World of Travel

and held some of the very white newborn lambs which were present in profusion. The Australian lambs' wool lives up to its reputation for softness.

Of course, we were treated to an "Outback barbecue" with a genuine Aborigine cook and the food was delicious. This was followed by a boomerang throwing contest, also led by a genuine Aborigine boomerang thrower. Bruce Markel, the Brownstown, Ind., attorney, won this contest as his curved stick really did complete a wide arc and return right to him.

Pierre Legeard of Honduras was first runner-up. He didn't speak a word of English but his excitement broke all language barriers when his boomerang came sailing back home. I think mine ended up in a dry gulch somewhere short of Ayer's Rock (that's the world's largest monolith in mid-continent Australia).

After the boomerang barbecue, we inspected a large cattle auction yard. Cattle prices are depressed in Australia with the grade nearest "choice" (as near as I could make out) bringing about fourteen cents per pound from a 700-pound steer — usually grass-fattened, as little grain is fed.

Our Outback trip was called a "Jolly Swagman Tour" after the hobo character made famous in Australia's near-national anthem, "Waltzing Matilda." The story told in the song is very interesting and dear to the hearts of Australians.

Even the opera at Sydney was not comparable to "Outback." "Fra Diavolo" was the name of the comic opera which detailed the romantic exploits of a defrocked monk. The men generally attended under the prodding of wives but the decorative plywood walls throughout the enormous building did make it a thing of beauty.

Canberra, Australia's capital, is a new and planned city. Its design beauty and precision planning is probably the world's best. Although all the central city is designed to support the government structure of activities and building, there is industry on the outskirts and we had a nice tour of Integrated Forest Products Pty. Ltd., which was conducted by Terry Connolly, the plywood plant manager.

It was now time to leave Australia and the group was dividing at this point to take off toward different but equally exotic ports. The Johns, McCoys, Howells, and Helen Livingston (Southeastern U.S. contingent) were heading north to the Fiji Islands.

Would you believe that resourceful Sylvia McDonald had arranged with Denis Cullity of Westralian Plywoods Pty. Ltd. to carry the group by twin-engine plane to his Fiji Plywood Plant. Charming Mildred Huey of Memphis and hubby pilot James were flying to Japan. The rest of us were heading north by west over 3,000 miles of Australia, across the Rabbit Wall, and across 1500 miles of Indian Ocean to Jakarta and Bali.

All together we joined in a rousing chorus of "Tie Me Kangaroo Down, Mates," led by Harry Howell and Thomas John in their best "Suthren" Australian and sparked with a few "Vivas" by Pierre, Marcel and Pierrette.

Bali is Island of Mystery
Singapore is Beauty and Business

Bali is a mysterious island, truly a place far away and still living in an era of long ago. It is called the Isle of Ten Thousand Temples (or Shrines). Either the Balinese can't count or the number is figurative, for there are many more than ten thousand shrines.

Bali is separated from Java to the west by the Bali Straits. It is a small state of the very large Republic of Indonesia which, with a population of 140 million, is the fifth most populous country in the world.

Indonesia now supplies a large percentage of the hardwood logs for the world's plywood. We came to Bali after a 4,600-mile Qantas Flight across Australia and over the Indian Ocean.

The "Bali Hyatt," a natural name for a very comfortable Sheraton Hotel, was a masterpiece of Balinese decor and atmosphere. We were soon caught up in this tiny land which most of us had regarded as a misty myth of beautiful and diminutive women dancing their classic angular ballets to the unfamiliar chords of the native "gamalang" or orchestra.

It is no myth. The women are not only beautiful with China doll figures, olive complexions and Polynesian features but also are highly skilled in weaving silk and cotton and even cloth of silver and gold thread.

Bargaining on the idyllic beach was a delightful pastime. Most of us were easy prey for the winning smiles of the young boys and girls displaying their exotic cloths and wood carvings. The goods were very desirable and money was cheap (about 400 Rupiah for $1 U.S.), so we were willing buyers.

The sun, sand and surf were all as delightful as anticipated, and again many of us took to the outriggers for short sailing trips over the fantastic formations of coral.

Deyde (Da'dee), our native guide, was a super-salesman for Bali. He started his pitch even as we drove toward our hotel from Denpensar or DenPasar (spell as you wish — it's nearly impossible to translate Balinese names, words and meanings into English).

He toured us through the terraced rice fields where oxen and water buffalo pulled the plows through the paddies. He pointed out the intricate design and artistry embodied in many of the centuries-old public and family shrines and explained many of the customs and manners of these unusual people.

The superb stone carving craftsmanship reflected in Shrines of Bali are fascinating to all those interested in sculpture or art forms, but especially appealing to anyone familiar with the stone industry or cognizant of the talent, time and effort necessary to produce such outstanding carvings. Some family shrines undoubtedly represented work of several generations.

Also of special interest was Tampakspring. This twelfth-century mausoleum and holy spring had attracted multitudes of bathers, many of whom were nude, hoping to cleanse their bodies and spirits in the grotesquely-decorated public baths fed by overflow water from the holy springs which were reserved for priests. It was a Holy Day and a very festive occasion.

At this point Deyde showed us his teeth — which were filed straight and level across the front in the Hindu-Polynesian ritual at 13 years of age.

Everyone looks forward to seeing the Balinese dancers and, after a great native dinner including shark steak and other delicacies, we were off to the Rama Ballet, commonly called the Ketchak (Monkey Dance), with origins reaching back into ancient rituals.

It is a form of Trance Dance and all principal characters are performed by the elaborately-costumed girls dancing in the center of a circular chorus of young men. The men maintain a hypnotic chant "Ketchak-Ketchak-chak," which is said to actually put the actors into a trance. I will verify that the whole thing (as with much of Bali at night) is rather spooky (there are few lights to turn on anywhere).

The Monkey Dance draws heavily upon the Indian-Hindu epic poem, Ramayana. The story depicts the struggles of the divine prince, Rama (incarnation of a God), and his beautiful wife, Sita, against the giant,

Rawana, king of demons. Rawana lusts after Sita. An unscrupulous prime minister, disguised as a golden deer, lures Sita into being kidnapped. The kidnapping precipitates many battles during Rama's attempts to rescue Sita.

At one point, Rama is entrapped by a python-like snake but Rama calls on a great bird to kill the snake and free him. In the last act, the good monkey army defeats the demon army; Rama succeeds in killing Rawana (at least temporarily) and returns happily to his kingdom with his wife.

After the Monkey Dance, we were privileged to meet and exchange greetings with the very attractive dramatic dancers. The girls who had been heavily made up and costumed, looked quite different in their western dress and they seemed pleased to meet those of us who had come to see this performance in the village temple. However, all communication was limited to sign language.

On Sunday, this time during the daylight, we attended another dance performance based on the ancient but still prevailing religious beliefs of Bali. The Barong Dance is the old story of eternal conflict between good and evil. The Barong is the mythical creature representing good while Rangda, queen of the witches, represents evil.

The principal dance, performed by the two girl stars, is called The Legong. During the play, the Good Queen's son is scheduled for sacrifice, but the prince is made immortal and immune to the powers of The Black Witch. Agile dancers, costumed as dragons, witches, snakes, wild boars and great birds appear on stage from time to time.

In the finale, the forces of good and the forces of evil engage in a great battle. There is no victor as the Balinese believe generally that good and evil must co-exist. At the end of the performance, the temple's priest sprinkles the dancers with holy water to end their state of trance.

Sunday night some of us discovered there was still strong belief in the power of evil, or what would be elsewhere called Black Magic and Voodoo.

We attended a very small church service held by two Christian missionaries — a native Balinese minister and his white wife, Joye, from New Zealand. Both were well-educated with traditional western theological background.

However, the Rev. Rus Alit testified to his belief that the Devil was very definitely walking to and fro upon that island and contesting Christian advances at every step. The preacher firmly believed that deaths of his brothers had been caused, at least indirectly, by acts of demons — men or spirits — and that one of his sisters had been hexed into at least temporary insanity.

To keep perspective, however, one must consider that in the anti-communist Indonesian massacres of the sixties probably more than a half million people were killed. The Indonesian government is considered on "our side" and is the largest single recipient of World Bank Aid.

President Suharto heads the country and the Golkar Coalition Party as he has "wahju," or the reflection of heaven's light which shines on a ruler. Suharto will undoubtedly be re-elected because of wide belief in this almost occult political structure.

Suharto has done many things for the republic, but a possible mystic opponent, Sawito, has supposedly had "visions" indicating he should be crowned "just ruler." These visions are taken seriously in Indonesia where ancient myths are regarded with much more respect and credibility than anything from modern civilization.

In a society and government born of recent violence (even if in just cause) one must make careful judgments of motivations and objectives. Our guide had told us that Hindu, Christian and Moslem exist side by side in harmony on Bali. That may be true by day, but by night it is probable that most of Indonesia is predominantly Moslem, that Bali is predominantly Hindu (with Polynesia modification), and that Christian natives have some special trials and tribulations.

These attitudes must also be remembered by those doing business in Indonesia — where there are fantastic resources already entering and ready to enter world trade. Indonesia is a very present factor in world politics. Bali fairly represents the mystery of that factor.

Singapore

The Singapore story begins before antiquity and continues with modern programs extending into the twenty-first century. After Bali, we had stopped for a brief stay in Jakarta, capital city of Indonesia, and continued on to the "The Island Marco Polo Missed" — now both a city and country located just across the narrow straits from the southern tip of Malaysia.

There are six million people in Singapore's 226 square miles, making it one of the most densely populated cities, and yet it is possibly the cleanest. The population is predominately Chinese with some Malays, some Indians and a few Englishmen left over from colonial times.

It is amazing that it has no natural resources — it thrives on trade, a cross-roads where East meets West and ships transfer cargoes and pass in the world's fourth largest port.

We had visited plants here in 1973 but changes were unbelievable. One can still find Chinatown, but the city is mostly like a New York-London combination and not like a typical Chinese city. Chinese food there is perhaps the best in the world — we were treated to a twelve-course Chinese meal in the Shangri-La Hotel (Beautiful Place) and it was extremely enjoyable — chopsticks notwithstanding.

Fortunately, the Raffles Hotel still stands — standing, in the words of Somerset Maugham, "for all the fables of the exotic East." Kipling, Coward and many others wrote often of Raffles and travelers stop here as a "must." We stopped to look over the famous Long Bar (where a tiger was once shot under a table) and sip a "Singapore Sling" at the place of its creation.

Sylvia McDonald, in her usual efficient manner, had scheduled our brief stay in Singapore to include not only most of the major points of interest (such as the fantastic Handicraft Center — showcase of Asian's Arts and Crafts — and the Tiger Balm Gardens), but also visits to most of the important veneer and plywood mills there.

Our chic Chinese guide was a young women of 21 — a Taoist (mixture of Hindu and Buddhist), very sharp and very pretty — a "liberated woman" in this place where only a few years ago women were seen occasionally and seldom heard.

She took us first to Starlight Timber Co., where another young lady, Esther Ng, escorted us on an interesting plant tour. Ron Lee, executive director of Southern Wood Products, showed us this efficient plant where several kinds of plywood, including "kitchen cabinet stock," were being manufactured.

The capacity of this plant is rated at 800,000 4' x 8' sheets monthly, four mm thickness basis, of plywood and blockboard. We understand wages at most Singapore plants to be about $1 Singapore per hour, equal to 40 cents U.S. per hour. Jurong Plywood, a Boise Cascade associate company, was especially educational due to an "American type" understanding between our hosts and ourselves. The plant was impressive and

A beautiful Chinese hostess is shown in the renowned writer's Long Bar of the Raffles Hotel in Singapore. Here is where Somerset Maugham met and sipped the famous "Singapore Sling," and where a tiger, real or ima-GIN-ed, was discovered underneath a billiard table.

Carlito Zaragoza, production manager, gave us new insights on Oriental manufacturing trends and attitudes.

At International Wood Products, Shen Ting conducted our tour, where we obtained perhaps more than the usual information on current oriental wood-gluing technology — my particular interest. As a note in passing, here we met Vic Kaplan and Mike Jennings of Champion Building products. Our J.D. Prince had run across these fellows earlier in the Bali Hyatt. "It's a small world."

At Bork Singapore Private Limited, we were treated in a most hospitable manner by Neil Rombaut and Freddie Clark. Here we witnessed production of some of the world's most beautiful, most wanted exotic veneers — Teak from Burma, Red Meranti from Indonesia, Ebony, African Mahogany and East Indian Rosewood.

And Jack Koss, president of Capital Machines, Indianapolis, was all smiles as we paused and posed beside the 225-inch Capital Veneer Slicer (largest in the world), which his company had recently installed there.

Time was pressing and we needed to press on northward to the jungles of the Malaysian Peninsula.

Touring a Real Sultan's Palace in Malaysia Can Be Interesting

Malaysia — Thailand

Ten thousand miles southwest of California there is a jungle book road. It is 200 miles long and follows a former jungle trail from Singapore to Kuala Lumpur.

This highway has been carved through the heart of the almost impenetrable rain forest of the Malay Peninsula along the western shore lapped by the Bay of Bengal and the eastern beach kissed by the surf of the Gulf of Siam. There are still man-eating Bengal tigers and mammoth elephants just a few miles back in the bush.

Our group of adventurers explored only 40 miles of this tenuous concrete ribbon, but that was enough to expose us to sights and experiences previously found only in story books, imaginations and dreams.

Who hasn't dreamed of visiting in a real Sultan's palace with a real live prince? Well, it happened to us, without announcement or anticipation.

On the very southern tip of the Malay Peninsula our plywood people had just been introduced to some of the directors of the Mados-Citoh-Daiken Plywood Company. His Highness, Raja Muda (for short), was present, we thought appearing only momentarily as a courtesy.

After the formal introductions and exchanges of card and greetings, "The Logging Prince," out of the blue, asked, "Would you like to visit the Sultan's palace?" Most of us were dumbfounded but not Susie Markel of Brownstown, Indiana, or Pierrette Lafleur of Victoriaville, Canada. These vivacious thrill seekers fairly shrieked, "Yes" and "Oui" respectively and immediately.

The palace was as fabulous as one might imagine. It was the official residence of the Sultan of Jahore and the recently-deceased Sultana. The Moslem period of mourning was still being observed. Shoes were respectfully deposited at the entrance and the prince escorted us through the great halls, dining areas and living quarters for the residents and guests of state.

Treasures beyond belief were shown to us with a casual and gracious hospitality — place settings for hundreds in silver and gold, crown jewels and ancient court costumes bedecked with precious jewels to see and touch. It is an understatement to say that we were awed. As we departed we noticed a rainbow in the bright sky which followed a short monsoon shower — we must have been at its end.

We were not, however, at the northern extremity of the road. After seeing only a few miles at the southern end, we flew north the 200 miles to Kuala Lumpur, the surprisingly modern, bustling capital of Malaysia.

Here is a great center of almost three million Malays, Indians, and Chinese. We were quartered in one of the most luxurious hotels in the world — the Kuala Lumpur (K.L.) Hilton. Entertainment and cuisine were native or sophisticated as desired.

Just a few days after our arrival, this elaborate hostelry hosted the 5th annual conference of Asian Plywood Manufacturers and we were pleased to meet several of the early-arriving delegates. During the roof restaurant floor show, one of our party, Don McCoy, Jr. of New York, was "discovered" by the performers.

Don, a handsome young world traveler, has a cultivated and pleasant speaking voice. One of the featured starlets called Don from the front row spectator tables to join her on stage. He obviously "stole the show" and the starlet's adoration.

In Kuala Lumpur we visited the Malaya Plywood and Veneer Factory and then were guided about 30 miles down "that road" where the important tin mines, rubber tree plantations and palm nut plantations separate the road from the untamed jungle.

Here we saw jungle timbers processed completely from the elephant-handled logs into beautiful plywood, packed, marked and ready for shipment to the docks at New Orleans.

The Chinese management entertained us with a delightful luncheon at a nearby club restaurant where food was "unusual" and the Malaysian hostess-waitresses anxious to serve our every whim — our wives were, of course, the only women customers or guests in the club.

J. D. Prince insisted that his wife, Doris, and this reporter demonstrate some American dances for our host — we complied, reluctantly of course, and all at least feigned enjoyment.

Our Indian guide took us to the Sin-Salvation Steps at the Batu Caves. Here sin-laden Hindus (Indian) may enter an emotion-controlled state as they proceed up the 372 steps enduring hooks in their chests without blood flow and needles or small knives through cheek or neck flesh without blood.

The previously "bad" Indians are then changed through priestly controlled rites into a Hindu sinless condition. We climbed the steep steps, surrounded by monkeys, to get a better idea of the ritual. We asked our guide when he intended to make the climb. He replied, "I'm a GOOD Indian."

The Malaysian minister of agriculture was reportedly killed in the December terrorist-caused plane crash near K.L. Malaysia (actually only about 15 miles from the Sultan's palace in Jahore Bahru). He was associated with an ambitious agricultural recovery plan based on the emerging palm nut plantations — the palm nut trees had been planted in profusion. This plan is "guaranteed" to yield Malaysian farmers 1,500 Malaysian dollars per month (about 500 American dollars) for their ten-acre plots. We could follow the economics of the plan but are doubtful that the project will turn out as well as anticipated. It is a world oil market factor, however, and one for soybean farmers to watch. These palm nut trees will yield much more oil per acre than soybeans and we have seen millions of these young trees in Asia and Africa.

Most Americans give little thought to Malaysia, but we might do well to remember that Japanese occupation of this land in WWII put tin on the critical metal list and brought about tire rationing in the U.S. — resulting in the growth of the synthetic rubber industry.

It is a different land of friendly, apparently happy and beautiful people. By our standards, their morals are extremely loose, but they follow natural inclinations easily and entertain gracefully with total dedication to pleasing the guests.

Thailand

Thailand and Bangkok, are much better known to Americans than Malaysia and Kuala Lumpur. Bangkok is often on the Hong Kong-Singapore-Bangkok tourist route, but this doesn't lessen its attraction. This, after all, is the locale and land of "Anna and The King of Siam," and the fact is that both are even stranger and more interesting than the fiction.

Although there are many modern buildings in Bangkok and the streets are clogged with motorized traffic, there are 300 "wats" (monasteries or temples) which surpass the expectation of all who enter here.

While buses, multi-rider motorcycles and cars clutter Bangkok streets, the waterways give one ready access to the pulse of the city. The Royal Temple, The Floating Market and a thousand other sights line the rivers and canals which carry the lifeblood of the city.

Beside the great "wats" or temples, the small ornate "spirit houses" seem to be everywhere. The spirits dwelling therein must be pleased with the floral wreaths and other appropriate offerings left there by the "true believers."

Monks are "in" in Bangkok and probably have been forever. As best we could determine, the monk fraternity had few formal entrance requirements. There appeared to be no clergical hierarchy and the monk tenure was extremely variable. One may be a monk if he decides that he should "serve" for a period (one day, one week, one month, or years), depending on his sins or his need to do something better.

One shaves the head, dons the white or orange robe (don't know the color code), and starts walking with his empty rice bowl ready to receive contributions from those inclined to give without solicitation.

The Temple of the Emerald Buddha is beyond even an imaginary vision of a legendary temple — magnificent architecture, elaborate sculpture, sky-reaching edifices and mysterious statuary.

Classical temple dancers are, of course, possibly the most famous feature of Bangkok, and rightfully so. The charming dancers dance and act as billed. Unlike the monks, they are pleased to pose and demonstrate their terpsichorean grace and skill on request.

We were lavishly entertained in Bangkok by Bunlue Yontrarak, president of Bangkok Veneer Company. Bunlue was associated with many

Following the Bangkok Veneer plant visit, hosted by U.S.-educated Bunlue Yontrarak, many of the HPMA study tour group were taken on a city river trip which included stops at several Thailand temples. The group included (left to right) Mary Koss; Don McCoy, Jr., Hasty Plywood; Sylvia McDonald, HPMA; Jack Koss, Capital Machine, Indianapolis; Virginia and Joe E. Robertson, Susie and Bruce Markel, all of Brownstown; Marcel Lafleur, Victo Veneers, Canada; J. D. Prince, Plywood and Panels, Inc.; Pierette Lafleur and Doris Prince, New Orleans.

A World of Travel 217

Our HPMA group (in front row) was met by members of the Federation of Indian Plywood and Panel Industry (FIPPI) delegates at the New Delhi Airport. Back row, left to right: Shri K. S. Lauly, Indian Plywood Mfg., Company, Ltd.; Shri K. S. Nair, Executive Director FIPPI; Shri Narendra Vithaldas, Indian Plywood Mfg. Company, Ltd.; Shri M. K. Saharia, M/s Assam Forest Products Ltd.; Shri B. N. Kapur, Pres./Mng. Dir., M/s Crossley & Towers and President of FIPPI; Shri B. K. Khaitan, M/s Andamans Timber Ind. Ltd.; Mrs. T. K. (Sally) Jacob; Shri M. M. Jalan, M/s Assam Saw Mills & Timber Company, Ltd.; Shri A. S. Vagh, M/s Hunsur Plywood Works; and Shri T. K. Jacob, M/s Veneer & Laminations (India) Ltd.

other family enterprises in Thailand. On meeting Bunlue, we knew immediately he was American-educated. He had learned his American-type English at Warren Wilson Presbyterian College in North Carolina.

It was most interesting to notice a "Spirit House" on the premises of Bangkok Veneer. Bunlue was Presbyterian but, insofar as the talented Thai workers were concerned, the goodwill of the spirits was more important than OSHA [*Occupational Safety and Health Administration*] regulations in assuring the safety program of the plant.

Our American press has reported a coup and political change in Thailand since our departure. Our American friends had assured us, however, that whoever holds the power in Thailand must first hold the hand of the King of Siam. Thailand traditionally has been friendly and helpful to the United States but Communist infiltration and influence is an ever-present threat from east and south-bordering Laos and Cambodia — only a short distance from Vietnam.

World politics and power have been linked to rivers of this country for many years — "The Bridge on The River Kwai" [*of movie fame*] is only a short distance from Bangkok and the Mekong rises in Thailand to cut southeasterly through the wooded mountains to the rice-rich delta near Saigon.

It was time to leave the problems and pleasures of this fabled land and fly "The Hump" over Burma into India.

A Person Can't Appreciate the Taj Mahal Until He Sees It

India

The flight into India was another long one covering more than 3,000 miles. We headed higher and northwest toward Shangi-La land.

The winding Burma Road, combat area of The Flying Tigers during WWII, zigzagged below as we moved above "The Hump" a few hundred miles to the north and the greatest of mountains, Mt. Everest.

This sky was one of many proving grounds for the men and machines of the U.S.A.A.F. during the forties. Fortunately for the U.S., the flyboys, the lumbering B-17's, 24's, 25's, and 26's and the shark-nosed P-40's and fast 38's and 43's passed the tests. Soon we were through the clouds of the past and had started our descent into Delhi, where we landed in darkness.

On our arrival into Delhi Airport, we were most plesantly surprised when we were met by a sizeable delegation of top executives from India's Plywood Industry. Some of these executives, from the farthest parts of India including Bombay, Calcutta and the Andaman Islands, had traveled as much as 3,000 miles and expended a great deal of time, effort and money to meet with our group representing U.S. plywood interests.

The next morning, in an atmosphere resembling a U.N. meeting — beautiful, large round wood tables with individual lighted microphones — we had a very informative and productive meeting with these men from the Federation of Indian Plywood and Panel Industry [*FIPPI*].

Mr. B.N. Kapur, president of the Indian Federation, addressed our assembly and contrasted the difference between the cheap labor-intensive technology of developing nations and the capital-intensive mass-production technology of the U.S. He suggested that a combination of the two technologies had tremendous potential for application in the timber-producing countries of the Third World.

All of the members of the Indian Federation and their wives were extremely hospitable and helpful in enlightening us regarding India. The sights of Old Delhi were especially intriguing with well-preserved antiquities illustrating Hindu and other Indian lifestyles reaching back 2,000 years.

Delhi, over the last twelve centuries, has served as the capital. The Qutb Minar stands in Old Delhi, perhaps a 13th century Victory monument, but perhaps another "Tower of Babel" attempt failing as another incomplete tower nearby, to reach the clouds but leaving gems of history in its ornate carvings reaching ever toward the heavens.

It was in and around Old Delhi where we could easily identify "The Untouchables." Of course, "Untouchables" are no longer officially recognized in democratic India, but the Caste System, practiced for centuries in this Hindu-dominated land, is not dead — legislation has banned and altered much of it and its recognition, but much of "the system" remains.

Although the lines of order and definition in the Caste System are muddled today, the Castes include the Brahmans (originally priests), The Kshatriyas (government or military), The Vaisyas (merchants), and the Sudras (working class) who make up 50 per cent of India's 620 million people. Then there are the Harijans, "The Untouchables," the "Children of God" who do the "unclean" jobs including removing the many

Between China and Nepal, the study group stopped for a visit at India's fabulous Taj Mahal, at Agra.

HPMA members pause beneath the Acropolis. From left to right, Joe E. Robertson, Bruce Markel, Susie Markel, Virginia Robertson, and Doris Prince, stop for a "breather" on the ascent to some of the ruins that were the "Glory that was Greece" during the Athens visit.

dead cows, tanning hides, and doing menial tasks considered beneath the dignity of many Caste Indians.

The Taj Mahal at Agra is The Jewel of India — truly a world wonder. It has been said accurately that one does not know whether to call it architecture or a gem. It is a peerless marble mausoleum built by a Mogul emperor, Shah Jahan, for one of his wives, Mumtaz, in the 17th Century.

A total of 20,000 workers labored for 22 years at building this elaborate tomb. The monument is all the more remarkable when one considers that the Shah was a Moslem and had many wives.

Most people know about the Taj, but one cannot really appreciate its beauty until he sees it. Of course, everyone takes pictures, and it is no time to be out of film — but I was. This at first seemed catastrophic and I had a cab driver cruising all through Agra in the early morning of a holiday looking for film. We ended up finding it in Agra's "New India Hotel."

It wasn't a Hilton, but it was interesting. Rooms were about 20 Rupees as best I could determine. A Rupee is about 11 cents. The only roll of film available, however, was priced at $15. That is more than many Harijans earn in one month, but I needed the film and bought it. Currency values do fluctuate these days.

Madame Gandhi was speaking at Agra while we were there and there were crowds to hear her. She was arrested that night. When we asked about the details, our guide said it was "something like Watergate and CREEP — a misuse of election funds." [*CREEP is an acronym for "Committee to Re-Elect the President.*]

However, we made no attempt to probe the imponderable politics of India — dealing with poverty in numbers and degrees beyond our comprehension. But, make no mistake, India is highly interesting and has much to offer the tourist or business visitor.

As we left the new Delhi Airport, we were fortunate to see another amazing occurrence. There he was — a real Guru, white robes, turban and all, with a dozen attractive young girls rushing and kneeling for the privilege of kissing his feet.

Greece

Greece is much better known to tourists than some of the other countries visited by the plywood group, but its charm and history have a great deal of attraction for all those who have interest in "The Glory that was Greece."

Cosmopolitan Athens is worth seeing, but the Acropolis overlooking Athens, the Parthenon and other ruins remaining from the times of Plato, Aristotle, and Socrates are most stimulating.

We visited three veneer plants in Athens where we found veneers of outstanding quality. Marcel Lafleur of Victo Veneers, Canada, a highly competent judge of veneer quality, was greatly impressed with the beauty of these veneers — some of which were being sold to our U.S. furniture factories for their finest pieces.

Pierre Legeard, the French plywood manufacturer from Honduras, was now getting to say something. Several of the Greeks were perhaps more fluent in French than English. India spoke English, although much less than before independence, and this same language situation prevailed in Singapore. At the other Asian countries, translation was required from native tongue to English — French was not usually in the translation.

The Greek port of Piraeus is not only scenic but also famous — the setting for [*the movie*] "Never on Sunday." It was Wednesday night when we were there but the calendar rules must still apply, for our mini-coach driver pulled a vanishing act while we stepped into a sidewalk cafe. We searched the area streets and taverns in vain — the driver showed up about 30 minutes later with no explanation.

The rest of the evening was spent in the picturesque night spots in Piraeus and the Plaka District beneath the Acropolis. Classical Greek folk dancing and an unexcelled "belly dancing" exhibition made for great entertainment.

Cruising the Greek Islands is an adventure in enjoyable relaxation. The Aegean is blue and the serenity is soothing. As one departs from Piraeus, a look to the west conjures up visions of the Phoenicians sailing their A.D. 50 vessels toward the Isthmus, now the canal at Corinth.

Although we were not on a "Paul's Journeys Cruise," Biblical history comes to life here just as it did when we looked down from the Acropolis toward Mars Hill and could almost hear Ol' Paul starting his "'Ye men of Athens' Sermon of The Unknown God."

As one sails the Aegean, with his eyes closed or open, a thousand sights stimulate the mind. Ten thousand fleets have swept by this center stage of

The sightseeing was pleasurable. Sylvia McDonald (left) and Virginia Robertson, followed by Pierette and Marcel Lafleur, tour the waterfront at Hydra, Greece.

history, and countless vessels have carried famous figures from one port of action to another.

Ulysses sailed by here . . . these islands were the playgrounds of the Gods — Poseidon, Aphrodite, Apollo and others frolicked and schemed in these bewitching islands. Hydra beckons one to step into the past and stay awhile. No automobiles, only donkeys or Shank's pony for moving along the harbor front or up the cobblestone walks.

Poros and Aegina were equally interesting and the cruising time in between was very pleasant with time for meeting interesting people from all over the world. For example, one attractive young couple from Iran — ancient Persia — but that's a story for another time. One leaves the Greek Islands reluctantly.

Paris and Home

Paris is, of course, one of the most popular tourist spots. Millions of U.S. visitors go to France every year to see the sights.

We came from Greece on Olympia Airlines (the one Onassis owned) and sailed right over the Eiffel Tower into the near-town Orly Airport, then through "The Streets of Paris" to our Paris Intercontinental. The streets were jammed here too.

We had an unforgettable evening on the Seine. We had a birthday party for Virginia (Robertson) on "Bateaux Mouches," a night-time river cruise on a delightful boat, with a superb French meal and the dazzling attractions of Paris, brightly illuminated on both the Right and Left Banks for our advantageous viewing from the famous river.

Twenty bridges were passed and the history of 2,000 years unveiled — Concord Bridge (stones from the Bastile), The Latin Quarter on the Left Bank and so many other places but particularly, the grand dame of all Cathedrals, Notre Dame.

Pierre Legeard was now in his home town and how he added to the party with his finger-snapping and "garcon" calls to the waiters who were attired in tuxedoes and French sailor uniforms. Lobster, steak, champagne and all kinds of wines were available for those who cared, as was Baked Alaska, ad infinitum.

Other night-time visits included, of course, Place Pigale, still as raw and brazen as ever, Moulin Rouge, and exquisite cuisine at incomparable

The Eiffel Tower was the last stop before Virginia's birthday party in Paris.

A World of Travel 227

The "FINALE" . . . Virgie Robertson's memorable birthday celebration aboard the *Bateaux Mouches* on the Seine River in Paris.

French restaurants. The daytime tours were outstanding too. We sat in the sidewalk cafes along the Champs Élysées — here one is either the "watcher" or the "watchee" in this favorite Parisian pastime.

Other points of interest included Arc de Triomphe, and the storehouse of art treasures at The Louvre, and "Mona Lisa" . . . later a half day at sad and beautiful Versailles.

It was time to leave here, too. At noon Sunday, October 9, we departed Paris on TWA No. 803 and arrived in New York only a couple of hours later EST. In 35 days we had circled the globe, and made a great many business and cultural contacts in many strange lands.

Perhaps two observations are most outstanding: (1) Despite all our problems, we all prefer "home", and (2) the world is a big place — we saw only a small part of it and hope to see more.

Chapter 8

Latin America and the Galapagos, 1987

*T*HIS ACCOUNT OF OUR Latin American travels was written by Sylvia McDonald, president of Clark E. McDonald Enterprises of McLean, Virginia. Sylvia is the super-resourceful international travel expert who arranged our itineraries to far-away places and exotic destinations on the world's roads less traveled. Clark was a long-time president of the International Hardwood Plywood Manufacturers Association and a U.S. Army Air Forces Major during World War II with a Harvard MBA, and was thoroughly familiar with the "Kilroy complex" throughout the world. Sylvia had been raised in the Banana Republics and Sugar Supply Stations of Central America and followed and led her family, friends, and associates through the Customs houses and cultures of many nations. Her linguistic skills were considerable. She, too, knew the implications and importance of "Kilroy's" accomplishments and their contribution to the making and maintenance of today's global community.

(In 1996, I again visited Ecuador to initiate the exporting and licensing of Robertson Products there.)

We arrived in Quito, Ecuador in the late afternoon of April 26, 1987, and saw a little of the city on the way to the Hotel Colon. Quito, the capital of Ecuador, is a lovely city carved by two ravines; the oldest of all South American capitals, it preserves much of its ancient atmosphere. Quito was already an ancient city when Spaniards arrived in the 16th century; before their arrival, it was an Incan empire; and prior to that time, it was inhabited by other Indian tribal confederations.

Monday morning, we left the hotel around 8:30 a.m. to visit Plywood Ecuatoriana, S.A. We were met by its president Señor Pedro Alvarez. A graduate of Notre Dame with an M.B.A. degree from Columbia University, Alvarez has also served as president of AIMA (Wood Industries Association of Ecuador). Plywood Ecuatoriana was established in 1963 and was the first plywood manufacturer in Ecuador. They produce 50 percent of all Ecuadorian plywood, and export much of their product to Mexico, Peru, Venezuela, and the United States. A sister company, "Codesa," is also involved in the plywood and particleboard business.

We left Plywood Ecuatoriana to visit Novopan Del Ecuador, S.A., a particleboard mill established in 1979, and operated by Señor Cesar Alvarez, brother of Pedro. Cesar is also American educated, having a B.S. from Notre Dame and an M.B.A. from Harvard.

Our tour included one more plywood mill, Endesa, whose products are used in the building industry and in the manufacture of furniture, wall panelings, cabinets, and architectural decoration.

The Galapagos Islands

The Galapagos is an archipelago in the Pacific composed of 13 major islands, 6 smaller ones, and more than 40 islets and rocks, approximately 600 nautical miles from the coast of Ecuador. The marine currents, including "El Nino," are an important element in the habitat of the Galapagos; together with the volcanic and the geographical isolation of the archipelago, they are the reason for the natural and unique conditions which characterize these islands.

History has documented the official discovery of the "islands lost in time" as March 10, 1535, by the Bishop of Panama. The islands were visited by others over the years — Spaniards, pirates, British and American whalers, Ecuadorians, but it was not until September 1835 that an important visitor arrived, the English naturalist Charles Darwin. He visited the islands for five weeks, and 24 years later, he presented to the world an authentic time bomb, "The Origin of the Species." This was the treatise that spawned The Scopes Monkey Trial and the acceptance of [*the theory of*] evolution as told in the movie *Inherit the Wind*.

Our Tame Airlines flight was late in arriving in Quito, and consequently late in departing to Guayaquil where we were to make connections to the island of Baltra in the Galapagos. It was raining when we arrived in Guayaquil and everyone was directed to the plane waiting on the runway. Armed with vouchers for the group, my instructions were to find our guide in transit for our "chartered flight." We finally located our "lady in white," and made — not an envisioned six-passenger plane — but the Tame plane that was rapidly filling up.

After arriving on Baltra (Galapagos) and being bused to the pier, we paid a park tax of U.S. $40 each and were taken to our ship, the *Buccaneer*, in a metal, diesel-powered boat, called a "panga," which was capable of carrying 25 passengers.

We had lunch on the ship shortly after arriving, and made our first shore excursion that afternoon to Playa Ochoa and saw our first frigate birds, sea lions, and blue-footed boobies.

We cruised during the night and after a 6:45 a.m. wake-up call, and 7:15 a.m. breakfast call, we were ready at 8:00 a.m. (no bells) for a wet landing excursion to Punta Suarez (Espaniola) on Hood Island. Each island seems to have several names. We saw mocking birds, uncommon red and green-trimmed marine iguanas, and colonies of blue-footed boobies and masked boobies.

We returned to the ship at 11:30 a.m., had lunch and rested, read, and enjoyed the island view from the ship until our 3:30 p.m. departure for our excursion to Point Cormorant, Floreana Island, where we saw pink flamingoes in a pink lagoon! The water was pink because of the tiny shrimp upon which the flamingos feast.

Recalling Samuel T. Coleridge's "The Rime of the Ancient Mariner" made seeing an actual albatross, many of them, one of the most exciting experiences I had on the trip. I thought it a most beautiful bird, and not at all as I had imagined an albatross to be from the poem. The albatross nearest to us walked even closer to take a look and then returned to where it had been originally.

The most amazing experience on the islands is that nothing — bird, fowl, or animal — displayed any fear whatsoever. We looked at them — they looked at us!

The next morning we had a pier landing at Puerto Ayora where we visited the Charles Darwin Research Station. Here we had a chance to read more about Darwin, and to see the giant tortoise. After lunch and a rest break, we visited South Plaza Island and were once more enchanted with the sea lions, Darwin finches, land iguanas, Sally light-foot crabs, petrels, and other unique flora and fauna.

Our last morning, Friday, May 1, was an early morning visit to North Seymour to enjoy the blue-footed boobies, swallow-tailed gulls, sea lions, lava gulls, land iguanas, and the varied vegetation.

It was here where "Honey" Howell Taylor and Joe Robertson were challenged to "Swim With The Sharks," by using dolphins for protection, and play with the seals. As we pulled into the island, we were excitedly watching alternately large schools of fish, then sharks, and then dolphins, always in that order. What a sight! On coming closer to the rock walls of the island's bay, the great calls of the large bull seals were rather fearsome. We could see them as they rested threateningly on the rocks watching their mates who, in turn, were watching the playful young frolicking in the foam-filled waves of the bay. The bay was literally filled with the mothers and young seals. Our guide encouraged us to jump in the water and play with the seals.

"Yeah," Joe said, "and I'm going to jump over the moon! Didn't you see those sharks out there?"

The guide replied, "You do not need to worry about the sharks. The dolphins will protect you."

"After you," Joe said.

At that point, the guide jumped in and played with the young seals. Joe was still reluctant to jump in. Honey (much younger than Joe) soon jumped in, and he thought "If she can do it, so can I!" So he jumped in and sure enough, soon the little 50 lb. to 100 lb. baby seals came up to be hugged and petted. It was a great experience! After this rare moment, we were ready to disembark and transfer by panga to the pier, and then by "endemic" bus to the airport to board our return flight to Guayaquil.

At this point, we discovered that the U.S. had built a submarine fueling station even at this remote outpost during WWII and an airfield to supply it. Undoubtedly, the script was on the sub stall walls: "Kilroy was here."

The M/N *Bucanero*

The M/N *Bucanero*, or *Buccaneer*, is no "Love Boat," but it is listed as the largest ship cruising the Galapagos; powered by twin diesel engines, 285-feet long and 2,244 tons displacement. This last measurement didn't mean anything to me, but I assume it probably did to some of the men on the cruise.

The *Buccaneer* contained superior and average rooms; a nice dining room in the bow of the ship; a boutique where one could purchase cosmetics, toiletries, film, wearing apparel, and books on what we were going to see on land; and a bar/lounge. There also was on the deck a small, but adequate pool that was filled daily with sea water.

Our room contained a double bed and private bath. The shower was tiny, with lukewarm water. The toilet flushed, but our instructions were to place toilet tissue in a pail that was provided. We were furnished one towel each, which might have been adequate — except for the wet landings.

As no fresh water is available in the Galapagos, we were asked to conserve water whenever possible. The drinking water on board was boiled and kept hot in an electric urn (coffee maker) in the *Caleta Bucanero* Bar and poured over ice cubes that were made from boiled water.

Trash disposal is extremely important, and we were alerted to not throw plastic baggies away. The turtles see the plastic in the water, eat it thinking it is jelly fish, and die. We saw the remains of one that had worked its way up on shore with the fatal plastic showing in the disintegrated carcass.

The Galapagos tour is a memorable one — an adventurous and once-in-a-lifetime experience. A tour to be prepared for, however.

To be prepared for this outstanding excursion, one should consider the "wet" and the "dry" landings. We departed the ship in a panga. For the wet landings, a bathing suit, or shorts is required wearing apparel. We climbed down a short ladder in the bow of the panga and dropped into the water —

up to our knees or our waists! We removed our shoes upon landing, and after drying off (using one of the towels) on the sandy beach, we donned our walking shoes for the hike over rocks and overgrown paths.

The "dry" landings I found difficult. The Pacific, although not rough *per se*, was turbulent enough that the panga rose and fell with the waves, and trying to land on rocks that were described as slippery, required considerable agility.

Things to take to make a more enjoyable shore landing are: waterproof bags for camera and binoculars, waterproof or water-repellent head cover for rain, tennis or walking shoes, towel, change of clothing (shorts or slacks or shirt to don over bathing suit), mosquito repellent, flippers (for snorkeling), and a plastic bottle with screw-on lid for water or soft drink while on shore. One of the young ladies in our group had a plastic backpack in which she carried her supplies, and we all wished we had been as clever!

There is no need for cash in the bar or on the ship, purchases and drinks are put on a tab, payable at the conclusion of your trip. Signing each tab will insure an exact accounting of one's charges.

Our naturalist guides were two of the most outstanding guides we have ever had. Both college graduates, Francis and Melanie Dimmer had been married only a few months, and were extremely knowledgeable about the flora and the fauna. Francis who had a degree in geology, led our group (called "The Boobies") most of the time; Melanie, with her knowledge of Spanish, conducted the Ecuadorians and other Spanish-speaking fellow passengers on most occasions. Their "Dance of the Web-Footed Albatross" at one of our twice-daily briefings was a delight to behold. The *Bucanero* is indeed fortunate to have them.

One needs to pause here to contemplate that we were much better equipped than Darwin on his HMS *Beagle*, better educated, had much more enlightened guides and could take 1,000 photos while he sketched one. We saw much more, covered more territory, and had access to broader background. Yet, he changed the world with his findings — timing is everything!

Panama

A desire to see the operations of a Panamanian mill enabled us to spend the weekend in Panama City. In 1534, Charles I of Spain ordered the first survey of a proposed canal route through the Isthmus of Panama. More than three centuries passed before the first construction was started — by the French.

Panama and the United States signed a treaty in 1903 and undertook to construct an interoceanic ship canal across the isthmus, and now, more than 70 years after the first official ocean-to-ocean transit of the waterway, the U.S. and Panama have embarked on a partnership for the management, operation, and defense of the Canal. The Panama Canal Commission, a U.S. Government agency operates the Canal with an administrator (the chief executive officer), who is a U.S. citizen, and the Deputy Administrator, a Panamanian citizen. Beginning in 1990, the positions will be (were) reversed. In December 1999, the U.S. will transfer the Canal to Panama.

It takes about nine hours for an average ship to transit the 50 miles from deep water in the Atlantic to deep water in the Pacific, being raised or lowered according to the locks. The airline distance between the two entrances is 43 miles.

We bussed from Panama City on the Pacific side to Colon (an almost deserted city) on the Atlantic side; we saw the ruins of the Spanish gold city of Porto Bello; and we walked along the path the buccaneer Henry Morgan used in 1671, when he led a band of about 1,000 men to capture Porto Bello and Panama on the isthmus. We enjoyed our visit to this natural short cut that divides the Pacific and the Caribbean.

Monday morning, we were met in the lobby of the Caesar Park Marriott by John E. Palmer, of the U.S. Agency for International Development in Panama, and Allan Randall, Consultant to the U.S. Department of Agriculture, who accompanied Clark McDonald and Joe Robertson to an early morning meeting with Señor Carlos Sanchez Fabrega, managing director of Uniply, a modern, well-run plant that makes many kinds of plywood. The ladies followed in the van with our luggage.

There are three hardwood plywood manufacturers in Panama. We drove by Maderas Laminadas, S.A. Plywood in Las Cumbres outside of Panama City. We did not get to visit the plant since it was a national holiday, Labor Day. Panama was presenting a placid and pretty picture at this time.

Aruba

We arrived in Aruba, one of the Holland-in-the-Caribbean islands off the coast of Venezuela, on Monday evening. Our hotel was located on the south side (nearest Venezuela) with its sandy beaches and palm trees. Our tour also took us to the north side where the trade winds have sculpted unusual rock formations and made the divi-divi tree a great natural rarity — its branches bend completely in one direction. This side of the island, mostly volcanic rocky cliffs, with the water deep and treacherous, and the dry, arid terrain covered with several kinds of cacti and very large rocks is reminiscent of the Arizona desert. It was here that Joe Robertson managed a short windsurfing trip.

We made brief stops at Bonaire and Curacao on this tour, thus completing the "ABC" group of the lower Caribbean. Our group was made up of Joe and Virginia Robertson, Beverly Howell, Honey Howell Taylor, and Clark and Sylvia McDonald. It was an interesting and informative study tour. We returned better informed about the (plywood) industry conditions in Ecuador and Panama, and as well as being forever impressed with the solitary uniqueness of the Galapagos.

Chapter 9

The Travelers' Century Club and Circumnavigators Club: Around the World in 18 Days, 1987

B Y 1987, Virginia and I had taken our third trip around the world and had visited some 100 countries — an accomplishment to be noted by the *Times-Mail* feature on our travels describing our newly gained status in the world of travelers.

Joe Robertson, Now in Century Club, Still Seeks New Ventures, Challenges

By Claude Parsons

Joe Robertson is now a member of the exclusive Travelers' Century Club.

His wife, Virginia, has joined him in this illustrious group.

Membership in the Century Club is attained when an individual visits 100 different countries. This was accomplished by the Robertsons in October during their third around-the-world trip.

"My first milestone to pass was being in all 50 states," stated Robertson. "The Century Club is the second one."

His 100th country was Yugoslavia. All the trips he has taken have been connected with his business, and his wife has traveled with him everywhere he has gone outside the United States.

Robertson's recent "Around-the-World in 18 Days" journey covered 35,000 miles and took him to Portugal, Italy, Greece, Indonesia, Borneo, and Turkey, as well as Hong Kong and Singapore.

While in Rome, Robertson was one of only four U.S. representatives attending the consultation of wood panel experts at the invitation of the U.N. Food and Agriculture Organization and the U.S. government.

He has often made other presentations or lectures abroad, or taken tours of various mills gathering information which has helped him to become an international expert in his field.

Robertson not only travels by air more than 50,000 miles a year in his business but also drives at least 35,000 miles annually. This includes a daily 50-mile round trip from his home in Brownstown to his office in Bedford.

"Kilroy" crept into Robertson's concept of travel importance during his military service. As the surviving warbird crews and pilots returned with incredible stories of experiences, of places, and of Kilroy from all over the world, he became infected with the urge to go and see. Although Robertson developed the "travel bug" while in the U.S. Air Force in World War II, most of his traveling abroad has been since 1966.

"I work hard at the business, but also enjoy it a great deal," commented Robertson. "Having fun is one of the major objectives in my life, and I have lot of fun in my business relationships."

He is always looking for a new venture, a new place to go — "another mountain range to look beyond, another sea to sail, another river to cross or forest to explore," he stated.

Which trip has Robertson enjoyed most or which country has he found the most interesting? "I'm a hopeless romantic," he explained. "I especially like to go to those faraway places with associations of adventure or intrigue — Timbuktu, Kathmandu, the slopes of Kilimanjaro, Kenya and the Serengeti, the Pyramids of the Nile, the Taj Mahal, the Himalayas, the

Casbah in Casablanca, the Great Wall of China, and the Trans-Siberian Express, to name a few."

"The great cities of the world are also interesting, but not as challenging," Robertson added.

He admits he has always been full of energy and is driven to follow opportunities and challenges wherever they may be. He has always been attracted to athletics, playing varsity basketball at Kansas State, as a member of an Air Force team and some semi-pro after leaving the military. He is an enthusiastic water skier, has done some parasailing, and follows a daily exercise program.

"You need to be in shape to go to the places we go and keep up with the schedule we follow," said Robertson. "The things I learned from the great coaches and the great players I played for, with, and against taught me valuable lessons of perseverance and dedication."

Articles about Robertson's travels have been published periodically in The Times-Mail since 1972. Prior to that time he did a weekly grain column for The T-M. In college he was on the newspaper staff and was yearbook business manager.

"I admit to having some printer's ink in my blood," he remarked. "Ray Snapp, retired Times-Mail editor, often said I was a frustrated journalist. I confirm some substance in his perception."

Robertson loves to read and is an enthusiastic student. His educational background as a cereal chemist headed him toward technical studies he still avidly pursues.

"As a result of my travels and the friends I have developed, I could probably find a friend or business acquaintance within 50 miles of anyplace in the U.S. where I might find myself," he remarked. "This would also probably be true in most of the top 50 cities in the world."

As for the future, Robertson said the demands of his business are always more than he can handle. The Robertson Corporation and its mills have been in the family over 100 years and have been engaged in many activities.

Robertson currently serves on the Indiana Port Commission, but is not a politician and has never had political aspirations. "I have had and still have lots of friends in both parties, although I am a Democrat of long-standing," he stated. "The late Republican Sen. Bill Jenner was one of my good friends."

The Robertsons have one son, Dr. Joe Robertson, Jr., an eye surgeon in Portland, Oregon, and two grandchildren.

"The GLU-X business has been very good to us," he explained, "but we're always looking for innovative ways to market new and different products or services. We have made corn meal, cake flour, animal feeds, been in the grain business, and tried many other things."

"We are looking to many new endeavors," he added. "After all, Col. Sanders didn't get started until he was nearly my age. Lee Iacocca, of my vintage, runs the Chrysler Corporation. Chuck Yeager, who was in the same war as I, still flies fighter jets, and President [*Ronald*] Reagan, who is older, runs the country." [*President Reagan was in office at the time this article was written in 1987.*]

"To some extent, youth is not a time of life, but a state of mind," Robertson commented. "I try to think young and about the next adventure."

In 1992, Virginia and I received an invitation to join the Circumnavigators Club. Claude Parsons, of the *Times-Mail*, wrote the following article for the December 17, issue:

CIRCUMNAVIGATORS INVITATION FOLLOWS CENTURY CLUB INITIATION

Circumnavigators Club

Joe and Virginia Robertson Have Completed Three Trips "Around The World."

After Joe and Virginia Robertson had visited over 100 countries, they were qualified to become members of the Travelers' Century Club.

But they were quite surprised a few weeks ago when they received word that they are now members of the exclusive Circumnavigators Club.

The Robertsons, who have now traveled to 120 countries, are among only seven Hoosiers in the club.

"When we first heard of the Circumnavigators Club, we were aware it was something more than just another travelers' club," Robertson explained. "But we were not prepared for the announcement of membership."

The membership was conferred by means of an invitation to the Magellan Award Dinner held at New York City's Metropolitan Club in November.

The Order of Magellan is the highest award of the club, and is presented to outstanding individuals who are dedicated to advancing peace and understanding in all parts of the world. A person is selected for the order only once every two or three years. The first recipient of the award was Gen. Douglas MacArthur in 1961. Among others honored have been Neil Armstrong, Barry Goldwater, Lowell Thomas and Sir Edmund Hillary.

The 1992 recipient is author James A. Michener. He was honored at the dinner, but the Robertsons were unable to attend.

"Michener's selection was especially interesting to me," Robertson said. "Company employees and associates presented me with Michener's latest book, "The World Is My Home." They knew we had visited many of the exotic places of which Michener writes."

Circumnavigator Jim Pirtle of Madison, Indiana, on Oct. 4, [*1992*] this year, flew into Seymour's Freeman Field to interview the Robertsons. Such an interview is a part of the ritual of acceptance into the club.

At the time of the interview, there were only five members of the club in Indiana. Included is Dr. John Ryan, former president of Indiana University.

Pirtle and his associate, Dr. Henry Riley, had qualified for their memberships through an unusual circumnavigation. Their round-the-world trip began when they flew a single-engine private plane across the Atlantic via the Charles Lindbergh route, with stops at Gander en route to Ireland. Robertson mentioned that this leg of the journey seemed rather risky. Pirtle responded that they had a better plane than Lindbergh, much better instrumentation, they were better trained pilots — and they made it. They then continued their easterly journey through Europe, parts of the Arab world, over the Malay Straits and even retracing some of what was believed to be Amelia Earhart's route over the South Pacific.

"We were as intensely interested in Pirtle's tales of the South Pacific as those of Michener," Robertson said. "We shared rare incidents of common interest such as their both knowing Yummy of "Yummy's Place" fame on faraway Truk."

The Robertsons submitted their 1987 easterly round-the-world schedule as their qualifying circumnavigation. This trip was completed in 18 days instead of the traditional 180.

In two previous Robertson round-the-world jaunts, they "chased the sun" to the west on trips requiring 35 and 31 days. The first was in 1977. The second was in 1981.

In 1988, *The Times-Mail* carried my record of our 18-day around-the-world trip that began at a United Nations Forest Products Conference in Rome.

Plenty of Prosperity, Concern for Poverty in Portugal

By Joe Robertson

Trans World Airlines' flight 900 departed New York's Kennedy International into an eastern dusk as a blazing western sunset surrounded the stern of our favorite L1011 aircraft. Our cruising altitude was 35,000 feet. The Atlantic horizon presented a view of the slight earth's curvature, a phenomenon visible only from near-stratospheric height over oceans or large and level land masses.

As we sat in our comfortable seats, served by bright and helpful people, I remembered some of my friends who tried to tell me of the rigors of international flight and the stress of "jet lag."

Surely, I thought, they must be kidding. After 100 countries and a million plus air miles, our solution to jet lag is sleep in flight and our answer to upset stomach is "don't drink the water," no ice, no milk, no salads, nor uncooked food.

We were bound for a U.N. Forest Products Conference in Rome. We had been called upon by the U.N. and by the U.S. government to present papers relative to wood panels. Thirty-one papers from both western and developing countries were on the program and many facets of politics and protocol were involved.

We had participated in a number of other international business meetings and technical conferences, but this was our first participating experience with a U.N. organization. En route we were stopping in Portugal for a lazy weekend.

After the Rome and U.N. experience, we were headed for plywood mill visits in Turkey and Indonesian Borneo, one of the most primitive of areas but part of the Indonesian plywood manufacturing community which now supplies perhaps 70 to 80 percent of the world's hardwood plywood.

Our itinerary then programmed us to continue our third round-the-world trip and on to Portland, Oregon for an American Plywood Association meeting.

Our trip included stops at some very interesting places along the global route: the Yugoslavian shore of the Adriatic Sea, the Turkish site of ancient Troy, the Temple of Diana or Aphrodite at Ephesus, Istanbul, the Acropolis in Greece, Singapore, Jakarta and Hong Kong, to name a few.

Beverly Howell of Howell Plywood, Dothan, Alabama traveled with us except when we split for her expedition to Bali and ours to Borneo. Mr. and Mrs. Clark McDonald joined us in Rome and provided some valuable guidance in Rome, Turkey and Indonesia.

The Portugal visit was all that one could wish. Lisbon was impressive with its beautiful harbor, cathedrals, castles, and contrasts of modern avenues versus the quaint and narrow cobblestone streets of centuries past.

A northern excursion included a visit to the Shrine of Fatima. It is said that the statue of the Virgin Mary here sheds real tears for the sins of men. Some Catholics have veneration for healing powers associated with the spring water and the shrine. The physical expanse of the facility seemed almost as large as St. Peters Square in Rome, and the parking and seating capacity must have provided for at least 100,000.

It is reputed to be second only to Lourdes in France as a sacred shrine of the faithful. Among the unusual things were the burnings of wax body parts such as arms and legs apparently to assist in direction of the healing. Of course, I don't understand such things, but they are interesting.

A trip to "The Algarve," Portugal's southern sea coast, or Riviera, was also most enlightening. It has, of course, a dominant Moorish atmosphere as the Islamic Moors ruled the land for some 400 years before the Middle Ages.

They left their marks on the architecture, the castles, and the mosques — now churches. The number of people and the extent of building on the sunny coast reminds one of the earlier days of Florida's boom development except there is less order.

I, of course, tested the water and checked the beach wear. I found the water warm and the beaches unusual, often with sharp and abrupt cliffs behind the coarse sand or fine gravel so typical of the Southern European seashore. Probably a more unusual feature of the beaches was a substantial number of bare bosoms. It seems all across the Riviera, as many as 30 to 40 percent of its many sunbathers and swimmers are going topless.

Our guide also directed our attention to the historical interest of the area. This was the haven of the fabled and famous Portugese Navy of the 14th and 15th centuries. It was the home of Prince Henry's Navigational School and the harbor from which sailed out many of the great discoverers — Columbus to North America, Balboa to the Pacific, etc.

All in all we found Portugal progressing, plenty of prosperity, a concern regarding poverty, and full of people doing better.

When in Rome, Attend Meeting
Yugoslavia a Delightful Surprise

The flight from Lisbon to Rome was very unusual. It was smooth and scenic.

On the way to Rome we landed at Milano (Milan) and passed through the transit lounge and back into the airplane — there was no luggage check. Then we flew on into the Rome Domestic Airport and so passed no checkpoint whatsoever. This was especially interesting since I had been told that Rome was in a state of "high alert."

The United Nations Food and Agriculture meeting in Rome was a stimulating experience. The meeting was, of course, involved with international protocol and politics. It was called an International Consultation of Wood Panel Experts.

Wood panels are now the world's major home building material. There were representatives from both "developing" and "developed" countries and discussions were generated regarding plans for advanced adhesive technology, wood processing technology, and market development.

Low-cost housing and furniture in developing countries is of great concern to all. It is a key international issue, for if populations are properly housed, then the local market for building material becomes the primary market, and exports develop only on the basis of actual value so that all countries are better served with lower subsidies.

I presented a paper related to the importance of extender milled from Lawrence County [*Indiana*] wheat in wood panel adhesives. In total, there were about 30 experts from such places as Brazil, India, Indonesia, New Zealand, Canada, China, Finland and Germany.

The security of the U.N. meeting place was tight. Attendance was absolutely restricted to participants and a minimum support staff. Spouses and other interested associates were not permitted entry.

The Eternal City is still a very interesting place. The food and atmosphere of the sidewalk cafes, the lure of the shops and the awe of the grand ruins are as unique as ever. However, the prices for reviewing "The Glory that was Rome" are now high — a direct and noticeable result of the weaker dollar. For example, $40 each way to and from the airport, is pretty steep.

The Adriatic seacoast of Yugoslavia was a delightful surprise. Yugoslav Airlines treated us nicely out of Rome and the airport arrival was routine.

Essentially all airports and airlines were handling full loads of passengers without apparent security inconveniences or unusual delays. We waltzed through easy custom formalities and were soon welcomed to the Holiday Bellevedere at Dubrovnik, a hotel of spectacular architecture built into a cliff overlooking the Adriatic.

We are often asked why we subject ourselves to the risks inherent in international air travel and particularly travel involved with Mediterranean ports such as Rome, Athens, and Istanbul — all have experienced terrorist activity in the last year or so. However, our reply routinely, and in truth, is that there is more danger inherent in getting to the airport than after one gets in the airport.

A recall of some of the taxi rides to and from airports certainly bears that out. We were taken at speeds up to 85 miles per hour in Jakarta. The cab driver at Dubrovnik must have been late for his date for he did the normal half-hour trip in 19 minutes. Requests for caution were always misunderstood.

Yugoslavia has been called the "Threshhold to Another Europe," and Dubrovnik properly named "The Pearl of the Adriatic." The old city has an impressive wall around the shops and houses which line marble streets!

After a delightful evening meal, we enjoyed a walk around the many viewpoints of the hotel. It seemed that every vista of the sea and tile-roofed city surpassed the previous one.

Early the next morning we were on our way South with the Adriatic Riviera on our right, the distant Balkans on our left, and Sweti Stefan, a legendary castle hideaway projecting into the sea, as our destination.

The harbor villages, the old Orthodox Cathedrals, the sun-bathers — as topless as those in Western Europe — and the ever-present hospitality were not what we expected in a Communistic Country.

We left Dubrovnik reluctantly and as easily as we had entered — no questions or hassles. However, in the Belgrade Airport we had a most unusual experience. We were waiting in line behind a well-dressed, English-speaking, gentleman who could not avoid overhearing our ever-enthusiastic conversation. He turned and opined that Beverly Howell was from Alabama, and possibly from Dothan? Of course, many well-traveled Americans could play 'Enry 'Iggins and identify her "Southernese" but possibly not pinpoint it.

Then he asked us where we were from in Indiana. When we replied, "Brownstown," as if we thought everyone should recognize it, he said, "I practically grew up there." Some coincidence! Although we had never met him, he knew everyone we mentioned and every landmark.

He was David Cross, President of International Offset Trading Corporation, and his grandfather had lived two doors from my brother's house in Brownstown. Moreover, the Cross and Robertson farms in the river valley were almost adjacent. He was on the same plane with us to Athens where we arranged to be photographed together with an "Athens Airport" sign behind us.

It really is a small world and this could qualify as "A Funny Thing Happened On The Way to The Forum" incident.

Istanbul: Visions of Mystery and Intrigue

Istanbul. Just the sound of the word brings visions of mystery and intrigue. It was always to me a "far away place" — the stuff dreams are made of — where Ottoman Sultans smoked water pipes and, on whim, summoned beautiful and exotic women from the harem to dance before the visiting Pashas and Princes.

A World of Travel 247

Here on the Golden Horn of Europe, the city guards from Europe the entrance to Asia and, as a major world crossroads, has for centuries looked upon the treasure-laden caravans coming from the silk and spice roads of the East to the cities of Europe, while ships from all nations, including the Russian fleet, move swiftly in crossing a constant flow of Northern water from the Black Sea into the narrow straits and on the warm waters of the Mediterranean.

The jewels of the Topkapi Palace constitute a display to stagger the imagination. Emeralds of grape size are heaped in plates. Rubies as large as half dollars, and an 86-carat diamond are only a few of the many pieces displayed in the rooms of pearled thrones and golden candlesticks.

Many may recall the movie, "Topkapi," in which Omar Sharif was involved in the theft and recovery of a jewel-covered dagger with a hilt of gold and a handle cut from a single perfect emerald. We saw the dagger. It was fascinating.

The City of The Star and the Crescent is just as exciting today as in the Middle Ages when Crusaders paused before entering upon their march toward Jerusalem.

We were met at the airport by an attractive and bright Moslem girl from the American University. At that time, I waded into the Bosporus where the on-rushing top current from the North flows over an in-bound current from the Sea of Marmara and the Dardenelles.

We were taken to the Grand Bazaar where goods from all the world are in hundreds of "stalls" or shops displayed and traded by sharp Turkish Moslems. Our guide here was a young Moslem mother who advised us in the bargaining ritual.

Oriental rugs and jewelry are among the most famous items offered in this fabled "mall."

After the Bazaar, we were hosted at dinner by another attractive Moslem woman, Osi Derbend, and by her husband. The Turkish cuisine was delicious — borsch, eel, caviar, Bosporus mullet, honey-laden Turkish sweets, and Turkish coffee.

The food in Turkey proved as unique and interesting as the atmosphere. Service was instantaneous and superb. The setting was most impressive — a formal atmosphere of Eastern decor including beautiful silver, china, and linens.

The clientele was "Istanbul society." Our seating was such that we dined in Europe while looking across the narrows of the Bosporus into the

The road to Istanbul. Beverly Howell is "up" on the camel Camellia enroute to the Far East. The beast is being lead by Virginia Robertson. The donkey belongs to man in rear.

A World of Travel 249

The legendary Wooden Horse stands in front of the real site of the Trojan War.

Istanbul of Asia. All of these factors weigh heavily in placing this restaurant, with the mysterious name of "S," near the top of my Ten Best Restaurants in the world. Dinner started late and finished much later which placed sleep at a premium before the early wake-up necessary for us to make a morning visit to a Turkish plywood mill.

The owners of the Pelit Arslan Plywood Mill were Hasan Turan and his brother Fuat. Hasan's two sons had spent some time in England and had learned their English well. Of course, our guide, Suat Ozyurek (Sue), was an excellent interpreter too, so we had little difficulty in communicating.

However, the "Southern Accent" of Beverly Howell created both interest and confusion for our interpreter and the two sons. For example, her "Y'all" and "reckon" didn't translate easily into Oxford English or Turkish.

"Plywood Manufacture" in Turkish is "Kontrplak Fabrikasi," but the machinery and process is much the same as in many countries. They were making hardwood panels ranging from about 3/16 inch to one and 1/4 inch thickness and about five feet by eight feet square. The panels contained veneer cores and faces of Luan, although some faces were of exotic African veneer.

Our hosts were most hospitable and cooperative. We had an enjoyable and informative plant tour and found it to be an unhurried but productive operation. The Turkish economy appeared to be very satisfactory.

After the plant visit, we moved on through the very heavy Istanbul traffic onto the rural highway in our very comfortable van with a competent driver. Sue, our guide, proved to be a veritable encyclopedia of information and provided us with a great deal of economic, political, historical, and religious information, which made us aware of the general ignorance of Americans regarding Turkey.

We traveled on good highways down the European coast and crossed the Dardenelles by ferry near the spot where, in ancient times, the Persian king, Xerxes, had made his famous entry into Europe by building a bridge across the Hellespont. We stayed in a delightful motel on the Asian beach of the Dardenelles.

Here an early morning wading expedition came upon fishermen casting their nets and pulling them in loaded with fish from Aegean waters.

A short trip from Cannakalee brought us to the site of ancient Troy, the very real site of the legendary Trojan Wars which pitted invading Greeks against the Trojans. The Trojans were attempting to protect Paris from losing his love, the beautiful Helen with "the face that launched a thousand ships" as recorded in Homer's "Iliad."

From Troy we proceeded to Pergamum, one of Paul's Seven Churches of Asia Minor, and again were astounded at the extensive ruins of this relic of antiquity. It was the site of a great city established by one of the generals of Alexander the Great.

By now we had covered several hundred miles of Turkish geography and were convinced that Turkish civilization deserved a place in history comparable in many respects to the civilizations of the Greeks and Romans.

Contrasting Cultures Fascinating

Our visit to plywood mills, adhesive chemical plants, and a particleboard plant in Borneo has to rank as one of the most interesting experiences we have had in visiting plants in more than 40 countries.

We were aware that Indonesia was now supplying 70 to 80 percent of the world's hardwood plywood, but we could not comprehend the scope of the total timber harvesting operation here until we were actually on the spot.

Our trip started from Jakarta, Indonesia, on the large island of Java, from where we flew about 1,000 miles to land at Balikpapan on the southeast side of Borneo, now called Kalimantan. The rich Kingdom of Brunei separates Kalimantan from the Malaysian-owned part of Borneo, now called Sarawak.

At Balikpapan we were picked up by a company plane, owned by the Kalimanis Interests, and flown upstream into the Borneo Jungles where we visited the plywood mills.

Don Cross, whom I had known in the States, was resident manager of three plywood mills, a chemical adhesive company and a particleboard plant. We were impressed with the quality and quantity of the hardwood plywood production. They were easily producing more than 100 million square feet surface of plywood annually.

Norman Pascual, a fellow we had also known from his previous Georgia-Pacific background at Savannah and in Brazil, proudly showed us the most modern plywood quality control lab in Southeast Asia.

The predominantly Meranti logs came out of the jungle under the direction of another American, Jack Boyer, who educated us on this tremendous tropical forest resource and entertained us with stories of fast-vanishing habitat of the great pythons, orangutans, bears, and near-mythical "wild men of Borneo."

The mythical Garuda, a great bird that carries the Gods, has replaced the "wild men of Borneo" as the symbol of the future in Southeast Asia.

All in all, we were highly impressed with the economic, industrial, and social structure of Indonesia. The contrasting cultures were fascinating.

We flew over dense forests after having been transferred through the crowded streets of Samarinda. Mini-motorcycles were everywhere with one to four Indonesians on each cycle. There were lots of "foreign" cars with a few rickshaws thrown in and even an occasional native carrying a beam with two baskets.

While there were a number of American machines in the plants, such as Coe Lathes and Globe Spreaders, most machinery was of foreign make. This brand new facility can make 4,000 layered panels daily.

Many of us in America think of Japan, Taiwan, and Korea as the "yellow peril" of U.S. plywood and furniture makers. We have not recognized the presence and potential of Indonesia — the fifth most populous nation in the world — with 170 million little, energetic and intelligent people living on many islands nurturing perhaps the most productive tropical rain forest in the world.

In the last decade, they have built over 100 large modern plywood mills and have essentially cut off log exports to 'treeless' Asia — Japan, Taiwan and Korea. They are now entering the international furniture market.

The wild jungles of Indonesia remain, but in one generation we have seen high-tech plants spring up in the campsites and on the canoe landings of perhaps the world's last primitive man.

Hong Kong

To most of us, Hong Kong, the Crown Colony, has represented the gateway to China and a place where East and West could meet. It is the island where unbridled Capitalism has flourished on the edge of a closed China and an open Pacific.

Today, the seething metropolis of James Clavell's [*novel*] "Noble

House" may be passing into the twilight of its reign with the ending of British rule and a return to Chinese control scheduled for 1997. [*After this article had been written, Hong Kong reverted to Chinese rule on July 1, 1997.*]

We made a weekend stop in this great port city on the last leg of our world tour. This time we stayed at The Mandarin which ranks in the top of the several "World's Best" Hotels in Hong Kong.

Our room overlooked the busy harbor and the Star Ferry, while Victoria Peak, in the background, was bright in the light of a full Harvest Moon shining down on China. It was a memorable scene never to be forgotten amid a realization that the next time, if there is one, it will not be the same.

The junks cluttered the harbor and the horns of the ships pierced the din of the busy night. Street and building construction was still going on, but there was a sense that another chapter in civilization was probably drawing to a close.

United's 747 Flight to California compared favorably with the super Singapore Airline service we had come to favor. We left Hong Kong at noon on the 11th and, after crossing the international date line, arrived in L.A. just 18 days after leaving the U.S.

Did we lose a day? Perhaps we had been in an Oriental Brigadoon. Perhaps, in circling the earth in 18 days, touching three continents, crossing the equator and date line and both the Atlantic and Pacific, dipping in the waters of the Mediterranean, Adriatic, Aegean and China Seas — almost as if the trip were a fragment of imagination.

Of course, we had seen more than we could remember. We were again highly impressed with our experiences in "far away" places, but we're always glad to return home. There's no place better.

We find the forests of our Northwest Mountains even more beautiful than those of the Asian Tropics, our seashores and our deserts as spectacular as any, and our plains and valleys more productive than any others.

It's true that exotic lands stir our imagination, but nothing is better than to look homeward to the beautiful hills and painted trees of Southern Indiana. Istanbul and Indonesia are exciting, but so are the sights and sounds, and people, of Lawrence and Jackson Counties.

Chapter 10

The Canadian Northwest and Alaska, 1989

IN JULY 1989, we traveled up across our North American continent to the Canadian Northwest and Alaska — land of the midnight sun. From *The Times-Mail* of August 15, 1989:

Yellowknife to the Yukon

The Canadian Northwest Territories and the Yukon stir visions of Arctic expeditions and experiences within those of us having adventurous spirits and the urge to look beyond the ordinary. For the traveler seeking comfortable sojourns and carefree rest, this is not the route or region.

The trip date is important. Summer is the time of "no night." We departed Indianapolis in the early morning July 5, 1989, accompanied by Dr. Joe and Jane Black of Seymour. The first overnight was in the beautiful Banff Springs Hotel on the Bow River, the next night was overlooking lovely Lake Louise.

The unusual excitement started with a snowbus tour on the Athabascar Glacier of the Columbia Ice Fields in Jasper National Park. Then it was back to Calgary and the world famous Calgary Stampede, the ultimate in rodeo and the modern equivalent of a chariot contest, the Chuckwagon Race. Stampede Park is only a few miles from the site of the '88 Winter Olympics. These places served as a prologue to a travel experience totally different.

Departing Calgary by jet, we flew several hundred miles almost due north, over green fields of wheat and yellow fields of canola to Edmonton, a world-class grain and oil center. The railroads stop here and one lone road heads north, asphalt first and then gravel, almost one thousand miles toward the Pole and our destination — Yellowknife on the Great Slave Lake, just below the Arctic Circle.

Our plane was now filled with both passengers and cargo. An unusual variety of people — a few in business suits, most in jackets and sweaters. Most were businessmen, engineers, or miners returning to "the North" to work. We were possibly the only "tourists" on the plane.

Below was barren wilderness to the horizon as the trees turned to dwarfs and the rock outcroppings interrupted the rolling tundra.

Yellowknife is a city of contrasts. There is still a very vital "Old Yellowknife" down on the flats — the lake and bay shore settlement where all types of float planes are tied up beside all kinds of boats — house, motor, barge, canoe, and kayak.

The buildings are mostly 1930-ish, mining camp small log and early miscellaneous material and architecture. To say they are interesting and unusual is an understatement. They were constructed originally from whatever could be carried in or scrounged from the area.

The dwarf trees made only very small logs and most rock was in boulders far too large for masonry. Tundra doesn't make good adobe. As time passed and fortunes improved, better houses were built in front or back of the originals, which then became storage or utility buildings. The "outhouses" were finally outlawed, as were the bawdy houses, but getting rid of either sewage or prostitutes in a mining town with winter temperatures under 40 below is difficult.

The "Modern Yellowknife," up the hill, is less than thirty years old.

After Yellowknife became the capital of the Northwest Territories, government people and planning moved in. Funds from government and gold made it possible to erect very modern buildings. The administrative and legislative buildings are, of course, impressive as is the hospital. The little log tourist information building is staffed by competent young women, well versed in the history, geography and sociology of the region.

We were confronted with interesting people and situations at every turn. On arrival, I presented my confirmed "4-door full size" reservation to Hertz only to be told that [*they were*] aware of the reservation specifications, but the only vehicle available was a pickup truck. Same story at Avis and Tilden, but we were rewarded by Budget's offer of a very dirty, high-mileage LTD with a dented rear fender and tail-light and an inadequate trunk with loose tire and tire tools. We accepted this offer at twice the Hertz-confirmed price and rattled off to town with the trunk lid standing open, bouncing against the stuffed bags, all in a very real "cloud of dust."

This pricing situation continued generally throughout Yellowknife as reflected meaningfully in the realtor's offer of a good mobile home on a small lot of rock and tundra for only one hundred and ten thousand dollars.

However, we should keep the modern relationship of the community in perspective with the fact that Yellowknife is in reality an outpost, a barren oasis of rock in the Arctic, a sector point in the northern frontier. From our hotel window we could look out over a sea of tundra, rivers, rocks, and lakes with dwarf trees soon to disappear a few miles out at "the Timberline."

We were thrilled to aim our cameras toward the Pole with light from the "Midnight Sun" and at a frozen horizon without elevation between us and the elusive goal of Robert E. Peary — he finally reached the Pole just ninety years ago.

The tales of Yellowknife go far back into the legends of the Dene and other Euro-American Indians and then even farther to the Asian ancestors, the Inuit (formerly called Eskimos). Our interest, of course, centered more upon the stories of gold discovery on the trapper's knife as he cleaned it on the shore of the river.

The Yellowknife Museum contains many exhibits about the great animals, past and present, of the land of the tree-line and tundra. We ate the steaks from the caribou and the musk-ox and filets from the Arctic char, but we were not fortunate enough to see them in the wild as we did the moose and mountain sheep in Banff.

However, in talking to the mining men returning from the camps less than a hundred miles north, there were tales of grizzly bears and cubs. And the associate of our Yellowknife guide outfitted and ran hunts for 52 polar bears last winter. I had my picture taken beside the beautiful, huge male at the museum. He weighed fifteen hundred pounds.

The "R&R" miners we met were a jolly and boisterous lot with incredible stories of the current camps. In symbolic jest, they reported flies as large as frogs, bees as big as birds, and mosquito bites requiring stitches. On some days bug clouds were confused with fog.

We flew back to Edmonton with some of the fellows. The booze is free on this Air Canada flight. It's a good thing the flight was slightly less than 1000 miles.

Edmonton, the capital of Alberta, is a city of some seven hundred thousand people. The lawns are green and homes well-kept. The Klondike Festival was coming soon to celebrate early Edmonton's role as a starting and outfitting point for one of the trails to the gold fields of the Klondike. The glass of the skyscrapers make Edmonton appear as a true jewel of the plains.

From Edmonton, we flew on West through British Columbia and then up the coastal range over the snow and ice fields of the Canadian Rockies to White Horse.

As we made our midnight approach in soft daylight, there below was the scene made famous by Robert Service's "The Spell of the Yukon" :

> *"There are strange things done in the midnight sun by the men who moil for gold. . . but the queerest ever to see, was the night on the marge of Lake Lebarge, I cremated Sam McGee."*

There it was, big as life, the real Lebarge. And, in another spot, a renovated paddlewheeler like a reborn "Alice May." It's fun to relive a legend, such as the miners' struggles, failures, and fortunes. It was unseasonably warm that July midnight in Whitehorse. Had Sam possessed the gumption to hit the trail in July instead of 60 days sooner or later, he could have traveled in the Tennessee temperature he loved and we would have missed his familiar quotation from the bowels of the boiler — *"It's the first time I've been warm."*

From Whitehorse we followed the Alaska highway for a few miles and did the White Pass Trail in reverse. Up the mountain to Lake Bennett where the Chilhoot and White Pass Trails of '98 converged. Down the Pass Canyon we rolled on the narrow-gauge White Pass & Yukon Railroad. We would stop, perched precariously on the cliff sides, to look down on the still-visible, impossibly steep, foot trails, where resolute men and mules formed human chains and climbed through waist-deep snows for days toward the top.

From there it was a downhill dog sled and water route to the Klondike gold fields. More than three thousand mules and uncounted prospectors perished in the scaling effort. Many items remain as stark evidence of the unreasonable lust born of desire for El Dorado. The bones, backpacks, belts and miscellanea will remain unburied until a future glacier kindly covers this trail of hope and hell.

At the end of the narrow-gauge line, we whistled into Skagway, Alaska. This town, historically preserved and authentically reconstructed, has about seven hundred and eighty residents. In 1898 it was the base camp for upwards of thirty thousand people — some women — outfitting for "the trail."

The names of the rivers and creeks — Skagway, Yukon, Dawson — in themselves create visions of booted men picking berry-sized nuggets from pans or brushing golden dust into small leather pouches. The Red Onion Saloon and the assayer's office still open their doors for gold — but now, from the pockets of people like us who come to see where others dug, or out of the casual jeans of the tourist from the nearby Loveboat docked in Skagway Harbor.

From Skagway, we took to the sky in a Piper Lance to view the great ice and snowfields and the glaciers spawned by the Pacific storm deposits on the towering coastal mountains. We have seen the snowfields of the Himalayas from a small plane flying around Everest, but the magnificent display of eternal snow scenery between Skagway and Juneau is possibly unsurpassed. Flying a hundred feet over great glaciers is thrilling — almost thrilling enough to smother the fear created by the bumpy ride and the thought of "what if" the little engine of this tiny plane conks out? Coming into the small Juneau airport, we passed directly over the stupendous Mendenhall Glacier, moving 10 feet daily into the sea and calving icebergs while one watches.

In Juneau, everyone flocks to the Red Dog Saloon. It was crowded, as

A *World of Travel*

it has always been since the Gold Rush started. There were many items of memorabilia on the walls, and a couple of would-be "dance-hall dolls" from a nearby cruise ship were swinging hips to the beat of the small, but loud, band. A sign on the wall told it all, something like this: "If you would live, laugh, and love even more, just cast your coin on the sawdust floor." (The floor was truly covered with sawdust.) We did.

From Juneau, we flew on south to Victoria, British Columbia where we enjoyed "high tea" in the lobby of the famed Empress Hotel. Then we "lucked into" an elaborate suite at regular high prices — fireplaces, dining table, bay view, etc., etc., right out of TV's "Rich & Famous." The Butchart Gardens of Victoria were beautiful.

It was an early morning ferry that took us across the San Juan Straits and over to Port Angeles, Washington. We drove down through North America's Temperate Zone Rain Forest on the Olympia peninsula and over to Seattle and on to Portland. It was good to be back in the U.S. of A. Northwest scenery cannot be beat.

We are settled in again in the comfort of Indiana living. We have our official certificates as "Arctic Adventurers" and have satisfied that urge to see the tundra and tree line of the Northwest Territories and the Yukon. The trip is over, but memories of the Midnight Sun remain and there will forever be a fondness and recognition of "The Spell of the Yukon."

Chapter 11

The Walls of the World: Our Travels in the 1990s

*T*HE FLIGHT OF TIME speeds ever faster, and the events of 1990 provided a benchmark, not a pause, in the constantly accelerating pace of change. The kings of the earth have always tried to "wall in" their familiar security zones and "wall out" the threatening and the unknown. Others, however, like children wishing to climb or fly over the garden walls, have both sought the security of walls and fought their restraint.

The Great Wall of China, the Walls of Jericho, the Maginot Line, the Siegfried Line, the Australian Rabbit Wall, and the Berlin Wall are only a few examples of important historical walls. All these, as well as many others, with the exception of the Great Wall and "Kilroy's wall," have gone with the winds of change.

Kilroy and his airfields did much to establish the futility of walls. The cartoon with the long nose over the inscripted wall not only says, "Kilroy was here," but also illustrates that any wall is a fool's bastion. Like Jonathon Livingston Seagull of Richard Bach's novel, men now soar over any wall to any destination, real or virtual.

Our 1990 travels began with a tour of the Pacific Islands and ended in Pamplona, Spain, for the annual "Running of the Bulls."

Joined by our friends, Dr. Joe and Jane Black, we were thrilled and moved by the Passion Play, which is presented every ten years in Bavarian Oberammergau. The larger-than-life historical account of Christ's last days is performed by people prepared by ten years of near-total immersion into the lives of the characters they portray. The staging is small, perhaps only 6,000 seating capacity in a day where high school basketball tournaments may have a greater draw. We have not described this great play here because many are familiar with the highlights of Christ's life between the Triumphal Entry into Jerusalem, through the Passion, Crucifixion, and Resurrection — a great story. The influence of this play in this picturesque German village has stirred the world since the 17th century.

In 1990, the world recognized that a politically fragmented Berlin had become one again and that "the Wall" had really tumbled down. The Iron Curtain, which had descended upon Europe from the Baltic to the Adriatic had been torn asunder and the lights of freedom had penetrated into the Communist regions.

Most of us were uncertain as to whether the gates were open to the countries of Eastern Europe. Even the national border officials were unsure. At some border gates, we crossed through elaborate but abandoned control complexes. At others, the bureaucrats were holding onto their jobs and going through the familiar control exercises without any real regulation.

In 1980, we had cleared Berlin's "Check Point Charlie" with real fear and trepidation. Ten years later, we crossed into East Germany through a "Check Point Charlie," which had turned into a place for souvenir shops featuring highly prized and priced pieces of the fallen Wall.

There were, however, still a few incidents, and we were one of them. We had a rented sedan chauffeured by a young Iranian emigrant. We passed freely from Austria into Hungary. However, as we returned from Budapest, the armed Austrian guards decided that the papers of our chauffeur-guide were not in order. All of our pleas, rationale, and arguments were refuted. Our driver was ordered out of the car and told to return to Budapest for clearance. We were told to get ourselves and the car out of there "in three minutes." There were many guns around us. We asked our driver if he needed more money. "No." We told him our route and that I was driving on into Czechoslovakia (still united at that time) on the authority of my International driver's license. It would require a long story to relate how it all worked out, but it did. Earlier I had assured Mrs. Black that travel through and between Communist countries was now no more difficult than driving from Indianapolis, Indiana to Louisville, Kentucky. She now thinks I might lie about other things as well.

The Gulf War prelude also reached a crescendo in the fall of 1990. U.N. resolutions and the build up of American forces very quickly placed a half-million U.S. troops in Saudi Arabia our ally — undoubtedly the highest concentration of state-of-the-art military might ever assembled. On January 15, 1991, attacks were launched on the heavily armed Army of Iraq. In 30 days, our awesome destructive technology had "won the war." But, peace results are still pending. As Americans, we should be proud that our military machine was able to accomplish objectives so quickly. The military leaders undoubtedly had taken some lessons from the Israel of 1967 when Israel neutralized an aggressive Egypt in six days.

After Virginia and I returned home, my review of our travels through the Pacific Islands and Spain was published in the *Times-Mail*, July 24 and August 20, 1990.

A "New Pacific"

Each trip unveils new insights, interests, and exciting revelations of faraway places that seem ordinary enough to those few who live and work there, but very extraordinary to those of us who visit them infrequently or not at all because they are not on the comfortable travel routes which most prefer. These little-known places may be important because they either did make a difference in the past, they may make a difference in the future, or both.

We just completed visiting a few such places in the Polynesian and Micronesian Pacific where U.S. fleets, air, and land forces engaged and prevailed in a death struggle with Japanese forces in WWII. The war in the Asian Theater, of course, was started with the Japanese bombing of Pearl

Harbor on Dec. 7, 1941, and essentially finished with the atomic bombing of Hiroshima and Nagasaki in 1945. In between these dates, the peaceful water, beaches, and atolls of the Pacific were filled with a million skeletons of ships, planes, weapons, and brave men who were lost in resolving the conflict and preserving freedom for our country in our time.

We felt our quest had really begun this time as we came dropping down over Pearl Harbor and landing toward Diamond Head. The weather was near-perfect — delightful, as expected. The congestion becomes much greater with each trip, as unexpected. The water and beach at Waikiki are still very enjoyable, but once off the beach and into the city, the traffic reminds one of Los Angeles, New York, or Miami. We drove across the island to the Polynesian Cultural Center for a little background briefing on Pacific Island Cultures. The traffic was almost bumper to bumper for forty miles. However, the young people and excellent displays for Tahiti, The Marquesas, Samoa, Tonga, and Fiji gave an excellent background for our journey.

As we said "Aloha" at Honolulu International Airport, the sun was just breaking over Diamond Head when our Air Micronesian Airline, Flight 957*, lifted toward the West. The sun chased us all day as we hopped islands, but we led the chase for almost fourteen hours. (*Note — #957 Puddle-Jump Pacific Flight was featured in the Center of Front Page, Wall Street Journal 10/24/96.)

Until this trip, I knew little of Micronesia and nothing of Air Micronesia, and here we were flying on it — liked it too, even though cargo was stacked in front of us in the first class space.

Johnson Island

Our first stop was about two hours out of Honolulu at Johnson Island. This appeared almost as a giant super aircraft carrier with a little more land available for a very few support buildings. One factory-type building was alleged to be a safe chemical disposal unit. The base is highly restricted and, on occasion, is totally closed to commercial air travel. This means it is only a touch-down spot but it is undoubtedly highly important to maintaining our lifeline of protection across the Pacific.

Majuro

As we approached Majuro in the Republic of Marshall Islands, (U.S. Protectorate — dollars and stamps) we had started to pick up knowledgeable friends, literature, and resources. Among these was an M.D. who had treated and checked those who were moved out of Bikini (like the swim suit) Atoll for the atmospheric atomic (nuclear) tests in the late 40's. There is still some contamination around the atoll. Some residents have made unauthorized returns to Enwietok [*Enewatak*]. U.S. authorities are still concerned about contamination there [*possible from drift from tests on Bikini Atoll*].

Majuro, (I could neither spell or pronounce it) with 20,000 people, is the capital of the Independent Republic of Marshall Islands. It is a thin coral reef about thirty miles long and an altitude of 3 to 6 feet (not 326). But what makes it important is its link between native Pacific Culture and our Western World. To keep distances in perspective, remember it was two jet hours to Johnson, three more to Majuro.

Kwajalein

At Kwajalein, one of the sporadic showers delayed our landing on the somewhat larger atoll — about 60 miles long. If one were blindfolded and removed from the mainland, he would have no difficulty in determining the difference between a Caribbean island and a Pacific atoll.

We also engaged in conversation with the airplane captain who had been flying in and out of Kwajalein on this route for years, and also with an Army helicopter pilot out of Kwajalein. From the press and the people we learned of the still-forming political restructure of the area and of the strategic importance of the area to the "Star Wars" missions — an accomplished fact in local minds. The missile interceptors here reportedly "shoot down" the practice missiles from the U.S. This defense posture could be turned toward the West if required.

Pohnpei

Pohnpei [*Ponape*] is the capital of the Federated State of Micronesia. It has a native population that often may still look and act "native," as in "South Pacific" (by James Michener). Many of the Pohnpeian women there still appear in grass skirts and with a red hibiscus in their jet black hair — nothing else. Others are in more complete and more Western dress. As in the other islands, the local economy is based on coconuts, breadfruit, and fish. However, there are possibilities for tourism in the future. Pohnpei is the site of Van Madal, a mysterious underwater city of stone. There is no satisfactory explanation of its origin, or of the purpose of the builders. It is said to be "Havaiki," the mythological fatherland of the Polynesians.

Truk

Coming into Truk was a wonderful experience. I had made the acquaintance of Bernard Dillemont, a several generation Truk native, and he sat beside me to describe the beautiful atoll as we approached. Virginia, by now, was sitting beside the wife of the plane's First Officer, so we both had plenty of local expertise available.

The atoll appears as a ring of islands about forty-five miles across with a large atoll housing the capital city, or town, Moen. The lagoon in the center of the ring has a number of battleship and submarine wrecks remaining from WWII action when our bombers surprised the Japanese fleet. This is a world-famous diving area and was declared by President [*Ronald*] Reagan to be the International Diving Museum.

The sunken fleet at Truk is known as the Ghost Fleet of Truk and it is involved with sea ghosts which are prominent topics of conversation at Truk. There are sea ghosts and there are the ghosts of love magic makers which have sure erotic powers in the secret love lives of many natives, young or old, wed or unwed.

There was a typical store there and the name was "Yummy's." Yummy was on the airplane with us. She sold everything from carvings to cloth. However, Yummy did not sell magic love potions because love magic is a clandestine activity. The love powder is not an item that we find in the local Wal-Mart. It is said generally, to be made from fish lips, and very, very effective.

Guam

Guam is Japanese! There is, of course, a powerful U.S. Military presence at each end of the island — the Navy base and the Air Force base; but in the middle where the people are, the language, the cars, and most of the people (90% at our hotel) are Nipponese.

Of course, the island is only about 1400 miles from Tokyo while nearly 7000 from L.A. For most Americans, it is too far away, and the memories of the decisive and bloody recapture too far removed to draw any but the most adventuresome of American tourists. For example, at our U.S. National Park Services Pacific War Memorial Headquarters and Museum, we were the only American visitors at 10 a.m. At the nearby

Japanese War Shrines there must have been more than two thousand visitors.

The hotels were jammed, the few main streets or roads on the island were crowded with two to four lanes of traffic.

A few years ago, the Japanese claim to fame was quality at low prices. I probably am not highly qualified to comment on quality, but I doubt that quality continues to be the same and obviously, prices are becoming outrageous. The Hilton Hotel did not recognize Hilton cards, the Hertz Rental Agency did not recognize Hertz discounts, and gas stations displaying the familiar yellow Shell sign would not accept Shell credit cards. The Guam companies must be Japanese owned.

From the above comments, we do not wish to imply that Guam is not an exciting and interesting place to visit. It is. But we were expecting an American atmosphere. It isn't. Japanese people are everywhere. The Japanese food is delicious — perhaps better than in Japan and the equal of that in Portland, Oregon. We saw the chef adding such U.S. goodies as butter to his cooking oil. I stuck with my chopsticks through a delicious many-course meal of Gengi salad, bean sprouts, eggplant, green pepper, sirloin steak, rice, miso soup, etc. It was outstanding, and we were able to watch a bunch of Japanese women sitting across the Flat Wok Grill as they manipulated steak, salad, and soy, without knife, fork, or spoon. So I did likewise.

There is much mystery and magic about Micronesia. The remote coral atolls in the Marshall Islands hold many interesting stories. The giant clams come from the northern Mariana Islands, including Saipan and Tinian, where so much American history was made. Of course Tinian is the island from which the atomic bombers were launched to end the war and introduce the Nuclear Age.

Guam is known as the place where the American day begins, fifteen hours ahead of Bedford, Indiana. It is at the southern end of the Mariana Archipelago. The local people are Chamorro and the language is Chamorro. There are many posh hotels or resorts on Tuman Bay in Guam. Here it is said that one feels the presence of good or evil. No visual appearance. Magellan landed here in 1521 and actually ended his personal voyage in the Philippine Sea as he was assassinated on the island of Cebu. "Gulliver's Travels" used a Micronesian setting. The real Gulliver was W. Dampier, made famous in the Jonathan Swift story. Dampier made his visit to Guam in 1686.

Native chiefs are buried under what they call latte stones, which are the foundation stones of their houses. The have a Latte Stone Park in Guam — somewhat like a cemetery. There are most interesting atolls north of Guam — Tinian, Saipan, and Rota.

The main highway on Tinian was built to carry bombs, atom bombs, too, from the port toward the B-29 Air Base on the opposite shore. There are still many submerged hulls of WWII shipwrecks in the area, but many are down in the world's deepest depths — the "Mariana Trench" 37,000 feet below the protruding volcanic cone which is Guam.

Every island we visited was either very significant in geostrategy for winning the war in the Pacific in 1945, or is very significant today in the U.S. Defense strategy, and particularly the "Star Wars" concept on which we now place reliance to shield us from nuclear missile attack.

Few today recognize that the Japan Empire Plan of 1940 was generally to establish a perimeter from our Alaskan Aleutians through the Pacific to Australia, and to exclude us from being a trade factor in that area. We thwarted that plan with our Pacific victory in WWII, but since the war we have generally opened our markets to most countries, including Japan, while permitting Japan to restrict our trade penetration — thus it appears that the 1940 empire goals of Japan have been accomplished to some extent with our agreement.

There is a "New Pacific" forming and we are not in close touch with a lot of it. We are all becoming globally oriented, but our attention has understandably been on Europe where we have seen the political Iron Curtain ripped asunder, and we avoid the economic uncertainties of the United European community in 1990.

But what of the Pacific? The Sleeping Giant of China is scheduled to move into the great trade center of Hong Kong; Indonesia is developing rapidly; and the inscrutable Japanese are becoming increasingly influential in the strategic Pacific Islands.

The islands such as Majuro, Kwajalein, Pohnpei, and Truk were occupied for good reason and at great cost in WWII. We may have already defaulted on our advantages and responsibilities there — today there are few Americans who know or care about either. Too long ago, too far away.

Guam, we still remember slightly. The others have become either the slighted names in history books or the romantic stuff of dreams.

It's Called "The Sport of Fools"
'Running of the Bulls' Hooks Hoosiers in Spain

The "Sport of Fools" is all the stuff that Hemingway made famous in *The Sun Also Rises*. Pamplona's "Running of the Bulls" is watched by a million and experienced by a few hundred foolhardy, not-so-bright individuals who remain in the streets when the "brave bulls" are turned loose at the Festival of San Fermin.

The mean monsters charge up Santo Domingo Street and around the Plaza at City Hall and into the "bounce wall" as they try to turn into Estafeda Street — "The Dangerous Corner."

It was here where my mentor led me, ahead of the bulls, to a totally exposed position as the thundering herd charged by. I had received thorough instruction on bull behavior by Tom and his four cohorts, and we had gone with the front runners about halfway through the route, but I was not prepared for the mass of bull meat bouncing off the boards not twenty feet from my "stand."

The sweaty hides and sharp horns truly struck fear into all hearts as one, then two turned their red and beady eyes toward us in search of path or prey. One bull went down and reversed field toward us, another slipped and fell on the slick cobblestone pavement. Although I had been shown an escape route through the boards across the narrow street and had been told how to fling my rolled-up newspaper to divert the bull's aim from my body, the cry of "Don't move" froze most of us in our tracks.

One white-clad runner lay prostrate in the street at our feet as the mini-maelstrom of bulls eyed first the crowd and then challenged one another briefly in confusion before galloping down the stretch toward the top of the run at the bull ring.

Our group then started to breathe again as the "clean-up" big-horn steers came up.

It was over. Probably two minutes had elapsed, or maybe it was two centuries. The was blood on the street in front of me from both man and beast, but no fatalities, and we were off to the bar in Castello Plaza where I gladly bought a round for all our "bull run buddies."

It was an interesting assemblage of characters. Jim was there, at 65 years and running since 1969, but I topped his age. He had come to Pamplona in the 1960's and never went home. Bud had been forbidden to come but "ran off" from his wife back in the States.

Tom appeared to be a mostly-sane American business man, and he was pleased by his accomplishment with me. "Oldest trainee I've ever had," Tom said, "and here I was considering retirement." (Tom is early forty.)

Dr. Joe and Jane Black and my wife Virginia had braved the mass of humanity to take up position at the top of the run at the bull ring. The action in and out of the ring was performed by at least three classes of people — adventurers, masochists, and drunks — there were a lot of the latter, but very few in the "run" streets where agility was a great help in staying alive.

The lure and excitement associated with this world-class event is unique. It is impossible to explain and very difficult for a non-runner to understand, but a million people came from everywhere to watch in the total discomfort of attendance while millions more see it on TV and read of it in other media.

The watchers can vicariously share in the event, but the actual experience of being one of perhaps two hundred running with fright and standing with fear in the barricaded bull streets is an unprecedented thrill. For some, it means an insatiable yearning to return again and again. For us, I'm quite sure, it's once in a lifetime.

Some 20 years after Virginia and I had visited the Far East, we returned to Southeast Asia and the Republic of China. We discovered dramatic changes in the development of the countries, which are chronicled in the following *Times-Mail* features.

Tigers, Chopsticks, and Forks

Clashing or Cooperating in 20th Century Southeast Asia

Returning to distant places can be disappointing or surprising, depressing or exciting. What was once exotic and mysterious may have become modern and familiar.

The nations once regarded as the sleepers in the menagerie of the world have become tigers of commerce and industry, and the awakening peoples will in large measure influence their own destiny and make their own decisions — chopsticks or forks or both on the table of international relations.

With the birth of the United Nations, attempts were made to classify or describe nations with some sort of definition nomenclature. "Developing Nations," "Third World," and many other terms were used to replace "primitive," "impoverished," and other not-so-nice terms. However, the changes have been so dramatic that the nations, places and peoples so described often prefer not to be reminded of their situation in 1950.

Knowing this, we embarked on a Southeast Asia trip with our usual high degree of anticipated enjoyment. We found a large region of the world not only fast maturing in global development, but also where the winds of change have swept across the South China Seas and engulfed the peoples and nations in a wave of upheaval in culture, customs, economics and environment, changing the very essence of their life and sending tremors reaching to the farthest corners of the earth.

We had been up nearly 36 hours when we witnessed our first sunrise of the trip. It was spectacular. We were approaching Taiwan in the great circle arc curving from the north when suddenly through the port ports (left cabin windows) a rainbow of bright gold and rose emblazoned a dawn of unsurpassed beauty. It revealed a sun springing into a beautiful blue sky over a Pacific Ocean that was a blue much darker than the sky and that appeared to reach almost to Hawaii.

We had taken off in a sunset, chased the sun through the darkness of the U.S. land mass and across the Pacific until Ol' Sol caught us again in a blazing sunrise 14 hours later off the China coast. We had gone maybe halfway around the world and the sun had lapped us.

Our flight from Cincinnati to L.A. was an enjoyable one. However, it is always something special for one's overseas airline to be an airline from the intended destination. It makes for a welcome into the culture of the host country. This is true whether it be Swiss Air, KLM, Japanese Air Lines, New Zealand Air, Qantas, or whatever, but it seems to us that boarding Singapore Air is a cultural special.

A Singapore Airlines flight to the Orient is an excellent prelude to the Eastern experience one is about to have. The decor, the vocal and body language of the diminutive and charming stewardesses, who are featured so prominently in SIA advertising, and the cuisine options (including chopsticks or forks) all strike a note of the welcome and surprise that awaits.

A very competent steward, a native Singaporian as they all were, explained many things Eastern to us in a curious blend of English, American and Malay with a Chinese accent. His given name was Tan Boon Chye: Tan like the color, Boon like Daniel Boone, and Chye like Ky.

You could call him "Boon Chye" or "Mr. Tan," but his Christian name was Jeffery.

His beautiful co-workers were Hin, Elaine, and Lei Mei Yi (with a Christian name of Jennifer). Later we encountered Tammy Li and Foo Slu Fung (love those names). They did everything possible to make the 14 hours between L.A. and the Far East comfortable, and they succeeded.

Singapore

Our daylight re-introduction to a new Singapore and a city tour brought us suddenly to the realization that "the island Marco Polo missed" was gone. Fortunately, the now-grand Raffles Hotel still presided over the original downtown district, and the flowers everywhere were as diverse and beautiful as ever.

The city is, of course, extra clean. Fines of up to $500 Singapore ($300 U.S.) are assessed for littering and, no foolin', signs everywhere warn seriously, "the penalty is death for dealing in drugs." Since laws are rather rigorously enforced in Singapore, one does not see litter and one does not see or hear of drug addicts. The crime rate generally is very low.

The many unusual and/or famous places in Singapore include an interesting nation-city (about the same) museum, Chinatown, Mt. Fabor — from where a very high cable car transports one across part of the very busy harbor to a resort island near the site of the World Trade Center, jewelry processing center, and the fascinating Botanical Gardens.

Sir Stamford Raffles established a settlement on the island of Singapore in 1819. Because it had been a fishing location with a lion-inhabited jungle, he named it Singapore — loosely translated as "place of lions" — and created a symbol with fishlike base and a lion's head. To keep things peaceful, it is said he paid the nearby Sultan of Jahore (Malaysia) about $3,000 and another heir-claimant about 5,000 pounds.

He then brought in a few British Tars and Tommies and let it be known this little island was to be a British Crown Colony whose mission was to protect the British Navy's passage and to control the spice and mercantile trade through the Straits of China (or Malay Straits) from the South China Sea to the Indian Ocean.

The refurbished Raffles Hotel remains as the social center of the Singapore 400, the elite high society of the city.

The city is located only one degree north of the equator, so the temperature is relatively constant at 75-90 degrees year-round with a rainy season (monsoon) centered in the first quarter of the year. It is easy for Americans to visit Singapore because English is the first language, followed by Chinese (Mandarin), Malay, and then a host of others. Of course, British English modified by Chinese and Malaysian accents is not typical American speech.

Sir Stamford Raffles brought in 100 huts-full of the nearby Malay natives for his first settlers and they were followed quickly by Chinese, Indians and others wandering down from the north and mixed breeds of Polynesians drifting in from the sea, as well as a few civil servants and noble class Brits to establish a civilized social order. These were joined by some Portuguese, French and Arab vagabonds either pursuing a dream or escaping pursuit by distant civil authorities.

The Raffles plan for multi-racial and multi-cultural harmony was almost the direct opposite of those we espouse today. He established several ethnic-cultural religious quarters or regions — Chinatown for the Chinese (Taoists, Buddhists), Little India for the Asian Indians (Hindu, Buddhists, Muslims), the Malaysian Quarter (Muslim), the Arab Sector (Muslim), and so on.

These peoples lived and worked in these quarters but traded freely in other sections of town. Of course, if they wanted to do well and sell to the British, it behooved them to master some of the King's English. We are told there was and is no prejudice in Singapore. An outsider's casual observation is not reliable, but we were surrounded by many Muslims and Chinese with no problems.

I attended the Singapore International Furniture Exhibition and the Asian Furniture Exhibition at the Singapore World Trade Center. This trade show was huge by any international standards. There were several hundred well-organized and elaborate exhibit booths representing the production of Asian countries. The show suffered some, in my opinion, from a relatively small number of prospective buyers compared to the large number of sellers from Singapore, Malaysia, Taiwan, Indonesia, Thailand, Korea and Japan. The trade show language was, of course, English and the marketing personnel was about 40 percent female — a far cry from the Oriental "women's place" concept of even 10 years ago.

We were entertained by Patsy Bong, operations manager of the Swedish Bank in Singapore. Patsy and her husband, Larry, are second generation

The two-mile long causeway provides a lifeline to Singapore from the mainland Jahore Baharu, Malaysia. The span carries not only vehicular and rail traffic, but also utility support cables and water pipes.

Chinese immigrants and have recently adopted a Chinese baby girl from the Mainland China province of their origin. Their story of the trials of the adoption procedure is certainly adequate material for a suspense novel or movie.

Patsy is a sharp, savvy and charming modern Oriental female filling a responsible role in the bustling business world of Singapore. She took us to the Long Bar of the Raffles Hotel where we sat in the high rattan chairs and, naturally, were served a famous Singapore Sling — the gin-based drink either made famous by the hotel, or vice-versa.

Following this we were taken to the Chinese dining room of the opulent Westin Plaza for a delicious and authentic Chinese dinner ordered by Patsy. Since WWII, the pace of change in the Orient has been a long road for Eastern women from the shadowy world of Susie Wong to the real business world of Patsy Bong.

Singapore housing is generally very good with necessary efficient utilization of space. With land worth $100 per square foot, comfortable apartment living prevails with "townhouse" type buildings available for higher incomes and a relatively few spacious single dwellings. Some of the townhouse units sell for $95,000 Singapore ($60,000 U.S.), and 86 percent of the population lives in good subsidized housing. The living in Singapore is good. The economy seems prosperous with less than two percent unemployment.

We attended a Presbyterian church with a very wide diversity of racial background in the congregation of around 1,000 — Chinese, English, Malay and Indians singing hymns familiar to all in Christiandom. The freedom of inter-race relationship was dramatically illustrated to us when a Japanese woman approached us in a restaurant and introduced us to her daughter, who was 17 years old. Her daughter had studied briefly in America at Salt Lake City. They apparently wanted to practice their English.

One of our most exciting experiences in Singapore was a short trip across the two mile-long causeway to Jahore Baharu in Malaysia. Singapore's lifeline water supply runs beside the highway and railroad across this causeway. The trip gave us a chance to see again the Sultan's Palace where, some 20 years previous, the then-crown prince (later to become sultan and king) had given us a personal tour of a palace with opulence only imagined in wildest dreams.

Joe Robertson stands in front of one wing of a sultan's palace in Jahore Baharu, Malaysia. Twenty years ago, on a previous visit, the Robertsons were personally shown through this same palace by the then-crown prince, who later became sultan and king.

Kuala Lumpur Seen At Work, Play

Kuala Lumpur is the melodic-sounding name for the bustling capital of Malaysia. This was our second visit, but it was not deja vu. We could not believe that in a dozen years this relatively small country with only 18 million "little" Malay people had exploded from a resource-rich tropical rain forest into a dynamic nation with highly technical development in electronics while supporting unbelievable industrial growth.

Education has not been the key, for although rapid strides have been made, formal schooling development does not approach that of the U.S.

The Protestant work ethic has not been the key, for this is a Muslim world where many stop to pray five times daily and they fast (and feast) for a month each year, take a week off for Hari-Raya (Islam's equivalent of New Year's Day), and observe many other holidays during the year.

The key isn't many other things, for although Germans invest here, there is little of German-type discipline. Perhaps it is related to family values and a moral code requiring individual responsibility. Criminals are punished severely with little thought of rehabilitation. There is plenty of poverty, but there is plenty of wealth being created.

There undoubtedly are many things wrong here, but the improvement in the last decade is beyond belief. Economic growth rate is about seven percent, inflation about three to four percent. Prime interest is around six percent (higher than Singapore or Hong Kong) with mortgage money (or whatever) available for subsidized housing at about 10 percent.

We entertained a group of seven native people for dinner at the Eden Village Malaysian Restaurant — reported to be one of the best in Kuala Lumpur — which offered a wide selection of Southeast Asian cuisine and a fine culture show featuring the people, songs, and dances of Malaysia, China, Thailand and India.

I was taken to the stage by a host of little people and thrust into a set-up dance routine with a beautiful and agile small-scale Malaysian woman, about 4 feet, 10 inches tall and claiming to be 24 years old. Her jet black hair, olive complexion and sparkling brown eyes qualified her to make me do about whatever she wanted — to the great amusement of my friends.

The desserts were mountains of fruit and sweets. My ice cream must have been 10 inches tall buoyed up by a bed of sweet sago and local nuts, berries and cherries. Drinks were colorful but reportedly not super-charged as is sometimes the case. Dr. Razali, a Muslim, did not drink anything alcoholic — as is the custom of Muslims — although we all promised him "we wouldn't tell" the muessin, Shah, Ayatollah, or whoever polices such things.

Although much of our specific business and technical discussion was reserved for the following days, there were many interesting observations. For example, the tin mines, which drew many people to the area, were in a descendancy despite the worldwide appreciation of the Royal Selangor Pewter. The pewter was sold well locally by savvy saleswomen such as Carol Sin. The principal commercial ministries today include oil (petroleum), lumber, tourism, rubber and palm oil.

The dinner was scheduled for 7:30 p.m. Dr. Razali, a U.S.-educated forest products academic from the University of Malaysia, was already at the table "breaking his fast" which, as is Muslim custom in the Ramadan month, he had been keeping since 5:30 a.m. Mr. Ong, wood adhesives research expert; Dr. Koh, Forest Research Institute of Malaysia; and Mr. Chew of Dynochem, tech service manager, arrived next without a fellow researcher, Tann En Eng, who failed to meet up with them in rush hour traffic.

Jennifer Wong showed up next. She had recently switched from resin chemistry for wood products to resin chemistry for cosmetics and pharmaceutical medicine derivatives. Then at about 8:30 p.m. our special friend, Ms. Kwee Lin, showed up — delayed for one hour by a not-uncommon KL traffic jam. Kuala Lumpur has less than 3 million inhabitants, and from traffic appearances, every KL inhabitant must have two cars — they can take eight years to pay.

The dinner was truly international. For example, Virginia started out with shark fin soup, Jennifer with escargot from the jungle. For entrees, I ordered sauteed prawns from the nearby sea (about 12 or 14 inches long and delicious) and others ordered lobster twice as large. The seafood selections, of course, were taken live from the holding tanks nearby. All kinds of odoriferous stuffs were brought to the table in rapid succession, and I suspect we had one server assigned to each guest.

Malaysian Business and Research Visits

We were made most welcome at the adhesive manufacturing plant of Norse Chem Resins in Shah Alam, Selangor State, about 20 miles from Kuala Lumpur. Norse Chem is associated with the Nestle Co., which is an active glue supplier in the U.S. Our hostess was the very competent Ms.

Kwee Lin, director of quality control, research and development. Kwee Lin, a sharp young woman of Chinese background, was very knowledgeable not only in adhesive technology but also in the economics driving the plywood and adhesive business.

We discussed many of the likenesses and differences of plywood adhesive technology in Malaysia and the U.S. One of her laboratory associates explained their laboratory equipment and procedures. The production superintendent, Ting Ong Hua, showed us around the formaldehyde plant, the urea and phenol manufacturing facility and the dry blending plant.

Some polyvinylacetate, melamine and resorcinols are being added for special urea and phenol adhesives. Norse Chem expects to soon complete a totally new plant of 90-ton capacity. Quality management and statistical control programs were discussed.

After the resin plant visit, we proceeded to the Forest Research Institute of Malaysia [*FRIM*], where we were invited to a lengthy discussion of Malaysian Forest Policy and Progress by Dr. Azizol Abdul Kadir, director of the chemistry division of the institute.

Dr. Azizol and his associates gave me a fine tour of the considerable acreage and facilities of FRIM. The business-science forestry people are very much into the economic yield and environmental management of the forest. They are almost fanatical in their pursuit of better methods of forest waste utilization — the palm fronds and the branches of all trees.

I was surprised to learn that no more plywood plant building licenses will be issued in Peninsular Malaysia nor in Eastern Malaysia — Sabah and Sarawak — which are part of former Borneo. They are encouraging investments and activity in Particleboard and Oriented Strand Board (OSB) because their perception is that such plants utilize secondary value of trees and more of the tree.

They are particularly excited about using mature palm nut trees after their oil nut days are over — Malaysia is the world's largest producer of palm oil and of course the copra (meat) is well utilized but much research has been directed for some time at the hull or shell.

Actually, as is often the case with waste utilization projects, efficient disposal can be a more economical and environmentally friendly procedure than trying to adapt unsuitable material to highly specialized uses in sophisticated processes. Coconut shell flour is not the best plywood adhesive filler in the world and sago flour is not the best extender.

There will possibly never be a decade of change in Malaysia to equal that of the last one. The teeming suburbs of skyscrapered Kuala Lumpur are still pushing back jungle where two hours away tigers and even rhinos are still wild and protected. Elephants are regarded by natives as crop destroyers — in the same manner as deer in the U.S. There are also orangutan, vipers and cobras.

In the nearby village there is always a mosque. There is also a Blue Mosque maybe only second or third to the Great One in Istanbul. It is strikingly beautiful and relatively new. The dome is unbelievably large and the building will house 25,000. The Malaysian Muslims are an interesting lot with a wide deviation of depth into the religious fundamentals.

There are many fully-covered women wearing the bnaju kuring [*outer garment worn by Muslim women*] and scarf. There are also those wearing beautiful Batki sarongs and blouses showing arm above the wrist and leg far above the ankle. These are mixed in with the many mini-skirts, and for a country with independence dating from only 1957, they "have come a long way, baby!"

The Orient - Hong Kong, Taipei Exhibit Old and New

Hong Kong

Fortunately, it was daylight as our jumbo jet dropped down into Hong Kong (actually Kowloon) by Victoria Harbor. We could see some of the famed Victoria Peak, the Lion Head Mountain and the New Territories, and even the tops of the skyscrapers, some now more than 70 stories high.

The buildings seem to share the atmosphere in Hong Kong, defying resolution by coming in and out of the fog. This is 1994 with building and developing still progressing rapidly, but local stocks are reportedly down 20 percent. What's in the future in 1997 when the People's Republic of China takes over control from the British? The Crown Colony will be no more.

Hong Kong is a delightful place to visit and, of course, a great commercial center for Asia and the world. It is difficult for Westerners to believe that nearly half of the world's shipping moves through the major Asian ports.

What we remember most of the old Hong Kong that has not changed is the Star Ferry. The ferryboats are probably the same ones we boarded for the six-minute ride to Kowloon in 1972. The landmark of the Hong Kong-Kowloon class hotels is the Peninsula, where in days past "everyone who was anyone" in the world paused for High Tea in the lobby or stayed in one of the few places where "gracious living" was still possible — a sign card greeting from a Rolls Royce chauffeur at the airport, a greeting at the door by a suave doorman, and a swarm of white-clothed "China boys" to carry oneself and one's baggage all the way past a key keeper room boy and into a room of beautiful Oriental appointments.

About 12 stories are being added to the historic low-rise building. One now passes through the airport to the hotel touring desk without escort. Perhaps this is a much-needed leveling, but the present treatment at this wonderful hotel presented as for "the rich and famous" cannot compare to the former uniqueness of the Peninsula of earlier times. Like Raffles of Singapore and the Empress of Vancouver, all had the classical air of the heyday of British Colonial Empire, when the sun never set on the empire and there were no barriers in the world to her majesty's uniform.

"East is East and West is West and never the twain shall meet" is now a mixed bag. They have met and there are many blendings, but great cultural chasms remain in some areas. We saw electronic superiority everywhere: TVs of remarkable clarity, CDs with unsurpassed tone quality, cellular phones being used everywhere — on the streets, in the lobbies, in the cars, on the ferries, even on some of Southeast Asia's innumerable motorcycles.

It seemed that every fourth store was an electronic outlet with computers, boom boxes, TVs, walkmans and whatever — all of these with an overall music background ranging from traditional sing-song Chinese and lots of flute to rock and roll and country.

Hong Kong offers the products of the world to the shopper. However, the attractive (cheap) prices of former days are gone. The Arts and Handicraft Center offers a bonanza of the products from mainland China but at Hong Kong prices. Taking the Star Ferry to Kowloon and visiting the Chinese shops on both sides is real fun, however.

We attended a Methodist church which had a large Filipino congregation. An excellent service with a retiring Scottish minister from New Zealand — that's the way it goes. We sat by and in front of people from Alabama and we met Rob Wigel of Notre Dame's '78 football team in the hotel elevator — a running back who played with Joe Montana. Every new meeting was interesting. Dull folks just don't frequent these places!

After church we came back to Chater Road by the hotel and found several blocks cordoned off for about 10,000 Filipino domestic maids. These are girls — mostly in the 18-25 range — and this is the way they spend the Sunday afternoon of their day off. They just poured in from the Star Ferry Tunnel, the subway, truckloads of them from the country. They just met to mill and talk — a usual happening every Sunday afternoon. Just one more sight and sound associated with the commercial and cultural connection of China to the World

The Republic of China
Taipei, Taiwan

Two Fords and two Chryslers. Taipei, Taiwan, is a city with more than 150,000 cars; 40,000 taxis; and 40,000 little motorcycles. Yet we noticed only four American automobiles in this surging sea of vehicles. We had noticed this when we attended a wood adhesives symposium here in 1992, and the car numbers had seemingly increased from an already over-capacity street system, but the U.S.-foreign car ratio had not changed. Still next to no penetration of a growing dynamic market with goods to trade and money to buy.

Taipei's C.K.S. (Chiang Kai Shek) Airport is enormous and modern. The airport is larger but air traffic probably not as congested as that in Hong Kong. However, for sheer size, it compares favorably with our big hubs at N.Y., L.A., Chicago and Atlanta.

If one looks on the map, one will see Taiwan as only a little island off the China Coast, but it is bustling with activity. The native Taiwanese (Formosans) constitute more than 80 percent of the population, but the government is largely operated by the minority descendants of the mainland Chinese who came from China and set up a government in exile. It has been a strong, active and effective government. It could possibly be described as an authoritative democracy where people vote, but are subject to a strict and unsympathetic system of law and justice. As a result, streets are usually safe for both men and women generally any time of the day.

The Tang family provides some answers as to why the Republic of China (Taiwan) has been able to make such economic, cultural, and academic progress. These people are motivated, dedicated and educated.

Joe Robertson in front of the Chiang Kai Shek Memorial Museum in Taipei, Taiwan, Republic of China.

Jung Lei Tang spent 11 years in the U.S. completing his education and gaining work experience in his field of forest products. An excellent undergraduate record enabled him to get employment as a quality control and research development person at Swain Industries (Flakeboard) in Seymour, Indiana. He worked four years there, learning much about the American-engineered wood products business.

During that time he met and married Jennifer Wang, also a Taiwanese, who was completing her master's in biochemistry at the University of Louisville, Kentucky. Again, their excellent academic performance and work records earned them entrance into the selective PhD. program at Colorado State.

There, under the guidance of Dr. Fred Wangard, an eminent educator from the Yale School of Forestry, Jung completed his doctorate and accepted a position with the Department of Forest Research in Taipei. Jennifer remained in Colorado to complete her PhD. while also looking after their young daughter, Paige. Today, Tang is deputy director of the department and Jennifer works there in researching derivatives from forest resources.

Our dinner with Jung Lei Tang, Jeny Wang Tang and Paige Tang was a delightful experience. Jung ordered many delicious Chinese dishes which we relished while enjoying the stimulating conversation (in English — probably the only English in the excellent restaurant). Paige was charming and with her nearly completed high school education at the American-Chinese school, her U.S. experiences and excellent academic record, we see her as eligible for acceptance, and probable scholarship assistance, at almost any of our highly-rated universities. (Note — She later enrolled in University of California and also visited in the Robertson Home in Indiana.)

The Taiwan Department of Forest Research provided us with a great deal of helpful information pertinent to our field of wood panel adhesives. We also were provided with a great deal of assistance and information from Steve Sandor and his staff at the offices of the Indiana Department of Commerce in the World Trade Center of Taipei.

Steve and his staff are very effective in introducing and enabling Hoosiers in Taiwan. We were furnished lists of all plywood and resin manufacturers in Taiwan as well as a great deal of other pertinent information. We were also introduced to the very able John Fu, who represents Amer-

A World of Travel

ican Plywood Association, Hardwood Export Council and other American interests in Taiwan.

We were now ready to depart from the lands of the "Southeast Asia Tigers" — booming countries of Singapore, Malaysia, Hong Kong and Taiwan. The economies, production, and living standards in these countries have been exploding, and stocks related to them have enjoyed substantial appreciation as a result of American, Japanese, and European investment. These high-flying Asian markets may be due for a pause, however, as interest rates edge up and Hong Kong approaches "Takeover Time."

As our airliner lifted from an Oriental night toward an approaching dawn in the U.S. across the Pacific, we again were pleased to be coming home to our country, which is still the best place. We also felt privileged and pleased to have observed a 1994 Asia far different from what we had experienced in the 1970's and 1980's. In the next century, the world will probably see another New Asia, with the Asian nations then taking their place as equals in world councils of peace and prosperity — without prejudice.

The May 4, 1995, issue of the *Jackson County Banner* (Bedford, Indiana) ran the following account of our trip to France, where we joined our friends, the Rossers for a train ride through the "Chunnel" under the English Channel to London.

Local Residents Take "Chunnel" Excursion

The Under-Channel Tunnel, or "Chunnel" Passenger Service between Paris and London began about Thanksgiving-time last fall (1994). We had been looking forward to participating in this new travel adventure for some time.

Dreams of this project were published as early as 1803 by Napoleon, and trial digs were made about 1870. Early tunneling on the present route was started about 1974 and made rapid progress in the late 80's and early 90's with the completion of the two major tunnels and the one service tunnel. We planned to take the longer passenger trip from Paris to London. It is possible to drive your car (ferry style) on a much shorter journey.

Our adventure plan began to turn into reality earlier this spring [*1995*] when Paul and Sally Rosser and their charming eight-year old daughter invited us to meet them in Paris and do the "Chunnel" together, with their handling the pre-trip Paris overview tour and the post-trip tour of London and Southwest England.

The Delta flight, direct, non-stop from Cincinnati to Paris, was hassle-free and reasonably comfortable considering the flight time — 7½ hours to Paris Orly [*Airport*] and 8 hours, 20 minutes returning from Gatwick Airport in London.

The morning light and adequate pre-landing breakfast had us in pretty good shape for arrival. The scenery during the cab ride from Orly to our hotel was very enjoyable. Taxi fares in Paris are high in dollar terms. The dollar would only buy 4.6 Francs; so when I watched the meter roll past 100 Francs and on toward 150, the importance of the exchange rate was again brought to our attention.

En route to our hotel we passed a great many famous works of art and architecture and, of course, the sidewalk cafes were doing business along the Champs Élysées and the Avenue of Charles de Gaulle and the Grand Armée. The beautiful, small (very small) hotel was a delight. Les Jardins du Tracadero was located on the right bank of the Seine just across the river from the Eiffel Tower where two carousels were running, and colorful street vendors plied their trade. The views from the tower were, as always, spectacular — in April even better.

Our hotel was furnished and decorated rather elegantly in period style with Napoleon draperies and painted muses decorating each of the only 15 room doors. The "La Petite Muse" Restaurant-Salon provided dedicated dining facilities and attractive menus.

The cab ride to the museums and early evening dinners provided opportunity to see why Paris is considered one of the world's most beautiful cities. Notre Dame still inspires, and the architecture at Sorbonne University is outstanding. The Louvre is very popular all day long and a lengthy but fast-moving queue is maintained in front of the entry pyramid. Both the Eiffel Tower and the Louvre had entry charges of nearly $10 each. The

Mona Lisa, Venus de Milo, and Winged Victory [*statues*] are still the most popular spots in the great museum.

The Rossers booked exciting and excellent, small, very French restaurants every night. The gourmet French food was excellent and varied, and the interaction of the proprietors, patrons, and waiters/waitresses was entertaining.

The Gallery LaFayette provided a glimpse of unusual architecture and a vast array of French goods. The Ospey Museum had works of many famous artists on display — Monet, Whistler, Renoir, Van Gogh, et al.

After our four days of highlighting the Paris scene, we were scheduled to take off on the Chunnel adventure on Easter afternoon. An early morning egg hunt was held for Carey in the Rosser room before our leaving the hotel for the train ride. The Nord Train Station was big, and boarding procedures much more strenuous than airline boarding. Help (porter), however, was available and capable.

We were very comfortably seated in sleek modern train cars. The train moved out with hardly a semblance of motion and soon we were moving across the beautiful French countryside at 186 miles (not kilometers) per hour. The ride was unbelievably smooth. We have ridden bullet trains in Japan and excellent superspeed trains in Germany, but the comfort of this train ride would be difficult to surpass.

The ride to Calais was beautiful. The countryside was mostly deep green meadows of cereal growth and grass highlighted by the blossoming fruit trees. The total time for the non-stop trip is about three hours with less than 30 minutes in the dark under the billions of gallons of water in the English Channel above. The train emerges almost in the middle of the White Cliffs of Dover, and the journey is then mostly urban through the County of Kent into London. The London terminal (Victoria Station) is just across the Thames from Big Ben, the Parliament Building, and Westminster Abbey. In London, it was obvious that the British Customs and Immigration Services were just putting us through an entry exercise to maintain their bureaucracy. We were not harassed, and the procedure was polite, but queues were long and passport stamping time-consuming and inconvenient. We had, after all, been cleared by Customs and Immigration at Paris entry — why do it again?

The only major hitch of the trip developed in London. Virginia and I and our considerable baggage were in one proper London cab — probably the only roomy taxis in the world outside the U.S. — along with Sally

Rosser. Paul and young Carey and considerable baggage were in another. Paul's cab delivered them to our flat site (Mayfair Apartments) and set the two passengers and their baggage outside the apartment door. The plan was for Sally to pick up the flat key at the apartment agent's residence en route and proceed. Well, the flat was not ready for occupancy as the employees didn't want to work Easter weekend. So, our cabbie drove us over to where Paul and Carey and baggage were standing in dejection beside the street. Being resourceful and having a cooperative cabbie, all five of us, plus driver and 10 pieces of baggage, were piled in the taxi and "the boot," and off we went looking like Okies and searching for rooms in a very crowded London.

We passed one Intercontinental Hotel and I shouted, "Stop the cab!" Rosser took my expired Intercontinental Six Continents Club Card and various and sundry other expired and worthless documents and bullied the staff into giving us "honors treatment" with two upgraded, fairly high but reduced-rate rooms. That night we visited the nearby Audley Pub-Restaurant and enjoyed fish and chips along with other British fare.

One of the objectives of the trip was to visit the village of Shanklin on the Isle of Wight in order to investigate the genealogical background of Sally Shanklin Rosser. Paul Rosser rented a car, a Rover, an adequate sedan but not the size of a London cab. We filled it with people and our baggage the next morning and started out for Portsmouth where many British ships were built and launched. The British countryside was even more beautiful than that of France. Flowers and blossoms were everywhere.

We were driving on the "wrong side" of the road, you know, and had to "think left" to avoid head-on collisions. Paul maneuvered the car into a starting slot on the Isle of Wight Ferry departure lot and soon we were on our way across 40 minutes of English Channel/Irish Sea. We landed at Fishbourne and started down the very narrow island roads to Shanklin. The houses at Shanklin are mostly old, seaside cottages, now owned by affluent retirees or occupied by sight-seeing tourists. There is a profusion of bed and breakfast inns and small hotels. Nearly everything, of course, is built to face the sea or else to service those who face the sea. Charles Dickens broke bread here and Henry Wadsworth Longfellow visited and wrote here. Many of the roofs are thatched, and there are footpaths that lead through "chymes" or gullies down through the chalk cliffs to the seaside beaches.

A World of Travel

We were most fortunate in meeting a sort-of assistant rector of the Shanklin Church. He gave us a tour of that church and then led us to the old original church and graveyard dating back several hundred years to the time of Cromwell and the Royalists (British Civil War). It was small and delightful, and our lady guide who unlocked the church for our private tour had a wealth of information. We lunched at The Crab (thatched roof) in Shanklin and had crab sandwiches and Shanklin tomato soup along with crusty British white bread. From there we continued to the glass factory to watch the glass blowers demonstrate their ancient skill as they crafted the beautiful glass pieces for which the island is famous.

A local suggested we go down and check out the sand point from where many of the emigrants, escaping persecution or prosecution, had embarked for America.

After the ferry trip back to the mainland we drove about 1½ hours to London's Gatwick Airport and secured accommodations at the Gatwick Hilton for the night. The next morning we took off for the U.S. on Delta Flight 37, a comfortable L-1011. The route back went across Oxford, Manchester, Ireland, Iceland, Gander, Quebec, and on over Cleveland to Cincinnati.

It was an enjoyable and exciting trip. The Chunnel must be classed as one of civilization's greatest engineering achievements, and the trip lived up to expectations.

In the fall of 1996, Virginia and I traveled to the Incan ruins of Machu Picchu in Peru, and then flew to Easter Islands to view the mysterious great stone statues. *The Jackson County Banner* of December 12, 1996, carried my article on our experiences.

By Helicopter to Machu Picchu and By Gosh to Easter Island

If someone says they want to go to Machu Picchu "in the worst way,"

The llama and alpaca are among many of the pack and wool animals found in the high reaches of the Peruvian Andes.

that's how they're going to do it. That doesn't mean it isn't a fabulous experience. It is! BUT, however one does it, it's not a stroll through Central Park.

Most folks prefer "leisure travel" such as a "Caribbean Cruise" or a trip to a comfortable resort-casino or even to the best hotels in the U.S. or Europe. The trek to Machu Picchu is not for them. It's only for the modern vagabonds who seek remote places less visited on roads and seas less traveled. Crowds we didn't see, but we did see a polyglot mixture of all ethnic and racial backgrounds and of wide age range including many Generation X unmarrieds, male and female together and single. It seemed that many who probably would not consider a "mistress" role or even a "living together" arrangement were enthusiastic and vocal regarding their role as "travel companions." The language was universal — "sign" — or "communicable babble" with nearby linguistic interpretation readily available through Spaniards, Frenchmen, Germans or whatever, into our Pidgin English — loud.

Our trip started comfortably in the very early morning at the Cincinnati Airport, on Delta. Our first transfer was in Spanish Miami where we bought a little Ecuadorean, Peruvian and Chilian "Ugs" or Sucres, Soles and Pesos respectively. Of course we "got skinned" by the money changers but that's routine, at least for us — time and convenience being more important than the best exchange rate. There in Miami we boarded comfortable American Airlines Flight #967 for the trip across water, Cuba, Panama, and northern South America to Quito, Ecuador. There it was a little hairy for we were supposed to transfer to Avianca Airlines and those bozos had all gone home — no one knew where the counter was, and when we did find it, no one was at the counter. Again with the linguistic assistance of several bystanders we got aboard and the plane immediately took off — ten minutes early and half full. Of course, our baggage didn't make it and so in Lima, Peru we filed a complicated claim with a lonely, pleasant but hesitant "claim agent" or something. However, with the help of "Cecil," we made it out of the airport and through Customs. Then we overnighted in the Lima Sheraton-Casino-Resort where we were the only ones going to bed early or getting up early. We did get up early and boarded a very nice Aero-Peru Boeing 757 for the trip up to Cuzco — without baggage — and in our initial clothing. Even though we didn't have much time in Peru, Cecil managed to tour us through the heart of the rejuvenated city. Of particular interest was the main square around which a Spanish ruler had built eight similar houses for his eight sons. This area is great shopping today.

Cuzco, Peru is the "Spiritual Center of The Andes" and "The Archeological Capital of South America." We were advised by our new, very good and pretty guide, "Patty" (these names of course are "English handles" for Peruvian names we can't pronounce) that we should observe three rules when in the 11,500 ft. altitude of Cuzco: 1) Eat light 2) Drink lots of water and 3) Rest. Well, maybe good advice but "tempus fugit" so we checked in at The El Dorado Inn and told Patty to put us on a tour at 1:30 p.m. For a fee, she did.

Cuzco reached its zenith under the great Inca ruler, Pachacutec, about 1450 A.D. A great stone probable-fort SACSAYHUAMAN (say "sexy woman") guarded the city and also served as a temple. It is mind-boggling to consider how the Incas, without any knowledge of writing or the wheel, could devise and execute ways to place tremendous stones (some over 100 tons) in place in this fort and other buildings. No mortar was used and the surfaces fit so well one cannot insert a knife blade between them. We looked in wonder at this place which flourished at about the time of Columbus. Nearby we had our picture taken with a Giant Peruvian Condor — having a wingspan of 10 feet! This bird is nearly extinct but perhaps will have a chance of rejuvenation. The llama and alpaca, however, appeared to be in plentiful supply. The scenery was very impressive looking down from the mountain perimeter into the high valley. From this high viewing spot we could conjure up visions of the Spaniard Francisco Pizarro's "Rape of The City" in 1533. Here Pizarro was not disillusioned about Cuzco's being "El Dorado" ("City of Gold"). The streets were not paved with gold but many walls were covered by a gold plating process known only to the Incas at that time. The Incas were Sun Worshipers and "The Temple of The Sun" is a great building that served as both an Inca Emperor's Palace and a Place of Worship. The Gold Medallion was the "Seal of The Sun" and in some instances the seal was so placed that the sun's rays would strike through a small window or slit and light the room. Unquestionably, "tons of gold" were removed from Cuzco to Spain and to other palaces of kings and pirates alike.

As one looks around the environs of Cuzco, many centuries-old stairways, walls and buildings are in abundant evidence. One can only wonder "How did such a few small people (Incas) do so much with so little?"

The Highest Helicopter

The helicopter ride from Cuzco to Machu Picchu was truly spectacular. The train is the conventional mode of travel along the savage Urubamba River Valley to Agua Calientes Village and to the mountain bus transfer. The train ride is a three-hour trip with many views and well worthwhile. However, the helicopter provided a 30-minute ride that was filled with excitement and even amazement from the take-off at Cuzco's convenient airport to an impossible landing on a soccer field by a rushing river at the village of "Cool Waters" where there were no automobiles — a junction city that served as the transfer point for train and helicopter to bus.

The helicopter was a fairly large one carrying about thirty people. We were given up-front window and aisle seats both ways to facilitate unrestricted viewing of surrounding, snow-capped mountain peaks stretching up to 18,000 feet. We were allowed to take pictures out and down from our windows and also over the pilot's head through the windshield of the cockpit. The copter had proceeded down the Cuzco runway for maybe 200 yards before very rapidly ascending to get over and through the surrounding mountain peaks. Often it seemed that we could almost reach out and touch near-vertical mountainsides while looking down into canyons deeper than The Grand Canyon around "every corner." Much of the time we were not flying higher than the mountains for I recalled my World War II flying instruction to break out the oxygen masks for sure by 12,000 feet and we were routinely flying at 15,000 feet plus but dropping down into beautiful and treacherous valleys to energize the oxygen level. When we did land, we walked about one half-mile to a mountain bus for a harrowing 30-minute ride over a good distance, zig-zagging up the near-vertical side of the mountain. At the top was the unbelievable village on Machu Picchu — "Ancient Mountain." Cuzco was perhaps The Gate to Machu Picchu much as Kathmandu served as the gateway to The Himalayas and "Shangri-La." As a matter of fact, the view of the terrain from the helicopter reminded us of the Himalayan view of Mt. Everest which we had from a problematical plane ride that took us up and around the world's tallest mountain. At the 14,000 foot level, the Andean scenery and the Himalayan scenery looked much the same, very steep, brown and terraced mountains with intervening sheer cliffs. We bought a flute-like pipe — the Kena — from a small boy there in the Andes, much in the same manner that we had purchased a "Morelli" from a Serpa lad on the slopes of Ever-

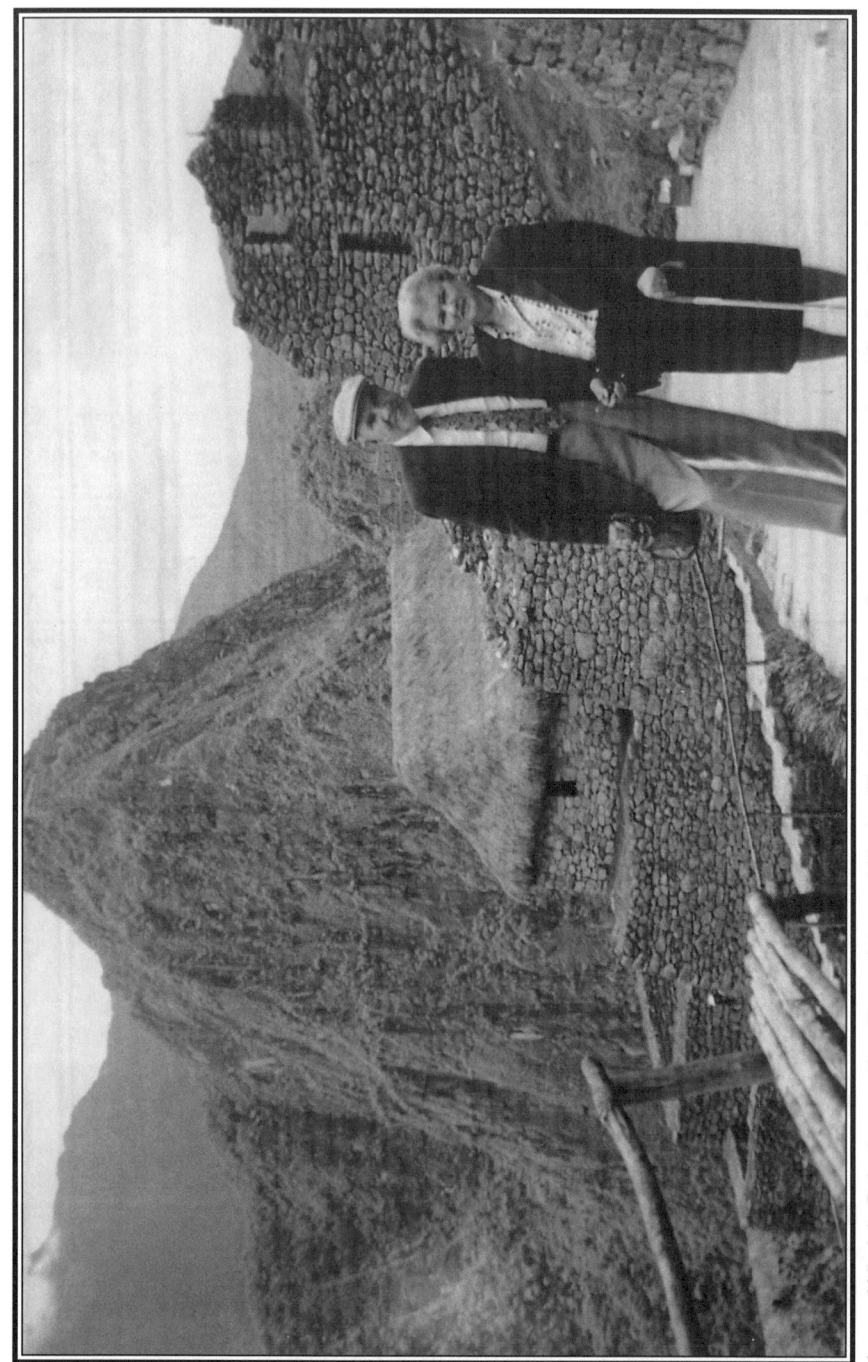

Joe and Virginia Robertson on the village plateau of Machu Picchu, the long-undiscovered nerve center of the Inca Empire.

est. The high-pitched tones of these pipes penetrate the region with a music heard nowhere else on earth.

No one had a totally satisfactory explanation of why or how the Incas wanted to locate and build this refuge-fortress-temple so high and inaccessible. It might help to recall that at the building time, the Inca Empire covered most of northern South America and much of Central America. Perhaps it was a center of communication. It was built at the divide of the torrid jungle from the western slopes to the Pacific. As one abruptly enters the Machu Picchu village plateau, located between two other "Picchus," it is undoubtedly a scene without duplication anywhere. How? Why? Impossible! The *very* steep terrace slopes on the *peaks* of surrounding mountains — to raise potatoes and other hearty vegetables. The other two Picchus — Huayna Picchu (Growing Mountain) and Huajana Picchu (Young Mountain) are the backdrop guardians almost totally obscuring the view of the stone-terraced city. There is much astronomical orientation within the city, and places of ritual abound. The achievements of the Incas were remarkable in totally keeping the knowledge of this "Place of The Sun" from the Spaniards. The Spaniards never discovered it nor made any reference to it. In later years, like the pyramids of Yucatan, it became covered by the invading jungle vegetation and was not really discovered until about 1911 by an expedition led by Yale's Hiram Bingham.

We walked through and around the terraces, temples, houses and garden area of Machu Picchu. Inside the enclosure was a vantage point with the same spell-binding view as that of the guard house-watch tower which covered all possible approaches. Virginia spent a good deal of her time there while our part-Inca guide, Percy, led me around some of the more inaccessible sites.

We had lunch at the restaurant on site and then boarded the bus, expecting it to take us back down the zig-zag mountain trail to the level place — where our helicopter was to be. Well, about 2 miles down the trail, the bus stopped abruptly in front of a barrier in the road. We were all ordered out and told there had been a landslide, a construction snafu, "or something." Anyway, we started walking, Virginia with a cane, and walking and walking on a very rough dirt and stone road. After about two and a half miles, we came to another barrier and beyond it, buses were waiting to finish the trip.

The helicopter ride back to Cuzco was again beyond belief. First, taking off with kids and dogs and soccer players all around was somewhat unusual, then going up almost vertically to avoid smashing into Machu Picchu's steep mountainside.

We returned to Cuzco's El Dorado Hotel and still no luggage — and now no water! We made do with lots of bottled water. The next morning, our local guide, Patty, was there to pick us up early and ship us back to Lima for a fresh start on another leg of the adventure.

To Easter Island

From Lima, Peru, we flew to Buenos Aires, Argentina on Aereolinas Argentinus. I had been a little uncomfortable in flying via unfamiliar national airlines, but the equipment was a brand new Airbus 310 — very spacious and more comfortable than most. The crew was friendly and helpful, and they arrived on time and guided us over to the Lan Chile VIP International Lounge to await departure for the one-hour-plus journey to Santiago.

Coming down to Buenos Aires from Lima we passed over the Atacamaean Salt Desert. This desolate but interesting desert of salt is vast and foreboding and covers part of Bolivia, northern Chile and western Argentina. It is presided over by the great volcano, Lican Cabur, and harbors many well-preserved archaeological treasures. Of course, we flew up and over the lower reaches of the Andes again on down the eastern slopes of the mountainous spine of South America. The foothills then rolled out into the Pampas leaving behind the Spanish-Inca legends and the fabled magic of the Shamans (rulers) of Atacama.

Now below was the green and brown prairie-like Pampas. The land of Tangerine and the Argentine Vaquero Cowboy. It appeared from the air much the same as Kansas. The Pampas then turned into the suburbia surrounding metropolitan Buenos Aires. We could also see across the fifty-mile wide bay to Montevideo, capital of Uruguay.

Our stop-over in Buenos Aires was brief and uneventful, only providing us a chance to contact the flavor of the land, to see some of its airport mercantile displays and to exchange greetings with many friendly people. Later we had the opportunity to discuss Argentine politics with a chemistry professor from the University of Argentina in Mendoza. Of course we were interested in Peron and Evita. The professor assured us the film and media representatives were more fantasy than fact. And, in his opinion, the government was now about as democratic, stable and satisfactory as most.

A World of Travel   297

Again across the Andes. This time flying westward while to the south lay the icelands of Patagonia down to the Straits of Magellan. As we passed over into Chile toward Santiago, I looked with longing to the far South — perhaps only a few hundred miles to Punta Arenas — "The End of Earth." I thought my urge to go and find the far out places was subsiding, but it wouldn't have taken much persuasion now to sell me a weekend ticket down there to watch the penguins paddlefoot around. We've done all continents except Antarctica, and we once missed a chance for a South Pole fly-over with possible fair weather landing — at the time only $400 round trip from New Zealand's South Island — but our fast-paced itinerary hadn't allowed the time.

Down into the beautiful valley surrounding Santiago. There we stayed at The Crown Plaza where there was plenty of hot water.

The next morning we still had no luggage. Our under-seat bag reserve was used up. So, we went on a fast shopping trip — quite an experience! We spoke no Spanish, only one or two store people spoke any English. So, we had everyone in the Hites Department Store helping us to find some basics. We just pointed and waved our credit cards. The buying procedure was about like Russia. First the goods selected were taken to a "line-up" counter for listing (on a computer no less) then I had to "stand in line" to have my credit card checked (each time I lined up) and everything listed on a computer and charged. Then, the goods and the goods list were laid out on another counter and checked against the charged items as the items were packaged. Anyway, the procedure almost caused us to miss our plane, but we ended up with a bag full of new, miscellaneous clothing necessities.

At 5:00 p.m. we took off into the sunset for Easter Island, Isla de Pascua, or Rapa Nui — take your pick. Toward a solitary speck 2400 miles out in the Pacific on a route to Tahiti another 6000 miles or so westward. It was a dark landing on a Kilroy-Yankee runway, which fortunately for the island, was an alternate emergency field for the space shuttles. Our simple, small hotel was just a few blocks from the airport — and I think all two thousand of the locals were there to meet the plane which came from Santiago going on to Tahiti twice a week. It returned from Tahiti twice a week and on back to Santiago. I saw no other airport activity during our four-day stay.

We were up early the next morning to preview the simple but enlightening museum and then to Ahu (statue) Akim where seven of the great

Easter Island is the remote Pacific island home of the Great Stone Heads (ahu statues) mysteriously carved and transported by primitive Polynesian peoples.

stone heads were on a platform. There were some "esoteric" cult types kneeling, meditating or whatever in hopes of gaining empowerment and understanding from the ancient stone figures.

Like cemetery monuments of today, the largest stoneheads are assumed to have belonged to the richest and most powerful people. The statues probably all had "top hats" when they were made and we visited the place where they quarried out the "top hats." We were then shown "caves" where some of the early dwellers lived and "hid" from the warrior tribal natives. At the Ahu Vim, there were incredible stone walls similar to those constructed by the Incas.

It's incredible to consider the mechanics of a people without the wheel moving the giant stone "ahus" (statues). There are several theories but most agree that the statues, ranging up to more than forty feet tall and weighing more than 100 tons, were carved right in the quarry mountain, then were skidded down the mountain into holes that had been prepared to make them stand upright. The great tombstones were then turned over on their backs and moved by skids, or on a sweet potato pulp lubricating mass, across the miles of island to wherever an owner might wish for his position in eternity — generally with his back to the sea and his "face toward his farm and family."

The first inhabitants of this remote speck are believed to have come from the South Americas — Peru or the Chilian Coast — about 600 A.D. Polynesian immigrants from the west in the Pacific apparently found the island in their reed, Kon-Tiki type canoes around 1000 A.D. There is strong evidence of war between not only the first and second waves of immigrants, but tribal wars between the Polynesians as well.

The high water mark of this statue carving came in the late 1400's and early 1500's. While not connected, the cessation of the "statue business" came at about the same time the Spaniards were overcoming the Central American Incas — 1530-1600.

The statues undoubtedly held some of both religious and political significance but were mainly Big Tombstones for Big People. The "hows" remain shrouded in the annals of history.

There was only one statue of a woman on the island. Perhaps symbolically, she had two heads!

Rano Raraku is the easily accessible and typical Pacific Island volcano. It is big and maybe only 5000 years since the last eruption. There are only three small sand beaches on the island. It is mostly large black volcanic rock shore where many times a high rolling surf comes crashing into the shore with spray leaping forty feet or more into the air and sporadic rainbows forming in the sunlight.

The Catholic Church on the island was crammed full — standing room only. We didn't understand a word of the Spanish Liturgy or Mass but did understand the spirit.

We routinely ate at our hotel "The Iorana" (meaning both "hello" and "goodbye" in Polynesian). The food was good, featuring local fish, papaya and banana-based dishes. Fish and chicken soups were common and good. On Sunday we ate at the Koa Kona, a French Polynesian Restaurant. It was French and it was good. We left Easter Island, Isla de Pascua, Rapa Nui on Monday with more appreciation of great accomplishments of earlier times but with little more understanding of how they did it.

We boarded the Tahiti-Santiago Express Plane on Monday around noon and arrived in Santiago in the sunset of late afternoon. It is a beautiful city. The next day we flew North between the Andes and the sea to a high-altitude field at Quito, Ecuador. "The Beautiful White City" is located at an altitude of 9,185 feet above sea level. It has a symbolic mountain and statue of "The Virgin of Quito" in the center of the city with a backdrop of the snow-capped volcano, Cotopaxi, the highest active volcano in the world. The surrounding ranges went up toward 20,000 feet with broad, beautiful and productive valleys between the ranges.

In Quito we had business objectives but had a great deal of pleasure while we were entertained and "shown around" by Cesar Alverez of The Codesa Plywood Company and his charming French-Ecuadorean wife, Maria Teresa Alverez. I visited very efficient particleboard and plywood plants where excellent boards were produced with cutting-edge technology. Mrs. Alverez and her driver helped Virginia tour many interesting points in the city. In the principal Catholic Church, many members of Mrs. Alverez's family are buried in vaults under the floor. The families on both sides have been prominent in the history and development of the country. For example, Mrs. Alverez's grandfather was the President of Ecuador.

The goldleaf, as in Cuzco, is unbelievable. Some overpainting is being done to the distress of some of the "preservationists."

Some churches and convents were closed because the "9th of October" is an Independence Day and a holiday. Furthermore, it was the day when the National Soccer Champs of Colombia had come to Quito to play the National Champs of Ecuador. 50,000-plus attended. The night before, the Colombian team had staged a very noisy celebration as they alighted from their airplane. Unfortunately for the Ecuadoreans, the Colombians did win, 1-0, in a wild and exciting game.

The delightful couple then took us out to visit their "hacienda" in the country where Mrs. Alverez manages a large herd of Holstein dairy cattle and feeds them concentrate from a soy processing plant in which the family has a substantial interest.

The Spanish-French-Ecuadorean ambiance of The Hacienda was very charming. Large fireplaces, beautiful paintings, tapestries and rugs, custom-made furniture pieces — all these contributed to the unique charm of the place.

The attractive meal, prepared in the large picturesque kitchen, was very delicious and appealing. We ate in the sun veranda. We were served a soup-meal, Ecuadorian — fresh grilled GIANT shrimp, salad and rice. The dessert was orange crepes. As an appetizer, we had homemade ranch cheese and broccoli fresh from the farm's produce. What an experience! It is said that an incredible 60,000 different dishes may be prepared in Ecuador — incredible but probable!

The Alverezes were doing a great deal to move their country and citizens into a prominent and progressive position in the world. The Alverez family provided us with a background of personal and native history which added to our understanding and appreciation of our South American neighbors. The impressions we gathered were most memorable.

Epilogue

THERE IS NO FORMAL Robertson plan for future travel, but Antarctica, as our last continent, was scheduled for 1998.

One remarkable part of the experiences of this book is that they touched four generations. My mother and father traveled a good deal for their time — in their early years via horse and buggy, and then in the horseless carriage — the automobile. Of course, railroads were available throughout their entire lives. They lived to see the end of the ocean-liner (not "cruise ship") age and had Dad been in a different age bracket, a different family situation, or occupation (military service — draft factors) he might have been on a troopship to Europe in 1918.

Travel potential exploded in my youth with cars, trains, and planes becoming available and affordable to go anywhere. However, the practicability and management of travel is a phenomenon of Baby

Boomer times. Today, the Boomers, in a large manner, can and do go about anywhere and everywhere often and quickly.

It is important that travel be managed — that it be the dessert and not the main course of life's banquet.

We took our first trip to Europe when we were about 50. Son Rob took his first trip there when he was 20! Granddaughter Katie took her first trip to Japan — escorted but without parents — when she was 13, and grandson C.J. is scheduled to go to Japan when he is 12!

Our travel attitudes have in some measures been passed on to our grandchildren — not only by oral transition of stories but by their traveling with us.

Through our travel accounts and memoirs, we are indeed fortunate to have been a participant in finding and following Kilroy's roots. If someone should point out someplace in the world where we haven't been, and Kilroy has, we'll probably go — even to the ends of the earth.

Appendix

The Robertson Corporation

C. A. Robertson
Founder, 1881

R. M. Robertson
C.E.O., 1930-1972

THE ROBERTSON CORPORATION stimulated, supported, and sustained the author's extensive travel, which the company recognized as one of the survival keys in milling. The milling industry is an inherently international trade.

The history of The Robertson Corporation begins with the Charles A. Robertson milling family and the ever-expanding industry of each succeeding generation. In 1881, C. A. Robertson and associates established the Ewing Mill at Brownstown, Indiana. In 1938, the company purchased the Lemon Mill in Bedford, and in 1942, added the Farmers Hominy Mill at Seymour, Indiana.

The Robertson Corporation is a small but vigorous cereal milling company that has always had broad and forward-looking interests, which have contributed to its strength of survival. In the early 20th century, thousands of small milling enterprises dotted the American landscape. As the millennium approaches, Robertson remains one of about a hundred family and corporate milling companies with significant production and sales.

GLU-X and SPRAY-X are the special and proprietary adhesive extenders, TM registered in the U.S. Patent Office, which are produced by The Robertson Corporation and internationally recognized by the wood panel industry as the premier extenders for phenol, urea, and other adhesive resins. When high moisture veneer gluing and spray application became popular, Robertson developed SPRAY-X to meet new and special needs.

Robertson Windmill, Historic Williamsburg.

The company's background of milling and cereal chemistry contributed to its establishment as a major manufacturer of adhesive extender for the plywood, panel, and furniture industries. It has *Fortune* 500 and other industry-leading customers throughout the U.S. It also is a part of a technical network of industrial, academic, and institutional interests associated with forest products throughout the world.

Prior to World War II, the company processed many cereals into foodstuffs. This focus changed, however, when the emerging plywood industry found that benefits could be derived from extending synthetic resins with natural protein-starch materials. The cereal chemistry know-how and technical background of The Robertson Millers contributed to the development of extender meeting the unfolding requirements of glue additives that would improve adhesive characteristics, control the viscosity of the glue mix, and eliminate several problems associated with neat or unextended resins.

Personnel of the company are actively associated with a number of professional organizations including the American Plywood Association (APA) — the Engineered Wood Research Foundation; the Hardwood Plywood and Veneer Association (HPVA); the Forest Products Society (FPS); the American Association of Cereal Chemists (AACC); and the Association of Operative Millers (AOM).

Robertson people have been major contributors to international technical literature regarding extender and have been responsible for most of the literature in technical and trade journals regarding extenders. An active Quality Control Program and a Research and Development Program have been involved with the continuous improvement policy of the company. Company representatives have appeared on panels of national and international meetings and made presentations related to extenders and non-resin additives to wood adhesives. They have studied adhesive technology and practices at plant sites in the tropical forests of Central and South America and East Asia; in the conifer forests of North America; Australia/New Zealand and Russia/Siberia; and in the temperate hardwood forests of North America and Europe. Samples and glue mix formulation information have been gathered from five continents, and when Phil Robertson or Joe Robertson or Bettina Coggeshall speak of these things, they draw on a decades-old data base of over 5,000 samples of extenders, fillers, and other adhesive additives and alternatives from all over the world.

Plywood extender has been the bread and butter market for Robertson, but much work has been done, independently and cooperatively, related to extender additions for economic and environmental benefits in particleboard, MDF (Medium Density Fiberboard), OSB (Oriented Strand Board), and other composite panels.

The Development of Environmental Emphasis — Enter Soy

The Robertson Corporation has been a long-term leader in wood adhesive extender technology. It has been engaged to some extent with developing and offering natural (renewable resource-based) additives and alternatives for synthetic polymers, (PF & UF), since the mid-1980s.

Soy-based adhesive technology systems were featured in the United Soybean Board (USB) exhibit at the Panel and Engineered-Wood Technology Conference and Exposition (PETE), in November 1996. Since that time, a number of cooperating entities have demonstrated not only the possibility of utilizing soy additives in plywood panel gluing, but also the potential advantages.

In mid-1996, the Robertson Corporation became a cooperator with USB in fostering commercial partnerships with commercial panel plants to make large and small commercial runs with some of Robertson's fortified and modified extenders and additives: Pan-X, Sepro-X, GLU-X MMS (soy bean), and Soy-Ply — all brands registered with the U.S. Patent Office.

Robertson has completed and documented a considerable body of favorable reports on commercial production runs of 1996 and 1997. Soy studies are conducted in cooperation with the United Soybean Board. Results in some measure have been presented at industry schools and conferences.

A report, "Back to the Future," regarding Robertson's soy extender/adhesive projects, in the April/May 1997, *Wood Based Panels International,* noted that most of Robertson's soy-related extender/filler/additives are modifications of GLU-X, (Robertson's Glue Extender), as companion products. These products were promoted, with the assistance of USB, as contributors to quality panel production, profit, economical environmental compliance, and resin conservation.

This very active soy interest has become an important part of the current development history of the corporation. Special extenders milled only for the forest products industry are routinely used in the adhesive mix in many hardwood and softwood plywood plants. Benefits of special extender in plywood gluing are well-documented. Analytical consistency of these extenders maintain the stability and predictable performance of the adhesive mix. Now that OSB and particleboard are important international building materials, they likewise could benefit from an adhesive mix that includes a special soy-enhanced extender that contributes to a more flexible glueline with less fracture tendency and brittleness.

Soy-based adhesives were used prior to 1950. Extenders fortified with Soy could enhance the performance of adhesive mixes in today's forest products in a world now highly concerned with forest ecology from forest floor to furniture.

Five Generations of Robertsons

Dick Robertson was a grandson of the founder. His milling experience started at age twelve and continued after his graduation from Wabash College. He worked "through the mill" as mill hand, marketing manager, accounting and finance manager, President and Chairman of the Board. He was past president of The American Millers Association. He was active in the business until his death in 1997.

Charles "Buck" Robertson worked on family farms as well as "In the mill" during his teens. Following in Dick's footsteps, he graduated from Wabash and returned to do sales work for the family milling firm. He handled much of the grain trading, as well as sales, during his progression to the presidency of the company.

After Phil Robertson's graduation from Kansas State University with a B.S. from the school of Milling Industry, he served as an Air Force officer, during which time he traveled extensively in the Pacific Rim. His active duty accomplishments and reserve assignments earned him the rank of Colonel before USAFR retirement. Phil is a widely recognized specialist in milling technology, and is active in the APA Engineered Wood Research Foundation.

With the exception of 39 months as an Air Corps officer, Joe Robertson has been involved in milling technology, administration, and cereal chemistry. He has visited plywood mills in many countries and has made presentations to international forest products conferences. He is a former Vice President and Director of the International Hardwood Plywood & Veneer Association.

Jerry O. Robertson obtained his graduate degree in Agricultural Economics at Cornell University. His business career was largely involved with international grain operations and U.S. and multinational grain companies. He is now retired. As a major shareholder, his grain expertise makes him a valuable member of the Robertson Board of Directors.

John Robertson attended Purdue University and Hanover College prior to his service in Vietnam. Since then his long experience in mill operation has served him well in assuming management responsibilities. He has also received a milling technology certification from the Department of Grain Science at Kansas State University.

Dr. Joe "Rob" Robertson worked in the Robertson mills and laboratories during his youth. He was graduated from Yale University and Indiana University Medical School, and completed residencies and fellowships in Portland and Memphis. He is now an Eye Surgeon and Director of the Casey Eye Institute and Chairman of Ophthalmology at Oregon Health Science University in Portland, Oregon. His Northwest location and business interest make him a valuable board participant, and a part of the plan for continuing family involvement. He recently completed an M.B.A.

The Robertson Corporation Board of Directors. Front left: Phil (Grain Science-Milling, Kansas State University, Colonel USAFR, Ret.), 4th generation; Joe E., Chairman (Cereal Chemistry, Kansas State University), 3rd generation; Jerry, Director (M.S., Cornell University, International Grain Trade), 4th generation. Back left: John, President, 4th generation; Joe, Jr., Director (M.D., M.B.A., Yale University, Indiana University, Oregon Health Sciences University), 4th generation; Jill, Director, first woman on Board (M.B.A., Depauw University, Indiana University), 5th generation.

Jill Robertson worked in sales and marketing for the corporation during summers of her undergraduate at DePauw University and graduate schooling at Indiana University. Jill has a M.B.A. Since then, she has been in several marketing and sales positions and currently serves in a position with a San Francisco securities firm.

The Robertson Corporation, with three processing plants in Indiana, may be the only U.S. wheat milling concern devoted totally to manufacture of adhesive glue extender for the building panel industry. Since plywood production is a major glue consumption segment of the wood panel industry, plywood manufacturers are top priority at Robertson's.

In 1938, the first shipment was to a hardwood plywood producer Hoosier Panel Company, in New Albany, Indiana. Jasper Wood Products and Jasper Corporation, both of Jasper, Indiana, and General Plywood (later acquired by Georgia Pacific) were early accounts.

Post-World War II developments saw GLU-X distribution expand into furniture manufacturing plants in the North Carolina area.

The shipment to the first southern pine plywood mill was made in December 1963, to Georgia Pacific's start-up plant at Fordyce, Arkansas. Since that date, carloads or trailer loads of GLU-X have moved into all but three or four of the 80 or 90 southern pine mills.

Today, some 50 or 60 of the nation's largest plywood producing mills, located in about 25 states from Texas to the Atlantic, and from Florida to New England, and 30 additional operations in other national and international areas use GLU-X.

U.S. Postage Stamp Featured Robertson Windmill

The 1720 Robertson windmill at Colonial Williamsburg, Virginia, was one of five early windmills featured by the U.S. Postal Service in a new booklet of small-size stamps commemorating historic windmills.

Coincidental with the new issue, the local Robertson Corporation, then in its 99th year, prepared for a Centennial Commemoration.

Although the Robertson windmill at Williamsburg, Virginia, dates from 1720, the roots of the local mill go back to the establishment of the Ewing Mill at Brownstown, Indiana, in 1881, by C. A. Robertson and associates. C. A. Robertson was the grandfather, great and great, great grandfather of the present mill officials.

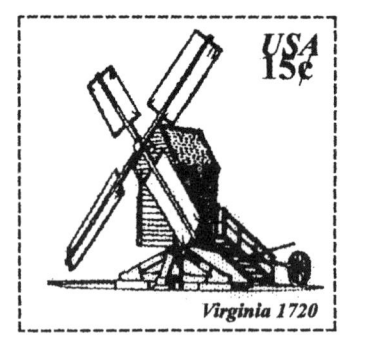

There is evidence that the current Robertson millers, who moved into southern Indiana about 1790, are related to the pioneer grain millers of Williamsburg.

The 19th century Indiana mill utilized millstones and steampower to grind grain for area farmers.

As the years rolled by, steel rollers replaced the stones and electricity replaced steampower in the same progression that colonial windpower was replaced by water-powered mills such as the "The Mill That Slept Awhile," originally constructed in 1814 and now restored on its original site in Spring Mill State Park near Mitchell, Indiana.

In 1938, the local company purchased the Lemon Mill in Bedford, and in 1942 acquired the Farmers Hominy Mill at Seymour. The mill's properties at Seymour and Bedford have been sold, but the Plainville Milling

Company of Plainville, Indiana, became an associate mill of The Robertson Corporation in 1986. Although many cereal products have been developed and produced by the Robertsons through the years, two modernized plants at Brownstown and the mill at Plainville are now engaged in processing wheat exclusively for the production of cereal glue extender. An excellent cooperation agreement has been continuing at Plainville with Boyd Grain Corporation.

The wheat germ and fiber by-product of this proprietary milling process is used in the manufacture of specialty feeds.

The Robertson Corporation is reportedly the oldest milling establishment in Southern Indiana and one of the same name and line as the founders. Several antique milling machines preserved by The Robertson Corporation were donated and placed in the Smithsonian Institute Museum in Washington D.C.

The 15¢ windmill stamp booklet was placed on sale February 7, 1980, at Lubbock, Texas 79408 – the site of one of the last American windmills, *circa* 1890. The stamps were issued only in $3 booklets containing two panes of ten 15¢ stamps each. The stamps were available for general distribution through the U.S. Postal system.

The Public Relations release below was printed in "The First 100 Years" desk planner published by The Robertson Corporation in 1981.

The Robertson Centennial Coin, 1881-1981

The motivation for striking this commemorative coin came from many sources but particularly from the 1981 U.S. Windmill Stamp which pictures the Robertson Mill in Williamsburg, Virginia. Struck in a limited number, the 1981 coin has been distributed to friends and associates of The Robertson Corporation. It commemorated the 100th anniversary of The Robertson Corporation which was founded as the Ewing Mill Company in Brownstown (Ewing Post Office), Indiana, by C. A. Robertson, John Robertson, and associates in 1881.

On the coin face is an exact replica of the Robertson *Windmill* Stamp, and continuing clockwise, a *water wheel mill*. Wind and water generated much of the energy for the birth of the Industrial Revolution epitomized by the grain milling industry. The *steam engine* is depicted as the invention which originally powered the Robertson Ewing Mill. Next the lightning bolt, symbol of *electricity*, is pictured as the present power which, of course, may be derived from many sources including water, wind, fossils, elements, and biomass. The *laboratory ware* symbolizes the research and analytical controls which have been important in developing quality products such as GLU-X and in carefully controlling the uniformity.

On the reverse side, the words common to U.S. Currency, "In God We Trust," are prominently inscribed. This motto certainly is appropriate not only for the coins of the period but also for the faith of the Robertson millers. In the center of the back is the *Circle R* trademark found on a number of Robertson products throughout the century. The *wheat stems* are symbolic of the cereal most often processed by The Robertson Corporation during "the first hundred years." The *millstone* represents the grinders used in the Ewing Mill erected in 1881, and *crossed rolls* beneath it represent the primary grinders used today.

The dates, 1881-1981 on the coin, represent the span of effort by four generations of Robertson and a team of associates who have vigorously engaged in processing wheat for industry, and who look forward to another hundred years.

The Robertson Corporation History Highlights

1881 Burr Mills started. R. M. Robertson born, son of founder.
1890 Steel roller mills for flour and meal.
1900 Wheat bran first sold as feed.
1918 First export sales.
1920 First "formula feed" mixed. "Emco Pig Meal."
1931 "Self-rising" flour.
1938 Development of first special "glue extender" flour, forerunner of "GLU-X" now used by plywood and furniture industry in 25 states.
1938 Purchased Lemmon Mill in Bedford, Indiana.
1939 Started buying soybeans.
1940 First "enriched flour" in Indiana.
1940 Purchased Ginger Feed & Elevator Co. in Jeffersonville, Indiana.
1945 Purchased Farmer's Hominy Mill in Seymour.
1948 Balanced dog feed produced.
1949 Discontinued corn meal production.
1951 Development of industrial cob processing.
1954 Leased Bloomington Elevator.
1957 GLU-X Reg. U.S. Pat. Off.
1960 Early computerized feed formulae.
1963 First Southern Pine Plywood Mill.

1966 "Triple-R" Feeds Reg. U.S. Pat. Off.
1970 Development of "Sepro-X" (soy-energy-protein-extrusion process).
1971 Research project with Kansas State University to develop new industrial starch.
1972 Record growth. R. M. Robertson died.
1973 U.S. Ag industry supplies world. Soybeans sell at $12.00 and wheat at $5.50. 100th anniversary of roller mills in U.S.
1974 100th anniversary of introduction of Turkey Red (Hard) Wheat in USA (Kansas).
1980 Robertson commended for shipping antique mill machinery to Smithsonian.
1981 C. R. Robertson died. Jerry O. Robertson named director.
1981 *Centennial*: Struck coin. Published commemorative planner.
1983 Invented and filed patent for Pan-X Composition Board Extender.
1984 Initiated computerized mail marketing of exotic bird and fish feeds.
1985 Marketed both GLU-X Extender and LIGNOFLEX Filler to panel industry, and published paper for Forest Product Research Society *re* role of these products in coming years.
1986 Jan.: Acquired "associate" mill in Plainville. Made large GLU-X shipments to Brazil. Remodeled Brownstown wheat elevator.
Aug. 5: Fire totally destroyed Bedford Mill. Made Patent Off. app. of "GLU-X West" Trademark. First continuing "bulk" GLU-X tanker shipments. Bedfore Marketing Office established at 1714 L Street.
1987 Marketing GLU-X West in Northwest by R.I.I.
1988 SPRAY-X Reg. U.S. Pat. Off. Developed and published commemorative calendar; continued international promotion.
1991 Jill Robertson, 5th generation from founder, appointed as first woman to serve on corporation Board. 4th generation Board members were R. R., J. O., J. E., Jr.
1992 Established total quality and process control systems.
1993 Moved Bedford office to new Marketing Office at 1032 W. Spring Street in Brownstown.
1994 Transfered Seymour Mill property through sale and contribution to Jackson County Community Foundation.
1995 DPB Corp. constructed new building at 211 Front Street, Brownstown, to facilitate transfer of Seymour equipment and operation to Brownstown. Significant SPRAY-X and GLU-X production started in August. Continued research on soy derivatives, tannins, and other adhesive additives.
1996 Significant extender-additive research initiated with objective of producing soy-modified GLU-X for improving benefits in wood panel adhesive technology. Robertson extender papers become industry references. Record high cereal prices: wheat $6.50+, corn $5.50+. Trademarks filed in U.S. Pat. Off. For Soy-Ply and Soy-Fill. Record growth.
1997 R. S. Robertson, chairman died. His eldest son, R. R. (Phil), elected president, and John, second son of R. S., was appointed to Board of Directors. Phil and John 4th generation from founder. Joe E. Robertson, Sr., 3rd generation, elected chairman. Sherrell Perry, elected assistant secretary-treasurer, became first female and non-family officer of The Robertson Corporation.

Index

by Lori L. Daniel

— A —

Aborigine, 205
Acton, Mary, x
Adriatic Sea, 243, 245-246, 253, 261
Aegean Sea, 189, 223, 250, 253
Aereolinas Argentinus, 296
Aero-Peru, 291
Africa, 137, 140, 154-162, 164-169, 171-172, 176-178, 180-187, 189, 214, 238
African, 137, 140, 155-157, 159-161, 164-167, 174, 177, 185-186, 212
African Timber and Plywood Mill, 171
African Timber Marketing Board, 165
Afrikaans, 178
Agha Khan, 148
AIMA (Wood Industries Association of Ecuador), 230
Air Canada, 257
Aircraft
  Aeroflot, 126, 130, 133
  B-17, 23, 29, 218
  B-24, 23, 27-29, 218
  B-25, 218
  B-26, 218
  B-29, 23, 28-29, 267
    Enola Gay, 24, 30
  Boeing 757, 291
  C-54, 78
  DC-3, 21
  DC-10, 190
  P-38, 218
  P-40, 218
  P-43, 218
  Piper Lane, 258
  Red Baron Link Trainer, 197
  747, 58, 116, 142, 190, 198, 253
  UTA (French) Airliner, 194
  Zero, 29
Air Afrique, 156, 167
Air Mali, 168
Air Micronesian Airline, 263
Air Moroc, 150
Alabama, 54, 81, 102, 117, 127, 146, 158, 191, 195, 197, 243, 246, 281
Alamagordo Air Base (NM), 30
Alaska, 31, 71, 254, 258-259, 267
Aleutian Islands, 267
Alexander
  J. B., 153
  Joan, 153
  Wood, 117
Alexander the Great, 251
Alit, Joye, 208
Alit, Rus (Rev.), 208
All-American Cities Contest, 38
Allegheny Mountains, 3, 7-8
Allen, Forest "Phog," 6-7

Allies, 12, 28, 137
Alsace-Lorraine, 96
Altman, Bill, xi
Alvarez
  Cesar, 230, 300-301
  Maria Teresa, 300-301
  Pedro, 230
America, 2, 11, 26, 28, 33, 35-36, 40, 42-44, 48, 50-51, 66, 71, 105-106, 110, 120, 157, 174, 203, 252, 275, 289
American, xiv, 10-11, 29-31, 35, 40, 42, 47, 50-53, 55, 58-61, 63-66, 68, 70-71, 73, 75-78, 88, 90, 98, 102, 104, 106-107, 111, 115-116, 122, 124, 126-129, 131-133, 139, 141-143, 146, 150, 155, 158-160, 165, 167, 170, 175, 178, 186, 193-194, 231, 210, 214-215, 218, 230, 246, 250, 252, 262, 265-267, 269, 271, 273, 282, 284-285, 304, 310
American Airlines, 291
American Association of Cereal Chemists (AACC), 305
American Colonization Society, 160
American Plywood Association (APA), xi, 243, 285, 305
American Revolutionary War, 35
American University, 247
Andamans Timber Ind. Ltd., 217
Andersen, Hans Christian, 103
Andes Mountains, 290, 292-293, 296-297, 299
Animist, 155
Annin-Bonso, B., 165
Antarctica, 57, 196, 297, 302
Antarctic Circle, 197
Antarctic Ocean, 196
APA Engineered Wood Research Foundation, 308
Appalachian Mountains, 111
Appomattox Courthouse (VA), 35
Arab, 140, 144, 146, 166, 273, 241, 273
Arabia, 166
Arctic Circle, 71, 255-256
Arctic Ocean, 129, 254
Argentina, 296
Arizona, 21-27, 42-43, 46, 116, 236
Arkansas, 309
Armstrong
  Burt, 99
  Mrs., 72, 87
  Neil, 241
  Pete, 72, 74, 87
Arnold, Henry H. "Hap" (General), 26-27
Aruba, 236
Aryal Shara Ram, 93, 95
Ashdod, 142
Asia, 23-24, 186, 188-190, 201, 214, 247, 250-253, 256, 262, 269-270, 277, 273, 280-281, 285, 306
Asia Minor, 251
Asian Furniture Exhibition, 273
Asian Plywood Conference, 201
Asian Plywood Manufacturers, 213
Askalon Plywood Ltd., 142

Assam Forest Products Ltd., 217
Assam Saw Mills & Timber Company, Ltd., 217
Association of Operative Millers (AOM), 305
Atacamaean Salt Desert, 296
Atchison, Darlene, x
Atlantic Ocean, 2, 16, 50, 156, 162, 175, 187, 235, 241-242, 253, 309
Atlantic Veneer Mill, 175
atom bomb, 21
Austria, 96, 113-114, 261
Australia, 188-190, 192, 198-206, 260, 267, 306
Australian, 201-203, 205-206
Austral Plywood, 202
Austrian, 113
Autobahn, 96, 113
Avianca Airlines, 291

— B —

Baby Boom, 302-303
Bach, Richard, 260
Balboa, Vasco, 244
Bali, 119, 206-209, 212, 243
Balinese, 206-208
Balkans, 246
Balle, Joe, 167
Baltic Sea, 103, 261
Bangkok, 215, 218
Bangkok Veneer Company, 215-216, 218
Bartlettsville Oilers/Phillips 66ers, 7
Battle of the Bulge, 28
Battle of Tipton's Island, 2
Baumann, Deiter, 111
Baxter
  Laura Falkenrich, x
  Mable, 40-41
  Virginia, 4, 8-10, 12
  see also Robertson, Virginia
Beach
  Marianna Kistler, 9
  Ross, 9
Bean, Maurice, 159
Beasen, Bill, 8
Beatles, 126
Bedford Daily Times-Mail (IN), xi, xiv, 57, 72, 97, 116, 135, 140, 176, 188, 237, 239-240, 242, 254, 262, 269
Begin, Menachem (Prime Minister), 143
Beijing Woodworking and Furniture Factory, 82
Beldon, Betty, 132
Belgium, 12, 72, 96
Bell, Don, 72, 81, 85, 87
Bermuda, 158, 167
Bernadotte, General, 107-108
Berry, John, 66
Best Wood Company, 194
Biggs Air Force Base (TX), 24, 26, 42-43
Bikini Atoll, 264
Bingham, Hiram, 295
Black
  Jane, 255, 261-262, 269
  Joe (Dr.), 255, 261, 269
  Lynn, 112

A World of Travel   315

Black *(continued)*
  Shirley Temple, 165
Blackadder
  Pat, 98
  Tom, 98
Black Forest, 96
Blackmore, Duncan, 196
Black Sea, 247
Blanchard, Doc, 20
Blanding, Don, 36
Bligh, Captain, 189, 192
Bliss Travel Agency, 203
Boise Cascade, 210
Bol
  Michael, 175
  Mrs., 175
Bolivia, 296
Bolshoi (Russia), 128
Bong
  Larry, 273
  Patsy, 273, 275
Bonitz, George, 81
Bonneville Salt Flats (UT), 46
Boonstra, W., 121
Borneo, 238, 243, 251-252, 279
Bosi, Domenico (Dr.), 141
BOSI, s.p.a., 141
Botang, Mr., 165
Bowers, Dick, 69
Boyer, Jack, 252
Bradford, Deborah, 18
Bradford Plywood, 100
Brazil, 154, 174-175, 245, 251
Brazilian, 174-175
Brink, Deane, 112
Briscoe, Mr., 40-41
Britain, 11
British, 158, 165, 179, 195, 231, 253, 271, 273, 280-281, 288-289
  Army, 35
  Commonwealth, 180
  Navy, 271
British Civil War, 289
British Customs and Immigration Services, 287
Broadley, A. L., 171
Brooke, Mr. and Mrs., 21
Brown
  Bob, 108
  Jeanne, 108
  Molly, 48
BruPly Board Group, 173
Bruynzell Multi-Panel Co., 120
Buck, Pearl, 88
Budapest, 261
Buddhism, 73
Buddhist, 68, 92-93, 210, 273
Bull Run (VA), 35
Bunge Corporation, Australian Division, 66
Burma, 65-66, 99
Burrell, Jim, 69, 71, 99, 108
Burton, Richard, 172
Bushmen, 186

— C —
Cable
  Betty, 22-23
  Ralph (Major), 22-25
Caine, Bill, 112, 146, 153
Calgary Stampede, 40, 255

California, 9, 26-28, 40, 43-46, 51, 54, 58, 60, 116, 156, 165, 173, 192, 195, 212, 253, 263, 265, 270, 282, 309
Cambodia, 218
Camera Bombing System, 26-27
Cameron, Phil, 202
Campbell, ____, 71
Canaanites, 143
Canada, 36, 39-40, 51, 69, 72, 84, 88, 98-99, 102, 110, 112, 146, 213, 216, 223, 245, 254-257, 259, 289
  Northwest Territory, 254, 256, 259
Canadian Hardwood Plywood Association, 97
Canadian Wood Products Association, 69
Cantonese, 64
capitalism, 73, 124, 252
Capital Machines, 212, 216
Capital Veneer Machine Company, 99, 157, 199
Caribbean Sea, 53-54, 175, 235, 264
Carter
  Howard, 147
  Jimmy (President), 127
"Casablanca," 150
Casanova, 139-140
Cascade Mountains, 39
Caste System, 219
Catholic, 114-116, 142, 243, 299-300
Cebu, 266
Central America, 80, 189, 229, 295, 299, 306
Chamorro (Guam), 266
Champaign Seed Co., 24
Champion Building Products, 212
Champion-International, 112, 167
Charles I of Spain, 235
Chennault, Claire L. (General), xi, 31
Chesapeake Bay, 8
Chew, Mr., 278
Chile, 291, 296-297, 299-300
China, xiii, 31, 63-66, 69-70, 72-90, 95, 132, 136, 215, 220, 238, 243, 245, 252-253, 260, 267, 269, 270-271, 275, 277, 280-285
China Airlines, 72
China Chronicles, 87
China Clippers, 90
China National Forestry Import and Export Corporation, 73, 82, 84
China National Forestry Import and Export Operations, 73
China Seas, 64-65, 75, 189, 253, 270-271
Chinese, 64-65, 68, 71-72, 74-78, 81-82, 84-85, 87, 132, 210-211, 214, 253, 271, 273, 275, 278-279, 281-282, 284
Chinese Air Cathay, 46
Chinese Exotic Veneer, 78
Ching, Chao Yung, 73
Chiricahua Mountains, 42
Chisholm Trail, 157
Cho, Madam, 74

Christian, 56, 103, 136, 142-144, 155-156, 161, 208-209
Christie, Agatha, 148
Chrysler Corporation, 240
"Chunnel" (England), 285-287, 289
"Chunnel" Passenger Service, 285
Church of Jesus Christ of Latter-day Saints, The, 47
CIB Veneer Mills, 162
Circumnavigators Club, 240
City College of New York, 18
Civil War, 35, 49
Clark, Freddie, 212
Clark E. McDonald Enterprises, 229
Clavell, James, 252
Codesa, 230
Coggeshall, Bettina, 306
Cold War, 127
Coleridge, Samuel T., 231
College of William & Mary (VA), 8
Colonial Era, 155
Colorado, 7, 9, 27-28, 48, 116
Colorado State University, 284
Columbia Forest Products, xi
Columbia University, 230
Columbus, Christopher, 53, 244, 292
Commonwealth Plywood Co., 112, 146
Communism, 61, 72, 96, 114, 122, 124, 136, 144, 218, 246, 261-262
Connecticut, x, 17-23, 99
Connolly, Terry, 205
Cook, Captain, 189
Cooke, Goodwin, 164
Coral Sea, 29
Cornell University, 308
Corregidor, 65
Cotopaxi (volcano), 300
Courts of Khan, 88
Coward, Noel, 210
Coyte, Tony, 194
Craig, Paula, 175
Crawford, John, 164
Cross
  David, 246
  Don, 251
Crossley & Towers, 217
Crusades, 166
Cuba, 291
Cullity, Denis, 205
Curry
  Dee, 159
  Jim, 99
Curry Veneer, 99, 159
Czechoslovakia, 262

— D —
Dampier, W., 266
Danish, 101-103, 110
Danzer Veneer Mill, 164, 175
Dardenelles, 247, 250
Dark Continent, 155, 176
Darlington Veneer Plywood, xi
Darwin, Charles, 231, 234
da Vinci, Leonardo, 139
Davis, Glen, 20
Davis-Monthan Army Air Base (Tucson, AZ), 21-23, 43

Dazzi
 Julian, 160, 161
 Laura, 160
Dead Sea, 47, 144
Death on the Nile, 148
Delta Airlines, 286
Demilitarized Zone (DMZ), 61
Deming Air Base (NM), 42
Denmark, 12, 98, 100-104, 125, 130
DePaul University, 6
DePauw University, 309
Derbend, Osi, 247
Deyde, 207
Diamond Power Specialties, 98
Dickens, Charles, 288
Dillemont, Bernard, 265
Dilton-Liberia Lumber, Inc., 160
Dimmer
 Francis, 234
 Melanie, 234
Disney, 44, 115
Dominion Products, LTD, 196
Donahue, Gilbert, 164
Donner Party, 45
DuBois, W. E. B. (Dr.), 165
Dutch, 119-120, 174
Dutch East Indies Company, 120
Dynochem, 278

— E —

Earhart, Amelia, 241
Earth
 George, 117, 128
 Shirley, 117, 128
Earth Veneer, 117
Easter Islands, 289, 296-298
Ecuador, 230-231, 233, 236, 291, 299-301
Ecuadorian, 231, 234, 291, 300
Egypt, 79-81, 85, 135-136, 143-149, 262
Egyptian, 144-145, 147
Eisenhower, Dwight D. (General), 8, 30
El Alamein, 156
Elefant, Marcel, 112
Elmore, Auna, 22
Endesa, 230
Eng, Tann En, 278
Engineered Wood Association, 305
England, 12, 24, 98-102, 104, 115, 165, 196, 210, 250, 271, 285-289
English, 27, 58, 66, 74, 78, 82, 93, 100-101, 107, 111-113, 121, 122, 124, 160, 162, 168, 170, 174, 178-179, 181, 189, 191, 194, 207, 210, 233, 231, 246, 250, 271, 273, 275, 284, 291, 297
English Channel, 285, 287-288
Enwietok, 263
EPA, 124
Eperson, L. G., 165
Erath, George, 69
Estonia, 125-127, 134
Ethiopia, 11
Eurasian, 68
Eurocomp Plywood Mills, 139
Europe, 11, 29, 82, 96, 98, 105-106, 112, 125, 130, 156-157, 166-167, 188-189, 241, 246-247, 250, 261, 267, 291, 302-303, 306

European, 11, 21, 28, 97-98, 104, 111, 113, 115-116, 129, 175, 186, 194-195, 244, 250, 285
 Common Market, 111, 114
 Theater, 23
 War, 29
Evans, 112
Evans, Larry, xi
Evans Products Company, 100
Ewing Mill Company, 10, 304, 309, 311

— F —

Fabrega, Carlos Sanchez, 235
Far East, 58, 186, 248, 269, 271
Farmers Hominy Mill, 304, 310
Fascist, 114
FDA, 124
Federation of Indian Plywood and Panel Industry (FIPPI), 217, 219
Fengzhu, Qin, 84
Fielding, Temple, 116
Fiji Islands, 190, 205, 263
Fiji Plywood Plant, 206
Filipino, 281-282
Finland, 12, 108-110, 113, 245
Finnish, 109-110, 131
Finnish Plywood Association, 111
Firestone rubber plantation, 158
Florida, 13, 16-18, 23, 32-34, 47, 51, 116-117, 142, 162, 192, 244, 263
Fluter, Frits de, 196
"Flying Tigers," xi, 31, 218
Folge, A. A., 121
Forbes Air Force Base (KS), 49
Forest Industries Conference, 96
Forest Products Society (FPS), 305
Forest Research Institute of Malaysia (FRIM), 279
Forestry Commission of New South Wales, 200, 202
Forde, Kata, 161
Formosan, 292
Formosa Straits, 64
Fort Myers Bugle (FL), 33
Fortune, 106
Fortune 500, 305
"Fra Diavolo," 205
France, 11, 12, 108, 225-228, 230, 243, 250, 285-288
Freeman Air Force Base (IN), 11
French, 104, 109, 155-156, 158, 168, 189, 223, 225, 228, 235, 273, 287, 291, 299-300
 Foreign Legion, 167-168, 171
 Protestant Church, 156
Fuller Presbyterian Seminary, 156
Fu, John, 284
Fu Manchu, 59
Funcke, Svante, 105
Furniture and Wood Products Department, 124

— G —

Gable, Clark, 180
Galapagos Islands, 230-233, 236
Gandhi, Madame, 222
Gardner, Jack, 6
General Plywood, 309
General Woods Company, 112

Genghis Khan, 132
Georgetown University (D.C.), 142
Georgia, 12, 51, 158, 282
Georgia-Pacific, 112, 167, 251, 309
 Savannah Plywood Mill, 53, 251
German, 26, 49, 66, 84, 104, 113, 164, 261, 277, 291
Germany, 10-12, 26, 28, 46, 72, 85, 96, 112-114, 126, 245, 260-261, 287
Gesellius, 109
Ghana Primeboard Products, 165
Ghost Fleet of Truk, 265
Giacobbi, Piero, 140
Gilfillin
 Millie, 162
 Paul, 162
Giza, 81
Glacier National Park, 39
Glen Island Casino, 11
GLU-X adhesive extender, 34, 36, 64, 105-106, 240, 305-307, 309-311
Gold Rush, 44, 259
Goldwater, Barry, 241
Golkar Coalition Party, 209
Gone With The Wind, 12
Gooch, Jim (Dr.), 200, 202
Goodman
 Benny, 126
 R., 69
Grace, Princess, 115
Grand Bahamas, 33
Grant, Ulysses S. (General), 35
Great Pyramid (Cheops), 145-146
Great Salt Desert (UT), 46
Great Salt Lake (UT), 47
Great Slave Lake, 255
Great Smoky Mountains National Park (SC), 34
Great Sphinx, 146
Greece, 221-225, 238, 243, 245-246
Greek, 223, 250-251
Greek Islands, 223, 225
Gross, Bob, 69, 163, 171
Guam, 29, 265-267
Guerrant, D. S., 7
Guihe, Li, 82
Gulf of Mexico, 51
Gulf Stream, 101
Gulf War, 262
Gulliver's Travels, 266
"Gunsmoke," 43
Guyer
 Charles "Charlie," 117, 133, 158
 Jerry, 117, 133

— H —

Hale, Nathan, 18
Hamann, Roland "Ding," 175
Hamlet, 103
Hammack, Roy, 54-55
Hammarskjold, Dag, 107
Han, Victor, 160
Hancock, John, 201
Hancock Brothers Pty. Ltd., 201
Han Dynasty, 79
Hanley
 Carolyn, 117, 130
 Ed, 117, 130

A World of Travel

Hanover College, 308
Hanschoten, Kees, 159
Hardaway, 158
Hardwood Export Council, 285
Hardwood Plywood and Veneer Association (HPVA), 305
Hardwood Plywood Manufacturers Association (HPMA), 57, 69, 72, 86-87, 97, 112, 116, 118, 135, 149, 151, 154, 157-158, 163, 171, 188-189, 203, 216-217, 221
Harlem Globetrotters, 23
Harrison, Karen, x
Hart, Freddy, 100
Hashish, Iman, 147
Hasty Plywood, 162, 198, 216
Hawaii, 11-12, 15, 71, 115, 263, 270
Hazard, Sue, 72
Hebrew, 143, 145
Heidi, 111
Hemingway, Ernest, 268
Henderson and Pollard Plywood Plant, 194
Henrichse, Egy, 120
Herald-Tribune (Germany), 113-114
Herb, C., 99-100
Hewitt
　Charlie, x
　Harriet, x
Hillary, Edmund (Sir), 241
Hilton, James, 93-94
Himalaya Mountains, 31, 74, 90-93, 218, 238, 258, 293
Hindu, 90, 92-93, 207, 209-210, 219, 273
Hirohito, Emperor, 30
Hiroshima (Japan), 263
Holland, 116, 118-121, 128, 160, 160, 236
Homer, 251
Honduras, 205, 223
Hoosier Panel Company, 309
Hottentots, 186
Howell
　Beverly, 102, 117, 128, 141, 153, 191, 197, 204-205, 236, 243, 246, 248, 250
　Clay Auburn, 117, 121, 127
　Clyde, 81, 141, 146, 153
　Harry, 81, 117, 158, 191, 195-197, 199, 204-206
　Mildred, 102, 117, 130, 197, 206
Howell Plywood, 243
"HPMA Tales of the Med Round Robin," 151
H. T. Plywood, LTD, 196
Hua, Ting Ong, 279
Huang, Qin Shi (Emperor), 8
Hubbard
　Carolyn, xi
　Reggie, xi
Huey
　James "Jim" (Captain), 71, 102, 111, 117, 130, 158, 197, 204, 206
　Mildred, 102, 117, 130, 197, 206
Hungary, 113, 261
Hunsur Plywood Works, 217
Hussein, King, 144

— I —

Iaococca, Lee, 240
Iberia Airlines, 115
ICAS, s.p.a., 140
Iceland, 289
"Iliad," 251
Illinois, 2-6, 9, 23, 38, 40, 48, 50, 112, 282
Inca, 294-296, 298-299
India, 72, 90, 96, 189, 217-220, 222-223, 245, 277
Indian, 2, 5, 13, 24, 42, 46, 50, 54, 56-57, 68, 207, 210, 219, 222, 230, 256, 273, 275, 289
Indiana, xii, 1-11, 15, 20-21, 23-24, 36, 38, 49-50, 72, 82, 88, 96, 98-99, 108, 112, 116-117, 137, 145, 157, 159, 163, 168, 172, 175, 193, 199, 203, 205, 212-213, 216, 238, 241, 245-246, 253-255, 262, 266, 284, 304, 309-310
Indiana Department of Commerce, 284
Indianapolis Capital Clippers, 109
Indianapolis Capital Veneer, 175
Indianapolis 500 Speedway Race, 2
Indiana Port Commission, 239
Indiana University, x, 7-8, 117, 241, 308-309
Indian Ocean, 187, 206, 271
Indian Plywood Mfg., Company, Ltd., 217
Indonesia, xiii, 67-68, 120, 136, 189, 206, 209, 238, 243, 245, 251-253, 273
Industrial Revolution, 311
Inherit the Wind, 231
Integrated Forest Products Pty., Ltd., 204-205
International Consultation of Wood Panel Experts, 244
International Dateline, 194
International Diving Museum, 265
International Forest Products Society, xi
International Hardwood Plywood and Veneer Association, xi, 308
International Hardwood Plywood Manufacturers Association (HPMA), xiv, 53, 229
International Offset Trading Corporation, 246
International Plywood and Panel Magazine, 54
International Wood Products, 211
Inuit (Eskimo), 256
Iowa, 9
Iowa State University, 9
Ipi Tombi, 174
Iran, 225
Iranian, 140, 261
Iraq, 262
Ireland, 98, 241, 289
Irish, 49
Irish Sea, 288
Iron Curtain, 121
Iseli
　Carlo, 111, 112
　Daniel, 111
　Rico, 111
　Thais, 111

Islam, 47
Islamic, 150, 243
Isle of Wight, 288
Israel, 47, 135-136, 140, 142-144, 153, 247, 262
Israeli-Egypt Wars, 144
Istanbul, 245-248, 250, 253, 280
Italian, 18, 104, 114, 137, 139-141, 153, 160, 162
Italy, xiii, 10-11, 114-115, 135-142, 238, 242-245
Ivory Coast, 156, 161, 163-164, 167-168
Iwo Jima, 29

— J —

Jackson County Banner (IN), xi, xiv, 57, 285, 289
Jackson, Robin "Lucky," 100
Jacob
　Sally, 217
　T. K., 217
Jahan
　Mumtaz, 222
　Shah, 222
Jalan, M. M., 217
Jamaica, 53-54, 57, 192
Jansen, Peter, 120
Japan, 10-11, 29-30, 46, 53, 58-60, 62-63, 68, 73, 97, 136, 201, 206, 252, 263, 265-267, 273, 287, 303
Japan Empire Plan, 267
Japanese, 15, 58-59, 62-63, 65-66, 68-69, 73, 214, 262, 265-267, 275, 285
Japanese Air Lines, 46, 58, 270
Japanese Plywood Manufacturers Association, 59
Japanese War Shrine, 266
Jasper Corporation, 309
Jasper National Park, 255
Jasper Wood Products, 309
Java, 206
Jelinek, Ernie, 194
Jenner, Bill, 239
Jennings, Mike, 212
Jewish, 18, 142, 144
Jews, 143
Jiang, Zhang Tung, 74
John
　Dibba, 102, 117, 167, 171, 199, 205
　Thomas, Jr. (Dr.), 117, 132
　Tom, 117, 127, 171, 172, 198-200, 204-206
"Johnny Carson Show," 107
Johns, Thomas "Tomjon," 69, 71, 107, 117
Johnson Island, 263-264
Joint Security Administration, 61
Jones, Buck, 42
Jones, Jimmy, 4
Jordanian, 144
Jurong Plywood, 210

— K —

Kadir, Azizol Abdul, 279
Kalimanis Interests, 251
Kalkhof, Albert, 112
Kalstrup, Per, 172, 175
Kamara, Nafi, 167-168, 170

Kansas, 1, 4-10, 12-13, 21, 34, 43, 45, 48-50, 157, 296
Kansas Prairie, 49
Kansas State Agricultural College, 49
Kansas State College of Agriculture and Applied Science, 3
Kansas State University, x, 3-4, 8-11, 23, 48-49, 239, 308
Kaplan, Vic, 212
Kapur, B. N., 217, 219
Kentucky, 2-3, 7, 13, 72, 81, 162, 262
Kessler Air Force Base (MS), 33
KGB (Russian Secret Police), 130
Khaitan, B. K., 217
Kikuyu, 180-181
Kilroy, xiii-xiv, 11, 14, 25, 30-31, 33, 35, 40, 42-44, 46-50, 53-54, 141, 148, 150, 176, 229, 233, 238, 260, 297, 303
King Arthur's Court, 99
King Christian 4th, 103
Kinley, 69
Kipling, Rudyard, 210
Kissinger, Henry A., 127
Kling Furnier-Werk, 112
KLM (Royal Dutch Airlines), 121, 270
Klondike, 258
Klopp
 Bill, 168
 Ruth, 168
Koenig, Paul, 69
Koh, Dr., 278
Korea, 61-64, 136, 201, 252, 273
Korean War, 62
Koss
 Jack, 66, 69, 81, 99, 109-110, 117, 128, 153, 163, 167, 171, 175, 199-200, 204, 212, 216
 Mary, 62, 66, 81, 110, 117, 153, 167, 170, 199, 204, 216
Kremerman, David, 142
Kroon, Rory, 173
Kuhn, Klaus, 173
Kwajalein, 264, 267

— L —

Lafleur
 Marcel, 72, 77, 84, 99, 153, 200, 203, 206, 216, 223-224
 Pierette, 72, 87, 153, 203, 206, 213, 216, 224
LaGuardia Airport (NY), 116
Lake, Victor, 97
Lake Bennett, 258
Lake Michigan, 2
Lake Wawasee, 2
Lama, 92-93
Laos, 218
Laserma Company, 175
Latin America, 229
Lauly, K. S., 217
League of Nations, 160
Lee
 Robert E. (General), 35
 Ron, 210
 Walter, 100
Legeard, Pierre, 77, 200, 205-206, 223, 225

LeHay
 Roland, 99
 Curtis (General), 42
Lemon Mill, 304, 310
Lenderink, Ted, 71, 109
Lenin's Tomb (Russia), 122
Lester, Jim, 101, 175-176
Lewis
 Dilys, 160
 Tony, 160
Liberian, 159-160
Lican Cabur (volcano), 296
Lihua, Zhang, 73
Lillard, Mike, 173
Lin
 Kwee, 278-279
 Mrs. Pei Yu, 64
Lindbergh, Charles A., 50, 57, 241
Lindgren, 109
Linwood, 109
Living Goddess, 93-94
Livingston, Helen, 162, 172, 192-193, 197, 205
Lockhart, Frank, 47
Loerts, B ., 121
Longfellow
 General, 24, 26, 29
 Henry Wadsworth, 288
Lord Derby, 100
Lorenz, Werner, 72, 84, 87
Lost Dutchman Mine, 43
Louisiana, 32-33, 39-40, 103-104, 195, 197, 214, 216
Love, Clydia, x
Lowrey
 Bill, 69, 104
 Mrs., 69
Lowry Field Air Corps Technical School (Denver, CO), 48
Loyola University (Chicago, IL), 6
Lutheran, 103
Luxembourg, 72, 96
Lynn, Sue, 203

— M —

MacArthur, Douglas (General), 241
MacInitch, Leroy, 4
MacMaster, Quay, 110
MacNeil, Jim, 18
Madagascar, 183
Maderas Laminadas, S.A. Plywood, 235
Mados-Citoh-Daiken Plywood Company, 212
Magellan, Ferdinand, 189, 266
Maginot Line, 96, 260
Maine, 51
Majorca, 115
Majuro, 263-264, 267
Malay, 65, 186, 210, 271, 275, 277
Malay Straits, 241, 271
Malaya Plywood and Veneer Factory, 213
Malaysia, 67-68, 189, 201, 209, 212-215, 271, 273, 274-280, 285
Malaysian Forest Policy and Progress, 279
Maleniecki, Lad, 157
Mali Empire, 167
Maloney, Tom, xi
Manchu, Fu (Dr.), 88

Manhattan Project, 21
Maori, 194-195
March Air Force Base (Riverside, CA), 28, 43-44
Marco Polo, 271
Mariana Islands, 29, 266
"Mariana Trench," 267
Marion, Francis "Swamp Fox," 35
Markel
 Bruce, 67, 72, 82, 87, 91, 96, 141, 153, 193, 205, 216, 221
 Susie, 72, 82, 87, 91, 96, 141, 153, 213, 216, 221
Marquesas, The, 263
Marshall
 Frank (Rev.), 168
 Mrs. Frank, 168
Marshall Islands, 263-264, 266
Martin, Billy, 7
Masai, 180-182
Massachusetts, 18, 24, 35, 45, 49, 69, 229-230
Mathers, 88
Matthews, Ernest (Dr.), 55-57
Matthews, Mrs., 55-57
Maugham, Somerset, 58, 210-211
Mau Mau, 180
Mayo Clinic (MN), 9, 23
McArthur, Douglas, 69
McCoy
 Don (Judge), 69, 119, 122, 128, 167, 192-193, 200, 205
 Donald, Jr., 192-193, 213, 216
 Kathryn, 119, 167, 192-193, 205
McCracken
 Branch, 7
 Jack, 99
McDonald
 Bwana, 172
 Clark, ix, xiv, 68-69, 98, 107, 109, 157, 163, 235-236
 Mrs. Bwana, 173
 Sylvia, ix, xiv, 62, 67, 98, 119, 141, 153, 203-205, 210, 216, 224, 229, 236
McEver, 88
McGee, Sam, 257
McIlvane, Jim, 18
McMaster, 158
McNair, Art, 88, 99
Medici family, 139
Mediterranean Sea, 114, 135-136, 142, 167, 188, 245, 247, 253
Mekong, 218
Mendenhall Glacier, 258
Mermelstein, Otto, 175
Methodist, 281
Mexican, 24, 56-57
Mexico, 26-27, 36, 50, 53-57, 69, 157, 230
Miami University (Ohio), 4
Michelangelo, 139
Michener, James A., 190, 241, 264
Michigan, 3, 104, 109
Micronesia, 262, 264, 266
Middle Ages, 243, 247
Middle East, 144
"Midnight Sun," 256, 259
Midway Island, 29
Milford Sound Expedition, 197
Military Police (MP), 42

A World of Travel   319

Miller
  Bill, 4
  Glen, 11, 19-20
  Ralph, 7
milling industry, 3
Ming Dynasty, 65, 84-85, 88
Minggang, Liu, 73, 87
Minnesota, 9, 23, 40
Mississippi, 33, 35
Missouri, 2, 4-5, 12, 50
Mix, Tom, 42
Mobley, Theo, 3
Moehring
  Karl Heinz, 175
  Mrs. Karl, 175
Mohammed Ali, 168, 170
Monaco, 114
Mongol, 85, 88, 92, 132
Monks, 215
Monnin, Agnes, 156-157, 160
Montana, 195
Montana, Joe, 281
Moorish, 243
Morgan
  Henry, 235
  Hubert, 153
Morgon, Margaret, 153
Mormon, 47-48
Mormon Tabernacle Choir, 48
Morocco, xiii, 31, 135-136, 150, 156
Moslem (Muslim), 68, 142-143, 147, 155-156, 161, 167, 209, 213, 222, 247, 273, 277-278, 280
Muda, Raja, 212
Muhammed, Askia, 167
Munene, Kamau, 180
Mussolini, Bonito, 114
Mycernius, Monarch, 146

— N —
NAACP, 165
Nadir-point Target Locater, 26
Nagasaki (Japan), 263
Nagle, Anne, x
Nair, K. S., 217
N & N Veneer Company, 175
Napoleon, 107-108
Natchez Trace, 40
National Geographic, 183
National Park Service, 265
NCAA Finals, 7, 117
Nebraska, 5, 21-22
Nepal, 72, 90, 92-96, 220
Nepalese, 93, 96
Nestle Corporation, 7, 278
Netherlands, 119-120
Nevada, 39, 45, 59, 90
New Delhi, 46
New England, 24, 35, 309
Newfoundland, 117
New Guinea, 31
New Mexico, 24, 27-28, 30, 42
New York, 2, 6, 18, 20-21, 50, 96, 101, 115-116, 132-133, 135, 142, 150, 192, 210, 213, 228, 241-242, 263, 282
New York Renaissance, 23
New York Times, 113
New Zealand, 188-190, 194-198, 201-202, 208, 245, 281, 297, 306

New Zealand Air, 270
New Zealand Forest Products, LTD, 196
New Zealand Manufacturer's Association, 194
Ng, Esther, 210
Nickel, Pete, 159
Nielson, Eric, 101
Nigerian, 171
Nipponese, 265
NIT, 117
Nobel House, 252-253
Nobel prize, 107
Norden Bomb Sight, 26
Normandy, 12
Norse Chem Resins, 278-279
North Africa, 150, 156
North America, 31, 100, 196, 244, 254, 259, 306
North Atlantic Treaty Organization (NATO), 8
North Carolina, 24, 34, 51, 72, 102, 107, 117, 127, 163, 167, 171, 192, 198, 218, 309
Northern Sawmill and Veneer Works, 101
North Pole, 255-256
North Sea, 101, 103-104, 119
Norwegian, 66, 197
Novopan Del Ecuador, S.A., 230
Nuclear Age, 266

— O —
Odom, Tom, 109
O'Donoghue, Bob, 69, 158
O'Hare Airport (IL), 71
Ohio, 2-3, 16, 21, 23, 270, 286, 289, 291
Ohio State University, 18, 60
Okaply, 112
Oklahoma, 5, 7-8
Old East, 65
Old Joppa, 142
Olympia Airlines, 225
Olympics, 60, 113, 125, 156, 255
Ong, Mr., 278
Operation Deep Freeze, 196
Oregon, 25, 240, 243, 259, 266, 308
Oregon Health Science University, x, 308
Oregon State University, 7
Oregon Trail, 49-50
Orient, 65, 67-69, 72, 98, 270, 280
Oriental, 64, 71, 76, 79, 131, 211
OSHA (Occupational Safety and Health Administration), 124, 218
Outer Mongolia, 129, 131
Out of Africa, 2
Ozyurek, Suat, 250

— P —
Pachacutec (Inca), 292
Pacific Islands, 261-263, 267
Pacific Ocean, 15, 29, 31, 44, 50, 53, 55, 129, 132, 188-189, 191-192, 194, 198, 230, 234-235, 241, 244, 252-253, 258, 262-264, 267, 270, 285, 295, 297-299, 308
Pacific War Memorial, 265
Palestinian, 144
Palmer, John E., 235

Pan Am, 46, 65, 90, 96, 175, 178
Panama, 54-55, 57, 231, 234-236, 291
Panama Canal Commission, 235
Panama Canal Zone, 54-55
Panamanian, 234-235
Panel and Engineered-Wood Technology Conference and Exposition (PETE), 306
Parsons, Claude, xi, 240
Pascual, Norman, 251
Patagonia, 297
Pearl Harbor (HI), 262-263
Pearson
  Gary, 160
  Mrs., 160
Peary, Robert E., 256
Pelit Arslan Plywood Mill, 250
Pendergast, Tom, 5
Pennsylvania, 2, 35, 50
Pennsylvania State University, 3
Pensacola Naval Air Station (FL), 33
Perron, Jean, 69
Perry, Sherrell, x
Persia, 250
Persinger, Joe, xi
Peru, 225, 289-296, 299
Peter The Great, 125
Philippine Airways, 65
Philippines, 64-65, 136, 281
Philippine Sea, 266
Phillips Oil Corporation, 7
Pickett, J. (Colonel), 179
Pirtle, Jim, 241
Pizarro, Francisco, 292
Plains Indian Wars, 35
Playboy, 121
Plywood & Panel Magazine, 71, 99
Plywood and Panels, Inc., 216
Plywood Association of
  Australia (PAA), 20-202
  New Zealand (PANZ), 201
Plywood Panels Inc., 103
Poland, 11, 121
Polo, Marco, 53, 88, 139
Polynesia, 191-193, 195, 206-207, 209, 262-265, 273, 298-299
Pompeii, 135, 137
Pope, 114, 140
Portugal, 115, 176, 238, 243-244, 273
Portuguese, 88, 273
  Navy, 244
Potter, Helen, x
Powell, Colin (General), 8
Presbyterian, 7, 55-56, 218, 275
Prince
  Donna, 103
  Doris, 196-197, 216, 221
  J. D., 71, 77, 103, 195-197, 212, 216
Prince Henry's Navigational School, 244
Protestant, 277
Purdue University (IN), xi, 66, 308

— Q —
Qantas, 270
Qin Dynasty, 79-80, 85
Queen Elizabeth, 180

Queen Margretha, 102

— R —
Raffles, Stamford (Sir), 271, 273, 281
Raffles Hotel (Singapore), 65, 67, 210-211, 271-272, 275
Railroad
  Baltimore & Ohio (B&O), 2, 5
  Beirut-Cairo, 144
  Burlington, 5, 39
  Canadian National, 39
  Chicago, Milwaukee, St. Paul and Pacific, 40
  Great Northern, 39
  Kowloon and Canton, 66
  New York and New Haven, 20
  Pennsylvania, 2
  Short Line, 5, 21-22
  Trans-Siberian Express, 239
  White Pass & Yukon, 258
Ralph Symonds, Ltd., 202
"Ramayana," 207
Ramses II, 147-148
Ramsey
  Esther, xi
  Jack, xi
  Jim, xi
  John, xi
Randall, Allan, 235
Rano Raraku (volcano), 299
Raphael, 139
Raute Machinery, 110
Raymond Plywood Company, 173
Razali, Dr., 277-278
Reagan, Ronald, 240, 265
Red Army, 132
Red China, 66, 73, 75, 77, 88, 90
Red Cross, 23
Red Square (Russia), 82, 122-123
Rembrandt, 120
Renaissance, 166
Reserve Officer's Training Corps (ROTC), 4, 8, 10-11, 23
Reynolds, Debbie, 48
Rhodes, John, 8
Riley, Henry (Dr.), 241
Rin Con Mountains, 43
River
  Amazon Basin, 175
  Blue, 48
  Blue Danube, 113
  Bosporus, 247
  Bow, 39, 255
  French Riviera, 114
  Ganges, 95
  Great Niger, 166, 170
  Hellespont, 250
  Holy, 95
  Huang Pu, 74-75
  Jordan, 47
  Kansas (Kaw), 5, 48-50
  Mississippi, 2, 5
  Missouri, 5, 50
  Nile, 145-146, 148, 238
  Ohio, 1
  Rhine, 96, 113
  Seine, 225, 227, 286
  Smoky Hill, 49
  Upper Nile, 85
  Urubamba, 293

River *(continued)*
  Yangtze, 75-76
Riviera, 243-244, 246
Robertson, 284
  C. J., 303
  Charles A., 304, 308-309, 311
  Dick, 307-308
  Jerry O., 308
  Jewell, 1
  Jill, 308-309
  Joe Edmond, xii, 19, 25, 58, 62, 69-70, 72, 77, 87, 91, 96-97, 117, 138, 141, 153, 163, 169, 176, 181-182, 184, 200, 216, 221, 232, 235-238, 240, 276, 283-284, 294, 306, 308
    Air Cadet, 11, 14, 17-21
    K-State Varsity basketball, 5-6, 14
  Joe, Jr. "Rob," ix, 34-35, 40-46, 50-51, 240, 303, 308
  John, 308, 311
  Katie, 303
  Lee, 1
  Margaret "Maggie" Hewitt, x
  Phil, 64, 306, 308
  Roscoe, 2
  Virginia, xi-x, 1, 14, 20-24, 30, 32, 38-44, 50-55, 57, 62, 72, 87, 91, 96-97, 110, 117, 135, 153-154, 167, 169-170, 176, 181-182, 184, 188, 199, 216, 221, 224-227, 236-238, 240, 248, 262, 265, 269, 278, 287, 289, 294-295, 300
Robertson Products, 230
Robertson Windmill, 305, 309-310
Robison
  Jon, 2
  Peggy Lucas, xi, 2
Rockne, Knute, 1
Rocky Mountains, 7, 9, 29, 48, 50, 90, 257
Rogers
  Bernard "Bernie," 8
  Roy, 42
Roman, 114, 143, 251
Romano, Sammy, 18
Rombaut, Neil, 212
Roosevelt Field (NY), 50
"Rosie the Riveter," 30
Rosser
  Carey, 287-288
  Paul, 286-288
  Sally, 286-288
Rota, 267
Roush, Mrs. Delbert, 168
Royal Lipizzaner stallion, 113
Royal Nepal Airline, 90
Royal Purple, 9
Royal Selanger Pewter, 278
Ruark, Robert, 181
Rudolph, Crown Prince, 113
"Running of the Bulls," 261, 268
Runyon, Damon, 49
Rupp, Adolph, 6-7
Russell, Sergeant, 27
Russia, 11-12, 49, 72, 108-110, 116-117, 121-133, 136, 148, 168, 247, 297, 306
Russian Air Lines, 46

Rutledge, Jack, 167
Ryan, John (Dr.), 241

— S —
Saarinen, 109
Sadat, Anwar, 146
Saigon, 218
Saipon, 265-267
Sahara Desert, 156, 166, 168-170
Saharia, Shri, 217
Samoa, 194, 263
Samuel
  Margot, 110
  Ted, 110
Sanders, Colonel, 240
Sandor, Steve, 284
San Juan Straits, 259
Santa Fe Trail, 49-50
Santa Rita Mountains, 43
Sato, Dr., 60
Saudi Arabia, 262
Sawito, 209
Scandinavia, 97-98, 100-104, 106, 109-110, 136, 159
Schneider, George (First Lieutenant), 13-14
Scotland, 97-98, 160
Scottish, 97, 171, 281
Seagull, Jonathan Livingston, 260
Sea of Marmara, 247
Sellers, Terry, xi
Senegalese, 156
Sepro-X, 60
Serengeti Plain, 177, 181, 183-184, 238
Service, Robert, 257
Seven Clouds of Joy band, 4
Shakespeare, William, 99, 103
Shanghai Light Industry Commission, 74
Shanklin
  Betty, 33
  Jack (Captain), 33
  Mary, 33
  Susan, 33
Sharif, Omar, 247
Shell Oil Refinery, 41
Sheridan, Frank, 101
Shinto, 68, 73
Ship
  African Queen, 144
  Arizona, 15
  Buccaneer, 231, 233-234
  Hartford (steamboat), 48
  HMS *Beagle*, 234
  Queen Elizabeth, 111
  Titanic, 48
  Wasa, 105
Shuman, Joe, xi
Shyrock, Deryl, 159
Siberia, 116, 126, 129-133, 136, 306
Siberian forest, 116
Siegfried Line, 96, 260
Silk Road, 53, 82
Silver Certificate, 143
Sin, Carol, 278
Sinai, 136, 144
Singapore, 53, 58, 65-68, 189, 206, 209-211, 212, 215, 223, 238, 243, 271-275, 277, 281, 285

A World of Travel 321

Singapore Air, 253, 270
Singapore International Furniture Exhibition, 273
Skelly Oil, 158
slave, 157-158, 160, 165-166, 168, 186
Slavic, 122
Smith, Joseph, 47
Smoky Mountains, 34
Snapp, Ray, xi, 239
Snow Brand, 60
Socialism, 73, 124, 190
Solomon Islands, 29
"Something of Value," 181
Song
  "Dixie," 127
  "It's a Sin to Tell a Lie," 4
  "Knuckle Down Winsocki," 19
  "San Francisco," 127
  "St. Louis Blues March," 19
  "Tie Me Kangaroo Down, Mates," 206
  "Waltzing Matilda," 205
  "Yankee Doodle Dandy," 127, 160
Songhai Empire, 167
Sons of Islam, 68
Sorbonne University, 286
South Africa, 172, 174, 177-178, 185-187
South America, 189, 230, 291-292, 295-296, 299, 301, 306
South Carolina, xi, 34-35, 51, 110, 158, 195
Southern Cross, 174, 191
Southern Wood Products, 210
South Pacific, 190, 264
South Pole, 297
Soviet Union, 42, 116
Spain, 12, 41, 115, 261-262, 268, 292
Spanish, 13, 53, 55-56, 65, 109, 115, 231, 234-235, 291-292, 295-297, 299-300
Spanish Civil War, 11
Spanish-Mexican, 27
"Spell of the Yukon," 257
Speltz, Pat, 102
Speltz, Rose, 102
Spicer, Ted, 103
SPRAY-X, 305
Stanford University (CA), 69
Starlight Timber Co., 210
Stasio, Anna di, 139
Statue of Liberty, 101
Steinbeck, John, 43, 48
Steinz
  Han, 160
  Maryke, 160
Stenerson, Jim, 69
Stipp, Mary Margaret, xi
St. John, Dick, 158
Stone Age, 65
Straits of China, 271
Straits of Magellan, 297
Strategic Air Command (SAC), 42-43
Strauss, Johann, 113
Streep, Meryl, 2
Suez Canal, 144, 183
Suharto, President, 209

Sui Dynasty, 79
Sullivan Principles, 186
Superstition Mountains, 43
Sutter, Madelon, 111
Swahili, 178
Swain Industries (Flakeboard), 284
Sweden, 103-108, 125
Swedish, 104-107
Swedish Co-Op, 106
Swift, Jonathan, 266
Swiss Air, 270
Switzerland, 72, 96, 110-111, 139

— T —
Tahiti, 188, 190-194, 202, 263, 297
Tahitian, 192-194
Tahiti-Santiago Express Plane, 299
Taipei's C.K.S. (Chiang Kai Shek) Airport, 282
Taiwan, 63-64, 66, 69, 81, 201, 252, 270, 273, 282-285
Taiwan Department of Forest Research, 284
Taiwan Plywood Manufacturers, 64
Taiwanese, 282, 284
Takoradi Veneer and Lumber, 165
Tame Airlines, 231
Tamiami Trail, 33
Tamier, Leonardo, 175
Tang Dynasty, 79-80
Tang Family, 282
  Jennifer (Wang), 284
  Jung Lei, 284
  Paige, 284
Tasi Dei, 65
Tasman Sea, 197-198
Taylor
  Elizabeth, 172
  "Honey" Howell, 232, 236
Tel Aviv, 142
Temperate Zone Rain Forest, 259
Tennessee, 12, 34-35, 100, 102, 108, 158, 197, 206, 257, 308
Texas, 24, 26-28, 30, 40-43, 46, 51, 309-310
Thailand, 189, 215-216, 218, 273, 277
Thames Plywood Co., 100
Thapa, Surya Bahadur, 90
The African Timber and Plywood Company, 165
The American Millers Association, 307
"The Bawdy Ballad of the Baltic," 134
"The Bridge on The River Kwai," 218
"The Celebrated Jumping Frog of Calaveras County," 44
The Codesa Plywood Company, 300
The Danzer Company, 162
The Diary of Anne Frank, 120
The Engineered Wood Association, xi
The Four Horseman, 1
The Gipper, 1
The Grapes of Wrath, 48
"The Great Barrier Reef, 202
"The Hump," xi, 31, 90, 218
The Old Ox Road, 5

"The Rime of the Ancient Mariner," 231
The Robertson Corporation, ix, xii, xiv, 10, 53, 57, 163, 239, 302, 304-306, 308-311
The Shanghai Bureau of Light Industry, 74
The Sun Also Rises, 268
The Tragni Brothers — Ettore and Giuseppe, 137
"The Unsinkable Molly Brown," 48
The World Is My Home, 241
Third World, 219, 270
Thomas, Lowell, 241
Thompson, 71
  Regina, 166
Thornton, Mabel, 117, 133
Thorpe, Jim, 50
Tibet, 92-93
Tibetan, 92-93
Timbuktu, 53
Ting, Shen, 211
Tinian, 266-27
Tjime, M., 60
Tobruk, 156
Tomb of King Tut, 147
Tonga, 263
Tortilla Flat, 43
Touchdown Jesus, 2
Tragni
  Ettore, 139, 153
  Fratelli, 137
  Josephine, 139
  Laura, 139
  Peppino, 153
Transco Industries, 162
Trans World Airlines, 242
Travelers' Century Club, 237-238, 240
Tritch, John, xi
Trojan War, 249-250
Troy, 243, 250-251
Truk, 31, 241, 265, 267
  Truk International Airport, 53
Truman, Harry S. (President), 5, 30
Tse-Tung, Mao, 84
Tuaregs, 170
Tubman, William, 160
Tucker
  B. G., 25
  Gerald, 8
Turan
  Fuat, 250
  Hasan, 250
Turkey, xiii, 183, 238, 243, 247, 250-251, 280
Turnstill, Bill, 112
TWA, 228
Twain, Mark, 44, 190
Tyler, Dan, 69

— U —
U.N. Food and Agriculture Organization, 238
Uniply, 235
United Airlines, 253
United Kingdom, 97-100, 104, 110, 195
United Nations, 219, 243, 245, 270
United Nationsl Food and Agriculture, 244

United Nations Forest Products Conference, 242
United Soybean Board (USB), 306-307
United States, ix, xiii, 11-13, 16, 31, 51-52, 57-61, 63, 66, 73, 77-78, 82, 84, 95, 97-98, 100, 104-105, 107-113, 115-116, 120, 123-124, 130-131, 133, 143, 147, 150, 155-156, 159, 165, 167, 174, 178, 186, 196, 198-199, 201, 203, 210, 214, 218-219, 223, 225, 230, 233, 235, 238-239, 242, 251, 253, 264-268, 270-271, 277-280, 282, 284-285, 287, 291, 305, 309-310
   Army, xiv, 8, 13, 262, 264
      Air Corps, 11-14, 19, 43, 48, 308
         Technical Training Command Band, 19
      Air Forces, 16, 19, 21, 28, 43, 64, 78, 218, 229, 238-239, 265, 308
         Aerial Photo Reconnaissance and Intelligence, 18, 21, 23, 42
         Air Transport Command, 22
         Military Occupational Specialties (MOS), 18
         2nd Air Force, 24, 27, 29
            Combat Crew Training, 29'
         16th Wing Bombardment Operational Training Wing Staff, 24, 26-27
   Consulate, 60
   Department of Agriculture, 235
   Department of Commerce, 69
   Emancipation, 186
   Embassy, 78, 141, 164
   Greenback, 98
   Navy, xiv, 54, 62, 196, 265
      Naval Intelligence, 11
      Pacific Fleet, 189
   Patent Office, 305, 307, 310
   Postal Service, 309-310
      Railway Postal, 2
   Seventh Cavalry, 42, 48
      Pony Soldiers, 42, 48
   Windmill Stamp, 311
University of
   Argentina, 296
   Arizona, 23
   Cairo, 147
   California, 284
   Florida, 191
   Georgia, 117
   Illinois, 23-24
   Louisville, 284
   Kentucky, 6-7
   Malaysia, 278
   Nebraska, 5
   Oklahoma, 5
Urals, 129
Uruguay, 296
U.S. G.R. Saunders, 173
U.S. National Park Services Pacific War Memorial Headquarters and Museum, 265
U.S.-U.S.S.R. Trade and Economic Council, 124
Utah, 28, 46-48, 275

— V —

"Vagabond House" (by Don Blanding), 36-38
Vagh, A. S., 217
Van Beuren, Mike, 69, 157, 157
Van Beuren, Lise, 153, 157
Van Buren, Martin (President), 36
Vanerply Mills, 105
Van Gogh, 120
VanHout, Adrian, 120
VanHout, Tony, 120
VanHout Veneer, Plywood and Furniture Complex, 120
Van Madal (Micronesia), 264
Van Ply, Inc., 158-159
V-E Day, 28
Veneer & Laminations (India) Ltd., 217
Venetian, 159
Venezuela, 230, 236
Verhoeven, J. H., 121
Vermont, 100, 130
Vetsera, Mary, 113
Victo Veneers, 203, 216, 223
Vietnam, 66, 218, 308
Viking, 101, 105
Virginia, 8, 34-35, 116, 163, 229, 305, 309-310
Vithaldas, Narendra, 217
Vogler, Karin, 146, 153
von Bonin, Bogislaw, 164

— W —

Wabash College (IN), 3, 307-308
Walters, George, 69
Wangard, Fred (Dr.), 284
War Between the States, 35
War Debt, 108
Warren Wilson Presbyterian College (NC), 218
Warsaw, 121
Warwick, Dian, 99
Wasatch Mountains, 48
Washington, 38-39, 100, 189-191, 203, 259
Washington, D.C., 2-3, 123, 310
Washington Post, 113
Weaver, Joseph, 36
Webb Co., 172
Weber, Dick, 69, 101, 158
Weinstein, 18
Welsh, Andy, 100
Welsh, Tom, 100
Wendover Air Force Base (UT), 28, 46
West Africa, 155-158, 165, 178, 181, 183-185
Western Civilization, 79
Western World, 166, 190, 264
West Point Military Academy (NY), 17
Westralian Plywoods Pty. Ltd., 20
Wheatley, Mary Jane, x
White
   Betty, 23-24
   John (Captain), 23-25
White Cliffs of Dover, 287

Whitehead, Helen, 153
White Sands Missile Range (NM), 24, 28
Wigel, Rob, 281
Wilco Machines, 102
Wilson Machines, Inc., 197
Wisconsin, 69, 101, 158, 176, 195
   Milwaukee, 2
Wong
   Jennifer, 278
   Susie, 275
Wood Based Panels International, 307
World Bank Aid, 209
World Council of Churches, 156
World Trade Center, 271, 273, 284
World War I, 11, 43
World War II, xi, xiii-xiv, 5, 10-12, 22, 33-34, 47, 49, 52, 54, 78, 96, 98, 108, 119, 141, 156, 197, 214, 218, 229, 233, 238, 262, 265, 275, 267, 293, 305, 309
Wu, Empress, 80

— X —

Xhosa, 174, 186

— Y —

Yale School of Forestry, 284
Yale University, 308
   Air Cadet Training (CT), 18-19
Yang Zhi Timber Factory, 75
Yankee Veneer, 117
Yeager, Chuck, 240
Yellowknife Museum, 256
Yellowstone National Park, 39, 195
Yontrarak, Bunlue, 215-216, 218
Young, Brigham, 47-48
Yucatan, 53, 79, 81, 295
   Mayan Pyramids, 79
Yugoslav Airlines, 245
Yugoslavia, xii, 238, 243, 245-246
Yukon, 254, 259
Yummy, 241

— Z —

Zaragoza, Carlito, 211
Zhizhenkov, N. M., 124
Zulu, 174, 178, 186
Zurich Veneer Mill, Ltd., 111
Zurich Sea, 111